CUT TO BLACK

Also by Graham Hurley

CUT TO BLACK

Graham Hurley

ORION

Copyright © Graham Hurley 2004

The right of Graham Hurley to be identified as the author
of this work has been asserted by him in accordance with
the Copyright, Designs and Patents Act 1988.

First published in Great Britain in 2004
by Orion
An imprint of the Orion Publishing Group
Orion House, 5 Upper St Martin's Lane,
London WC2H 9EA

A CIP catalogue record for this book
is available from the British Library

ISBN 0752850989 (cased)
ISBN 0752850997 (trade paperback)

Typeset by Deltatype Ltd, Birkenhead, Merseyside

Printed in Great Britain by Clays Ltd, St Ives plc

'There's no shame in wealth, my dear.'
'Indeed, but does it not depend on how it's carried out?'

Mansfield Park – Jane Austen

To
Bob and Di Franklin
With love

My thanks to Glen Barham, Alan Betts, Caroline Cawkill, Dave Cook, Roly Dumont, Jason Goodwin, Norman Feerick, Di Franklin, David Horsley, Andy Harrington, Dave Hunter, Michelle Jacolow, Richard John, Gary Linton, Tim Lucas, Andy Marker, Bridget Munro, John Molyneux, Julie Mortimer, Laurie Mullen, Simon Paine, Tim Robinson, Jane Shuttlewood, Colin Smith, Paul Thatcher, Tony West and Martin Youngs. Others, to whom I owe an equal debt of gratitude, have taken a discreet step into the shadows. Anyone wanting to learn more about the colourful history of away support for Pompey should buy a copy of *Rolling with the 6.57 Crew* by Cass Pennant and Rob Sylvester. Excellent read. My editor at Orion, Simon Spanton, was enthusiastic about this project from the start and guarded it against all-comers. Likewise, my wife Lin kept our bellies full, our hearts warm, and our heads below the parapet. Pompey Till We Die . . .

Prelude

He slowed in the darkness, the breath rasping in his lungs, trying to think of a thousand reasons not to draw the obvious conclusion. The car looked like a Vauxhall, maybe a Cavalier. The two shapes bent to the driver's door had the edgy slightness of kids. And the music through the open car window, as if this were some movie, was perfect: gangster rap with a heavy bass line that pulsed away into the night, drowning the nearby murmur of the sea.

He finally came to a halt, annoyed at losing the rhythm of his nightly run, aware of the chill kiss of the wind as it cooled the sweat on his body. Seven hard miles had drained the strength in his legs but already little knots of adrenalin were swamping his exhaustion. After the endless months of paperwork – of audit trails and expenditure profiles, of asset calculations and restraint preparations – it had come to this: the sordid little drama played out across dozens of cities, hundreds of estates, thousands of similar patches of urban wasteland. The Cavalier, he thought grimly, had replaced the ice cream van. Stop me and buy one. Same time tomorrow night. And the night after that. And the night after that. Until your new friend in the beaten-up Vauxhall had you phoning him every four hours, pleading for your life.

He began to circle the car on the driver's blind side, still fifty metres out, moving slowly, balls of his feet, stepping lightly through the tangle of scrub and marram grass. In these situations, anyone with half a brain would be thinking risk assessment. How would he take the guy behind the wheel? How would he contain him afterwards? What were the dangers of the kids getting hurt? These were important questions. He needed a plan, and a fallback, but there was something about this little tableau – how blatant, how fucking *insulting* – that had cut him loose. All of a sudden, he had the chance to make a difference. Not much of a difference but a difference nonetheless.

He was ahead of the car now, aware of the line of street lights half a mile away. Silhouetted against the orange glow, every move he made betrayed him. He began to backtrack, hunting for cover, meaning to close on the car from the passenger side, then he froze as the driver stirred the engine into life. The music, abruptly, had gone. In its place, the throaty bark of a dog and a yelp of laughter from one of the kids. The child was barely an adolescent. His voice had yet to break. What kind of animal sold gear to thirteen-year-olds?

He began to run, suddenly oblivious of the need for cover. Anything to get between the Cavalier and the distant street lights, between the driver and the next sale. One of the kids had seen him, yelling a warning to his mate. Two shapes melted away into the darkness as the car began to move. Abreast of it now, he drove himself forward, legs pumping hard. He reached for the passenger door and wrenched it open. There was someone else in the car, slumped back against the headrest, the seat half reclined. The thin figure jackknifed forwards. A hand lunged at him, a fist in his windpipe, a choking pain that blurred his vision. Abruptly he lost his footing, fell head first, felt cinders tearing at his face, heard a squeal of brakes and the dog again, barking fit to bust. The car was ahead of him, metres away, briefly motionless. The passenger door was still open. A face appeared, contorted by a grin. Then a voice, thick accent, Scouse.

'Run the fucker over.'

The engine was revving. Then the brake lights dimmed and for the briefest moment, as he tried to will his body to move, he had a perfect view of the Cavalier reversing towards him and the zigzag pattern of the tyre tread, inches away. Moments later, a wheel crushed his ankle and he screamed as it happened again – another wheel, his lower leg – and for a second or two he must have lost consciousness because the next thing was a moment of surreal terror as the blaze of the headlights and the roar of the engine bore down on him. This time, somehow, he was able to reach out, trying to fend it off, flailing at the oncoming monster with his bare hands, flesh against metal, then he was aware of his body arching backwards, a gesture of defeat, before the pain thickened and the darkness returned, unfathomable, beyond comprehension.

Chapter one

The aircraft appeared well after midnight. It approached high from the west, droning over the sprawl of suburbs around Gosport then sideslipping down in the gusty onshore wind as the black mass of Portsmouth Harbour disappeared beneath the nose.

Beyond the harbour and the gaunt shadows of the naval dockyard lay the city itself, the shape of the island necklaced with street lights. Away to the south, there was a queue of cabs for the fares spilling out of the late-night clubs by South Parade pier; further inland, the cold, blue wink of an ambulance picking its way through the maze of terraced streets.

At 1000 feet, the aircraft levelled off then dipped a wing and began to fly in wide, lazy circles, taking its time, each new circuit overlapping invisibly with the last. Households in its path stirred, dreams broken by the steady, pulsing beat of the engines overhead. Even half asleep, groping towards consciousness, this was a noise you'd recognise at once, familiar city-wide. Boxer One. Pride of the Hantspol ASU. The Air Support Unit's all-seeing eye in the sky.

The aircraft remained over the city for the best part of an hour. After a while, the circuits tightened and on two occasions the pilot took it low enough for startled insomniacs in Fratton to report the rush of air over the wings. Then, abruptly, the beat of the engines changed pitch, and the aircraft lifted and climbed away towards the west, returning the city to silence.

Awake in the stillness of the Bargemaster's House, Faraday had heard it too. And began to wonder.

It fell to DC Paul Winter to put the obvious into words.

'There's sod all here. We blew it.'

'The Stanley blades? That bit of clothes line? Blood on the lino down in the corner there? More blood on the sofa? Is it your age, Paul? Doesn't violence excite you any more?'

'I thought this was supposed to be a drugs bust?'

'It was. Is. And a tenner says we'll get a good hit on the DNA.'

'Taking us where? Some scroat they tied up and put in a Tarantino movie? What's he going to tell us we didn't know already? These blokes are off their heads, Cath, but we can't do them for that.'

Winter's use of her Christian name drew a cautionary look from DI Cathy Lamb. The rest of the squad – three DCs and a dog handler – were still out of earshot, banging around in the chaos of the bedrooms upstairs, but even so Lamb was wary about letting Winter too close. The proactive CID team – the Portsmouth Crime Squad – was barely a week old. The last thing she needed just now were the kind of liberties detectives like Winter were only too happy to exploit.

'We were unlucky,' she said flatly. 'We took every reasonable precaution but sometimes . . . it just doesn't work out.'

'Is that for my benefit, boss? Or are you rehearsing for tomorrow?'

'Tomorrow?'

'The post-mortem. Secretan's going to love this. All that overtime. All that hype. And we come away with a couple of Stanley blades and a million pizza boxes.' He poked at the litter of greasy cardboard with the toe of his shoe. 'What is it with kids these days? Don't they know about real food?'

There was a thump overhead as someone tripped but Lamb ignored it. She was looking again at the detailed target analysis supplied by the Air Support Unit, the result of a casual fly-by the previous weekend. The colour still, in perfect focus, showed a mid-terrace house in Pennington Road, one of the maze of streets in the heart of Fratton. Every relevant feature was helpfully labelled – the boarded-up first-floor windows, the TV aerial adrift from the chimney stack, the abandoned fridge in the tiny back yard. There was no rear access and only one front door. In theory, as she'd been reckless enough to claim at this evening's pre-bust briefing, it should have been a breeze.

Yet somehow the two bodies they'd come to nick had both legged it. An area car was still quartering the nearby streets but the ASU's Islander – Boxer One – had thrown in the towel and flown home. The two white blobs on the thermal camera had split up as soon as the aircraft secured a fix. The ASU guys had tracked one of them as he scaled garden wall after garden wall before emerging at the end of the terrace. Sprinting the length of the neighbouring street, he'd ducked into the shelter of a garage. After that, in the dry commentary of Boxer One's observer, no further contact.

The area car had checked out the garage. A rusting Ford Escort with two flat tyres, half a lifetime's collection of paint tins, and a plastic dustbin full of fishing gear. No sign of an eighteen-year-old drug dealer with a taste for extreme violence.

The youngest of the DCs came limping down the stairs. His name was Jimmy Suttle. His suit was filthy and his face was smudged with dirt but his obvious glee brought the faintest smile to Lamb's face. More hope than expectation.

'Well?'

'Cracked it, boss.' He sounded out of breath. 'There's a hatch into the roof space. Little bastards had knocked through to next door. And then through again. Must have gone out via their back garden. I'm thinking number 34. That's the empty one down the street.' He paused, confused by Lamb's reaction. 'Boss?'

'You're telling me they had time for all that? We were in here in seconds. You know we were.'

Winter nodded. The front door had surrendered to the House Entry Team without a fight. No way could the targets have legged it into the roof ahead of the cavalry.

Suttle stuck to his story. Crawling across the intervening attic, he'd let himself down into number 34. Fully furnished, the place was either up for let or awaiting the return of the owners. It had fitted carpets, nice pictures, widescreen TV, the works.

'And?'

'They'd obviously been using it. Or someone had. The place is a shit heap. Beds slept in. Empty bottles. Telly on. Old food—'

'Pizzas?' Winter enquired drily.

'Everywhere. Kitchen. Lounge. Pepperami, bits of onion, HP sauce. These blokes are animals.'

'Yeah . . . like we didn't know.'

'Gear?' It was Lamb again, almost plaintive.

''Fraid not, boss.' The young detective was rubbing his knee. 'Bit of charlie, bit of draw, but we're talking personal, not supply. They must have taken it with them. Dunno.' He frowned. 'What I'm thinking, they probably kipped at number 34, used the place like a hotel. Bloody sight nicer than this khazi.'

'So why didn't we know?' Lamb was looking at Winter. 'About number 34?'

'No idea.' Winter looked round, pulling a face. 'What's that smell?'

'Dog shit, mate.' Suttle lifted his shoe, and then nodded up towards the bedrooms. 'Knee deep, it is. Bloody everywhere.'

The phone call came minutes later. Winter was first to the mobile, half hidden beneath a pile of unopened post. He picked it up in his handkerchief and then turned his back on the watching faces, grunting from time to time.

'So who might you be?' he queried at last.

The conversation came to an abrupt end. Winter wrapped the mobile in the handkerchief, then laid it carefully on the plastic milk crate that served as an occasional table.

Cathy Lamb raised an enquiring eyebrow.

'Our absent friends.' Winter grunted. 'Definitely Scousers. They've got an address for us. Bystock Road. Number 93. They think we ought to pay a visit.'

There was a brief silence. Cathy Lamb was looking ever more resigned. Some jobs left you feeling worse than useless and this was definitely one of them.

'They're taking the piss.' She sighed. 'Aren't they?'

Bystock Road was a three-minute drive away, another of the endless terraced streets that had turned this corner of the city into a playground for double-glazing salesmen, dodgy roofers, and enforcers from the less scrupulous credit companies.

At Lamb's insistence, Winter took Suttle and two of the other DCs with him. Turning into Bystock Road, he nearly collided with a patrol car. Winter got out and walked across. Number 93 was way down the other end of the street but already he could hear the music.

'Neighbour complaint. Rang in couple of minutes ago.' The young PC at the wheel was Asian. 'Bloke says he's going to take a hammer to next door if something isn't sorted.'

'Address?'

'91.'

The two cars drove on, double-parking in the street outside 93. The upstairs window was wide open but the house was in darkness and there was no sign of a party. Winter's knowledge of music didn't extend much beyond Elton John but Suttle helped him out.

'Dr Dre,' he said briefly. 'You're lucky you're so old.'

The PC was already talking to the neighbour who'd rung the complaint in. He was a huge man in his forties, crop-haired with a two-day growth of beard, and Winter couldn't take his eyes off the blur of tattoos beneath his string vest. He said he hadn't a clue who lived next door, dossers always coming and going, but he meant it about the hammer.

'What do you think, then?' The Asian PC had turned to Winter.

'Me?' Winter was still eyeing the man next door. 'I'd kick the door down and let him get on with it.'

'You're serious?'

6

'Always. Except the paperwork would be a nightmare.'

The PC offered Winter an uncertain grin. There were issues here – maybe drugs, maybe weapons – and the night-shift skipper was manic about playing it by the book. Maybe they ought to be thinking about a risk assessment.

Winter walked across to the front door. Twice, he shouted up at the open window but his challenge was lost in the thump of the music. Finally, he rapped at the door. When a second knock had no effect, he took a step backwards and motioned to Suttle.

'You're uglier than me.' He nodded at the door. 'Open it.'

The young DC needed no encouragement. His third kick splintered the wood around the lock and a shoulder charge took him inside. Winter followed, fumbling along the wall for a light switch. A gust of something stale and acrid made him catch his breath. When he finally found the switch, it didn't work.

'Here.'

It was the man next door with a heavy-duty torch. Winter took the torch and told him to get back outside.

'No fucking way.'

Winter tracked the beam of the torch back along the narrow hall and into the neighbour's face.

'I said get outside.'

The big man hesitated a moment, then shrugged and stepped back towards the pavement. Winter was already in the tiny lounge. The torch found a single mattress on the floor, one end surrounded with empty mugs, half-crushed milk cartons, and a small mountain of cigarette ends. There was a pool of vomit under the window and more vomit crusting in the fireplace. Two o'clock in the morning, thought Winter, and there have to be better things to do than this.

The kitchen occupied the back of the house. A tap dripped in the darkness and there was a low whirring from what might have been a fridge. A single sweep from the torch revealed a table, two bicycles, and a catering-sized tin of Nescafé in the sink.

It was obvious by now that the music came from upstairs, the entire house shuddering under the heavy bass. Another hour or two of this, and number 93 would explode.

Winter climbed the stairs, Suttle behind him. There were three doors off the narrow landing at the top, two of them ajar. Winter checked quickly in both, then turned to the third. This room was at the front of the house.

'Again?' Suttle nodded at the door and mimed a kick.

'No.' Winter shook his head, then patted the young DC on his arm. The heavy torch at the ready, Winter turned the handle and felt the

7

door give. The music came at him like a wave, a wall of noise. He stepped inside the room, aware at once of a panel of lights in the darkness. Snapping on the torch, he found himself looking at the hi-fi stack in the corner, an amplifier flanked by enormous speakers. He swung the beam towards the window, almost expecting someone to lunge out of the darkness, but saw nothing but an iron bedstead standing on the bare floorboards a couple of feet in from the open window. Lying on the springs of the bedstead was a woman, naked except for a pillowcase draped loosely over her head.

Winter stepped towards the bedstead, then changed his mind and sorted out the hi-fi. A cable ran to a point on the skirting board. When he tore out the plug, the silence flooded in, an almost physical presence. From the street, the voice of the neighbour.

'What's happening?'

Winter ignored him. The woman was alive, shivering in the draught from the open window. Winter could see the rise and fall of her chest, hear the faintest sound from inside the pillowcase. Both ankles were tied to the bed frame with cable ties, and more ties had chafed her wrists where she'd tried to struggle free. Winter stared down at her for a moment, trying to guess at an age. She was young, certainly, with the kind of body that deserved a better setting than this. Goose-pimpled white skin, big breasts, flat belly, and the faintest bikini marks from her last encounter with serious sunshine. Recent bruising had purpled her ribcage on the left-hand side but there was no sign of other injuries.

Winter reached down, telling her that everything was going to be OK, that everything was going to be fine, and eased the pillowcase off her head. A pale, almond-shaped face. A slash of scarlet gag across her mouth. Eyes that began to swim with tears.

Winter felt a jolt of recognition. For a second, the beam of the torch wavered. Impossible, he thought. Not here. Not like this.

'Lost a bit of weight, love.' He smiled in the darkness. 'Suits you.'

Chapter two

Faraday's second sweep with the Leica Red Spots revealed a flash of white amongst the scrub and gorse around the freshwater ponds a stone's throw from the Bargemaster's House. Racking the focus on the binoculars, he eased slowly left, convinced already that he'd spotted the season's first wheatear. Seconds later, the little bird broke cover again, staying low, scurrying a few feet at a time, finally hopping up onto the back of one of the old wooden benches that ringed the pond.

A couple of months back, this tiny creature would have been wintering south of the Sahara. Late January would have found it in Morocco. Days it devoted to finding food. Nights, often alone, it sped north again. Only now, in mid March, had it finally returned to its nesting ground, bringing with it the promise – the guarantee – of spring. Faraday made a second tiny adjustment to the focus. Carved into the bench below the spread of claw was another message that had survived the winter. *Deano's a wanker*, it read. Welcome to Pompey.

Faraday settled himself beside the pond, hoping for a glimpse of the bearded reedlings that were rumoured to be making their way south from the low smudge of Farlington Marshes. It was still barely seven o'clock, the air still, the sky cloudless, barely a ripple on the blue mirror of the nearby harbour. In a couple of hours, after a leisurely breakfast, he'd drive into work where the clear-up on a recent high-profile murder awaited his attention.

A psychopath in his mid forties had taken out a lifetime's frustration on a foreign language student, a Finnish blonde unlucky enough to cross his path. Stranger murders were never supposed to be easy, but the Major Crimes Team had blitzed the backstreets of Fareham where the girl's severed head had been found in a Londis bag, and scored a result within seventy-two hours.

Caged by the evidence, mainly DNA, the suspect had thrown in the towel after barely an hour's interview. The transcript of what followed, while dark in the extreme, had put a smile of satisfaction on the face of

Willard. This, he'd grunted, was a classic MCT investigation, conclusive proof of the linkage between resource, effort, dedication, and justice. A couple of years back, they'd have been months trying to get a result. Now, thanks to a major reorganisation, they'd redrawn the time lines. Faraday, who had profound doubts about trophy-talk and management-speak, was just glad the bastard was locked up.

The wheatear had gone. Faraday had begun to search the nearby scrub, wondering whether it was too early for a sedge warbler, when the peace of the morning was disturbed by the roar of an approaching aircraft. Faraday swung the binos in time to catch a blur of shadow as the military jet crested the distant swell of Portsdown Hill. Seconds later, it was almost on top of him, blasting south over the harbour, the noise so physically shattering he could feel it in his bones. Then the plane had gone, leaving clouds of black-headed gulls squawking madly, and several rafts of brent geese doing their best to get airborne. Any more stunts like that, thought Faraday, and the wheatear would be back in North Africa.

Faraday's mobile began to chirp. It was Eadie Sykes. The plane had got her up and she wanted to know what on earth was going on.

'You think it's started? You think the Iraqis are getting theirs in early?'

Faraday found himself laughing. Eadie feigned outrage.

'What's so funny? You think we ought to get married? Before it's too late?'

'I think you ought to go back to bed.'

'After that? Listen, you remember the Sixties, Cuba? What do you do with those last four minutes?'

'I still think you ought to go back to bed.'

'Yeah . . . but it's more fun with two, eh? Ring me later.'

The line went dead. Faraday slipped the mobile back in the pocket of his anorak, then began to search half-heartedly for the wheatear again. He'd been with Eadie last night, tucked up on the sofa with *Newsnight* and a bottle of Rioja. The past couple of months, they'd watched the government – Blair in particular – shepherding the nation to war. Bombing Iraq back to the Stone Age made absolutely no sense whatsoever, yet here they were, in lockstep with the Americans, hours away from releasing the first fusillade of cruise missiles.

Eadie, behind the wry one-liners, was incandescent with rage. Bush was a retard. Blair was an arse-licking con man. The Brits should be ashamed of themselves. Only the fact that her own prime minister seemed as hell-bent on Armageddon as the rest of them had kept her from packing her bags and phoning Qantas for a ticket home.

Back in February, at Eadie's insistence, they'd taken the early train to

Waterloo and joined a million and a half other people who felt less than convinced about killing Iraqi women and kids. The river of protesters stretched for miles, stopping traffic, filling bridges, swamping the Embankment, and Faraday, who'd never been this side of the bararicades in his life, found it an oddly comforting experience. Students, mums, kids, pensioners, asylum seekers, nurses, civil servants, a huge slice of Middle England shuffling slowly towards Hyde Park under the watchful gaze of a couple of thousand policemen.

To Faraday, that was the oddest experience of all. Not that he was himself under surveillance, a copper coppered, but that he found this single act of protest so natural, so long overdue. *Ex-Labour Voters Against The War*, read one placard. Too bloody right.

He stirred at the sound of the mobile. Expecting Eadie again, instead he found himself listening to an all-too-familiar voice. Willard.

'Joe? Something's come up. Where are you?'

Faraday glanced at his watch. 07.22.

'Still at home, sir. I can be in by eight, maybe earlier.'

'Don't bother.'

'Why not?'

'I'm still waiting to talk to the medics at the QA. Ask for Critical Care.'

The Queen Alexandra Hospital was on the lower slopes of Portsdown Hill, a 1300-bed goliath with views across the city towards the Isle of Wight. The Department for Critical Care was on the third floor, two open wards with side rooms for solo occupancy. In the corridor outside, Faraday spotted the tall, bulky figure of Willard deep in conversation with a young nurse.

Faraday paused to peer into the nearest of the open wards. Most of the beds were occupied – propped-up, comatose shapes moored to life-support machines, monitoring equipment, and an assortment of drips. At this range, it looked like an audition for the city's undertakers. No one seemed familiar.

'Nick Hayder.' Faraday found Willard at his elbow. 'Third bed on the left.'

Faraday, astonished, took another look. Last time he'd seen Nick was a couple of days back. As fellow DIs on the Major Crimes Team they'd been obliged to attend a headquarters briefing on a recent change to CPS protocols. Afterwards, they'd gone down the road for a snatched pint at a Winchester pub. Now this.

'What happened?'

'Good question. You know that patch of scrub round Fort Cumberland? He was found there last night. Unconscious.'

Faraday was still gazing at the bandaged figure Willard had pointed out. Fort Cumberland was an MOD site on the south-western tip of the island, acres of brambles and couch grass, as remote a spot as you could find in a city as densely-packed as Portsmouth.

'So what happened?' Faraday repeated.

'No one knows, not for sure. He was in running gear. It was dark.'

'Any witnesses?'

'One old boy, late sixties, walking his dog. Says he saw some kind of fracas but he was a fair distance away. He thinks there was a car involved but that's about as far as we've got.'

'Make? Colour?'

'He can't say. We'll start on the CCTV this morning but don't hold your breath. Nearest camera's the far end of Henderson Road.' Willard was watching a doctor in green scrubs who'd paused at Hayder's bedside. 'There must have been a car because they're saying he's been run over. He's got compound fractures, both legs, a broken pelvis, ruptured spleen, and query brain damage. They took the spleen out in theatre but it's the head injury that's bothering them.'

'How bad is it?'

'They won't say, but they're talking a three on the coma scale.'

'What's normal?'

'Fifteen.'

'He's unconscious?'

'Very. He was brought in around nine thirty last night. Still hasn't surfaced. He—'

Willard broke off. The nurse had returned and was indicating an open door down the corridor. The consultant, she said, would be in touch with him as soon as he was free. Willard looked pointedly at his watch, then led Faraday to a small, bare office. There was a poster advertising yachting holidays in the Peloponnese on the wall, and a list of names and bleep numbers on the wipe board. A plant on the window sill was fighting a losing battle against the central heating.

Willard shut the door, eyeing Faraday for a moment before settling into the chair behind the desk. Three kids beamed out of a stand-up frame beside the PC.

'Mates, weren't you? You and Hayder?'

Faraday nodded. 'Mates' wasn't a term he'd applied to many men in his life but in Nick Hayder's case he liked to think it was close to the truth.

'Pretty much,' he agreed.

'Did he have any personal problems that you'd know of?'

Faraday hesitated. Willard's use of the past tense was beginning to irritate him. Critical Care was high tech. Critical Care was where they hauled you back from the brink. So why the rush to consign Hayder to the Recycle Bin?

'Nick has a partner,' he said carefully.

'That wasn't my question.'

'I know, but that's the situation. I can give you her number. Why don't you—'

'Don't fuck around, Joe. I'm asking you about his love life. Someone tried to kill him. It may be they've done just that. Does the word "motive" ring any bells? Or do you think you're doing him some kind of favour? All this buddy-buddy shit?'

Faraday held Willard's furious gaze. The Det-Supt was as armour-clad as any detective when it came to the flesh and blood consequences of serious violence, but this was family and family was different.

'Nick's been living alone for a bit,' Faraday said at last. 'Gutty little bedsit off Albert Road.'

'Why was that?'

'Problems between him and Maggie. They were trying to work it out ... Are trying to work it out.'

'Was he over the side?'

'No.'

'Was she?'

'Not that I know of.'

'You're sure about that?'

It was a fair question and Faraday wondered how much further he should go. Monday's lunchtime drink in Winchester had stretched to two pints and a coffee, chiefly because life in a Southsea bedsit was driving Nick Hayder nuts. Faraday had never met a fellow detective so self-contained, so centred, so sure of his own judgement. Yet here he was, totally lost.

'There's a problem with Maggie's boy,' he said. 'Nick would be the first to tell you he hasn't been handling it brilliantly.'

'Let's hope he gets the fucking chance.' Willard was still angry. 'What was the problem?'

'Nick thought – thinks – the kid's doing drugs. Nothing heavy but enough to get Nick going.'

'Like what drugs?'

'Cannabis mainly. Speed and ecstasy at the weekends.'

'How old's the boy?'

'Fourteen.'

'And his mum? What does she think?'

'Maggie prefers to deal with it in her own way. She's a teacher, one of the local comprehensives. This kind of stuff's meat and drink in schools like hers. She thinks wading in's the last thing you do.'

'Which Hayder couldn't handle?'

'Exactly.'

Willard nodded, saying nothing. He had no kids of his own, though his long-term partner, a Bristol psychologist, was rumoured to be contemplating IVF.

'So no one else?' Willard mused at last.

'Not to my knowledge. I've been round to see her a couple of times. She's a strong woman.'

'Attractive?'

'Nick thinks so.'

'And he dwells on it? All those nights banged up by himself? No wonder he went running.'

'He's been doing it for years. He got the bug from Brian Imber and thank God he did. If you want my opinion, running was the best—'

Faraday broke off, hearing a soft knock at the door. Brian Imber was the DS with the Force Intelligence Unit.

The nurse at the door was full of apologies. The unit manager needed her office back. The nurse was about to suggest an alternative when Willard shook his head and got to his feet.

'We're through, love.' He turned to Faraday and then glanced at his watch. 'Back to base? Ten o'clock at Major Crimes?'

The operational heart of the Portsmouth Basic Command Unit lay in a suite of offices on the first floor of Kingston Crescent police station, a stone's throw from the Continental Ferry Port. These offices, stretching the length of the corridor, housed the Senior Management Team, including the uniformed Chief Superintendent who headed the BCU. To these men and women fell the everyday challenges of policing Portsmouth.

For several years, Pompey's top cop had been Chief Supt Dennis Hartigan, a diminutive martinet who'd made no secret of his determination to end his career in an ACPO job. In this respect, an Assistant Chief Constable's vacancy with the Cleveland Constabulary had been the answer to his prayers, and he'd stepped briskly out of Portsmouth after a burst of valedictory e-mails and the most cheerless leaving party in living memory. Few regretted his promotion, and a couple of dozen survivors from Hartigan's routine bollockings held an impromptu celebration in the top-floor bar the day after he'd gone. Lucky Middlesbrough, went the first toast.

Hartigan's successor was a quietly spoken West Country copper in his mid forties called Andy Secretan. Taller than Hartigan, with a bluff outdoors face and an obvious impatience with the dressier rituals of higher command, Secretan had quickly won respect across the BCU for his preparedness to put common sense ahead of New Labour performance-speak. Unlike his predecessor, there were no genuflections before the latest blizzard of Home Office diktats. Neither did he have the slightest interest in self-promotion or belittling his staff. As a result, morale on the first floor had been transformed. The Corridor of Death was no more than a memory.

DI Cathy Lamb, summoned this morning from her desk in the same building, rather liked the new boss. After Hartigan's mania for meticulously prepared risk assessments and the correct use of the apostrophe, it was refreshing to work under someone who treated all paperwork with profound mistrust and was prepared to throw the wider issues open to something approaching real debate. Not that Secretan didn't have views of his own.

'Barmy, wasn't it? Not knowing about the house up the road?'

Cathy had spent most of the night asking herself the same question. The newly established Portsmouth Crime Squad had been one of the first BCU initiatives to win Secretan's backing. She had fought hard for the post of DI on the squad and last night's operation should have been the first of her battle honours. Yet here she was, well and truly on the back foot.

'My responsibility,' she said at once. 'And my fault.'

'Very noble. Where did it go wrong?'

'I haven't a clue, sir. As soon as I find out, I'll let you know.'

'You were happy with the intelligence material? And the surveillance package?'

'There wasn't a problem.'

'And the guys were all briefed properly?'

'Of course.'

'Then –' Secretan held his hands wide '– what bloody happened?'

Cathy glanced down at the single sheet of precautionary notes she'd brought with her. A bunch of young Scouse drug dealers had turned up after Christmas, bored with life in Bournemouth. Within weeks, they'd dropped a very large boulder into the peace and quiet of the Portsmouth drug scene. There were reports of rival street-level dealers – Pompey kids – being kidnapped and tortured. There was talk of Stanley knives and electric drills. The word on the estates, with just a hint of admiration, was 'ultra-violence'.

Secretan, alerted by one of his Drugs Intelligence Officers, had sensed this sudden rise in temperature and knew at once the probable consequences. The last thing he wanted was a full-scale turf war, a major nightmare in a city already plagued by drug-related crime. Hence the clarity of the task he'd handed to Cathy Lamb. Get these guys sorted, he'd told her. I want them locked up before it all gets out of hand.

Cathy, well versed in the difficulties of getting any kind of result in court, had been painstaking in her preparation. The DIO had devoted countless man-hours to establishing supply patterns. The surveillance team had installed a camera in a property across the road and organised a round-the-clock watch. Yet not once had they sussed the house that the Scousers were using as an annexe. Hence last night's disaster.

In theory, by now DI Lamb should have had bodies in the Bridewell and a sizeable stash of Merseyside Class A narcotics – mainly heroin and cocaine – in the property lock-up. In practice, the moment the House Entry boys had done the business, the Scousers had abandoned the late movie two doors along and fled.

Secretan wanted to know about the later incident at Bystock Road. Who owned the premises?

'DC Winter was onto the housing benefit people first thing,' Cathy said at once.

'And?'

'It belongs to a Dave Pullen.'

'We know him?'

'Very well. He's just done two years for supply. Came out the back end of last year.'

'He's had the property a while?'

'No, sir. Winter says he only signed the contract a couple of months ago. The place was a repo.'

'So where did he get the money? You're trying to tell me he stashed it away? Little nest egg for later?'

'No, sir. Pullen's big mates with Mackenzie.'

'Meaning?'

'Mackenzie staked him when they auctioned the place. Or at least persuaded him to act as nominee. Either way, it puts Pullen alongside Bazza.'

'And our northern friends would have known that?'

'Must have done.'

'Because they wanted to get in Mackenzie's face?'

'Yes.'

'Ah . . .' Secretan reached for a sheet of paper and wrote himself a note. 'Just what we didn't need.'

He paused a moment, staring down at the scribbled names. Then Cathy offered an apologetic cough.

'I'm afraid it gets worse, sir.'

'Really?' Secretan glanced up. 'How?'

'The girl we found on the bed, the one that went to hospital. Her name's Trudy Gallagher. According to Winter, she's the daughter of a woman called Misty Gallagher.'

'And Misty?'

'Is Mackenzie's shag. Or certainly used to be.'

There was a long silence. Then Secretan, in a tiny spasm of anger that took Cathy by surprise, screwed up the sheet of paper and tossed it into the bin.

'I warned you the Scouse kids were trouble,' he said quietly. 'Didn't I?'

Det-Supt Willard's Major Crimes Team also operated from Kingston Crescent, a neighbourly arrangement that put the Basic Command Unit and the MCT closer than – in practice – they really were. While Secretan's brief was getting on top of so-called 'volume crime', the small print of policing a challenging and frequently violent city, it fell to Willard's squad to take on crimes that attracted a more generous helping of CID resources, unavailable to the likes of Secretan. The bulk of murders, stranger rapes, and complex conspiracies were thus referred to the MCT's secured suite of offices, which occupied an entire floor in a newish block to the rear of the Kingston Crescent site. The largest of these offices, a south-facing room dominated by a long conference table, naturally belonged to Willard.

Faraday found him in his shirtsleeves, his massive body bent over the phone. Mention of house-to-house parameters and a POLSA search suggested a sizeable operation already underway out at Fort Cumberland.

Willard nodded towards the conference table and Faraday took a seat. Driving back from the hospital, he'd managed to raise Hayder's partner on his mobile. Maggie had spent most of the night at the hospital, waiting in Critical Care for some returning flicker of consciousness, and now she was at home, excused classes until she felt able to face the real world again. The conversation had been brief, Faraday offering whatever help he could, but before Maggie had rung off she'd told him that what had happened had come as no surprise. 'He'd been working up to it,' she'd said. 'Something had really got to him.'

Quite how this squared with the facts of the case – some kind of confrontation, injuries consistent with being run over – wasn't remotely clear, but Faraday understood at once what she'd meant. The times the two men had met over the last couple of weeks, Hayder had struck him as reticent to the point of preoccupation. He felt, he admitted at one point, 'under siege', a state of mind that seemed to have absolutely nothing to do with his domestic situation.

Willard had finished on the phone. He left the office without a word and returned minutes later with three mugs of coffee.

Faraday nodded towards the phone.

'How's it going?'

'It isn't. Not yet. Scenes of Crime are talking multiple tyre tracks and we don't even have a proper fix on where it might have happened. It's a famous shagging spot. Half the city uses it.'

Faraday was curious to know who was coordinating the inquiry.

'Dave Michaels is sorting it out.'

'SIO?'

'Me.'

Faraday nodded, not beginning to understand. Dave Michaels was a Detective Sergeant. Senior Investigating Officer on a case like this was a role for a DI. There were three DIs on the Major Crimes Team. With Hayder off the plot and the other DI flat out on a domestic in Waterlooville, that left Faraday. He had nothing pressing on his desk. He knew Nick Hayder well. So why wasn't he out at Fort Cumberland, marshalling the troops?

There was a tap at the door and Faraday glanced round to find Brian Imber stepping into the office. He must have driven over from the Intelligence Unit, Faraday thought. And he must have been expected.

'Black? Half a sugar?' Willard nodded at the third mug.

Imber sat down, parking his briefcase beside the chair. A lean, combative fifty-four-year-old with a passion for long-distance running, he'd spent a couple of controversial years banging the drum for an aggressive new approach to the drugs issue, and for the first time Faraday had the smallest inkling of what might lie behind Willard's early-morning call. There was a sub-plot here, something more complex than sorting out a serious assault.

Willard had opened his file. He quickly scanned a page or two of notes, then told Imber to get on with it.

Imber glanced across at Faraday.

'You've seen Nick.' It was a statement, not a question.

'Yes.'

'Not good, eh?'

'No.'

'OK, so here's the problem we have.' He reached down for his briefcase and produced a thick file of his own. 'Nick has been putting a case together. I'm sure the boss will be going into the whys and wherefores in a minute but the point is this: Nick won't be around for a while. Not the way we'll need him.'

'So?'

'So the boss is after a replacement.'

Willard's finger was anchored on a page halfway through his file. He glanced up at Faraday.

'We're talking serious covert. You won't have come across it and neither will anyone else, not if Hayder's done his work properly.' Willard paused. 'We're calling it Operation *Tumbril*.'

Faraday could only nod. He'd never heard of *Tumbril* in his life. 'What is it?'

'Number one, it's long-term. A year now?' Willard was looking at Imber.

'Fourteen months, sir.'

'Fourteen months. That's a lot of resource, believe me, and there's days I regret even dreaming we could run with something like this. *Tumbril*'s been like the bastard kid no one really wants. I can name you a dozen people in this organisation who wanted it strangled at birth and most of them are still putting the boot in. If you're looking for serious grief –' he tapped the file '– be my guest.'

'So what is it?' Faraday asked again. 'This *Tumbril*?'

Willard abandoned the file and sat back in his chair, briefly savouring this small moment of drama. Normally the most undemonstrative of men, he even allowed himself the beginnings of a smile.

'It's Bazza Mackenzie,' he said softly.

'He's the target?'

'Yes. The way we've played it, there are other names in the frame, names that'll make your eyes water, but, fundamentally, yes, we're talking Bazza.'

'You finally decided to take him on?'

'Had to. NCIS were talking full flag level three if we got the spadework under way. Even our lot couldn't turn that down.'

The National Criminal Intelligence Service was the body charged with ranking the UK's major criminals. To Faraday's knowledge there were only 147 full flag level threes in the country. With the extra funding that came with trying to tackle that kind of notoriety, Willard was right: a major investigation was irresistible.

Faraday glanced at Imber, beginning to wonder how many other *Tumbril* files were in his briefcase.

'But we're a bit late, aren't we? Mackenzie's made his money, gone legit. These days he's just another businessman . . . No?'

'No way.' Willard was emphatic. 'That's what we thought to begin with, but it's not true. What no one ever takes into account is the nature of these blokes, the way they're made. You're right about the money. Mackenzie's millions in, squillions in, but the truth is he can't leave it alone. The guy's programmed to break the law. That's what he does. That's what he's best at. He's a local boy, Pompey through and through. He's done it his way, right from the off, and the bottom line is, he doesn't care a toss. If it isn't hard drugs, it'll be something else. And that's why we're going to fucking have him.'

This, from Willard, was a major speech. In terms of investigative style, the Det-Supt had the lowest blood pressure Faraday had ever come across yet the mere mention of Bazza Mackenzie seemed to put a blush of colour in his face.

Faraday was about to ask a question about last night, about some kind of linkage to *Tumbril*, but Willard had already handed the baton back to Imber. According to the DS, there was money-laundering legislation they could use. They'd employed a forensic accountant. They'd acquired truckloads of paperwork from various sources and spent months and months crawling over hundreds of transactions, trying to unpick the web of deals behind which Mackenzie had hidden his profits. None of this stuff was easy, and lots of it – to be frank – was a pain in the arse, but piece by piece the jigsaw was coming together, and that was what mattered.

As Imber warmed to his theme, pausing over a page in his file to make a particular set of points, Faraday let the details wash over him. Soon enough there'd be time for a proper briefing. Just now, here in Willard's office, he wanted to dwell a little on Mackenzie.

Everyone in Pompey knew the name. Bazza was the man who'd first brought serious quantities of cocaine into the city. Bazza was the one-time football hooligan who'd turned kilos of 95 per cent Peruvian into cafe-bars and tanning salons, and countless other legitimate enterprises. Bazza was the guy at the wheel of the latest SUV, at the launch of the latest theme restaurant, in the best seats in the South Stand at Fratton Park. Bazza, in short, was living proof that crime – serious crime – paid.

Faraday, unlike many other local detectives, had never had any first-hand dealings with the man, but his control of the city's cocaine and ecstasy market had been so total, so carefully secured, that it sometimes seemed impossible to come across a drugs-related crime that didn't, in the end, link back to Mackenzie. Over the years the man had become a legend. He gloried in his notoriety, in his reputation, and the more visibly successful he became, the more it seemed to some that the forces of law and order had simply given up. Bazza, as one DC had once remarked, was a bit like the weather. Always there.

Watching Imber, Faraday was more heartened by this sudden development that he could possibly express. Like others in the force, he'd been bewildered by Mackenzie's seeming immunity, failing to understand why he'd never been taken on. Slowly, this bewilderment had turned to frustration, then anger, then – to his own quiet shame – resignation. In contemporary policing, he'd finally concluded, certain battles simply weren't worth fighting. Maybe it was a question of resources. Maybe it was the pressure of a million other things to do. Either way, Bazza seemed to have slipped effortlessly into a prosperous middle age, well connected, beyond reach, a role model for every little scroat in the city.

Until, it seemed, now.

Imber was talking about a recent trip to Gibraltar. Faraday touched him lightly on the arm, struck by a sudden thought.

'How come Nick managed to keep the lid on this?'

'I'm not with you.'

'His office is next to mine. I know he's always shutting the door but there are limits. Surely . . . ?'

Imber glanced at Willard. Willard hadn't taken his eyes off Faraday. There was a long silence.

'You're telling me *Tumbril*'s run from somewhere else?'

'That's right.'

'Another nick?'

'No.'

'Why not?' Faraday looked from one to the other. 'You're serious?'

Chapter three

Winter loathed hospitals. Ever since he'd been a kid, they'd represented authority. People who'd tell you what to do. People who'd strip you half naked and take the most amazing liberties. People who'd hurt you. A couple of years back, he'd lost his wife to the men in white coats. More recently, after a vehicle pursuit that had gone badly wrong, he'd spent a couple of painful days under NHS care, fantasising about Bell's whisky and the possibility of a decently-cooked spud. Show Paul Winter a hospital, and he'd be looking for the door.

The A & E Department, for a Wednesday morning, was already busy. Winter showed his warrant card to the woman manning the reception desk.

'It's about last night,' he said. 'Girl called Trudy Gallagher.'

'What about her?'

'She was brought in by ambulance. Three, half three, this morning something like that. Bit of an incident.'

'And?'

'I need to talk to her.'

The woman tapped a command into her keyboard. The other side of the waiting area, Jimmy Suttle was sorting out small change for the coffee machine.

'As far as I can tell, she went.' It was the receptionist again, still gazing at the screen of her PC.

'*Went?* We talking the same girl?'

'Here.' The woman turned the screen towards Winter. Trudy Gallagher had been booked in at 03.48. She'd complained of a headache and period pains, and the duty streaming nurse had marked her low priority. The pre-midnight rush had thinned, but with half a dozen patients ahead of her in the queue that still meant a wait of a couple of hours. At least.

'She had bruising. Here and here.' Winter touched his ribcage. 'She'd

22

been tied up half the night, terrified out of her head. She was in shock. You're telling me she just walked out?'

'We can only go on what we're told. It's her body, not ours.'

'Yeah, but . . .' Winter shook his head. Last night he'd known he should have ridden up to the QA with Trudy but, looking at her, he'd concluded there was no point. She was past talking, past saying anything remotely useful. They'd keep her in at the hospital, bound to. Next morning would be better. Then she'd have something to say.

'Here . . .' It was Suttle with the coffees. Winter ignored him.

'So where did she go?'

'No idea.'

'She give you an address?'

'Yes.' The woman was peering at a box on the screen.

'And?'

'No chance.' She gave Winter a withering look. 'You blokes ever bother with data protection?'

Winter obliged her with a smile.

'Never,' he said.

He leaned across the counter, trying to check out the screen, but she turned it away. Finally, he gave up.

'So that's it?' He pocketed his notebook. 'She arrives in an ambulance? She sits here for an hour? Then legs it?'

'That's the way it looks.'

'What about the people who dealt with her? The streaming nurse you mentioned. Where do I find her?'

'At home, Mr Winter.' The woman was already clearing her screen for the next patient. 'Asleep.'

Winter phoned Cathy Lamb from the car park. Back from her head-to-head with Secretan, she'd sent him a text message. Secretan was looking for an action plan, some clue to where the inquiry might be headed next, and the DI wanted to know about Trudy Gallagher.

'It's fine, boss. Favour?'

'What does "fine" mean?'

'We're setting up to take a statement. Could you do a CIS check for me? Dave Pullen?'

'What about him?'

'I need a current address.'

'93 Bystock Road.' There were limits to Cathy's patience. 'You were there last night.'

'That's his rental property. He lives somewhere else. Has to.'

There was a pause while Lamb accessed the Criminal Intelligence System. Simple checks like these took less than a minute.

'They're giving 183 Ashburton Road, Southsea,' she said at last. 'Flat 11.'

Driving back into the city, Winter couldn't rid himself of the image of Trudy Gallagher crouched in the bare bedroom minutes after Suttle had taken his penknife to the plastic cable ties. Last time he'd seen her, a couple of years back, she'd been a dumpy little schoolgirl with a passion for Big Macs and anything featuring Leonardo di Caprio. Her mum, with more money than sense, had given her a big, fat allowance and let nature take its path.

Now, a stone thinner, a couple of inches taller, young Trudy had stepped into womanhood in the dodgiest company imaginable. First, according to a trusted local source, had come a live-in relationship with a Farlington car dealer twice her age. Then, for reasons the source didn't begin to understand, Trudy had picked up with Dave Pullen. Share a bed with that kind of arse-wipe, thought Winter, and you shouldn't be surprised by the consequences.

Last night in Bystock Road, the neighbour had come in with a couple of blankets while Trudy had huddled in the corner of the bedroom, white-faced, her whole body shuddering with cold. When Winter asked her what had happened, she said she didn't want to talk about it. Nobody had hurt her. Nobody had sexually molested her. It had all been a joke and the last thing she needed was an examination by a police surgeon. In the end, once Suttle had found her clothes, she'd agreed to let the ambulancemen take her to hospital for a check-up, but what she really wanted was everyone to go away and leave her alone.

'You saw her, son. She was wrecked, wasn't she?'

'Yeah, right state.' Suttle was at the wheel, nudging eighty on the long curve of motorway that fed traffic into the city.

Winter was still brooding, still working out how he'd managed to abandon a key witness in favour of rescuing a couple of hours' kip.

'Observation, at least. Isn't that what we thought? Couple of days tucked up in some ward or other? Amazing.' He shook his head, staring across the harbour at the pale spread of Portchester Castle. 'Just goes to show, eh?'

'You're thinking she conned us?'

'I'm thinking my arse is on the line.' He reached for the packet of Werthers Originals on the dashboard. 'Again.'

Suttle grinned. As a young DC, barely twenty-four, he was new to Portsmouth. He'd grown up in the New Forest, one of a huge family of country kids, and to date his police service had taken him to postings in Andover and Alton, neither of which had prepared him for the likes of Paul Winter. Their month together, to his delight, had been the steepest of learning curves and he was still trying to disentangle truth from legend.

'It was DI Lamb before, wasn't it? When you totalled the Skoda?'

'It was, yes.'

'Good job you've got me to drive you round, then, eh?'

Winter shot him a look. While it was true he'd lost his taste for driving, he'd still emerged from the Skoda incident with his licence intact. Better still, with Traffic finally choosing not to charge him with reckless driving, he'd even won reinstatement to CID. Two long months in uniform, waiting for their decision, had been the pits. Nothing, he'd recently told Suttle, could prepare a man for the excitements of the community foot patrol on a wet winter day in deepest Fratton. One more nicked bicycle, one more rogue pit bull, and he'd have been fit for the locked ward at St James.

Suttle checked his mirror, easing into the middle lane to let a motorcyclist through.

'What do you think, then?' He glanced sideways at Winter. 'About the girl?'

'I think we find her.'

'And then what?' The grin again. 'We tie her down?'

Ashburton Road was one of a series of streets which led north from the commercial heart of Southsea. Back in the nineteenth century these imposing three-storey terraced properties would have housed naval families and wealthy businessmen, the social foundations of fashionable seaside living, but successive tides had washed over the city since, and the results were all too obvious. There wasn't a house in this street that hadn't been overwhelmed by multi-occupation. Properties spared by the Luftwaffe had surrendered to three generations of Pompey landlords.

Dave Pullen lived at the top of a house towards the end of the street. When two attempts to raise him through the speakerphone failed, Winter sent Suttle up the fire escape at the back. Seconds later, he was leaning over the rusting balustrade.

'There's a note,' he yelled. 'He'll be back in half an hour.'

'Who's it to?'

'Doesn't say.'

They waited in the car, parked on a double yellow at the end of the road. As curious as ever, Suttle wanted to know about Pullen, and about Bazza Mackenzie.

'Pullen's a knobber,' Winter said at once. 'Complete waste of space. Could have made a decent footballer once but pissed it up against the wall.'

'You're into football?' This was news to Suttle, who was a Saints fan.

'God forbid, son, but it helps to pretend in this city. Those with a brain aren't a problem but all the rest think about is bloody football. Sad but true.'

'So how good was this bloke?'

'Pullen? Half decent, certainly. Used to turn out for Waterlooville before they merged with Havant.'

'That's the Doc Martens League.' Suttle was impressed. 'What position?'

'Come again?'

'Where did he play? On the field?'

'Ah . . .' Winter frowned. 'Up front, I suppose. I know he was forever scoring. That's how he got his nickname. Or partly, anyway.'

'Pull 'em?'

'Exactly. On the field, he just blew up. Too many fags. Too many bevvies. Too much stuff up his nose. With women, though, it stuck. Dave Pullen. Screwing for England. Young Trudy should have known better.'

'Maybe he talks a good shag.'

'Doubt it. I don't know about the rest of him but there's fuck all between his ears. Not that Trude's any intellectual, but then at eighteen you wouldn't be, would you?'

Suttle was watching a man of uncertain age weaving towards them along the pavement. He had a Londis bag in one hand and a can of Special Brew in the other. Scarlet-faced, glassy-eyed, he paused beside the car, raising the can in a peaceable salute when Suttle told him to fuck off.

'About this Bazza, then.' He'd closed the window.

'Bazza . . . ?' Winter glanced across at him, then settled back in the passenger seat, a smile on his face, the pose of a man savouring the meal of his dreams. 'Bazza Mackenzie is the business,' he said softly. 'Bazza Mackenzie is the closest this city gets to proper crime. It's blokes like Bazza make getting up in the morning a real pleasure. How many people could you say that about? Hand on heart?'

'He comes from round here?'

'Home grown, through and through. The authentic Pompey mush.'

'You ever nick him?'

'Twice, in the early days.' Winter nodded. 'D and D both times, once on the seafront, broad daylight, necked too many lagers on the pier. The other time late at night, club in Palmerston Road, well shantied on Stella and bourbon. Bazza couldn't see a fight without getting stuck in. If we were involved, so much the better.'

'Lots of bottle, then?'

'Lunatic. Complete lunatic. I knew the woman he married – pretty girl, bright too – and she couldn't believe what she'd taken on. Total head case, she used to tell me. Knows absolutely no fear.'

'Big guy? Physically?'

'Small –' Winter shook his head '– small and up for it. But that's always the way, isn't it? You ever notice that, looking at a crowd of them, itching to take you on? It's always the small ones you have to watch. Maybe they've got more to prove. Christ knows.'

Suttle had his eyes on the rear-view mirror. The drunk was rounding the corner, swaying gently as he debated whether to cross the road at the end.

'And Pullen and this Bazza are big mates?'

'Mates, certainly. They go back forever. But then that's the way it works in the city. Same school, same pubs, same women. They ran with the 6.57, both of them. That was Bazza's major career move, took him to the big time.'

The 6.57 had been a bunch of hooligans, Pompey's finest, taking the first train out every other Saturday and exporting a very special brand of football violence to rival grounds all over the country. According to Winter, it was the 6.57 who'd pioneered the major import of serious drugs into the city.

' '89' He grinned. 'Summer of love. These guys had been kicking the shit out of each other for Christ knows how long, then suddenly they're blowing kisses and dancing together in the nightclubs and we're wondering what the fuck's going on.'

'What *was* going on?'

'Ecstasy. They were bringing it in by the truckload, scoring from the rival firms in London. Some of the raves they organised that summer were awesome. Thousands of kids, out of their skulls. Law and order-wise, we never had a prayer. Made you proud, though, just being there. The girl he married was right. Blokes like Bazza, completely fucking reckless, really put the city on the map.'

'Nice.'

'Yeah. Didn't last, though. They took to cocaine after that and it all got ugly again.'

'He stuck to cocaine? No smack?'

'Cocaine and rave drugs, plus amphetamine if you fancied it. Bazza had the odd dabble with heroin but much less than we thought at the time. Wrong image. Smack's for losers.'

Suttle was still watching the mirror. He touched Winter lightly on the arm.

'Tall bloke? Skinny?'

Winter glanced over his shoulder, then nodded.

'Let him get to the front door,' he murmured, 'then we'll say hello.'

But Pullen didn't go to the front door. Instead, he walked straight past the car and began to climb the first flight of steps on the fire escape. Winter watched him for a moment or two, wondering about the limp, then got out of the car. By the time Pullen realised he was being followed, he was nearly at the top.

'Dave. Long time.' Winter was out of breath. 'This is DC Suttle. We'd appreciate a word.'

'Sure. Why not?' Pullen tried to head down again. Winter blocked his way.

'Upstairs,' he said. 'In your place.'

'Why not here? Or down there?'

'Because I'd prefer a bit of privacy. And because I'm bloody knackered.'

Pullen looked suddenly haunted. He had a narrow, bony face, thinning hair that badly needed a trim, yellowing teeth. His sunken eyes were bloodshot and when he made a big show of checking his watch he had trouble keeping his hand steady. If this guy was an advert for the drugs biz, thought Suttle, then there must be better ways of earning a living. Give him a year or two, and a can of Special Brew, and he'd be just another item of street furniture.

'Well, old son . . . ?' Winter was still playing the jovial cop.

'No way.' Pullen shook his head. 'You ain't got the right.'

'No? You'd prefer I popped round the corner for a warrant? Left Jimmy here to keep an eye on you?'

'You can't do that.'

'Try me.'

'What do you want to know?'

'I want to know about Trudy Gallagher. And about what happened last night. Dave, you know the score. Easiest says we get it over with.' He nodded up towards Pullen's peeling front door. 'Half an hour max and we're gone.'

Pullen was doing his best to figure something out. A late night and untold helpings of unlawful substances clearly didn't help. At length, another shake of the head. Winter reached forward, brushing the dandruff off the shoulders of his jacket. Humiliation always talked louder than threats.

'Nice leather, Dave.' He nodded towards the door again. 'After you?'

The flat was three rooms with a tiny kitchen jigsawed into the back of the lounge. Potentially, the place had a lot of potential – south-facing, a hint of a view – but Dave Pullen clearly preferred living in the dark.

Winter wanted to pull the curtains back and throw open the windows. He wanted to invest a bob or two in a nice air freshener and a bunch of flowers. Instead, he sank into the only armchair, wondering how many roll-ups it took to recreate the authentic stink of prison life. Maybe this flat was an exercise in nostalgia. Maybe Pullen couldn't survive without the memory of B Wing.

'So where is she? That nice Trudy?'

'Ain't got a clue.'

'You're lying, Dave. She was in that dosshouse of yours, well fucking kippered. You'd have known about that. They'd have told you.'

'Who says?'

'Me. These Scouse kids are in the wind-up business. They send little messages. That's what she was, Dave: a message.'

Avoiding Winter's gaze, Pullen limped across to the kitchen and opened a drawer. Two fat tablets needed half a glass of water from the tap.

'Headache?'

'Migraine.'

'Same thing.' Winter paused while Pullen swallowed the tablets. 'So tell me about the Scousers. They weren't gentle, you know. Or has she told you that already?'

Pullen didn't answer. Suttle was over in the shadows, inspecting a headline Sellotaped to the wall. The back page had been ripped from *The News*, the city's daily paper.

'Super Blues?' Suttle queried.

Pullen turned on him, a spectral presence in the gloom.

'You got a problem with that?'

'Yeah.'

'Like what?'

'Like Pompey are shit. Half the fucking team are on a bus pass.'

Watching from the armchair, Winter started to laugh. He loved this boy, loved him. There was a kind of madness in so much of what he did. Like Winter himself, he pushed and pushed until something snapped.

'Shit?' Pullen was outraged. 'Top of the Nationwide? Top all fucking season? How does that work, then?'

'You'll find out, mate. If you ever get to the Premiership.'

'So what are you, then?'

'Saints.'

'Scummer?' Pullen started to laugh. 'Well, fuck me. No wonder you end up in the Filth.'

Winter struggled to his feet. There was a pile of twenty-four-can slabs of Stella wedged against the open door, doubtless trophies from a

Cherbourg booze run. Stepping carefully round the tinnies, he disappeared for a moment or two. Seconds later, he was back with something black and boxy in his hand. When he switched on the overhead light, Suttle recognised it as a car radio.

'State of the art, Dave.' Winter examined the back. 'And security marked.'

'It's legit.'

'I'm sure it is. What about the rest?' Winter caught Suttle's eye and nodded towards the door. 'Only we've been having this problem with vehicle breaks. Figures have gone through the roof. You wouldn't believe the grief it's giving our Performance Manager.'

Suttle was back with a cardboard box. After the first five car radios, he gave up counting.

'Worth a bit, eh Dave?' It was Winter again. 'No wonder you never invited us in.'

'She hasn't been here.'

'I don't believe you.'

'It's true. Not since a couple of days back.'

'Then where is she?'

'Fuck knows.'

'You've got a mobile number?'

'She never answers.'

'You had a row or something? Bit of a tiff?'

Silence.

Winter consulted his watch, then settled back in the armchair, steepled his fingers over the swell of his belly, and closed his eyes.

Pullen stirred.

'Her fucking fault,' he muttered. 'Little slag.'

'What did she do to you, Dave?' Winter's eyes were still closed. 'Ask for a decent conversation?'

'Bollocks to that,' Pullen said hotly. 'She can talk her fucking gob off when she wants to. Doesn't take much. Couple of Smirnoffs in Forty Below and you can help your fucking self.'

Forty Below was a cafe-bar and nightclub complex in Gunwharf Quays, immensely popular for chilling out.

'Was that the way they did it?'

'Who?'

'Your Scouser friends? Tenner across the bar and a car ride when she's up for it? Pop round to Dave's place? Listen to some music? Is that what happened?'

'Haven't a clue.'

'Not worried? Not the least concerned? They're taking the piss, Dave. They're telling you you're not up to it any more. Whatever's yours, they're helping themselves. And if you think it begins and ends with young Trudy then you're even more stupid than you look.'

'I don't know what you're talking about.'

'Bollocks you don't. It's not about fanny, you know it's not. It's business, Dave, and we're not talking nicked fucking car radios. I don't know how much charlie Bazza trusts you with these days but something tells me your dealing days might be over. Trudy was a redundancy notice, Dave. These kids are telling you you're past it. You with me? Or am I going too fast?'

'You're off your head.'

'Am I?' Winter got to his feet again. He beckoned Pullen closer. 'We paid these kids a visit last night, Dave. I won't bore you with the details but we came away with more Stanley knives than you'd ever believe. You know all those rumours about local dealers getting slapped around? Kidnapped? Cut? All true, Dave.'

Pullen retreated towards the kitchen. He didn't want to hear any of this. Winter, warming up now, pinned him in a corner.

'You've got a choice, Dave, you and your mates. My boss wants these kids out of the city. I dare say Bazza does, too. We can either go the official route, in which case you'll be giving me a statement, telling me everything you know. Or you can sort something out on your own behalf. Either way, me and Jimmy here are having these.' Winter picked up one of the radios. 'We've got a whole squad on vehicle break-ins. Operation *Cobra*. You might have seen it in the paper. Shall I spread the good word? Tell my mates you've got the beers in?'

Winter let the message register, then told Suttle to repack all the radios in the cardboard box. A visit to the tip that Pullen used as a bedroom produced more booty, enough to fill a pillowslip. On his way out of the flat, back in the sunshine at the top of the fire escape, Winter made Pullen write out Trudy Gallagher's mobile number. He studied it a moment, then folded it into his pocket.

'Best to Bazza, eh?' He gave Pullen a little punch on the shoulder, picked up the pillowslip, and followed Suttle down towards the street.

Mid morning, the conference with Willard over, Faraday followed Brian Imber's Volvo estate out of the parking lot at the back of the Kingston Crescent police station. At the start of the motorway, Imber indicated left, leaving the roundabout for the Continental Ferry Port. North of the port complex lay a cluster of naval establishments known locally as Whale Island. At the far end of the causeway connecting the island to the mainland, Imber coasted to a halt at the red and white barrier. A squaddie approached both cars, an assault rifle slung from his neck.

Faraday wound down his window. Imber had already given him a pass but Faraday had yet to open the envelope. When he did so, he found himself looking at a recent head and shoulders shot taken for an out-of-county inquiry. It showed a grizzled white male in his mid forties with a mop of greying curly hair. The expression on his face, at first glance, gave nothing away but the few people who knew him well would have wondered about the little creases around the eyes. This was a man trying to gauge exactly what awaited him next. Small wonder.

The squaddie glanced at the pass, checked the image, and then waved Faraday through.

Imber was in the nearby car park. Faraday brought the Mondeo to a halt beside him, pocketing the pass. Imber nodded towards a low, brick-built structure a couple of hundred metres away. Beyond lay the harbour and the naval dockyard.

'Welcome to *Tumbril*.' Imber was enjoying this. 'It's a bit cramped, I'm afraid, but we've done our best.'

The building belonged to the Regulating School, the establishment charged with training the navy's police force. A temporary arrangement with the Admiralty, financed from the *Tumbril* budget, paid for an open-plan office on the south side of the building which was normally used as a lecture theatre. Attached to this was a smaller interview room, which now housed the inquiry's ever-growing archive. Carefully labelled files crowded a wall full of shelves. There were also three battered filing cabinets, all fitted with heavy-duty locks.

Imber was explaining about the rest of the security arrangements. There were double locks on the main door, accessible by code and swipe card, plus the eight-foot barbed-wire fence that surrounded the entire site. At Nick Hayder's insistence, the office was regularly swept for bugs, the cleaner had been security-checked, and every member of the five-strong team had signed a binding undertaking never to discuss the operation with anyone else. In terms of paranoia, thought Faraday, this operation was in a class of its own.

'You think we've gone over the top?' Imber was watching him carefully.

'Just a bit.'

'You saw Nick this morning? Unconscious? Legs a mess? Crushed pelvis?'

'You're telling me that was related?'

'I'm telling you we took every conceivable precaution and someone still managed to switch his lights out. Whether that's just coincidence, who can say? All we've tried to do is give ourselves a bit of privacy.'

From the adjoining office came the sound of a door opening, and then the bustle of heavy footsteps. Moments later, Faraday found himself looking at a familiar figure: low-cut dress, huge bosoms, thick gloss lipstick, long purple nails flecked with glitter, and – beneath the mountainous body – a pair of shapely legs that had never failed to take him by surprise.

'Joyce.'

'Sheriff.'

'You're part of this?' Faraday gestured round.

'Too right I am. Archivist, doughnut supplier, hangover cures and light maintenance. Plus I deal with the ruder phone calls. Unless you're nice to me, you get a spanking.' She grinned at him. 'Did I hear yes to coffee?'

Without waiting for an answer, she stepped back into the office. Imber rolled his eyes.

'You two know each other?'

'Very well. Joyce took over at Highland Road a couple of years back when Vanessa got killed.'

'And you survived?'

'More than. Joyce was priceless. Has she still got the agency for Beanie Babes?'

'I'm afraid so.'

'And German porn?'

'In spades, big Jiffy bag from Hamburg every fortnight. We get the trainee reggies queueing at the door. They think she's something else.'

'They're right. She is.'

Through the open door, Faraday could hear her singing as she sorted out mugs for the coffee. Peggy Lee had always been a favourite; regret stitched through with a silky courage.

While Imber fielded a phone call, Faraday perched himself on the edge of a nearby desk. Joyce had disappeared from Highland Road after a cancer scare. Faraday had phoned her a couple of times, checking on the progress of the radiotherapy, but she'd always trivialised the whole thing the way you might dismiss a headache. Sure there was a little lump. Everyone got them. No big deal.

Faraday had never been quite sure whether this optimism of hers was uniquely American or whether she was simply being brave, but either way – to his eternal shame – Joyce had dropped out of his life, forgotten beneath the daily torrent of volume crime that surged through Highland Road.

'You made it then?'

'Sure. Zapped the little bastards.'

'Bastards? Plural?'

'Breast, lymph nodes, couple in the neck.' The purple nails traced the progress of the tumours. 'Got real interesting when they started talking mastectomy.'

Faraday stared at her. Her breasts looked real enough to him. 'So what happened?'

'I told them no way. They could try anything else, didn't matter what, but we'd all go down together. Worked real good. Chemotherapy you wouldn't believe. Couple of weeks of that shit and the little bastards came out with their hands up. Bang, bang, bang. Full military funeral but theirs not mine.' She glanced up. 'Still take sugar?'

Faraday nodded. For the first time, he noticed the display of photos on the far wall. Imber was still deep in conversation.

'Here.' Joyce handed him a mug of coffee. 'Let me give you the tour.'

Faraday followed her across the office. The biggest of the photos was an aerial shot of a sizeable property, red-tiled roof, big double bays, tall sash windows. There was a Mercedes convertible and an SUV on the patterned brick drive in front of the double garage, and a newish-looking swimming pool occupied part of the garden at the front. Certain features – security cameras, intruder-resistant thorn bushes, remotely operated double gates – had been identified and labelled, and there was a circle around a small wooden hut tucked beside a child's swing.

'That's a kennel. The guy just loves his dogs.' Joyce was demolishing her second chocolate biscuit. 'Two ridgebacks. Clancy and Spud.'

'This is Mackenzie's?'

'Sure. 13 Sandown Road. Now isn't that cute? And don't you just want to ask how they ever gave him planning permission? Nice area like that?'

Faraday followed her pointing finger. Above the first-floor bedrooms, a huge balconette had been built into the roof. A skirt of chromium and smoked glass hid the balconette from view but the angle of the photograph revealed four sun loungers with a couple of tables in between. Faraday nodded. Sandown Road lay in the heart of Craneswater Park. Craneswater was as select as Southsea got, street after street of generously proportioned Edwardian villas with plenty of garden and views across the Solent. People who'd made it to this middle class enclave guarded their heritage with a fierce passion. Joyce was right, Faraday thought. How come Bazza Mackenzie had been allowed this sudden splash of Florida?

'And here, look, the ASU boys have done us proud.' Joyce was indicating an object in the garden. 'You know what that is?'

Faraday stepped closer.

'Some kind of floodlight?'

'Gold star for the sheriff!' Joyce was beaming. 'He's got five of them.

Evenings you get the full works, and believe me we're talking serious gels. Mondays it's mauve, Tuesdays puke green, and Wednesdays ... my favourite ...'

'Purple?'

'Cerise. We'll end up with a charge sheet long as your arm but good taste won't figure.'

Imber, his phone call over, had joined them. Faraday nodded at the house.

'You've paid him a visit?'

'Not yet.' Imber shook his head. 'That photo's in case we have to at short notice, but the ASU have promised an update if we give them enough warning.'

'Where does the documentation come from?' Faraday glanced back towards the smaller room that housed the files.

'Production Orders. We're using the DTA. So far we've concentrated on property deals and transactions in and out of Gibraltar. Going back ten years, that's a lot of paper.'

The Drug Trafficking Act offered an investigation like this the power to raise Production Orders from a judge sitting in chambers. These, in turn, would have enabled Hayder to seize a huge range of documentation, from bank records to mortgage deeds. In theory, the target should remain ignorant of this ever-widening trawl. Fat chance.

'He'll know ... won't he?'

'Of course he will. His accountant will have told him. His bank. His brief. Being Bazza, he's probably flattered. There's not much we can do to shake him. Not yet.'

'Why didn't Nick go for supply?'

'Because Mackenzie's arm's length now, doesn't let the stuff anywhere near him. If we wanted to make a supply charge stick, we should have been doing this years ago.'

'But he still controls it all?'

'Of course he does. That's the way business works. He bankrolls supply and helps himself to a fat percentage. The richer you get, the more the other blokes do all the running around. Arm's length, he's laughing.'

Faraday was looking at the other photos. One showed Mackenzie getting out of the sleek convertible, a small, stocky, eager-looking figure with a broad grin on his face. Another showed a good-sized motor cruiser nosing into a marina berth. Both bore the imprint of a surveillance operation, the photographer working from a distance at the end of a powerful telephoto lens.

'These are his?'

35

'In reality, yes. He hides everything behind nominee names because he's not stupid, but yes. These are what keep us going. We've got loads more in the drawer. Properties abroad, local businesses, you name it. Joyce rings the changes every Monday. Just in case we lose motivation.'

'That's envy, isn't it?'

'Of course. And frustration, too. If you'd been banged up here all year you'd pretty much feel the same way.'

'So who does the legwork, figures-wise?'

'Bloke called Martin Prebble. He's a forensic accountant. Costs us a fortune but he's shit-hot. Give him three million documents and he'll know the ones to sling out. Without him around, we'd still be at base camp.'

'So where is he?'

'London. He works for one of the big City firms. We get him two days a week.' He glanced round. Joyce had returned to her desk. Imber bent towards Faraday. 'I know what you're thinking, Joe, but believe me this is the only way. We've tried everything else – the covert, surveillance, informants, plotting the supply chain – but like I say, Mackenzie's beyond all that. He's clever, brighter than you might think. He's well advised and he's listened to that advice. The guy's walled himself off from the sharp end. All we're left with is the money. But that's where we can hurt him. By following the money.'

Faraday was trying to reconcile this little outburst with something that had stuck in his mind from Willard. *Mackenzie's programmed to break the law*, he'd said. *That's what he does. And that's why we'll have him.*

'You really think it's all down to the paperwork?'

'I do.'

'No point trying to set him up?'

'None. Like I said, he's too well protected. This way we at least have a fighting chance. As long as we all keep the faith.'

'Who's "we"?'

'Who do you think? It's means and ends, Joe. And, to be fair, we've had our share of resources.'

'You're telling me there's pressure for a result?'

'Of course there is. There's always pressure for a result. That's why Nick was close to blowing up. A job like this takes time, years and years. We've never thought like that before but then we've never had to. What it boils down to is blokes like Bazza. The man's a billboard. He's up there in lights. He's telling every kid in this city there's no point going to school, no point keeping this side of the law, no point getting your head down and trying to lead a half-decent life. Leave Bazza alone, put him in the Too Difficult basket, chuck in the towel, and we might as well call it a day.'

Faraday nodded. He'd heard this from Imber before, almost word for word. For reasons the DS had never revealed, he'd won himself a reputation as a crusader when it came to the drugs issue. Since the mid-eighties, he'd been warning about the impending apocalypse, not simply because of his worries about his own kids, but because his intelligence work had taught him very early on that Class A narcotics would – one day – fuel an entire economy. Ignore the drugs issue, he'd said, and the consequences would be catastrophic.

Imber's bosses at every level, besieged by the pressures of volume crime, had paid lip service to this relentless lobbying. They read the reports he put together. They even circulated his more measured assessments of developments to come. But it had taken a figure like Bazza Mackenzie to persuade them to give Imber his head. Why? Because Mackenzie's wealth was beginning to taint every corner of the city. And that, in Willard's phrase, was a cop-out too far.

Faraday watched Imber pour himself a glass of juice from the fridge. Marathon training evidently forbade him any form of caffeine. Finally, he looked up.

'Willard's stuck his neck out,' Imber said. 'And I admire him for that.'

'Easy sell?'

'You're joking. It's not just the resources, it's other coppers. Every one thinks you're trespassing in this game.'

'You're supposed to be invisible.'

'I know. And thanks to Nick we largely are. But blokes know something's up and they get extremely pissed off.'

'Like who?'

'Doesn't matter. I'd give you a list of names but there's no point. I'm just telling you this thing isn't easy. We're out here on our own and we've got a bloody great mountain to climb. Take on someone like Bazza and you'd be amazed the people you upset.'

'Does that bother you?'

'Not in the least. As long as we get a result.'

Faraday studied him a moment, aware that Joyce had stopped typing.

'And you think we will get a result?' he said at last.

'I think we have to.'

'Despite all the –' Faraday frowned '– aggravation?'

'Of course.' Imber gave him a long, searching look. 'You are up for this, aren't you?'

Chapter four

Winter left his Subaru in the underground car park at Gunwharf Quays and led Suttle up the escalator towards the shopping plaza. It had taken two conversations on the mobile to coax a meet from Trudy Gallagher and, hearing the squawk of seagulls in the background, it gave Winter no comfort at all to realise the obvious. Misty Gallagher lived in one of the Gunwharf apartments overlooking the waterfront. Trudy had gone back to mum.

The Gumbo Parlour had only just opened. A harassed-looking waitress was at the back of the restaurant, polishing glasses. Winter selected a table by the window and took the seat with the best view.

Beyond the walkway, on the very edge of the harbour, contractors were working on the first stages of the Spinnaker Tower, a 500-foot extravaganza that would, hoped the council, put Pompey on the national map. Winter watched as another bucket of concrete was winched slowly into place, wondering what kind of difference a structure like this would really make. Fans of the tower banged on about the boldness of the gesture, how it spoke of confidence and a new start for the city, but Winter was rather fond of the other Portsmouth, scruffy, blunt, and perfectly happy to muddle through.

Suttle was already browsing the lunchtime choices. *Moules à l'Americaine*, he thought, sounded nice.

'We're having coffee,' Winter told him, 'unless you're paying.'

He settled back in his chair, watching a sailing dinghy on the harbour fighting to get out of the way of a huge inbound ferry. Trudy had promised to meet them at noon, and she still had ten minutes in hand.

'You should meet her mum,' he told Suttle. 'In fact you probably will.'

'That's a promise?'

'Health warning. Anything in trousers under thirty, you're talking serious risk assessement.'

Misty Gallagher, over the years, had become a legend. Winter had been to parties where she'd taken three men to bed, two of them CID, one a convicted bank robber, and left all of them the best of friends. Bazza Mackenzie, impressed by her contacts as well as her looks, had been shagging her since the mid nineties, setting her up in a series of properties he'd bought for development. More recently, he'd installed her in a third-floor apartment in one of the Gunwharf blocks beyond the shopping complex, a £600,000 gesture to say she still mattered. Lately, though, explained Winter, the relationship appeared to have come under some strain.

'How?' Suttle was still eyeing the menu.

'Italian bird, much younger than Mist. Bit of style, bit of class, doesn't need a bag over her head.'

'Misty's a dog?'

'Far from it, body to die for even now, but the woman's got a real mouth on her, never knows when to shut up. Pompey girl . . .' Winter beckoned the waitress. 'Comes with the territory.'

The waitress took the order. Two cappuccinos. Suttle watched her making her way back towards the coffee machine.

'So where's the father?'

'Trudy's dad? Christ knows. His name's Gallagher but I can't remember ever meeting him. Mist's real name is Marlene, by the way, and there are blokes in the job still call her that. Drives her mad.'

'So why Misty?'

'You don't want to know.'

'Go on.'

Winter shook his head, telling him it didn't matter, but Suttle was insistent and Winter finally gave in, recounting another party trick Misty used to pull. The story revolved around Misty's chest, of which she was extremely proud, and Winter had got to the bit where Misty removed her top when he became aware of a tall, striking figure in a tight red skirt and high leather boots.

'You're really fucking sad, Paul Winter.' She sank into the spare chair. 'You know that?'

Trudy was unrecognisable. Last time Suttle had seen her, stumbling into the back of an ambulance in the middle of the night, she'd stepped out of a Salvation Army poster. Now, barely half a day later, she might have graced the cover of a fashion magazine. Suttle couldn't take his eyes off her.

'Coffee? Something to eat?' He was already on his feet.

'Latte. With tons of sugar. And one of them Danish pastries. No –' she was fumbling in her bag for a cigarette '– make that two.'

With Suttle gone, Winter leaned forward across the table. Trudy catching him in mid story hadn't embarrassed him in the slightest. Quite the reverse.

'How is she, then, that mum of yours?'

'Off her trolley. As usual.'

'Seeing lots of her, are you?'

'Not if I can help it. She's pissed me off, if you want the truth. Seriously pissed me off.'

'Why's that?'

Trudy didn't answer. She lit the cigarette, and Winter watched her as she tipped her head back, expelling a long plume of blue smoke.

Trudy's eyes had followed Suttle to the counter.

'What's his name, then? Your mate?'

'Jimmy.' Winter was looking at her right hand. 'What happened to your nails?'

'What?'

'Your nails? There and there?' He reached across. The nails on her index and ring fingers had been savagely trimmed. 'Your new Scouse friends, was it? Fighting them off?'

'What are you on about?' Trudy rolled her eyes. She'd come here as a favour. Any more of this shit, and she'd be out the door.

'I'm trying to find out what happened, love. We're on your side.'

'Yeah?' She was watching Suttle again, weaving his way back through the tables with a coffee and a plate of pastries. 'Is he local then, your mate?'

Winter ignored the question. He wanted to know what had happened last night. Trudy had been the subject of an assault. It was Winter's job to find out how and why. Doing it over coffee was one way. There were others.

'That's a threat.' She moved her bag to make a space for the pastries. 'I don't do threats.'

'It's not a threat. I'm just telling you the way it is.'

'That's my business, ain't it?'

'Wrong, love. Last night made it ours.'

Trudy ignored him. The smile was for Suttle.

'Mr Grumpy here says you're local. That right?'

'Yeah.' Suttle nodded. 'Sugar?'

'Three.' She pushed the cup towards him. 'Where d'you live then? Somewhere nice?'

'Petersfield,' Winter grunted. 'And he's married.'

'Bollocks am I.' Suttle grinned at her. 'Has he asked you about last night yet?'

'Yeah, and I told him to fuck off so don't you start.'

'Can't have been nice, though, can it? Dr Dre's crap enough with

40

your clothes on. Naked, trussed up like a fucking turkey, you wouldn't have a brain left.'

In spite of herself, Trudy began to laugh.

'That kind of shit's for white kids wishing they were black. That's even sadder than him.'

'Who?'

'Him. Uncle Paul.' She nodded at Winter. 'He used to come sniffing round my mum. Still does when he's desperate.'

'You never said, boss.' Suttle raised an eyebrow.

'You never asked.' Winter had developed an intense interest in the Gosport ferry. 'And don't jump to conclusions, either. Mist and I? We were never more than—'

'Good friends?' Trudy started to laugh again. 'That's Chinese for disappointment, ain't it? That's what my mum says. No time for all that good friends shit, not her . . .'

'Meaning what?'

'Meaning she'll shag anything if she thinks there's money in it. And, believe me, I should fucking know.'

There was an abrupt silence while Trudy took a bite of pastry. Suttle glanced at Winter, then offered her a paper napkin from the sheaf in the middle of the table.

'Listen,' he began. 'About last night . . .'

Trudy shook her head, wiping her mouth with the back of her hand.

'There's no way you're gonna get me to talk about it,' she muttered. 'So don't even try.'

Winter ignored the warning.

'What about Dave Pullen, then?'

'Dave Pullen's a wanker.'

'He says he hasn't seen you for a couple of days.'

'No, and he won't either. Not if I have anything to do with it.'

'Why's that?'

'None of your business.'

Winter studied her a moment, then leaned forward and helped himself to the second pastry. When Trudy tried to get it back, he told her to behave herself.

'Listen, Trude, we're trying to help you. Maybe you met the Scouse kids here, Gunwharf, Forty Below. Maybe it was Southsea, Guildhall Walk, some club or other. Tell you the truth, it doesn't matter. All you need to know is it wasn't you they were after, not the lovely Trudy. But then you've probably worked that out yourself.'

'Yeah?' For the first time she sounded uncertain.

Winter leaned forward again. The pastry was still intact.

'What you have to understand, Trude, is this. There's a war on out there. The Scousers started it. They were the ones who—'

'But they were really nice. Really funny.'

'I'm sure they were. And then they tied you up and left you. You're not telling me you've forgotten all that?' He paused, letting the question sink in. He had her attention now, he knew it.

'No,' she said at length. 'I ain't forgotten that.'

'And the other stuff?'

'What other stuff?'

'The bruises.' Winter touched his lower body. 'Here and here. Where they whacked you. We had a torch, remember. You want to tell us how it happened?'

'No.'

'Not even if there's a chance they'll be back for more?'

'They won't be.'

'How do you know?'

'I just do.'

'Hundred per cent certain?'

'Yeah.' She nodded bitterly. 'One hundred fucking per cent.'

Winter looked at her for a long moment. Then he returned the second pastry to her plate.

'Here.' He tried to cheer her up with a smile. 'Compliments of the house.'

'No, thanks.' She shook her head and began to get up. 'You have it.'

Faraday found Eadie Sykes wolfing a sandwich in her office. She worked out of three small rooms above a solicitor's practice in Hampshire Terrace. Faraday's phone call from Whale Island had produced an invitation to share her take-out lunch but it was obvious at first glance that Faraday had arrived too late.

He was looking at the debris on the desk beside the PC, suddenly realising how hungry he was. Two pots of beans. A salad. Something with rice and little chunks of chorizo. All gone.

'Your boy,' Eadie said through a mouthful of cheese and sun-dried tomato. 'You ought to feed him in the mornings.'

'I would if he was ever around.'

Faraday found a perch for himself on a corner of the desk. J-J had been working part-time for Eadie for more than a year, first as a stills photographer on a Dunkirk anniversary film, and now as a researcher and cameraman on her latest production. Some weeks, he saw more of J-J's boss than his son.

'So where is he?'

'Out.' She glanced at her watch. 'Gone to look for more junkies.'

'He was doing that last week. And the week before.'

'Yeah, and the week before that. Finding them's one thing, trying to do anything half sensible is quite another. They're hopeless, all of them. Never out of bed. Never turn up. Never do what they've promised. Still, if it wasn't a problem, we wouldn't be doing a video about it, so I guess there's an upside.'

She was a tall, big-boned woman with the grace and ease of a natural athlete. Too much Australian sun had wrecked her complexion but she cared as little for make-up as she bothered with fashion. Most days, she wore jeans and a sweatshirt. This morning's was a souvenir from a cheap week in Fuerteventura.

Faraday swopped the desk for a chair in the corner, waiting for her to finish sweeping J-J's debris into a black plastic sack. After Marta, he'd promised himself never again to make any assumptions about a woman, yet here he was, back in a relationship that felt all too real. Part of it, he'd concluded, was simple admiration. Never had he met anyone, male or female, so single-minded, so gutsy, so undaunted by whatever odds life stacked against her. Even Nick Hayder was a pale imitation of Eadie Sykes.

'So how's it going?' Faraday nodded towards the PC but Eadie's attention had been caught by a tiny television on the other side of the office.

'The UN have abandoned the border and Reuters are reporting explosions in Basra.' She shook her head, disgusted. 'It's definitely going to happen, Joe. Tomorrow morning at the latest.'

'I meant your video.'

'Ah . . .' Eadie looked briefly confused. 'In that case I'd have to say slowly.'

'Because of the junkies?'

'Because of the absence of junkies.' She finally abandoned the television and turned to face him. 'This is a beautiful city, my love. Smack, cocaine, whatever you fancy, it's all there. Show me a junkie, one I can trust, I'll write you a cheque.'

Faraday felt as if he'd been sharing this battle for an entire year. Eadie was determined to make the definitive video about hard-core drug abuse. She wanted to explore, in the bluntest possible terms, what narcotics actually did to young people. No gimmicks. No fancy camera angles. No homilies. Just a candid account, passed on to a generation who – in Eadie's opinion – deserved a glimpse or two of the unvarnished truth.

To this end, with infinite patience, she'd stitched together a series of grants to fund the project. She'd twisted arms and bent ears. She'd knocked on doors and refused to take no for an answer. And slowly, cheque by cheque, the sheer force of her conviction had begun to bring in the cash.

Contributions had come in from prominent Portsmouth businesses. The Hampshire Police Authority had made a grant. The city council's Crime and Disorder Partnership had offered support. Other monies had turned up from God knows where until finally it fell to a govenment body – the Portsmouth Pathways Partnership – to match-fund the rest. With nearly £30,000 in the bank, Eadie Sykes was ready to shoot the documentary that would make her name. All she needed now was junkies.

'So where's the boy?'

'Down in Old Portsmouth. He came across someone at the Students' Union who thinks they've got the perfect answer. Happens every day. All you can do is say yes.'

'And J-J's hopeful?'

'J-J's always hopeful. Christ, you should know that. It's your fault.'

This was as close as Eadie ever got to offering a compliment, and Faraday took it as such. J-J's deafness had been with him since birth, and Faraday had spent most of the last two decades trying to reassure his son that it didn't really matter. Blind, he'd have been in some difficulty. Lame, he'd be dependent on someone else to push him around. Deaf, he simply had to figure out other ways of hearing. Having a mother around would have helped but sadly that had never been possible.

'When's he due back?'

'When he turns up. You know J-J. Give him half a chance, he'll talk the guy to death.'

They both laughed. J-J had loaded standard British Sign Language with a repertoire all of his own and Faraday, on occasions too numerous to count, had watched him transform potentially embarrassing encounters into wild flurries of body language and laughter. For reasons he didn't fully understand, his son had the gift of getting through, of using his smile and his eyes and those extraordinarily gawky limbs to do the work of his poor mute tongue. Had he not been handicapped, the boy would probably be earning a fortune selling real estate or double glazing. Thank God, Faraday often thought, for deafness.

'So who was this contact?'

'Her name's Sarah. She knows a guy called Daniel Kelly. Heavily into smack.' Eadie was back in front of the television.

'Who?'

'Daniel Kelly. J-J thinks he's a student, too.'

44

Daniel Kelly? Faraday tried hard to place the name but drew a blank. Eadie was still peering at the tiny screen.

'Blair's banging on about a just war again.' She shook her head. 'Can you believe that?'

J-J had the address written down. Chantry Court was a sought-after block of flats within sight of the cathedral. The parking space beneath the building was visible from the street and few of the residents had settled for less than a BMW. After weeks of nosing round squats, bedsits, and chaotic student lets, J-J found it difficult to believe that his contact at the university had sent him here.

The speakerphone beside the locked front door controlled access to the flats. J-J checked his piece of paper again and pressed number 8. He counted to five, then held his tiny Sony cassette player to the microphone beneath the row of buttons. The tape played a pre-recorded message from Eadie Sykes establishing the fact that the young man outside was deaf and dumb, and that he'd appreciate getting inside to meet the tenant. This message, repeated four times, was Eadie's idea, one of the many bridges she'd thrown up between J-J and the realities of video pre-production.

J-J had his hand on the door. A tiny tremor told him he'd won access. Number 8 was on the first floor. A door at the end of the corridor was already open, a stooped figure silhouetted against the light from inside. He looked older than the usual student, mid twenties, maybe more.

'Sarah said you'd be round.' He stepped back. 'Come in.'

The flat, though smaller than J-J had expected, was expensively furnished with chintzy covers on the plump armchairs, a big widescreen TV, and piles of books everywhere, many of them brand new. J-J stood before a watercolour on the back wall. A livid sunset hung over a skyline he recognised: the tiny squat church steeple, the pitch of the neighbouring roofs, the gleam of the enveloping creek, the memory of curlews stalking the mudflats at low tide.

J-J glanced over his shoulder. Daniel was wearing stained corduroy trousers and a pink button-down shirt that hadn't seen an iron for weeks. His head was unusually large, a cartoon head too big for its body, and there was a strange puffiness about his face. Discount the absence of bruises, and he might just have been in a fight.

Daniel plainly hadn't a clue what to expect next.

J-J nodded at the picture on the wall, then mimed taking a photo, briefly touching his chest in ownership before clapping his hands. His enthusiasm for the watercolour was all the more convincing for being genuine.

45

Daniel looked from one to the other, then came the beginnings of a smile.

'You know Bosham?'

J-J nodded at once. Lip-reading had been an early skill, the key that unlocked conversations like these.

From the depths of his denim jacket he produced a single typed sheet he'd printed and photocopied weeks ago. Three briefs paragraphs set out the thinking behind the video.

Ambrym Productions wanted to explore the realities of drug-taking. They wanted to know how, and why, and where next. They wanted to get inside the heads of the people at the sharpest end and offer them the opportunity of sharing their experience.

The video was destined for schools all over the country. Kids would see it and make judgements of their own about the rights and wrongs of using drugs. Print material – posters, teaching notes – would complete the package.

Saying yes to J-J meant agreeing to a videotaped interview, an hour at the most. The questions would be straightforward. The interviewee would do most of the talking. No one was interested in point-scoring, or preaching, or any form of sensationalism. Was that too high a price for the good a video like this might do?

Daniel sank onto the sofa beside the audio stack and studied the single sheet of paper. When he finally looked up, his eyes were swimming behind the thick-rimmed glasses.

'You know Sarah well?'

J-J shook his head.

'But you liked her?'

J-J nodded. When his hands shaped an hourglass, Daniel at last managed a smile.

'She used to be my girlfriend.' He picked up J-J's sheet again. 'How do I know this is for real?'

J-J's hand returned to his jacket. Eadie had given him a sheaf of business cards. He passed one across, miming a telephone call.

Daniel examined the card.

'I can keep this?'

J-J nodded.

'When do you need an answer?'

J-J touched his watch, then raised his hands, palms up, thumbs turned out. Can't say.

'Soon?'

J-J gestured round, encompassing the entire room with a sweep of his arm. Then he mimed the camera, the lights, the microphone, the whole circus that would commit this man to videotape. Daniel looked up at him, watching the performance, saying nothing. Finally, J-J touched his watch again and pressed his hands together, a supplicatory gesture that the student seemed to understand.

'Very soon?' His eyes went back to the sheet. He read it for a second time, then put it to one side. Eadie's card still lay on the arm of the sofa.

'I'll have to think about it.' He picked up the card. 'OK?'

It took Cathy Lamb to voice what Suttle was trying to get across. The DI had convened the meeting immediately after lunch in her office at Kingston Crescent. Other members of the Crime Squad were still out, scouring the city for the Scousers.

'We agree the girl won't say anything about last night.' She was looking at Suttle. 'What else isn't she telling us?'

'I don't know, boss. But you're right, there's lots going on there. She's well pissed off.'

'So would you be,' Winter said. 'The way those animals treated her.'

'I'm not sure sure it was them, though.'

'They phoned us,' Winter reminded him. 'They gave us an address. How did they know where to find her? Coincidence? Just happened to be passing by?'

'Of course not. But what if they'd gone looking for Pullen? What if they thought he was the guy who'd grassed them up?'

'He lives in Ashburton Road.'

'Yeah, but he also owns the place in Bystock Road. Maybe they confused the two. Easily done.'

Lamb hadn't taken her eyes off Suttle.

'Go on,' she said.

'OK.' Suttle leaned forward, clearing a space on the low table Lamb reserved for her dieting magazines. 'We do the door in Pennington Road. They bail out of number 34. Pretty soon after that, they turn up in Bystock Road. They want a word with Pullen. They knock on the door. Somebody answers. They get inside, find the girl upstairs tied to the bed.'

'Who's this somebody?'

'God knows. Pullen's got half the world in there. Asylum seekers, blokes on the dole, all sorts. You know the way it works, benefit cheques made out to the landlord, hundreds of quid a week for doing sod all.'

'So why was the place empty when you arrived?'

'Because the Scouse kids put the fear of God up them. Middle of the night. Threats and menaces. Half a brain, you bail out, don't you?'

'And the music?'

'Didn't happen till later. Remember the statement we took off the

47

bloke next door? Said it woke him up round two in the morning? The music was the Scouse kids' contribution. They found the girl on the bed, turned on the music, then fucked off and belled us. The rest –' Suttle shrugged '– we know about.'

Lamb was still putting together the chain of events, testing it link by link.

'So who tied the girl up?'

'Pullen.' It was Winter at last. 'The boy's right. It was probably Pullen that gave her the whacking as well. I must be getting old.'

'But why would he want to whack her?'

'Because she'd let the Scouse lads chat her up. They'd all met earlier, some bar or other. The Scouse kids got alongside her. She liked them. You could tell that when we talked to her just now. She thought they were OK. They made her laugh. Am I right, Jimmy?' Winter's question drew a nod from Suttle. Winter turned back to Cathy Lamb. 'So from there on, it kicks off. A couple of pints does it for Pullen. He's seen what's going on and he takes it personally so, bosh, he has her out of there. Big row. Toys out the pram. He takes her round to Bystock Road, gives her a hiding, then ties her to the bed in case she has any other plans, and buggers off. He loves her really, of course he does, but there's just so much a bloke can take. Who knows? Maybe he was planning to come back later. Maybe he was thinking flowers and a nice pot of tea, but we'll never know because the Scouse kids beat him to it. Prat that he is.'

'We can prove this?'

'No way, unless any of them talk. Pullen won't, for sure. The Scousers we can't find. That leaves Trudy.'

'No chance?'

'None. Kids in this city, kids with her background, they'd walk on broken glass before they talked to us. Any case, what are we trying to stand up? Kidnap? Assault? Happens all the time, blokes making a point or two.'

'You're saying he tied her up, Paul. You're telling me he beat her.'

'Sure, but it's easier than conversation, isn't it?'

There was a long silence. Winter was right and they all knew it. Nailing down the truth about Trudy Gallagher could swallow hundreds of hours of CID time without the faintest chance of a conviction.

'OK.' Lamb got to her feet. 'Here's the way it goes from now on. Secretan's a realist. He wants the Scouse kids out of here. He's not fussed about court, he just wants them gone. Doesn't matter where but it has to be soon.'

48

'Sane man.' Winter was looking positively cheerful. 'So what's the plan?'

'In plain English, we get up their arses. That's Secretan's phrase, not mine. From now on, he wants a car outside. He wants them watched, high-visibility. He wants them hassled. He wants us in their face. He wants them so pissed off they call it a day.'

'Outside where, boss?' It was Suttle.

'Pennington Road. They'll come back, bound to. They know we've got nothing on them. You were there, both of you. Plastic wraps, pair of scales, bicarb, icing sugar, but bugger all else. They must have kept the gear with them.'

'Scenes of Crime?' Winter this time.

'Jacked it in an hour ago. DNA by the yard from the blood but it takes us nowhere. This is a war, Paul, and neither side has any interest in talking to us.'

'OK.' Winter nodded. 'So what do we do?'

'You're the guys in the car.' She smiled down at him. 'Outside.'

J-J was back in Hampshire Terrace by the time the girl from the university put her head round Ambrym Productions' office door. He recognised her at once. Small, pretty, Prada T-shirt, big silver earrings. Sarah.

Eadie Sykes was looking at video rushes on the PC, a pair of headphones giving her the privacy she needed. J-J touched her lightly on the shoulder. He'd found a chair for Sarah.

'Coffee?' he signed.

By the time he returned from the tiny kitchen along the corridor, Eadie and the student were locked in conversation. She'd just been called by her friend Dan. She'd felt slightly guilty giving J-J his name in the first place and now she wanted to be absolutely sure that this video of theirs, this project, was for real.

'Absolutely for real.'

Eadie went through the funding, showed her letters of support from local luminaries, outlined the plans they'd made for distribution once the video was ready. She and J-J were facilitators, she kept saying. On the one hand there was a country flooded with drugs. On the other, nationwide, millions of kids potentially at risk. All Ambrym wanted to do was level the ground in between. No ego trips. No exploitation. Just the truth.

The girl nodded. She wanted to be convinced, J-J could tell. She was on a media course herself, she understood about documentary work, she'd be more than happy to lend a hand, but still there was something holding her back.

Eadie was pressing her about Daniel. How come he'd got into such trouble with drugs?

'He's a strange man. It's difficult . . .' She shook her head.

'How do you mean, strange?'

'It's like . . .' She frowned, hunting for the right phrase. 'It's like he's really unstable, you know what I mean? I've been around him now for a couple of years and I've watched him getting worse. It's partly his age, partly the fact he's got so much money. That makes him an outsider at the uni. It shouldn't but it does.'

Daniel, she explained, had come to higher education late. His father was a Manchester media lawyer, incredibly successful, incredibly busy. His parents had divorced when Daniel was ten, and he'd spent his adolescence with an elderly aunt and uncle in Chester. After A levels, in a doomed attempt to break free, he'd gone to Australia where his mother was contemplating the wreckage of her third marriage. The last person she'd wanted to see was her son, and after a couple of years wandering around on a generous allowance from his dad, Daniel had returned to the UK, more introverted than ever. Then came a long period of drift, totally aimless, before he woke up one morning and decided to go to university.

'Here?'

'Bristol. Portsmouth was his third choice.'

'What did he want to read?'

'Russian literature. He wanted to be a novelist. He thought the Russian might help.'

Sarah had bumped into him one night when she was celebrating a friend's twenty-first. Dan had been sitting by himself in a pub called the Still and West. And he'd been crying.

'Why?' Eadie hadn't touched her coffee.

'I've no idea, not the first. I talked to him a bit, even let him buy me a drink.'

'You don't think that was a ploy? Crying?'

'Not at all. Dan doesn't do ploys. He's just not that . . .' She paused again, looking down at her hands.

'Clever?'

'No, he's clever, definitely, probably too clever. No, he just doesn't do all that manipulative stuff. Maybe that's half the problem.'

She'd begun to see more and more of him. Thanks to his rich dad he'd had the flat in Old Portsmouth from the start, and she used to go round for coffee and a chat. He'd made no demands on her, nothing physical, no anguished pleas to stay the night, but at the start of the next academic year she'd found herself with nowhere to live and when he'd offered her the spare bedroom she'd said yes.

'I was grateful. I still am. He saved my life last year. Decent accommodation in this city can be a nightmare.'

'And you were close to him?'

'We were friends. Good friends. But that's all.'

'And now?'

'We're still good friends.'

'You still live there?'

'No.' She shook her head. 'It became impossible after he got really heavily into the drugs. I couldn't bear it. He's killing himself. He just doesn't care any more. That's hard to take.'

'Did you ever score for him?'

The question took her by surprise. So direct.

'Yes,' she said at last. 'A couple of times I made a phone call, if you call that scoring. It's like pizza really. You phone a number. Then the stuff just turns up.'

'This was recently?'

'No. Back last year before I moved out. Both times he was desperate, just couldn't get anything together. It's pathetic really. I hated it, hated doing it, but it made him better for a bit so I suppose . . . I dunno . . .' She shrugged.

'Did you ever try and get him off it?'

'All the time. He knows what I think about drugs.'

'What was he using?'

'Heroin. Sometimes cocaine, too, but mainly smack.'

'Regularly?'

'Every four hours. I used to count them. He said it was the best friend he'd ever had. Heroin? A friend? Can you believe that?'

'And now? He's still using?'

'Definitely. I go and see him from time to time and it's obvious. I've still got a key to the flat. Dan made me keep it.'

'You're absolutely sure he's still using?'

'Yeah. Like I just said, he has to – it's the only way he can keep functioning.' She paused. 'He's got money. He knows how to use a phone. What else do you need?'

Eadie pulled an editing pad towards her and scribbled a note. Sarah looked suddenly alarmed.

'You're not going to . . . ?' She nodded at the pad.

'No, of course not. Memory like a sieve.' Eadie looked up. 'What about his father?'

'Dan never sees him. His dad pays a standing order every month but that's it.'

'Have you ever thought of getting in touch yourself?'

'I did once. He drove down from Manchester, took me out for a meal, told me how worried he was. That was after I'd moved out.'

'Did he go and see Daniel?'

'No.'

'How do you know?'

'I checked with Dan later. His dad hadn't even rung.'

Eadie finally reached for her coffee. J-J stood behind her, wondering where this story might go next, beginning to understand the kind of cage Daniel Kelly had made for himself.

Sarah was still staring at the notepad. 'I'd never have mentioned Dan in the first place,' she muttered, 'except he's so articulate. He'd be perfect for what you need. Perfect.'

'Is that why you got in touch with us?'

'Partly, yes. But it's more than that. Something has to happen in Dan's life. Something has to give him a shake. He'd be good on your video. He'd be excellent. Maybe that's what he needs.'

'Bit of self-respect?'

'Exactly.'

The thought prompted a slow nod from Eadie. She put the pad to one side.

'I get the impression that some of this decision's down to you.'

'What decision?'

'Whether or not Daniel agrees to be interviewed. Would that be right?'

'Yes, I suppose it would. He has to be the one to say it. It has to come from him in the end. But yes, he's definitely asked my advice.'

'So what do you think?'

'Me?' Sarah's eyes strayed to the light stands propped in the corner, to the neat little Sony digital nestling in the open camera box. 'I think J-J should go back to the flat again. After I've made a call.'

J-J returned to Old Portsmouth within the hour. He didn't have to bother with the entryphone because Daniel was up in the window of his flat, watching the street below. J-J felt the lock give under his fingers and pushed in through the big front door. Daniel was waiting for him upstairs, pale and fretful. His palm was moist when he shook J-J's outstretched hand.

'Sarah phoned,' he said at once. 'And the answer's yes.'

J-J reached out to pat him on the shoulder, a congratulatory gesture that made Daniel retreat at once into the safety of the flat. J-J watched his hands, the way they crabbed up and down his bare arms. The insides of both elbows were livid with bruises.

Daniel had something else to say, something important. He fixed J-J with his big yellow eyes. He spoke very slowly, exaggerated lip movements, spelling it out.

'I need a favour.'

J-J cocked an eyebrow. What?

'I have to make a phone call but the number won't answer.' He stumbled through a clumsy mime. 'You understand me?'

Another nod from J-J, more guarded this time.

'I've got an address. I'll call a cab. All you have to do is knock on the door and ask for Terry. Give Terry my name. Tell him Daniel from Old Portsmouth. That's all you have to say. Terry. Daniel from Old Portsmouth. Then we can do the interview. OK?'

J-J glanced down and found himself looking at a fifty-pound note.

'Difficult,' he signed.

'What?'

'Hard.'

'I don't understand.' Daniel plunged his hand into his pocket. Two more notes, twenties this time.

'Please . . .' J-J tried to fend him off.

'Just take the money. Go on, take it. Terry. Daniel from Old Portsmouth. Then we can do the interview. Is that too much to ask?'

He produced a mobile. J-J guessed he was phoning for the taxi.

Daniel folded the phone into his pocket. Patches of sweat darkened his shirt.

'Why don't you wait in the street?' He tapped his watch and held up five fingers. 'The cab'll be here in no time.'

Chapter five

Faraday's third meeting with Willard took place in mid afternoon. One of the management assistants from the Major Crimes Team had raised Faraday on his mobile, telling him that the Det Supt would be parked in Grand Parade for a brief get-together at 3.15. There didn't seem much room for negotiation.

Grand Parade was a recently refurbished square in Old Portsmouth and once the bustling centre of garrison life. Lottery money had paid for stylish seating and a brand new ramp, quickly adopted by local skateboarders. The ramp led up to the Saluting Base, an area on top of the fortification walls that overlooked the harbour narrows.

Faraday arrived early, his anorak zipped up against a bitter wind, and spent a minute or two gazing down at the churning tide. A lone cormorant sped past, barely feet above the water, and he watched it until the tiny black speck was swallowed up by the enveloping greyness.

Cormorants had always been one of J-J's favourite birds. He'd drawn them since he was a kid, page after page of weird, prehistoric shapes, and he'd often pestered his dad for expeditions to watch the real thing. The way the birds bobbed around on the ocean, abruptly submerging in search of food, had always fascinated the boy, and one of the first times Faraday had recognised J-J's strange cackle as a laugh was when the hungry cormorant resurfaced, seventy metres down-current, with an impatient little shake of its head. He doesn't understand, J-J would sign. He's down there in the dark and he can't see a thing. Too right, thought Faraday, pulling up the hood of his anorak against the first chill drops of rain.

Willard took him by surprise, arriving in a brand new Jaguar S-type. Faraday got in beside him, curious to know why they were meeting here. There was a perfectly good suite of offices at Kingston Crescent. What was so wrong with central heating and a constant supply of coffee?

Willard ignored the question. He'd spent most of lunchtime with Dave Michaels out at Fort Cumberland. The DS had got his house-to-house team working through the neighbouring estate and the preliminary reports were beginning to inch the Nick Hayder inquiry forward. Several households – especially young mums with kids – had talked of after-dark comings and goings on the single road that led towards the Hayling ferry. Some of the cars that pulled off the tarmac and onto the scrubland that stretched out towards the beach were there for sex. You knew they were at it because afterwards they chucked their debris out of the car window, littering the place with used condoms, but recently there'd been other visitors, even less welcome.

According to the mums, some of the older kids on the estate were talking openly about scoring cheap drugs off dealers who'd driven in from elsewhere in the city. For less than a tenner, you could evidently take your pick – anything from ecstasy to smack – and the trade had become so brazen that the kids had taken to calling one of the dealers Mr Whippy. All he needed, said one harassed single mother, was one of those recorded chimes and a nice little fridge for the younger kids who might fancy a choc ice with their £10 wrap.

Faraday was watching the bridge and funnel of a passing warship, visible above the nearby battlements. No point resisting the obvious.

'You're thinking Mackenzie?'

'No way. Mackenzie uses dealers, of course he does, always has, but they're mostly local. More to the point, he doesn't deal smack any more.'

'And this lot?'

'Out of town. Definitely. And they'll sell you anything.'

'Who says?'

'It's what the kids tell their mums. One said he'd bought a snowball, smack and crack cocaine. Another thought they all sounded like Steve Gerrard. That says Merseyside to me. Scousers.'

One night last week, enraged by what was going on under their noses, a couple of the mums had decided to intervene. They'd marched into the darkness, determined to have it out with the intruders, but the dealers had had a dog in the car, big bastard, really vicious, because the next thing they knew they were trying to fend the bloody animal off. Only a prompt retreat had saved them from a serious mauling, and when the dealers had called the dog off and driven away, they'd made a point of winding down the car window and laughing in their faces.

'They get a number at all?' Faraday could picture the scene.

'M reg. XB something. And maybe a seven.'

'Make?'

'Cavalier.'

'They report it?'

'Yeah. Highland Road sent a couple of DCs round next morning. Took statements and left a number to ring. Last night one of the same women swears blind the same car was back again, couple of young blokes inside.'

'She get a good look at them?'

'Yes.'

'Why didn't she phone in, then? After it all kicked off?'

'She won't say but Dave's guess is her own boy's been at it, maybe last night.'

'Buying?'

'Yeah. Dave's got a list of repeat visits for when the kids come out of school. That's the ones who can be arsed to turn up, of course.'

'At home?'

'At school.'

Willard produced a toothpick and began to stab at something lodged between one of his back molars. Nearly a decade of policing the city had left him with a limited faith in secondary education.

'Highland Road ran a check on the plate number. We've got twenty-six possibilities, including four from Liverpool, two from Birkenhead, and one from Runcorn. Dave's organising a trawl through last night's tapes.'

'*All* of them?'

'Every single one.'

There were more than a hundred CCTV cameras in Portsmouth, each one of them generating hours of videotape. If anyone needed a clue to just how seriously Willard was taking last night's assault, then here it was.

'So you're thinking out of town?'

'I'm thinking we have to find the car. If it ties up with the Scousers, then we pull Cathy Lamb into the loop. Give her a chance to put the record straight.'

Briefly, he told Faraday about last night's abortive bust in Pennington Road. As the senior CID officer for the city, he'd received a full report, agreeing with Secretan that the new Crime Squad needed to shake down in a very big hurry. Any more disasters like that, and the city would become open house for any passing scumbag.

'So what did you make of *Tumbril*? Imber give you the tour?'

The abrupt change of subject took Faraday by surprise. He began to frame a reply but thought better of it. In a situation like this, it was wiser to check your bearings.

'Brian Imber seems to think you've rattled a few cages,' he said carefully.

'He's right. We have.' Willard was close to smiling.

'Like who?'

'Like Harry Wayte, for starters. Seems to think he owns the bloody drugs issue in this force.'

'I thought that was down to Brian?'

'It is. It always has been. Harry was late to the party. In fact I can remember a time he was telling everyone Imber was off his head. It's only now the penny's dropped that he's started to see the full potential.'

Until a recent reorganisation, Harry Wayte had been Imber's boss, the DI in charge of the Tactical Crime Unit, a dozen or so detectives working out of secured premises in Fareham, an old market town engulfed by the mainland conurbation that sprawls towards Southampton. The TCU had won its battle honours in the early nineties, tackling an explosion in drug-related crime, and had since become the fiefdom for a succession of hard-driving DIs who made the most of its reach and independence. Harry Wayte was the longest-serving of these DIs, an abrasive, plain-spoken ex-Chief Petty Officer, barely a year off retirement.

'You don't think he'd be in with a shout?' Faraday enquired.

'Never. And what's more, he knows it. The only way he's going to get promotion at his age is by lifting something really tasty off Imber and then claiming it for himself. He's doing his best, I'll give him that.'

'But Imber's out of the TCU now.'

'Sure, but that never stopped Harry.'

'You're telling me he knows about *Tumbril*?'

'I'm telling you he's been busting a gut to find out. And I'm telling you something else, too. It's guys like Harry who put the word round. This job's hard enough as it is. What we don't need is half the force behaving like bloody kids, thinking we've stolen some kind of march on them.'

'We?'

'Nick Hayder, Imber, now you.'

He broke off, and Faraday found himself nodding. Most policemen were cursed with an acute sense of territory and Harry Wayte was clearly no exception. In his rare moments of leisure, the DI indulged his passion for naval history by building exquisitely crafted model warships. Faraday had come across him several times, crouched on the edge of Craneswater boating lake, launching his latest radio-controlled frigate into the thick of battle. Faraday had envied his peace of mind, alone in his private bubble.

'What are you up to this evening?' Willard was checking his watch. 'Any plans?'

'None that I can think of.'

'Good. There's someone I want you meet. You know the jetty alongside *Warrior*?'

HMS *Warrior* had been the navy's first steam-driven ironclad. Fully restored, she dominated the view from the harbour station. The neighbouring jetty lay within the historic dockyard. Faraday was to be there for six o'clock. With luck, they'd be back by nine.

'Back from where?'

'Tell you later. Bring something warm.' Willard nodded across the row of parked cars towards the High Street. 'For now I want you round to the Sally Port Hotel. Room six. There's a guy waiting for you, name of Graham Wallace. He's u/c. I've authorised him to brief you. OK?'

Faraday turned to stare at Willard. Operations like this were trademarked by what the Force Media Unit termed 'a variety of specialist investigative techniques'. Imber had already tallied covert surveillance, phone intercepts, and forensic accounting. So why hadn't anyone mentioned undercover officers?

'Is that a direct question?' Willard was fingering the leather steering wheel.

'Yes, sir. It is.'

'Then here's the answer. Imber doesn't know.'

'Doesn't *know*? Why on earth not?'

'Because Hayder wanted to keep it tight.' The smile was back on Willard's face. 'A decision with which I totally agreed.'

The taxi dropped J-J off in the heart of Fratton. He stooped to the window, waiting for his change. When the driver glanced again at the address on his dashboard computer and told him to watch his back, J-J pretended not to understand. All he was doing, he told himself, was running an errand for a friend.

He set off down Pennington Road, his heart lumping away beneath the thin cotton of his Madness T-shirt. Like it or not, he'd suddenly found himself skewered on what Eadie Sykes liked to call the sharp end. The statistics he'd memorised from a thousand magazine articles, the transcripts he'd read from other peoples' research projects, the confessional truths he'd tried to wring from interviewee after potential interviewee, all this carefully filed information had finally boiled down to a single address, 30 Pennington Road. If you wanted to mess with your life, if you wanted to end up in Daniel's state, then this was where you started.

Parked cars lined both sides of the road. Walking beside them, J-J counted the houses until he got to number 30. Someone, he thought, must have given the front door a good kicking. The splintered panels had been crudely battened and there was a sheet of old plywood nailed over what must have been a square of glass. There was no number on the door and he had to pause a moment, rechecking the houses on either side, before he ventured a knock.

Being deaf, he never knew how loud a knock he was making. Normally, this wouldn't matter. When it came to handicap people were amazingly forgiving but on this occasion his nerve ends told him he needed to get it right. Too soft, and no one would hear. Too loud, too aggressive, and God knows what might happen.

J-J closed his eyes a moment, swallowing hard, wondering whether it wasn't too late to beat a retreat. Daniel, back in Old Portsmouth, had warned him about the guys in number 30. The word he'd used was rough. Rough, he'd said, but OK. OK meant they delivered. Rough, as the taxi driver had pointed out, meant watch your step.

Nothing happened after the first knock. Shivering now, J-J reached out again then froze as someone pulled the door open. A face appeared. Unshaven. Pierced eyebrows. Nose stud. And young, younger even than J-J himself.

'Yeah?'

J-J stood rooted to the pavement, suddenly oblivious to the rain. For the first time in his life he didn't know what to do, what signal to send, what expression to adopt. Then he saw the dog. It was a black pit bull, lunging out of the gloom inside. A length of rope tied it to one of the bannisters at the foot of the stairs and every time it threw itself towards the open door the bannister bowed.

J-J was terrified of dogs, the legacy of a long-ago encounter with a neighbour's alsatian, and he knew that this one couldn't wait to tear him apart. His instinct told him to turn and leg it. No video, no name on the credits, was worth this.

'Fucking say something, then, yeah?'

J-J couldn't take his eyes off the dog. He could smell it now, the rich sour smell of fear. The alsatian had put him in hospital for the night. This one would probably kill him.

'Fucking deaf are you? Lost yer tongue?'

At last, J-J managed to summon a response. He'd made Daniel write down his own name and address. Now he unfolded the scrap of paper. A hand shot out and grabbed it. Bitten nails. Heavy rings. A tattoo of some kind, blue dots across the knuckles. The head came up, eyes scanning the street beyond J-J's shoulder.

'If this is a fucking stitch-up . . .'

J-J shook his head with a violence that took him by surprise. No stitching-up. Promise.

'You know what I'm saying?'

J-J nodded at the scrap of paper. Trust me. Please.

'He told you where to find us?'

Yes.

'You some kind of friend of his?'

Yes.

'He gave you money?'

Yes.

The door opened wider and J-J stepped inside. The smell of the dog was overwhelming, the animal more frenzied than ever at this sudden intrusion, and J-J kept his distance, his back against the wall, praying that the bannister would hold.

Someone else appeared from a room at the back, boxer shorts, tattoo on his neck, and a red number 9 football shirt with *Carling* scrolled across the front. There was a brief conversation, an exchange of grins, a nod. The face at the door gave the dog a kick, then turned back to J-J, his hand extended, palm up. Gimme. J-J produced the £50 note. The face wanted more. Out came the two twenties. More still. J-J shook his head, gestured helplessly, nothing left, then he felt a sharp crack as his head hit the wall. Hands dived into the pockets of his jeans, searching for the rest, and he shut his eyes, forcing himself to submit, to go limp, praying that this nightmare would end.

Finally, a handful of coins richer, they left him alone. He backed towards the front door, away from the dog, uncertain what was supposed to happen next. Street prices in Portsmouth had never been cheaper. Everyone was telling him so. £90 should keep Daniel going for a couple of days, nine wraps at least. So where were they?

The face stepped past him and pulled the front door open. For a second or two, J-J was tempted to resist, to protest, to demand their end of the deal, but then he felt the sweet chillness of the street, and he was out in the rain again, gladder than he could imagine. The face was back inside, the mouth framing a message for his rich friend. Later, he was saying. Tell him we'll be round later.

Parked three cars up the street, DC Paul Winter was trying to work out how many shots they'd taken.

'Six.' Jimmy Suttle was studying the panel on the back of the camera. 'Four when he first turned up. Two just now.'

'Full face?'

'A couple at least. We should pull him now. He has to be carrying. Has to be.'

'Leave it.' Winter was watching the tall, awkward figure hurrying away down the street. Last time he'd seen Faraday's son, the boy had got himself mixed up with a bunch of young lunatics from Somers-town. A couple of years later, he'd evidently graduated to Class A narcotics.

'No?' Suttle had started to open the car door. 'The guy's on a nicking. That wasn't a social call.'

'You're right, son. Give me the camera.'

'Why?'

'Because one of us has to stay here.'

'And me?'

'I'd move sharpish if I were you.' Winter nodded towards the end of the street. 'Follow him and bell me.'

'*Follow* him? I thought we were into bodies? Scalps?'

'We are.' Winter was examining the camera. 'Do you know who that boy belongs to?'

Faraday made his way to the Sally Port Hotel, resisting the temptation to enquire about Graham Wallace at the tiny reception desk. Had this latest rabbit from Willard's hat been in residence long? Did *Tumbril* have a permanent booking on room 6?

Climbing the carpeted stairs to the first floor, Faraday couldn't rid himself of the image of Nick Hayder, unconscious in his hospital bed, helpless in a cat's cradle of monitor leads and transfusion lines. Managing an investigation this complex, trying to remember who was supposed to know what, would have been enough to drive any detective to the edge. No wonder he'd felt under siege.

A soft knock at room 6 drew an instant response. Faraday found himself looking at a tall, well-built man in his late twenties. He was wearing an expensive shirt tucked loosely into a pair of well-cut dark trousers. The silk tie, loosened at the collar, was a swirl of reds laced with a vivid turquoise. Despite the laugh lines around his eyes and the tiny gold ring in one ear, he looked tense.

'You are?'

'Joe Faraday.'

'Come in. Graham Wallace.' He had the briefest handshake.

Faraday stepped into the room, closing the door behind him. The desk beneath the window was spread with paperwork and a linen jacket hung on the back of the chair. Beside the bed, a pair of Gucci loafers.

'Tea? There's one bag left.'

'No thanks.' Faraday eyed the empty packet of biscuits beside the kettle. 'I could use a sandwich, though.'

'Ring down. They'll bring something up.' Wallace stepped across to the phone and dialled a number, then handed it to Faraday. Faraday ordered two tuna salad sandwiches, adding he'd pay for them on the way out.

When he'd put the phone down, Wallace gestured towards the empty chair.

'I'm sorry about Nick.' He had a flat London accent. 'Your guvnor said you were mates.'

'That's right.' Faraday nodded. 'And we still are.'

There was a moment of silence while the men eyed each other, then Faraday sank into the chair. U/c officers were notoriously wary, often more paranoid than the targets they were tasked to sting. Their very survival frequently depended on the lowest possible exposure to fellow officers.

'How tight did Nick keep all this?' Faraday gestured towards the desk. 'Only it would be helpful to know.'

'Very tight. The only guys I ever deal with are Nick and a handler from Special Ops, Terry McNaughton.'

'What about Willard?'

'Your govnor?' Wallace glanced up towards the door. 'Never met him till just now. He says he's filling in for Nick.'

'I thought that was my job?'

'It is. That's what he came to tell me.'

'Why didn't Special Ops pass the message?'

'Good question.'

'Did you ask him? Willard?'

'Of course I did.'

'And?'

'He said he was SIO on the job so there was no way he wouldn't know about me. Thought face-to-face was better than a phone call from Special Ops.'

'And you?'

'Me?' He offered Faraday a thin smile. 'A phone call from Special Ops would have done just fine.'

Faraday nodded. Special Ops was a tiny department of the Hantspol intelligence empire that supervised the deployment of u/c officers. Terry McNaughton would be the handler charged with running Wallace, sharing the debrief with Nick Hayder after each new instalment of the *Tumbril* story.

'You could help me here,' Faraday said slowly.

'How?'

'By telling me exactly the way it's gone so far. There's no point me trying to snow you. Twenty-four hours ago I was looking at a pretty much empty desk. Now this.'

'No one's briefed you?'

'Willard's handed me the file. I've talked to the team. This isn't a three-day event.'

'You're right.' Wallace appeared to be on the verge of saying something else, then shrugged and lit a small, thin cheroot before settling himself full-length on the bed. 'Where do you want me to start?'

Faraday hesitated. In cases like these, Nick Hayder and Terry McNaughton would deliberately limit the background knowledge shared with the u/c. The last thing they wanted was Wallace – in conversation with the target – unintentionally revealing more than he should have known.

'Nick and your handler would have sorted a first meeting.'

'That's right. We met in London.'

'When was that?'

'Before Christmas. Second week in December.'

'What did they tell you?'

'They said they were mounting a long-term op against a drugs target, major dealer. Full flag, level three. Bloke called Mackenzie. The way Nick told it, this Mackenzie was into some serious business. Nick said he'd been pouring washed drugs money into all kinds of local investments – bars, restaurants, property, hotels, all the usual blinds. Everything was sweet, ticking away, lots of nice little earners, but there was something missing. Nick called it profile.'

Faraday nodded. He'd heard Imber use the same word. Mackenzie, he'd explained drily, wasn't just interested in owning half of Pompey. He wanted more than that. He wanted to *be* Mr Portsmouth, to have his name up there in lights. King of the City.

'So?'

'So my job was to make it hard for him to get that profile. Nick said he was after a particular property, really hot for it, a place that would give him everything he'd ever wanted. According to Nick, he was already halfway there. I'm the bloke that comes in with a counter-bid.'

'And the property?'

'No one's told you?'

'No. That's why I'm asking.'

'Right.' Wallace was studying the end of his cheroot. 'It's Spit Bank Fort.'

'You're serious?'

'Absolutely.'

'It's inhabited?'

'Yes. I've been out there. There's a German woman in charge, Gisela Mendel. She's running some kind of language school.'

'And she's in on this? Or is the place really for sale?'

'I've no idea.'

'That means no.'

'That means I've no idea.'

There was a knock on the door. Faraday got to his feet. A woman gave him a plate of thick-cut tuna sandwiches and told him she'd left the bill at reception. Back in his chair, attacking the sandwiches, Faraday tried to puzzle his way through this latest development.

Spit Bank was one of three Victorian sea forts guarding the approaches to Portsmouth Harbour. Half a mile out to sea from Southsea beach, it had been built to keep the French at arm's length. If Nick was serious about Mackenzie's thirst for profile, it was the perfect choice: a stubby granite thumb the size of a modest castle. Take a walk along the seafront and you couldn't miss it.

'So you've come in as a rival bidder?'

'That's right. As far as I can gather, Mackenzie opened negotiations after Christmas.'

'At what price?'

'I haven't a clue. The asking price is one and a quarter mil and she's definitely been negotiating him up, but I don't know where the bidding stands right now.'

'And you?'

'I came in about a fortnight ago. £900,000 contingent on a full survey.' He smiled. 'Mackenzie can't believe it.'

'How does he know?'

'Gisela told him.'

'And you've talked to Mackenzie?'

'Twice. Both times on the phone.'

'He called you?'

'For sure, straight after he hassled Gisela for my number.' Wallace rolled off the bed a moment, reaching for an ashtray, then lay back again. 'He thought he'd squared the woman away, nice clear run. Believe me, I'm the last guy he needs around. *Nine hundred grand? You must be off your fucking head.*'

Wallace's take on Mackenzie's Pompey accent was faultless, and Faraday found himself grinning. The dim outlines of Nick Hayder's sting were at last beginning to emerge.

'You think he'll try and take care of you?'

'One way or another.' He nodded. 'Yeah.'

'How?'

'No idea. The perfect endgame has him bunging me a kilo or two of charlie but don't hold your breath.'

'How would that work?'

'No one's explained the legend?'

'No.' Once again, Faraday shook his head.

Every undercover officer has a legend, an assumed identity which must take him over. The best of them, Faraday knew, were indivisible from their new personalities. They lived, ate and slept what they'd become.

Graham Wallace was playing a twenty-nine-year-old property developer. He'd made his fortune with a hefty commission on a £98 million shopping plaza in Oman and was back in the UK to enjoy the spoils. He had an office in Putney, a flat overlooking the river, and a Porsche Carrera for his expeditions out of town. A couple of investments had already caught his eye. One of them was a Tudor manor house in Gloucestershire he planned to turn into a health spa. Spit Bank Fort was another.

'As far as Mackenzie's concerned, I'm thinking five-star hotel – gourmet cooking, de luxe accommodation, helicopter platform on the roof for transfers from Heathrow, the works.'

'That's huge money.'

'You're right. But that's the point. I told him about the Cotswold place, too. It's got fifteen acres. They're asking three mil five.'

'Why the detail?'

'Nick wanted him to check me out. The Cotswold place is part of the legend. The bloke that owns it is onside. Nick warned him to expect a call from Mackenzie.'

'And?'

'Mackenzie phoned him a couple of days ago. They had a long conversation and the bloke finally admitted he'd turned my offer down. Said he'd made calls of his own and the Oman story didn't check out. Said he thought the money was dodgy.'

'Drugs money?'

'Has to be. He didn't say it in those terms but Mackenzie will draw his own conclusions.'

'He thinks you're in the same game?'

'With luck.' He nodded. 'Yes.'

Faraday was eyeing the last of the sandwiches. A legend within a legend. Neat.

'So Mackenzie really does need you off the plot?'

'Exactly. For one thing, I'm after his precious fort. And for another, I'm potential competition. The way I understand it, he's got this city pretty tied up. Me, he doesn't need.'

'And you're thinking he'll compromise himself?'

'That was Nick's bid, sure. I just play along.'

Faraday reached for the sandwich, impressed by the lengths to which Nick Hayder had gone. Set up a sting operation like this – the false ID, the credit cards, the Porsche, the London office, the flat to go with it – and you were looking at a six-figure bill. Putting Mackenzie away and confiscating all his assets would dwarf that sum but there was absolutely no guarantee that this would ever happen. No wonder Nick hadn't been sleeping at night.

'Has this survey of yours happened yet?'

'No.'

'But it's kosher? You've got it organised?'

'Oh yes. Structural engineer, architect – the lot. Last time I talked to Mackenzie he told me I should forget it. *Why piss away all that money, mate?*' The Pompey accent again. '*Why give yourself the grief?*'

'And you?'

'I just laughed.'

'So when's the survey due?'

'End of next week.' Up on one elbow, Wallace nodded at the phone and flashed Faraday a smile. 'Which is why our friend will now be wanting a meet.'

It took three attempts on the mobile before DC Jimmy Suttle managed to get through to Paul Winter.

'Where are you?' The older man sounded half asleep.

'Hampshire Terrace.'

'What's happening?'

'It's pouring with bloody rain.' Suttle was doing his best to find shelter beneath a dripping lime tree across the road. Rush hour traffic was beginning to back up from the nearby roundabout, blocking his view of the terrace. 'The lad went into an office. Number 68. There's a solicitors' on the first two floors and something called Ambrym Productions at the top. Haven't seen him since.'

'Ambrym belongs to a woman called Eadie Sykes.' Winter smothered a yawn. 'She makes videos.'

'Should I know her?'

'Only if you're a mate of Faraday's.'

'The DI? On Major Crimes?'

'Yeah. She's his shag. Big woman. Australian.'

'And the lad?'

'Faraday's son You could try for an interview but don't hold your breath.'

'Why not?'

'He's deaf and dumb. Only speaks sign.'

Suttle was still trying to work out why a DI's son, Major Crimes for God's sake, should be keeping such bad company. Winter beat him to it.

66

'Kid's got a reputation for getting himself in the shit. You should have been around a couple of years back.'

'So what do I do now? Any suggestions?'

'Stay there. Cathy's sending a relief on this job. I'll pick you up.'

'Like when?'

'Like soon.' Suttle heard Winter laughing. 'Looks evil out there.'

J-J had waited nearly half an hour for Eadie to finish her phone call. She'd signed that one of the video's backers, the Portsmouth Pathways Partnership, were demanding an update on what was going on. It was taxpayers' money they were handing out and Ambrym were a month late sending in the quarterly progress report. Without the right ticks in the right boxes, there'd be problems releasing the next tranche of funding. And if that happened, according to the Ambrym spreadsheet she'd been obliged to share with the agency, her cash flow would turn to rat shit.

Eadie went through the agreed project milestones for the second time. Yes, they'd completed the initial research. Yes, they'd touched base with each of the city's drug abuse organisations. Yes, they'd circulated full details of the project to a thousand and one other interested parties including every school in the city, every further education college, every youth group, every neighbourhood forum. And yes, she'd even managed to comply with the positive discrimination requirements by hiring someone with a registered disability.

'That's you,' she signed, at last putting the phone down. 'How did you get on?'

J-J had spent most of the last half-hour wondering just how much to tell her about Pennington Road. In the end, he decided there was no point even mentioning it. He'd come away empty-handed. With luck, he'd never see the guys with the dog ever again.

'Daniel's sick,' he signed.

'What do you mean, sick?'

'Strung out. Hurting.'

'Strung out enough not to do the interview?'

J-J hesitated. £90 worth of heroin was the price of the interview. He wasn't at all sure what would happen if they turned up without the accompanying wraps.

'I don't know. He looks really bad to me.' He shrugged lamely, then mimed a state of imminent collapse.

Eadie watched him, scenting an opportunity.

'A real mess, you mean? The shakes? The sweats? Clucking?'

J-J nodded, an emphatic yes.

'You think he's got anything stashed away? Emergency supplies?'

A shake of the head.

'And this was when?' She glanced at her watch. 'An hour ago?'

With the greatest reluctance, a nod.

'Excellent.' Eadie was on her feet. 'I'll give you a hand with the lights and tripod. The car's out the back.'

Chapter six

Faraday, alone in Eadie Sykes's seafront flat, gazed out at the rain. Ten minutes ago, he'd finally brought the session with the u/c officer to an end. In an hour or so, he'd have to drive down to the historic dockyard for yet another meet with Willard. For now, though, he owed himself a pause for thought.

Eadie rented her flat from her ex-husband, a successful accountant, and the block lay on the seafront within sight of South Parade pier. It had once been a hotel but the kind of holidaymakers who booked for a week or a fortnight had long since fled to Spain, and the building, like so many others in the terrace, had been converted into apartments.

Eadie's was at the very top, a big, open space that she'd floored with maple wood and garnished with the bare minimum of furniture. Over the last year or so, Faraday had sometimes wondered about an extra chair or two, something to make it cosier, but Eadie always insisted that the whole point of the place was the view, and in this, as in so much else, Faraday knew she was right.

Four floors up, a stone's throw from the beach, the apartment offered a seat in the dress circle. Away to the left, the rusting gauntness of the pier. Offshore, the busy comings and goings of countless ferries, warships, fishing boats, yachts, their passage fenced by the line of buoys that dog-legged out towards the English Channel. Beyond them, the low, dark swell of the Isle of Wight.

Faraday had lost count of the number of times he'd stood here, marvelling at the play of light, at the constant sense of movement, at the way a line of squall showers could march up the Solent, bringing with it a thousand variations of sunshine and shadow. Today, though, was different. Today there was only a grey blanket of thickening drizzle and the grim, squat shape of Spit Bank Fort.

Eadie kept her binoculars on a hook beside the big glass doors that opened onto the recessed balconette. They'd been a Christmas present from Faraday, an unsuccessful down payment on birding expeditions together, and now he slid back one of the tall plate-glass doors and raised the binos. The optics were excellent, even on a day like this.

The skirt of green weed around the bottom of the fort told Faraday it was low tide. Above the weed, an iron landing stage looked newly painted. A big grey inflatable hung on a pair of davits and a staircase ran upwards to double doors set into the granite walls. One of the doors was open, an oblong of black, and higher still Faraday's binoculars found a white structure the size of a mobile home perched on the roof of the fort.

He lingered a moment, wondering what it might be like to live on a site like this, to wake up every morning to views of Southsea seafront across the churning tide, then he let the binos drift down again until he was following a line of open gun ports. Spit Bank Fort, he thought, looked exactly the way you'd imagine: unlovely, purposeful, thousands of tons of iron and granite dedicated to the preservation of the city at its back.

Faraday permitted himself a smile. Over the years, he'd talked to old men in Milton pubs who remembered the last war. There'd been ack-ack guns on Southsea Common, barrage balloons ringing the dock-yard, and Spit Bank Fort would undoubtedly have played its own part in protecting the city against the swarms of Luftwaffe bombers. Odd, then, that a German should find herself in charge here. And odder still that Bazza Mackenzie, Pompey born and bred, should choose this sturdy little piece of military history to mark his coronation. King of the City indeed.

Wallace's two phone conversations with Mackenzie had been taped, the transcripts and cassettes locked in Willard's office safe. According to Wallace, Mackenzie had been up front, even matey, one business-man talking to another. He'd wanted to gauge the strength of Wallace's interest and he'd been blunt enough to ask whether Wallace really knew what he was getting into.

Mackenzie said he'd been out to the fort three or four times and taken a good nose round. The place, he warned, was damp as fuck. The roof needed a total sort-out and some days – if you talked to the right people – they didn't have enough buckets to cope with all the leaks. Health and Safety would be taking a hard look at some of the exterior ironwork and he wouldn't be at all surprised if they red-carded the lot. On top of that, there were problems with the well that supplied the fort with fresh water and if he was honest you'd be looking to rewire the whole place as well as shelling out for a new generator. That's why his bid was so low. Pay anything close to the million and a quarter quid she was asking, and you'd be adding half that again – easy – for the refurb.

Wallace had ridden out the warnings and when Mackenzie, in the most recent conversation, had begun to press him about his own funding he'd kept things deliberately vague. He said he'd been lucky with a shopping development in Oman. Currency fluctuations had gone in his favour. A big investment in euros had netted him a small fortune and there were other bits and pieces that kept his bank manager more than happy. This last phrase had stopped Mackenzie in his tracks, and shortly afterwards he'd dropped his conversational guard to offer what – to Wallace – sounded like a buy-off. 'What would it take,' Mackenzie had mused, 'for you to pull out?'

Wallace had parried the offer with a chuckle. Money, he told Mackenzie, was the last thing he needed. Neither was he up for a compensatory slice of whatever business Mackenzie had in mind for the fort. No, his own interest was quite clear. Various trips abroad, he'd seen what a good architect could do with a site like this. He wanted to turn Spit Bank into one of Europe's most unusual five-star hotels. On Nick Hayder's prompting, he'd added that he might even be considering gaming facilities.

This last conversation had hit the buffers shortly afterwards but one phrase in particular had stuck in Wallace's mind. 'This is a funny town,' Mackenzie had said, 'but you won't know that until you've lived here a bit.' This observation had struck Wallace as a warning and he'd pressed Mackenzie on the kind of timescale he had in mind. What did 'bit' mean? Mackenzie, it seemed, had laughed down the phone. 'A lifetime,' he'd said. 'Anything less, and you're fucking playing at it.'

Faraday's own session with Wallace had concluded with a hand-shake and an exchange of mobile numbers. The u/c, it turned out, was keeping his visits to Portsmouth to an absolute minimum. Faraday got the impression Wallace had another u/c job on the go, different legend, but he certainly seemed to have plenty to keep himself occupied. Wallace had reported Mackenzie's interest in a face-to-face meeting and he'd been waiting for Nick Hayder to make some kind of decision. With Hayder now in hospital, that decision would presumably pass to Faraday.

Now, Faraday stepped back into the big living room, closing the glass door behind him. His previous experience of undercover operations had given him none of Nick Hayder's confidence and he'd heard enough about Bazza Mackenzie to suggest he'd be an exception-ally difficult target to sting. The problem with jobs like *Tumbril* was their very isolation. Walled off from real life, it would be all too easy to talk yourself into a result.

Faraday helped himself to a banana from the fruit bowl in the kitchen. The TV zapper lay beside the bowl and he pointed it across the room towards the widescreen television.

The TV was tuned to BBCNews 24. In Paris, according to the presenter, President Chirac was expressing shock and dismay at the American build-up on the Iraqi border. UN Resolution 1441 was not an authorisation to go to war and even at this late stage he found it inconceivable that President Bush would put the framework of international order at risk. Thank God for the French, Faraday thought. He slipped out his mobile and dialled Eadie's number, watching yet more footage of British tanks on the move. To his surprise, she didn't answer.

To J-J.s relief, getting back into the Old Portsmouth apartment block was no problem. Daniel Kelly was standing in his first-floor window, visibly anxious, and the street door yielded at once to Eadie Sykes's touch. She led the way upstairs, carrying the camera box and a lightweight tripod. J-J followed with two lights on stands and an armful of cabling.

Daniel met them halfway down the hall. Pale and sweating, he blocked the path to his flat, ignoring Eadie. J-J looked down at his outstretched hand.

'What's going on?' It was Eadie. 'Someone like to tell me?'

J-J edged past Daniel, fending him off with the light stands. When the student pursued him down the hall, he made an awkward bolt for the open door at the end. The flat smelled of burning toast and the air was blue with smoke. J-J dumped the light stands and the cabling in the lounge, reaching the kitchen in time to rescue the grill pan. Two slices of Mighty White were on fire and he smothered them with a washing-up cloth. Daniel stood in the door, oblivious to this small domestic drama.

'Where is it?' he kept saying. 'Where's the gear?'

J-J had tipped the remains of the toast into the sink. The grill pan hissed beneath the cold-water tap. He turned back to Daniel and began to sign, tapping his watch. Maybe an hour, maybe two, but soon, I promise. Then came a movement in the lounge next door and Eadie appeared behind Daniel. She was staring at a plastic syringe and a battered old spoon readied on one of the work surfaces. Daniel was still demanding an answer. It wasn't hard to connect the two.

'You *scored* for him?'

J-J shook his head.

'Then how come . . . ?' She'd spotted the belt Daniel would need to raise a vein. 'Are you out of your mind?'

The student turned on her, angry now. He hadn't a clue who she was but this was his flat, his property. She had absolutely no right to barge in or pass judgement. He'd thought J-J was interested in realities, in what it meant to make certain decisions, certain choices. If that was still the case, no problem. If it wasn't, he could go and poke his camera into someone else's life.

Eadie blinked. Few people ever talked to her like this.

'We came because I understood we were invited,' she said. 'And it's *my* camera. Just for the record.'

She looked witheringly at J-J, then stepped back into the living room. Through the open door, J-J watched her beginning to unpack the Sony Digicam. Daniel ignored her. He demanded to know what the guys at Pennington Road had said. He asked whether there was any point trying them on their mobile number. Curiously, thought J-J, he never once mentioned the money.

'You ready, guys. . . ?'

It was Eadie again. Calmer now, she wanted to know where Daniel would like to sit, the spot where he felt most comfortable.

'*Comfortable?*' The word raised a bitter smile. 'You really don't have a clue, do you?'

'You're right. That's why we're here. Chair by the TV be OK?'

Daniel shrugged and turned away, shaking his head. Then he began to hug himself, rocking backwards and forwards, his body hunched, his eyes shut, a man caught naked in a bitter wind.

'They drop it off by car,' he muttered. 'They ring the bell three times and I just go down.' Daniel looked up at J-J, those big moist yellow eyes. 'You'll stay with me? Help me?'

J-J nodded, easing Daniel gently out of the kitchen. Maybe an hour or two in bed might help.

Back in the living room, Eadie had set up the tripod and the camera. Lights ringed the armchair beside the TV and now she was arranging a line of books on the shelf behind.

'Daniel,' she said brightly, 'I think we're about ready. That OK with you?'

The student paused, looking blankly at the waiting filmset.

'Anything.' He began to shiver again. 'I don't care.'

The interview, according to the time code generated by the digital camera, started at 17.34. Eadie Sykes, after the earlier bump in the road, was determined to smooth out any differences between them. She was grateful for Daniel's trust. What they were about to do was enormously important in all kinds of ways and she wanted to repeat what J-J had doubtless already established: that this was Daniel's video, Daniel's views, Daniel's life, and no one else's.

73

'You understand me, Daniel?'

In the camera's viewfinder, J-J watched her big freckled hand reach out. The student shuddered under her touch. The way he kept moving in the chair meant holding the shot wider than J-J would have liked, though it felt a mercy to be able to spare him the usual close-up.

'You want to start by telling me how it all began?' Eadie might have been talking to a child.

Daniel stared at her, uncomprehending. It was hot under the lights, and his big waxy face was bathed in sweat. Eadie prompted him again, an edge to her voice this time, and slowly he began to claw his way backwards through his life, picking up fragments here and there, trying to tease some sense, some logic, from the decisions he appeared to have made. Strangely enough, thought J-J, the very effort this involved seemed to ease some of his pain.

He'd first tried smack in Oz. He was staying in a youth hostel in Queensland – big place, popular with students. He'd plenty of money but he'd chosen the youth hostel because he was lonely. A backpacker from Dublin had scored some heroin in Brisbane and sold him enough for an introductory smoke.

To Daniel's surprise, it was no big deal. He'd felt pleasantly sleepy, maybe a bit queasy afterwards. He certainly had no great desire to repeat the experience and remembered asking his new Irish friend what all the fuss was about. Given a choice between smack and a good bottle of Hunter Valley Chardonnay there was, he said, no contest.

A couple of years later, give or take, he'd tried it again. By now he was back in the UK and this time it was very different. He'd fallen in love with a dropout student from Godalming, a girl called Jane. She was already developing a sizeable heroin habit and had a real mistrust, almost a hatred, of straights. Just to stay alongside her, talk to her, be with her, meant using smack. To Daniel, it had seemed a price worth paying.

Within a couple of months Jane had dumped him for a failed rock musician. All Daniel was left with was a broken heart and a four-wrap-a-day heroin habit. Oddly enough, the smack helped. It was at this time that he stopped smoking it and began injecting. Injecting was a buzz. All his life he'd been afraid of needles but now, to his great satisfaction, he couldn't wait. There was an art to it, a right and a wrong way. He always used a sterile works. He always washed the spoon in boiling water. It was, he said, almost sacramental.

He turned his head away from the camera, wiping his face with the back of his hand. Eadie had visibly relaxed. For weeks, she'd been hunting for a junkie, any junkie, who was prepared to make a stab at an interview. Finding someone as articulate and self-deceived as this was manna from heaven.

'Sacramental how?'

Daniel seemed surprised by this voice beyond the lights, this sudden intrusion. He shifted in the chair again and began to scratch himself.

'I had respect for it,' he said at last. 'It held my life together. I could depend on it. It was my friend.'

'Smack had become your friend?'

'Yes.'

'Your best friend?'

'My only friend.' He closed his eyes. 'People don't understand about heroin. Treat it right and it looks after you. You can rely on it. You know what I'm saying?'

'I think so, yes.' Eadie was picking her words with care. 'Tell me how you feel at the moment.'

'Horrible. Cramps. Pains. Everything.' His eyes were still closed.

'And heroin?'

'Heroin will take the pains away. That's what it does. It makes it possible to be me again. It gives me peace. A peace –' he was staring into the far distance now, his face a mask '– so vast it's like waking up in some cathedral. It's huge. It's yours. It belongs to no one else. If you've never been there, never had this feeling, it's impossible to describe it. Like I said, a sacrament.' His chin went down on his chest and his whole body began to shudder.

Eadie glanced up at J-J, who stepped back from the camera, meaning to offer Daniel some kind of privacy, but Eadie caught him by the arm.

She signed, 'We haven't finished.' She turned back to the student. 'Daniel? You're OK to carry on?'

He nodded slowly. He looked bewildered.

'Is it time yet?'

'Time for what?'

'Time for the guys . . . You know . . .' He nodded, pleading, towards the street.

'No, not quite yet. Soon, Daniel, but not quite yet. You really think heroin is a friend? The way you're feeling now?'

'That's not smack. Smack makes that better.'

'How much better?'

'That's a stupid question. Feel what I feel and you'd know.'

'But I'm not feeling what you feel, Daniel. That's why I want you to talk about it.'

He stared at her, his hands crabbing along the arms of the chair.

'This is hard,' he mumbled at last. 'You can't believe how hard this is.'

75

'I know, Daniel. Just try.'

'I don't know what you want.'

'I want you to talk about now, about the state you're in, about the way you feel. Can you do that for me?' Eadie was leaning forward. 'Daniel?'

The eyes had strayed towards the window again and J-J suddenly sensed where this interview was going. Heroin really was Daniel's friend. As his life had closed around him, taking him prisoner, it was the one thing, the one sensation, the one constant, on which he could depend. Take heroin away, and there'd be nothing left.

'I used to think I could stop.' The voice was barely a whisper. 'But I can't.'

'Why not?'

'Because I don't want to. Sarah says I'm crazy. She may be right but that's not the point, is it? Maybe I like being crazy.'

'And feeling like shit?'

'Yes, but shit happens, everyone knows that. Shit happens and then everything is OK again. You know why? Because I get to shoot up. That's all I want to do just now. Go into that kitchen and shoot up.'

'And the next time?'

'I'll do it again. And the time after that. I'll do it forever and then I'll die. Hey . . .' He forced a smile. 'Nice thought.'

'Dying?'

'Doing it forever.'

His hand went to his mouth. He sat absolutely still for a moment or two, then jack-knifed forward in the chair and began to retch. Instinctively, J-J panned the camera slowly down, following a thin green thread of vomit onto the patterned carpet. Glassy-eyed, Daniel wiped his mouth and tried to apologise. Eadie had spotted a box of tissues. She leaned across, mopping up the vomit, stealing a glance at the camera to make sure J-J was still taping.

From the entryphone on the wall in the hall came a single ring, then two more. Daniel was on his feet, heading out of the room. Seconds later, Eadie heard the door open and the sound of footsteps as he ran for the stairs.

'You got it all?' she signed.

J-J nodded. He knew exactly what was going to happen next and he knew as well that he wanted no part of it. Watching someone in this kind of pain had begun to disgust him.

'Ready?' Eadie signed that she wanted the camera off the tripod. Shoulder-mounted, J-J could follow the action wherever it led.

J-J shook his head. You do it.

'You're serious?' Eadie stared at him a moment, then abandoned the soiled tissue and began to unclamp the camera. By the time Daniel reappeared, she'd wedged herself in a corner of the room, the shot nicely framed on the open door. J-J retreated to the window. In the street below, a red Cavalier was disappearing in the direction of Southsea. He watched until it rounded a distant corner. For once, he was glad he was deaf.

'Just ignore me, Daniel. Pretend I'm not here.'

Eadie had followed Daniel into the kitchen. The student was fumbling with one of the wraps. In the background stood the kettle he'd just plugged in. He tore at the Sellotape and began to empty the contents of the wrap into the waiting spoon. In the viewfinder the heroin was dirty brown, the colour of dried mud. From a plastic Jiffy container came a squirt or two of lemon juice, beginning to dissolve the powder.

Daniel tested the kettle with the back of his hand, then decanted a little of the water into the bowl of the spoon before propping the handle on a box of matches. Next, in close-up, came the belt. He wound it round his upper arm, leaving it loosely secured while he stirred the concoction with the end of a match. Moments later, he un-capped the syringe with his teeth and drew swampy liquid into the barrel. A biro lay beside the spoon. He slipped the biro beneath the belt he'd wrapped round his arm and began to twist. A vein appeared, a tiny blue snake amongst the yellowing bruises below his elbow. Trapping the tourniquet against his ribcage, he prodded the vein with the flat of his thumb, then retrieved the syringe and laid the needle against his flesh before working it slowly in.

A single drop of blood formed. There was a brief moment of absol-ute silence and then, as Eadie slowly panned the camera up to Daniel's face, there came a sound that was to stay with her for days to come. It began as a gasp and expired as a sigh. It spoke of surprise, of delight, of relief, of immense satisfaction, and she caught the clatter of the falling biro as she swung round with the camera, following Daniel out of the kitchen. He still had the syringe in his arm, empty now, and he began to sway and stumble as he made his way to bed.

His bedroom was next to the bathroom. The single bed was unmade, a flower-patterned duvet in a heap on the floor, and Eadie paused in the open doorway, the shot perfectly framed, as Daniel, still fully clothed, climbed into bed. He looked like a drunk, every movement slowed to half speed, a man easing himself through an ocean of sweetness. He struggled briefly upright and leaned out of the bed, plucking at the duvet, missing, plucking again, then finally dragged half of it off the floor. Flat on his back again, his eyes were closed. Eadie's finger found the zoom control and the shot slowly tightened. By the time his face filled the viewfinder, Daniel Kelly was smiling.

Faraday sat on a bollard on the quayside overlooking the harbour, waiting for Willard's Jaguar to appear. The rain had stopped now and the sky was beginning to clear from the west. Evenings like this, mid March, the sunsets could be spectacular, shafts of livid sunshine slanting across the city, and he thought of Eadie Sykes out on the balconette, toasting the view with her first glass of Côtes du Rhône.

Recently, watching her with J-J, he'd concluded that she'd become the mother his son had never had. She'd built a real kinship with the boy. She'd become his mentor, his pathfinder, his guide. She was teaching him all she knew. She stuck by him in difficult situations. And all of that, in Faraday's view, probably added up to motherhood. Janna had died when J-J was barely a couple of months old. Only now, twenty-three years later, had he discovered a woman he could rely on.

Rely on? Faraday shook his head. Relationships, as he knew to his own cost, could be brutal. A woman called Marta had made him happier than he'd ever been in his life. Losing her had taken him to places so dark he shuddered to remember them.

J-J, too, had tasted this kind of despair. His guileless passion for life, the unconditional trust he put in virtual strangers, exposed him to all kinds of risks and a year-long relationship with a French social worker had nearly broken his heart. But his son had somehow emerged from this encounter more or less intact and was still hungry for the next of life's little tests whereas Faraday was increasingly aware of his own vulnerability.

Eadie Sykes had blown into his life with the force of a gale. He loved her gutsiness, her candour, her absolute refusal to compromise. She surprised him constantly, and he loved that as well. But, unlike J-J, he was always alert for the unforeseen twist. In ways he was ashamed to admit, he almost expected betrayal.

Willard had left his Jaguar outside the dockyard. He was wearing a heavy-duty sailing anorak and a pair of yellow waterproofs to match. He stole up on Faraday, standing over him as he stared out across the harbour.

'The rib should be here any minute. I belled them just now.'

Faraday looked up at him, faintly surprised at the interruption.

'Rib?'

'Big inflatable. They use it to ferry stuff back and forth. Wallace tell you about the fort?'

'Yes'

'Neat, eh?'

'Let's hope so.'

'And the chats with Mackenzie? All that?'

'He told me they'd spoken a couple of times on the phone.' Faraday got to his feet. 'Mackenzie wants him out of the running. No surprises there.'

Willard was beginning to look irritated, and Faraday forced himself back into the world of Operation *Tumbril*. According to Wallace, the idea for the original sting had come from Nick Hayder but Willard would have been quick to spot the potential. Scalps were important to Det-Supts and Mackenzie's would be a serious battle honour. There were rumours on Major Crimes that Willard had his eyes on promotion – maybe even head of CID – and putting a full flag level three away would do him no harm at all.

Willard was watching the harbour entrance, his eyes narrowed against the flaring sun. When Faraday asked him how much the fort's owner, the German woman, knew about the sting, he smiled. Spit Bank, he said, had been offered for sale by the Ministry of Defence in the '80s. The buyer, an ex-boatyard owner, had spent a fortune getting it into some kind of shape. Fifteen years later, he'd sold it on to a wealthy businessman, eager to find a project for his wife.

'This is the German woman?'

'Gisela Mendel. You'll meet her in a minute. Peter Mendel's an arms broker, covers the gaps between the defence salespeople in the MOD and the dodgier foreign governments. It's a semi-Whitehall job. He's security-cleared, full PV.'

The positive vetting, Willard said, made him a perfect partner in the sting against Mackenzie. Given his relationship with the MOD, there was no way he'd hazard the operation.

'And the wife?'

'She runs a series of language modules for Fort Monkton. Four-week total immersion courses out on Spit Bank, any language of your choice. She charges the earth.'

'Monkton's MI6.'

'That's right. That's why she's PV'd as well. Hayder couldn't believe his luck. All he had to do was write the script.'

Faraday could imagine Nick Hayder's glee. Fort Monkton was a government-run training establishment across the harbour in leafy Alverstoke. Screened by trees and an eight-foot wire fence, it turned out spies for MI6. Posted abroad, languages were a must. Hence, Faraday assumed, the success of Gisela Mendel's little enterprise.

'So how did you play it?'

'Gisela put the word round a couple of local estate agencies, pretending the fort was up for sale, just the way we asked her. Mackenzie was onto her within a day.'

'She knows who Mackenzie is? His background?'

'No, he's just a punter as far as she's concerned, someone who's made a pile of money and now wants somewhere really high-profile.'

'And you think she believes that?'

'She's never told me otherwise.' Willard permitted himself a rare smile. 'You hear about the football club?'

'No.'

'Mackenzie tried to buy in. He was after an eleven per cent stake. With that kind of holding, he'd be looking to take Pompey over.'

'And?'

'They saw him coming and knocked the deal on the head. After that, he made a play for the pier.'

'South Parade?'

'Yeah. Problem there was he put in a silly bid and tried to snow them with all kinds of pressure. They got so pissed off in the end, they pulled the plug, and you can hardly blame them. Mackenzie's so used to dealing with low life that he forgets his manners. Quote the guy an asking price, and he instantly divides by ten. *Ten.* That's not negotiation, that's robbery. The pier people walked, big time, and then one of them found himself talking to Nick.'

This conversation, according to Willard, sowed a seed in Nick Hayder's ever-fertile mind. By this time, *Tumbril* had abandoned any thought of baiting the usual investigative traps. There was no way Mackenzie allowed himself anywhere near the distribution system and therefore no prospect of scooping him up with half a kilo of uncut Peruvian. The other strategy – following the money – might, in the end, achieve the same result via a money-laundering conviction but *Tumbril's* hotshot accountant was talking another three months minimum with the calculator and the spreadsheets and both Hayder and Willard himself were nervous that headquarters' patience might not stretch that far. Somehow or other, there had to be another way.

'So?' Faraday was beginning to warm to this conversation. At last, he thought, the pieces are beginning to fit.

'So Hayder took a good look at what happened with Mackenzie over the pier. Number one, the guy's determined to get his name up there in lights. He owes it to himself, to his mates. He wants the world to know there's nothing he can't buy. Number two, he's after a casino.'

'A casino?'

'Sure. Make Mackenzie's kind of money and the big problem is washing it all. You can carry it out of the country and stuff it in foreign accounts. You can treat yourself to a couple of Picassos. You can buy into legit businesses, bricks and mortar, whatever. If you've got the patience, you can even launder it through *bureaux de change*. Brian Imber will be giving you the full brief tomorrow but the truth is we're knocking all these options on the head. Believe me, it's getting hard to wash dodgy money. A casinos solves a lot of that. Plus –' he smiled '– there was still the question of profile.'

A casino on the pier would have been the answer to Mackenzie's dreams. Punters would flood in, the tables would magic dirty money into legitimate winnings, and everyone in Pompey would know that Bazza Mackenzie had finally made it.

'So Nick started looking for another property, another proposition. You know he used to go running?'

'Still will, when he's better.'

'Sure. So he was out there one weekend, hammering along the seafront, when – bosh – he's staring out to sea and he suddenly realises the answer. Spit Bank Fort. This is him talking, not me.'

Faraday knew it was true. He could hear Nick Hayder's voice, picture him leaning into the conversation, his head lowered, his hands chopping the air. This was the way the man had always operated, total conviction, turning a gleam in the eye into a string of successful prosecutions. The latter happened way down the line, but without the wit and the balls to pull some truly original stroke, the bad guys were home free.

'Mackenzie put a bid in?'

'At once. £200,000. Said it had to be rock bottom because sorting the place out would cost a fortune. Gisela wouldn't drop a penny under the asking price. One and a quarter million.'

Slowly, week by week, Mackenzie had gone to £550,000, each new trip to the fort confirming the vision that had begun to obsess him. A glass dome, he'd told Gisela, would seal the interior from wind and rain. Punters could look down on the gaming floor from the upper deck. Croupiers would be dressed in period blue artillery tunics. Girlies in naughty Parisian gear would serve drinks and canapés. And every night, with the gaming over, there'd be yet more boodle stashed away in the thick-walled cartridge magazines deep in the bowels of the fort. Spit Bank, to Hayder's delight, had become Mackenzie's dream fantasy, the clinching evidence that the Copnor boy had well and truly made it.

'That's why Wallace came as a bit of a shock. He was Mackenzie's wake-up call.'

Faraday was trying to put himself in Mackenzie's shoes. After all the plans, all the gloating phone calls to his mates, came the sudden news that some total stranger had stepped into the city and virtually doubled his bid. As a wind-up, it was undeniably sweet. But as a potential sting, thought Faraday, it still had some way to go.

'Mackenzie's after a meet. Before Wallace puts the surveyors in.'

'I know.' Willard nodded. 'We needed to back Mackenzie up against a deadline, make him sweat. That's why Wallace has the surveyors on standby for Friday next week. My guess is we're probably talking Wednesday or Thursday for the meet.'

Faraday smiled. He was thinking of Wallace in the hotel room earlier. The over-loud tie, the ear stud, the brash little touches. Young guy on the make. Clever.

'You really think Mackenzie has him down as a dealer? Same line of business?'

'That's the plan.'

'And you think he believes it?'

'I'll be disappointed if he doesn't.'

Faraday turned the proposition over in his mind. Turf was important, whatever line of business you happened to be in. The last thing Mackenzie needed was serious competition, and in a city like Portsmouth there was an added complication. Pompey belonged to her own. Intruders like Wallace needed reminding of that.

'So how will Mackenzie play it? Violence? Half a dozen mates round the corner?'

'Maybe.' Willard shrugged. 'Or he might just try buying him off. If he's silly enough to talk drugs, or some kind of co-distribution deal, we're home and dry. If it's a straightforward bung, he's still exposed himself. Either way, we end up with evidence. And not before time, eh?'

Willard broke off. He'd picked up the distant thump-thump of a fast inflatable and he turned in time to catch the rib powering down for the passage up-harbour. The controls were manned by a slight, solitary figure in a blue anorak. Minutes later, Willard was doing the introductions.

'Gisela Mendel.' Willard nodded towards Faraday. 'Joe Faraday. I mentioned him on the phone.'

Faraday smiled hello. Her handshake was businesslike. The big outboards were still idling below them. She needed to be back at the fort asap.

'No problem.'

Willard had taken charge, bending to slip the rope she'd made fast to the bollard, and Faraday sensed at once that there was something between them. He'd rarely seen Willard so animated, so eager. He seemed to have shed years.

Faraday clambered down into the inflatable and zipped up his anorak. Gisela, behind her dark glasses, was waiting for Willard to cast off. Her hand was ready on the twin throttles – perfect nails, blood red. When she turned to check the clearance beyond the bow, the last of the sunshine shadowed the planes of her face. Mid forties, thought Faraday. Maybe less.

Once Willard was on board, she eased away from the jetty, burbling out towards the harbour. The wind was stronger here, the slap of halyards against the masts of a line of moored yachts, and once they'd cleared the harbour entrance, she pushed the throttles wide open against the stops.

The inflatable responded at once, surging forward, and Faraday braced himself, glad he'd rescued a woollen scarf from the Mondeo. Willard was sitting beside him, oblivious to the freezing spray. Twice he shouted something to Gisela but the wind and the roar of the outboards carried his words away. Watching her at the wheel, Faraday realised how often she must have made this journey. She rode the inflatable like a horse, with immense skill, driving it hard at the oncoming waves then nudging left and right as she felt for the grain of the flooding tide. Over towards Ryde, Faraday could see the bulk of a container ship, outward bound from Southampton, and when he looked back towards the shoreline he thought he could just make out the line of apartments next to South Parade pier, white in the gathering dusk.

The tidal stream around the fort, a foaming river of water, made berthing tricky. Faraday could smell the dampness of the place, sense the history behind the glistening granite blocks. Willard was playing the sailor again, doing his best to grab a stanchion as the inflatable surged up and down, and Faraday caught the expression on Gisela's face as she nudged the bow towards the waiting pair of hands on the landing stage above them. She looked amused.

A rope ladder provided access to the landing stage. Willard caught a wave as he waited a second too long and was soaking wet by the time Faraday hauled him upwards. Gisela was the last off, leaving the inflatable to be secured for the return trip.

They followed her into the fort. It was nearly dark now, and the vaulted passageway that led to the central courtyard was softly lit by wall lights cleverly recessed into the granite walls. There were more of these feminine touches in the courtyard itself – tubs of year-round flowers, a sturdy little palm tree, tables and chairs warmed by a thicket of space heaters – but there was no disguising the essence of this place. A sense of military purpose hung over everything. It was there in the brick-lined casemates around the edge of the courtyard, in the iron spiral staircase that disappeared into the bowels of the fort, in the hand-lettered notices that Gisela had so carefully preserved. *Number 14 Store Hammocks*, read one. *Caution – Shell Lift*, warned another.

'We use these two as classrooms. The rest is accommodation.' Gisela had paused outside one of the casemates.

Faraday peered in. Perhaps a dozen figures sat at individual desks. A tutor was standing at the front, a map of the Balkans on the blackboard behind him. One of the women in the class had her hand in the air.

'You want to eavesdrop?'

'No.' It was Willard. The soaking on the ladder had tested his sense of humour. He wanted a towel and something hot to drink.

'So.' Gisela's English carried the faintest trace of a foreign inflection. 'Upstairs, then.'

She led the way across the courtyard and up another flight of steps. At the top, Faraday recognised the white structure he'd glimpsed earlier from Eadie's flat. A newly painted door opened into a tiny lobby. It was suddenly warm inside and there was a smell of fresh flowers. This was obviously where Gisela lived.

'You know where the bathroom is. I'll make tea.'

Willard disappeared and Faraday followed Gisela into a living room. The wide picture windows faced north, across the deep-water shipping lane, and Faraday could make out the line of coloured lights that ran the length of Southsea promenade. Beyond them, in the gloom, the black spire of St Jude's church.

'You drink tea?' Her voice came through a hatch from the galley kitchen.

'Please. Two sugars.'

Faraday gazed round. The room had been furnished with some care, neat rather than cosy. A compact, two-seat sofa faced the window. There was a television in one corner and a fold-down table in another. The laptop on the table was open and the screen saver featured a view down an Alpine valley. Faraday's attention was caught by a framed photo propped beside a row of paperbacks in the bookcase above the table. It showed Gisela in a striking yellow hat beside a heavy-set man in his middle fifties. The man was bowing. Gisela was performing an elegant curtsey. The third figure in the photograph was the Queen.

'Buck House garden party.' Willard had emerged from the bath-room. 'Hubby got the CBE.'

'For?'

'Services to the nation. Merchant of death.'

'He lives here, too?'

'Visits very occasionally. They've got a place up in Henley, river

84

frontage, paddocks for the horses, the lot. You could fit Kingston Crescent into the walled garden with room to spare.'

Faraday at last turned round. Willard had found a sweater from somewhere, an expensive polo neck in black cashmere wool, almost a perfect fit. The man in the photo, thought Faraday. Similar build.

Gisela returned with a tray of tea. She turned off the laptop and made space on the table. Willard organised another couple of chairs from the room next door and then got down to business. For Faraday's benefit, he wanted Gisela to describe her dealings with Bazza Mackenzie.

Gisela was looking amused again, that same expression, and Faraday found himself wondering quite where this relationship parted company with *Tumbril*. Willard never let anyone in the job anywhere near his private life but there'd always been rumours that the partner in Bristol wasn't quite enough.

'He phoned first, very friendly. That was a couple of months ago. Just after Christmas. He'd heard this place was for sale and he wanted to come out and take a look. He arrived next day.'

'Alone?'

'No. He came with a couple of friends, both of them older. Tommy?' She was looking at Willard. '*Ja?*'

'Tommy Cross.' Willard nodded. 'Used to work in the dockyard. Bazza uses him as a cut-price structural engineer, sorts out the conversions when Mackenzie's in the mood for another cafe-bar. It was Tommy who gave this place the once-over. Stayed most of the day, didn't he? Drove you mad?' He flashed a smile at Gisela.

'That's right. Lunch and supper. It was dark by the time they went.'

Within twenty-four hours, she said, Mackenzie had been back on the phone. He'd drawn up a contract. He had a price in mind. All Gisela had to do was sign.

'As simple as that?' It was Faraday's turn to smile. This was where Mackenzie's list of problems must have come from. Letting Tommy Cross loose on a structure like Spit Bank Fort might have been the best investment Mackenzie ever made. Except that Gisela wasn't having it.

'I turned him down. £200,000 was a joke and I told him so. It cost me £385,000 before I even started.'

'What did he say?'

'He laughed. He said he didn't blame me. He also said something else.'

'What was that?'

'He said I was a nightmare to do business with.'

'Why?'

'Because I was tasty as well as clever.'

'He said that? *Tasty?* That was the word he used?'

'Yes. I think he meant it as a compliment. To be honest, I didn't care. That's the kind of person he is. In your face. Right *there.*' She held her hand in front of her nose. 'After some of my husband's clients, believe me, that's a relief.'

'You liked him?'

'Yes, I do. He's not frightened of women. And he's straightforward, too. A silly offer like £200,000? All I have to do is say no. I can live with that.'

Within a week, Mackenzie was back on the phone. He'd had a bit of a think. He could go to £250,000. Once again, Gisela just laughed.

'And it went on,' she said. 'Another £10,000, another £10,000. In the end I said there were easier ways to chat a woman up. He agreed.'

'So what happened?'

'He invited me out. We went to Gunwharf, Forty Below. You know it?'

Faraday nodded. Forty Below featured in most of the weekend disturbance reports. Ambulance crews set their clocks by Friday night's first call to a serious affray. This woman could take her pick of Europe's finest restaurants. Only Bazza Mackenzie would treat her to Forty Below.

'How did you get on?'

'Fine. He made me laugh. I liked that.'

'And the fort? The business?'

'He said he had to have it. He told me all about his plans, the casino, the decor, the kind of food he wanted to serve, special suites for honeymooners. He was like a kid with a new toy. It was sweet, really.'

'And the price?'

'He'd got to £400,000.'

'So what did you say?'

'No. He said he couldn't go another penny higher but he offered to sleep with me. That would take it up to half a million.'

'Sleeping with Mackenzie's worth a hundred grand?' Faraday began to laugh.

'You can hear him on the tapes.' Willard was gazing out at the lights of Southsea. 'Can you believe that? *Mackenzie?*'

'He's funny,' Gisela said again. 'I think he meant it as a joke.'

Willard ignored this mild reproof. What was important just now was the presence of Wallace in the bidding. By upping the price to £900,000, he explained to Gisela, *Tumbril* had put the screws on Mackenzie.

'Deep down, the guy's unstable. Everyone knows it. What we need is a deadline. That's where the survey comes in. Part of me says we agree to meet before Friday. He might just compromise himself to sort the whole thing out. Otherwise we leave it a week or so. Wallace gets the thumbs-up from the survey and makes a decision to go ahead. At that point, Mackenzie has to make a move. Either he tops the offer or gets rid of the opposition.'

'You really think he'll pay another half million?' Gisela was gazing out into the dark.

'To be frank, no.'

'Pity. . .'

'Oh?' For the first time, Willard was on new ground. 'Why's that?'

Gisela studied him a moment, the way you might assess a child's preparedness for bad news, then she touched him lightly on the hand.

'I'm afraid the story's changed. I really do have to sell the place.' She smiled. 'And £900,000 in cash would be more than acceptable.'

'You're serious?'

'Perfectly.'

'May I ask why?'

'Of course.' The smile faded. 'Peter and I are divorcing.'

Misty Gallagher was drunk by the time the cab dropped her off at the Indian Palace. Paul Winter had phoned her earlier, planning to drive down to Gunwharf and pay her a social call, but Misty was adamant that she'd had enough of the apartment. She and Trude had been at it since late afternoon. Another hour of that kind of abuse and she'd take a carving knife to her mouthy daughter.

Winter had his usual table at the back of the restaurant. He'd been coming here for months now and he liked the people who ran it. He gave them all kinds of bullshit but they knew he was lonely and they treated him well. At forty-five, robbed of a wife you'd taken for granted, you appreciated that kind of courtesy.

'Misty. Long time.'

He got to his feet and guided her into the waiting chair. She was wearing a see-through black top over a pair of spray-on jeans. Unless Winter was bloody careful, the waiters would be selling tickets at the door.

'Paul . . .' Her eyes were glassy. 'They do wine here?'

'Sure. White?'

'Rosé.'

'Of course. Mateus OK?' He signalled towards the bar without waiting for an answer. When the waiter came over, he pointed to number 7 on the wine list. 'And another Stella for me, son.' He turned back to Misty. She was trying to find a lighter for her cigarette. 'How's tricks, then, Mist? Still getting it?'

'Fuck off. You know, don't you?'

'Know what?'

'Me and Bazza.' She'd found the lighter. 'Man's a prick.'

Winter did his best to look reproachful. It had been common knowledge for more than a year that Bazza Mackenzie had decided to trade Misty in for a newer model, but he'd somehow assumed that Misty would cope. Evidently not.

'I caught him in Clockwork the other night with that Italian bitch. Had it out with him then and there.'

Clockwork was the hottest of the late-night clubs down by South Parade pier, currently fashionable amongst the city's more successful criminals. Misty, on the wrong end of a bottle of Moët, had found Bazza at the bar with the lovely Lucia and a bunch of his best mates. Robbed of the power of speech, Misty had ordered another bottle of Moët, hosed him down, and left him with the bill.

'His mates loved it.' She had a smile on her face. 'Told me I should have done it months ago.'

Bazza, enraged, had pursued Misty onto the seafront. Lucia had locked herself in the toilets and half the fucking town was in stitches. Didn't Misty know that times had moved on? Didn't she have any sense of style? Of occasion? These were strokes you just didn't pull any more. Certainly not in public.

'He sent the agent round next day.'

'What agent?'

'The estate agent. Bloke I even *knew*. Told me Baz had decided to put the flat on the market. That fucking day. Vacant possession. Can you believe that? After all the shit I've had to put up with?'

Winter pulled a face. The wine had arrived and he steadied Misty's glass as the waiter did the honours. Given the state of the woman, he estimated he had maybe half an hour to coax any sense out of her. Tops.

'Tell me about Trude, Mist.'

'What about her?'

'We found her in a bit of a state last night. She might have told you.'

'She tells me fucking nothing. Except what a cow I am. Can you imagine? That kind of language? Your own fucking *daughter*?'

Winter reached out, closing his hand over hers. For once in his life he was serious.

'Listen, Mist. We found her in a dosshouse in Fratton. Someone had given her a thumping and tied her to a bed. You wouldn't have any idea who, would you?'

'Thumping?' Misty was trying to make sense of the word. 'My Trude?'

'That's right.' He watched Misty reach for the glass. 'What do you know about Dave Pullen?'

'He's a shag. At it all the time. He's a disgusting man.'

'I know. So what's Trude been doing with him? She's a good-looking girl. Christ, Mist, she could have the pick of blokes her own age – decent blokes, bit of education even. What did she ever see in an ape like Pullen?'

Misty blinked at him, the lightest touch on the brakes. She reached for the glass again, and emptied it.

'Mist . . . ?'

'I dunno.'

'But you must have known, must have wondered.'

'Of course, yeah.' She nodded. 'Of course I wondered.'

'So what's the answer?'

'I'm telling you, I don't know.' She tried to focus on another table across the restaurant, and then stifled a hiccough. 'He's an older guy,' she said at last. 'They know how to listen sometimes, older guys. Bit of sympathy, bit of a shoulder, know what I mean?'

Winter was watching her carefully, remembering Trudy at lunchtime in the Gumbo Parlour. Mother and daughter had fallen out, big time, and Trudy seemed to know exactly where to put the blame.

Misty was splashing yet more Mateus into her glass. Winter hadn't seen a bottle disappear so fast since the last time they met.

'What happened to that nice motor dealer Trude used to live with?' he said at last. 'Mike Valentine, wasn't it? Up in Waterlooville?'

'Pass.'

'You're telling me you don't know?'

'I haven't a clue. I've told you, I can't get a word out of her. Who she gives it to is a mystery to me. Always has been.'

'But she came back to live with you, Mist. And she did that because she must have fallen out with Valentine. There's no way you didn't ask her. I don't believe it.'

'Bollocks did I ask her. If you knew the first thing about Trude you'd know she keeps herself to herself. It was like living with a stranger, if you want the truth. Just a shame she hadn't got anywhere else to go. Fucking gloom bag.'

'She's angry, Mist. Angry at you. Now why would that be?'

'No idea. Ask her.'

'I did.'

'When?' The alarm in her eyes told Winter he was getting warm.

'Lunchtime, Mist. Today.'

'And what did she say?'

89

'She didn't. And she wouldn't, my love, because she's careful when she opens her mouth. Unlike her mum.'

He held her eyes over the table. Alarm had given way to a cold fury. Misty got to her feet, clutched the table to steady herself, then yelled at the waiter. She wanted a taxi. She'd had enough of talking to this wanker. In fact she'd had enough of everything.

Winter gazed up at her, wondering how far to take the rest of the conversation. Aqua would have a cab here in moments. Just time to take a punt or two.

'Mike Valentine's in deep with Bazza, Mist.' He leaned back in the chair. 'Maybe shagging someone that close isn't such a great idea.'

'You mean Trude?'

'No, love.' He offered her a matey smile. 'I mean you.'

It was gone eleven by the time Sarah made it round to the flat in Old Portsmouth. She'd spent the last couple of hours at the Students' Union, celebrating the end of the first draft of her degree dissertation. There was still stuff to do, lots of stuff, but the shape of the thing was there and fifteen thousand plus on the word count deserved a couple of pints of cider.

She kept Daniel's spare keys in a special pocket in her day sack. She stepped in through the street door and made her way upstairs. Outside Daniel's flat, she paused and knocked. This time of night, unless a miracle had happened, he'd be dead to the world, but it still felt more comfortable to announce her presence.

When there was no answer she turned her key in the lock and pushed the door open. The flat was in darkness, but the moment she switched on the light she saw that the furniture had been rearranged. This, she knew at once, was confirmation that the video crew had been round. The way the armchair had been positioned – nice sense of depth behind the interviewee – was exactly what she would have done.

'Dan?'

There was no response. She hesitated a moment, wondering whether to leave him to it. He'd be in bed by now, bound to be, and it might be better to come back tomorrow to find out how the taping had gone. With luck, the whole experience – something new in his life – might have given him a bit of a nudge. He might even have offered the kind of performance, the kind of analysis, she knew lay within him. That's why the smack was such a tragedy. The guy had a brain. The guy was clever. She'd never met anyone so thoughtful, and so articulate.

She began to turn to leave, then had second thoughts. His bedroom was down the corridor. She paused outside the open door. In the faint spill of light from the lounge, she could just make out the shape of his body, prone beneath the duvet. There was something else, too. A terrible smell.

'Dan?'

The smell was vomit. She knew it.

'Dan? Are you OK?'

Nothing. Her hand found the light switch beside the door. Daniel was lying on his back, his eyes open, staring up at the ceiling. A thick stream of vomit had caked on his face, on the side of his neck, on his shoulder.

'Dan?' Her voice began to falter. 'Dan . . . ?'

Chapter seven

The first mid-March London-bound train leaves Portsmouth and Southsea town station at 04.38. This particular morning, the trickle of early commuters included one of the city's two MPs, a cheerfully resilient Lib Dem who never tired of pushing Portsmouth's new image as the south coast's must-visit heritage attraction.

Pompey, he'd recently assured a visiting journalist from one of the broadsheet Sunday supplements, had at last shed its post-war reputation for poverty, planning mistakes, and limitless aggression. This was no longer the city where a shopping centre – the Tricorn – was annually voted Europe's Ugliest Building. Neither were Friday nights infamous for sailor-bashing and huge helpings of recreational violence. On the contrary, thanks to inward investment and a forward-looking council, the city was fast acquiring a well-earned reputation for meshing the old and the new. The historic naval dockyard offered a world-class collection of antique warships. The harbour had been given a multi-million-pound refurb. And in the shape of the Spinnaker Tower, the new Gunwharf development would soon boast the tallest structure in southern England. Portsmouth, in short, was on the rise.

The MP, already late for the 04.38, found himself amongst a gaggle of fellow passengers halted on the concourse by a line of *Police Caution* tape. Peering over the shoulder of a WPC, he watched two ambulance paramedics bending over a body slumped at the foot of one of the turnstile entries. The youth was wearing jeans and a red football shirt. There were livid splashes of blood around his scuffed trainers, and a brief glimpse of his face revealed the kind of damage you'd associate with a high-impact car smash. Only when the WPC moved, did the MP realise that one of the youth's wrists was shackled to the turnstile by a pair of handcuffs.

Pressed for details, the WPC did her best. The fire brigade were on their way to deal with the handcuffs. The paramedics were confident the young man would survive the trip to hospital. As so often with these incidents, the damage appeared worse than it probably was.

'These incidents?' The MP had noticed a blood-soaked pillowslip on the concourse beside one of the kneeling paramedics. 'What incidents?'

'Can't really say, sir.' The WPC was looking grim. 'Except it's getting worse.'

Faraday awoke to an empty bed. He lay there for a moment, gazing up at the ceiling, tuning in to the cries of the early-morning seagulls. Living in the Bargemaster's House beside Langstone Harbour, he could map the view from his window by a medley of different calls. The piping of redshanks and the bubbling call of a flock of oyster catchers would suggest low tide on the mudflats, but Eadie's seafront location lacked that kind of variety. A morning like this you had to put up with the angry squawk of black-headed gulls battling for their share of pavement debris from last night's take-outs. From the birding point of view this was a serious disappointment but Faraday had enjoyed enough early mornings in this bedroom to draw a subtler conclusion. As a prelude to his working day, the clamour of warring scavengers was near-perfect.

The crack between the curtains suggested it was barely dawn. Rolling over, he checked the bedside alarm clock. 06.03. From the nearby living room, came a low murmur from the television. BBCNews 24 again, Faraday thought.

Past midnight, with Eadie still working at her office, the news from the Gulf had finally driven him to bed. US and UK forces had been pounding the Iraqi port of Umm Qasr. Oil wells were blazing around Basra and there appeared to be every prospect of a counter-attack deploying Saddam's ample supplies of chemical weapons. By now, God help us, the Americans would be fingering the nuclear button.

Retrieving a towel from the carpet beside the bed, Faraday padded through to the living room. Eadie was kneeling in front of the television, wrapped in Faraday's dressing gown, consulting a clipboard on her lap. Paused on the screen, a single juddering image, was a face Faraday didn't recognise. Definitely not BBCNews 24.

'Tea?'

Eadie spun round.

'Shit.' She was grinning. 'Watch this.'

She glanced down at the clipboard, then zapped the video recorder into fast forward. Seconds later, Faraday was watching the same figure dragging himself along a badly lit hall. He disappeared briefly through a door at the end. By the time the camera caught up, he was clawing his way into bed. Eadie froze the image again.

'There.'

'Where?'

Faraday followed her pointing finger as she touched the screen.

'It's an empty syringe,' She said. 'Guy's off the planet.'

Faraday at last recognised the barrel of the syringe hanging from the bloodied forearm and as Eadie pressed the play button again he found himself drawn into what followed. There was a terrifying helplessness in the sight of this young man's battle to capture the duvet on the floor. Time and again, he reached down for it. Time and again, he missed. Finally, he caught one corner, hauled it agonisingly up towards him, then – barely half-covered – gave up.

'You found your junkie, then?'

'Big time.'

'Pleased?'

'Just a bit.'

'Lucky, eh?' Faraday was watching the eyes slowly close. 'Got there just in time.'

'You're joking.' Eadie busied herself with the zapper again, putting the video into reverse until there was nothing on the screen but a bulging vein and the slow plunge of the needle. Eadie played the sequence twice. Faraday had never seen anything so graphic.

'You were there.'

'Obviously.'

'And this is for real.'

'Too right. Real is what I do.'

He nodded, still riveted to the screen. 'What happens beforehand?'

'I do an interview with him.'

'Good?'

'Better than good. Excellent. The guy was a gift, articulate, strung-out, totally blitzed. Watch this, and no kid in his right mind will go anywhere near drugs. Any drugs. Watch this, and you'd probably give up shandy. Are we whispering *result* here? Or is it just me?'

'You said you did an interview with him.'

'That's right. Little me.'

'So who was behind the camera?'

'J-J.'

'And the other stuff? Afterwards?'

'Me. J-J wimped out. Couldn't hack it. Major disappointment. Still –' her eyes returned to the screen '– I think I did OK. No?'

Faraday didn't answer. Only when he'd filled the kettle and found the milk did he feel confident enough to continue the conversation. Anger would get them nowhere. Facts first.

'We're talking heroin?'

'Obviously.'

'And you know where this stuff came from?'

'Federal Express. Guy knocks on the door, you sign the little form, and, hey, it's candy time.'

'I'm serious.'

'OK.' Eadie was laughing now. 'You don't have to sign the form.'

'You're telling me you were there when it was delivered?'

'Of course. That's why the interview was such a knockout. These people run on tramlines. Four hours between fixes is comfortable. Anything over that, it starts to show. Six, seven hours, you start clucking. This guy?' She nodded towards the screen. 'Clucking fit to bust. The moment that entryphone went off, he was down the stairs. You really think I'm going to ignore what followed? I couldn't have scripted it better. Give me an actor and a million dollars and you wouldn't get a result like that. People sense reality. They sit up and take notice. That's the whole point.' She stared at him a moment, uncomprehending. 'So what's the problem, Joe? You find all this offensive?'

Faraday shook his head. It was far too early in the morning to feel so weary.

'You want to know the problem? The problem is, I'm a cop.'

'I know that. You're after the bad guys. This guy's not a bad guy, he's a victim. That's the whole point. Give him a stage, let him make his case, show what this stuff *really* does, and you're going to have fewer victims. Trust me. I've just spent a year rehearsing that little speech. Something else, too.'

'What?'

'I fucking believe it. And so should you.'

Her anger was sauced with disappointment. She'd served up her tastiest morsels, the dish of her wildest dreams, and Faraday had dumped it in the bin. After all this, she seemed to be saying, you've copped out. Literally.

'Let's start with the legal position,' Faraday said softly.

'Sure.'

'You were involved in supply. You were party to possession. They're both offences.'

'Supply? Crap. I kept the lights on, sure, while he dived downstairs but it wasn't me out in the street. That would have happened anyway. It's how all this stuff works.'

'Possession, then. You had a duty to stop him.'

'Stop *him*? If I'd strapped the guy down, he'd still have made it into that kitchen. We're talking chemistry, Joe, not rights and wrongs. That man needed to shoot up. If that wasn't the case I'd still be making videos about Dunkirk fucking veterans. Need is what this movie is about. Need is what those guys out in the street trade on. Need is—'

Faraday cut in.

'Guys? Plural?'

'Guys? Guy? Shit, I don't know. Stop playing the cop on me, Joe. I thought you understood. I thought we'd been through some of this together. It's open and shut, my love. It's means and ends. There's a problem out there, a problem like you wouldn't believe, and my little bit of the jigsaw, my responsibility if you like, is to try and put it on tape. That's what I do. That's my contribution. Get this thing right and I just might make a difference. Better that than playing the lawyer.' She paused. 'Any other crime I might have committed?'

'Aiding and abetting.'

'Like how? Like he couldn't do it by himself? Like he hasn't done it by himself half a million times before?'

'Like you could have stopped him. As I just suggested.'

'Are you serious?' She got to her feet and stepped towards him. 'Don't you listen to *anything* I say? I know I'm some dumb fuck from down under but give me credit, my love. The whole point of this circus, this little adventure, is that *nothing* stops these guys. Offer them detox and there's a shortage of beds. Get them into rehab and most of them do a runner. Put them in jail and you're guaranteed a junkie for life. Little me? I just point my camera and watch. Why? Because a classful of kids might just come to the conclusion, way down the line, that junk isn't worth it.' She glowered at him, still furious. 'Is anyone at home? Or am I wasting my time?'

Faraday busied himself with the teapot. He'd seen Eadie in these moods before but he'd never been on the receiving end. Her anger was truly volcanic. It had an almost physical impact. Spill it on the carpet and the flat would be in flames.

Reaching for the sugar bowl, he watched her prowling up and down. Twice she reached for the zapper, then changed her mind. With it finally in her hand, she stabbed savagely at the BBCNews 24 button. Another volley of cruise missiles. Terrific.

Faraday abandoned the tea and stepped towards her. When she turned to confront him again, he nodded down towards the screen.

'Show me everything,' he said. 'From the start.'

Winter was early for the nine o'clock conference in the cluttered first-floor office at Kingston Crescent that served as a base for the Portsmouth Crime Squad. Settling himself at his desk beside the window, he fired up his PC and logged on. A couple of mouse clicks took him into the Daily State, a constantly updated tally of incidents that kept a finger on the city's rough pulse. Amongst last night's excitements – a couple of D & Ds, a warehouse break-in, and a neighbour dispute – was something else that caught his eye.

Checking the name of the attending DC, he reached for the phone. This time in the morning, the divisional CID office over at Highland Road should be filling up.

'Bev?' He recognised the voice at once. 'Paul. Dawn there, by any chance?'

'Duty last night, mate. She's gone home.'

'Cheers.'

Winter put the phone down. Dawn Ellis was a young DC on division, one of the few detectives in the city for whom Winter had any respect. Recently, after a troubling encounter with a rogue newcomer from the Met, he'd developed an almost fatherly concern for her well-being.

When he finally got through, it was obvious she'd been asleep.

'I don't know why I bother with the tablets,' she muttered. 'Think of the money I'd save.'

'Sorry, love.' Winter was still peering at the overnight log. 'This smack overdose in Old Portsmouth last night, was that yours?'

'Yes.'

'What happened?'

There was a pause while Dawn mustered her thoughts. Cathy Lamb, meanwhile, had appeared at the office door. She looked even more fraught than usual.

'Student called Daniel Kelly.' It was Dawn again. 'Girlfriend found him dead in bed with a works in his arm. Uniform attended first, then me.'

'And?'

'I took a statement. Tango One sorted an undertaker. I was out within the hour.'

'Anything dodgy?'

'Not that I could see. According to the girl, he'd been shooting up for years. Rich kid, nothing better to do with his money. You should have seen his flat. Puts my place to shame.' She paused again. 'What is this?'

'There's mention here of a video crew.'

'That's right. According to the girl, he'd been involved in making a video. She thinks the crew may have been with him at some point last night. I left the details in the office. Needs sorting.'

'You've got a number for these people? A name?'

'Can't remember. It's some kind of production company, begins with "A". Talk to Bev.' She smothered a yawn. 'Night, night.'

Winter looked up to find Cathy Lamb standing over his desk. For once she didn't seem remotely interested in the details on Winter's screen.

'My office,' she said. 'Now.'

Jimmy Suttle and another squad DC were already occupying most of Cathy's tiny office. Winter joined them, shutting the door and wedging himself in the corner. Cathy, it turned out, had just spent an uncomfortable half-hour with the Chief Superintendent. The town railway station had been sealed off at four the morning while fire and ambulance did their best to disentangle an assault victim from one of the entry turnstiles on the main concourse. The young man in question was now occupying a cubicle in the Queen Alexandra Hospital A & E Department.

'He's one of our Scousers,' Cathy said wearily. 'And Secretan's drawn the obvious conclusion. What didn't help was a bloody MP on the station.'

'At that time in the morning?'

'He was going to a conference in Birmingham. Anti-Social Behaviour. And if you think that's funny . . .'

Secretan, she said, was chewing the furniture. The turf war had now gone very public indeed and the last thing he needed was yet more grief from headquarters. He wanted a full report on his desk by noon, and an action plan within twenty-four hours.

'Action plan?'

'We have to seal this off, nip it in the bud. So far the MP's agreed not to talk to the press but there were other punters there and they undoubtedly will. Secretan's writing the headlines already.'

'How are we so sure about turf wars? They leave a note? Name and address?'

'Good as.' Cathy summoned a weak smile. 'Someone had taken the trouble to adjust the lad's watch, then stamp on it. Any guesses?'

Jimmy Suttle stirred.

'6.57?'

'Exactly.'

Winter beamed his approval. The boy was learning fast. He turned back to Cathy Lamb as she listed the immediate actions. The Scouser had so far refused to offer a statement. A search of his clothing had revealed a set of car keys, a single wrap of heroin, and a scribbled list of mobile numbers. A couple of squad DCs up in A & E were waiting to take a statement but a fractured jaw and a mouthful of broken teeth didn't help and it wasn't looking hopeful. As far as witnesses were concerned, a postman had rung in with details on a van. He'd been en route to the start of his shift in the nearby sorting centre and had

98

noticed the van backed into the side entrance to the station. The rear doors were open and there was some kind of fracas going on. The van looked like a Transit – old, maybe a builder's wagon.

'There's CCTV on the concourse.' Cathy was looking at Winter. 'And another one outside across the road. According to the postie we're looking at half two in the morning. OK?'

Winter nodded. The CCTV control room in the bowels of the Civic Centre was his least favourite destination but already he'd put money on a rapid result. Secretan was right. Odds on, these were the beginnings of a serious turf war. This was about trespass, about the bunch of young lunatics who'd descended on the city and torn up the rules. If you were local and your patience had run out, then there ways of sending a message. Giving one of the Scousers a hiding and dumping him at the railway station didn't leave much room for ambiguity. Fuck off or else.

Winter was still wondering about the Transit when Suttle caught his eye.

'Bazza?'

'Has to be.' Winter returned to Cathy Lamb. 'Anything else, boss?'

Already late for a scheduled conference at the *Tumbril* HQ on Whale Island, Faraday found himself caught in rush-hour traffic. Inching towards his fourth set of red lights, he turned over the morning's events. The row with Eadie had shaken him more than he cared to admit, not simply because he hated letting the job get between them but because – in some important respects – he suspected she might be right.

Her junkie interview had been a revelation. As a divisional DI, he bumped into the drug problem every day of his working life, largely because junkies needed to burgle and shoplift to feed their habit. The same names cropped up time and time again on the charge sheets, cutting an ever-deeper groove in the monthly volume crime stats, and in clear-up terms it helped a great deal to know where to look for nicked laptops and help-yourself perfume. But watching the torment of this sweating, moon-faced junkie, with his quietly desperate conviction that heroin was doing him some kind of favour, was the first time that Faraday had truly understood the power of the drug. Getting seriously fond of smack, as Eadie had pointed out, was opting for a form of life imprisonment. No charge, no trial, no jury, no chance of appeal. Just the daily four-hour trek between fixes, with the strongest possible motivation for getting hold of the next wrap.

In this sense, Eadie's video rushes had spoken for themselves, perfectly capturing the chokehold that was heroin addiction. Strung-out and visibly distressed, Daniel had done his best to rationalise what smack had done to him, to defend the drug the way you might protect a best friend, but even at his most articulate you couldn't avoid the physical realities: the hands crabbing up and down the arms of the chair, the constant scratching, the haunted desperation in his eyes. Add to this the sequence that followed, and Eadie might have a point. Put these images in the right order, let them speak for themselves, and no one in his right mind would go anywhere near the stuff. That, at least, was the theory.

This morning, they'd argued the issue to a standstill. From Faraday's point of view, Eadie had been reckless. If it ever got to court a good lawyer might be able to limit the damage, but she'd sailed desperately close to the wind and taken J-J with her. Sooner or later he'd catch up with the boy and get another perspective on last night's little adventure but on the evidence to date he was amazed that Eadie should take a risk like that for a couple of minutes of video footage. It was, he told her, crazy.

At this, she'd simply laughed. She'd spent half her life taking risks for whatever had seemed to matter at the time, and this movie of hers, this video, was simply another example. From where she was standing it was simply means and ends. If the light at the end of the tunnel was truly important – and it was – then she didn't care a toss about how dark it got. Whatever it took, however big the risk, it would be worth it. For Daniel's sake. And for all the other kids who might end up burying themselves in smack.

At this point she'd had to take a call on her mobile, retreating to the privacy of the bedroom. Faraday had caught the name Sarah, but by the time Eadie re-emerged, minutes later, Faraday was on his way out. They'd exchanged a brief kiss at the door, Eadie plainly preoccupied, and Faraday had made a mental note to ring her later. He thought they were still friends but something new in her face had made him wonder.

Now, at last on the move again, he pondered the obvious irony. Eadie knew nothing about the Bazza Mackenzie operation. He seldom discussed work with her and would never taint pillow talk with something as sensitive as *Tumbril*. Yet, in her own way, simply by plunging in at the deep end, she probably knew a great deal more about the reality of the drugs scene than he did.

He smiled to himself, remembering Joyce's guided tour of the *Tumbril* premises. Shelf after shelf of files. Hundreds of surveillance photos. Thousands of documents. Hard disks brimming with audit trails and details of company structures. Countless evidential bricks to cement a case that might, God willing, put the city's major dealer away. All of this material was doubtless important, and over the coming days he'd have to get to grips with it, yet he was already sure that none of it was as compelling and vivid as the moment Eadie's young junkie lost his battle with the duvet and sank into unconsciousness.

Stopped yet again by traffic, Faraday eyed his mobile. The lights up ahead were still red. He owed her a call. He knew he did. He reached for the phone and punched in her number.

Engaged.

Still in the flat, perched on a kitchen stool, Eadie knew it was important to let this man talk about his grief. He'd known about the death of his son for barely three hours. Greater Manchester Police had sent round a WPC first thing, briefed by Southsea CID. Eadie, alerted to what had happened by a long phone conversation with Daniel's friend Sarah, was frank about the reason for her call. She wanted to express her sympathy. And she wanted to know how he was feeling.

'*Feeling?*' He paused. 'I don't know. I can't describe it. You ask a question like that, and I simply can't give you an answer. In one way I feel nothing, absolutely nothing.'

'Numb? Would that cover it?'

'Numb would be good. Numb is right. Excuse me . . .' He broke off a moment and Eadie wondered whether the sudden catch in his voice was entirely authentic. There was something slightly stagey about this man, something the lingering remains of a down-home Lancashire accent couldn't quite disguise. Did he really care about the son he'd just lost? She couldn't decide.

'How well did you know Daniel?' He was back again.

'Barely at all. We only met yesterday.'

'*Yesterday?* How was he?'

'Terrible. I shouldn't be saying this, Mr Kelly, but he was in an awful state. You'll know he'd been using for a while?'

'Yes.'

'Well, I think it had got on top of him. He was a very unhappy man.'

'You're a friend of a friend?'

'I'm afraid not. I was making a video.'

'A what?'

'A video.'

'With Daniel?'

'Yes.'

'About Daniel?'

'As it turns out . . . yes.'

She began to explain about the video, where the idea had come from, the support she'd lined up city-wide, and how that support had eventually translated itself into funding.

'That was the easy bit. The hard bit was finding Daniel.'

'What do you mean?' The question, this time, was unfeigned. She had this man's total attention.

'Most people in his situation you wouldn't want to meet. Daniel was the exception. In a strange way he knew exactly what he was doing to himself and he had the guts and intelligence to get that over.'

'Guts?'

'He was a brave man, Mr Kelly. I couldn't have made the video without him.' Eadie paused, waiting for some kind of reaction. As the silence deepened, she realised that she might just be an answer to this man's prayers, some tiny hope of rescuing something from the wreckage.

'So what exactly were you doing with Daniel?' he asked at last. 'This video thing?'

'I did an interview with him. Then I taped him shooting up.'

'Shooting up? You mean the stuff that killed him?'

'I'm afraid so. He'd have done it anyway. We just happened to be there.'

'You didn't bring the stuff with you?'

'God, no.'

'And when you left him?'

'He was asleep.' She paused a beat. 'And smiling. If you ever want to see the footage . . .' She let the invitation trail away.

There was a long silence. Eadie rubbed at a grease spot on the kitchen work surface, biding her time. Finally, the voice returned, barely a whisper.

'I don't know what to say. Truly, I don't. This is bizarre. I'm a lawyer. I get to meet all kinds of people and, take my word for it, not a lot gets by me. This is just . . . I don't know . . . Jesus . . . You don't pull your punches, do you?'

'I'm afraid not. This is going to sound very tactless, I know, but there's to be a post-mortem. Daniel was a known IV user so they have to take various blood tests, HIV, Hep B, Hep C. Assuming he's clear, they'll be doing the PM tomorrow.'

'And?'

'I'd like your permission to tape it.'

'The post-mortem?'

'Yes. I'll need to talk to the coroner as well but your support will make that a great deal easier. And when you come down I'd like to do an interview.'

'With me?'

'Yes.'

'Why?'

'Because we have to see this story through. We have to know where it ends. The post-mortem is part of it. That's where junk leads. To the mortuary, to the dissecting table, to all of that. And afterwards, of course, there'll be the funeral.'

'You want to tape that too?'

'Of course.'

'You said "we" just now. Who's "we"?'

'You and me, Mr Kelly. I'm simply the messenger. You're his dad. Together, I think we owe him.'

Another silence, even longer this time. Then Eadie bent to the phone again.

'This video will be selling into schools,' she said quietly. 'With some of the proceeds I'd like to propose a memorial fund in Daniel's name. I know this can't be easy for you, Mr Kelly, but we have to make some sense of a tragedy like this. Not just for Daniel's sake but for the millions of other kids who might put themselves at risk. I know you understand that and I'm not asking for a decision now. May I call you back in a while? Once you've had a chance to think it over?'

The answer, when it came, was yes. Eadie smiled.

'Yes to phoning you back?'

'Yes to the post-mortem. And yes to all the rest of it.'

'You're sure about that?'

'I'm positive. I don't want another conversation like this in my life but I admire you for asking. Does that make sense?'

'Perfectly.' Eadie was still smiling. 'And thank you.'

Chapter eight

Faraday couldn't take his eyes off Martin Prebble. For some reason he'd expected *Tumbril*'s forensic accountant to be older, greyer, and altogether more in keeping with the painstaking business of teasing a successful prosecution from a million and one pieces of paper. Instead, he found himself introduced to an exuberant figure in his late twenties with gelled hair, designer jeans, and an expensive-looking collarless shirt. Oddest of all was a circular purple blotch, the size of a five-pence coin, high on his forehead. Half close your eyes, and it might have been a caste mark.

'Paintballing,' Prebble explained at once. 'Mate's stag do last night. Guy I was up against thought he'd pop me at point-blank range. He's an investment banker. Brain-dead since birth.'

'You're telling me it's permanent, honey?' It was Joyce arriving with a plate of chocolate biscuits, plainly concerned.

'Haven't a clue. Half an hour with a packet of frozen peas says no but I wouldn't rule out cosmetic surgery . . .' He reached up to help himself to one of the biscuits. 'Clever, though, eh? Tough shot from three feet.'

Brian Imber was waiting for the meeting to settle down. The space he'd cleared in the middle of the *Tumbril* conference table was promptly commandeered by Joyce. The way she bent low over Prebble, depositing the tray of coffees, told Faraday she'd fallen in love again. Young, good-looking, and funny. Never failed.

'We've got most of this morning.' Imber was looking at Prebble. 'Like I said on the phone, we need to get Joe up to speed.'

'No problem.' The words just made it through a mouthful of biscuit. 'My pleasure.'

Prebble, it turned out, had spent the early months of his involvement with *Tumbril* burying himself in every last shred of evidence until Mackenzie had become as familiar to him as a member of his own family. Only with a picture this complete, he told Faraday, did he feel confident enough to apply the appropriate financial protocols – pursuing particular audit trails, leaning on conveyancers and the Land Registry for details of umpteen property transactions, chasing up invoices and bank payments – in a bid to build a day-to-day profile of Mackenzie's expenditure, and thus get the measure of his real wealth.

Imber, recognising this young man's talent for getting inside the head of *Tumbril*'s principal target, had decided to turn the entire briefing over to him. Only when it was absolutely necessary would he contribute thoughts of his own.

'Have you ever met Mackenzie?' Faraday was still watching Prebble.

'Never had the pleasure. I know him on paper – figures mainly, intelligence files from Brian, surveillance snaps, gossip – but that's pretty much it.'

'Informants?'

'Very little. Brian says that's unusual but my guess is these guys are tight with each other, always have been. That's what you breed down here. The place feels tribal to me.'

Faraday smiled. It was a shrewd judgement.

'And do you like what you see?'

'In some ways I do, yes. I'm an accountant. I know the way money works. This guy's been well advised, and more to the point he's listened. That's not always the case, believe me. I've done legitimate audits, big corporate stuff, where the guy behind the big desk listens to no one and blows a big hole in the bottom line. Mackenzie's not like that. Most of the time he watches every penny. He's a peasant at heart, and that's served him well. Plus, I understand he can be ruthless. Two reasons why he's a rich man.'

'How rich?'

'Last time we counted? Including all the nominee assets?' He frowned. 'Nine million four, give or take. And that's discounting narcotics in the pipeline, either on order or unsold.'

'You're telling me he's still dealing?'

'God, no. He's well past that. But analysis tells me he bankrolls others and takes a slice. It's standard practice, happens all over. You get to a point where you can't be arsed with all the running around. Ten years ago, he might have been closer to the front line but the last couple of years he's been back in the chateau. Ninety-five per cent of what he's up to now is totally legit, just like any other businessman. Which I guess explains why I'm here.'

Faraday's attention had strayed to the big colour blow-up of Mackenzie's Craneswater mansion on the wall. Prebble was right. With a multi-million-pound business empire to look after, Mackenzie was far too busy to stoop to simple criminality. Hence Nick Hayder's contortions baiting the Spit Bank trap. Only by threatening his bid for the big time could *Tumbril* hope to manoeuvre Mackenzie into compromising himself.

Prebble said it was worth an hour or so just talking about Bazza, and apologised in advance if he was repeating what Faraday already knew. Faraday waved the apology away. It was something of a relief to find someone who was prepared to walk him, step by step, through the entire story.

Mackenzie, Prebble explained, came from a Copnor family, a tight-knit area of terraced streets in the north-east corner of the city. His dad had been a welder in the dockyard and had scraped to get young Barry into St Joseph's College.

This came as news to Faraday. St Joe's was a Catholic boarding school in Southsea, high academic standards plus a dose or two of discipline from the Christian Brothers.

'His father could afford the fees?'

'No way. The boy won a scholarship. I told you just now, the man's bright. Wayward, but bright.'

Bazza, he said, had hated the school. For one thing, they played rugby when he was mad about football. For another, he couldn't stand wearing the same uniform as all those poncy rich kids. By the age of fourteen he'd been suspended twice, once for persistent smoking, and again for running a rudimentary protection racket, extorting everything from Bounty bars to Clash albums. After a monumental row with his disappointed father, he chucked in the towel at St Joe's and joined his Copnor mates at the local Isambard Brunel comprehensive. Three scraped passes at GCSE provoked another family row, and at the age of sixteen he left home to doss down with his elder brother Mark, who was by now making a living as a painter and decorator.

'Bazza went in with him?'

'Far from it. He's never fancied physical labour. Not then, not now. He joined an estate agency, got himself a junior selling job, mainly on the phone.'

From his desk in the estate agency, Bazza watched the early '80s property boom gathering speed. Weekends, he partied hard, swallowed bucket-loads of whatever was available, and re-established his social roots. What Prebble termed a leisure shag with a high school dropout called Marie resulted in a baby, Esme, but Bazza never took much interest. By this time he was playing serious football, turning out for a Pompey League Sunday side called Blue Army. The '83/'84 season took them to the top of the league, earning a fearsome reputation for on- and off-pitch violence on the way.

'What about the 6.57?'

'He was in it from the start.' Prebble glanced at Imber. 'Am I right?'

'Spot on.' Imber nodded. 'The 6.57 was pub-based to begin with, half a dozen groups coming together for the away games. There was no real leadership, not at the start. Bazza and his mates drank at a Milton pub, the Duck and Feathers. They went along for the laugh, just like the rest of them, and the thing just got bigger and bigger.'

By the late '80s, with Pompey briefly elevated to the old top-flight First Division, the sheer anarchy that fuelled football violence had opened Bazza's eyes to the possibilities of a life of crime. By now he'd abandoned the estate agency after a senior partner had caught him in bed with his second wife, but Bazza's years selling property had taught him a great deal about the commercial logic of toshing and selling on. What he needed was ready cash to buy crap properties and, on away days to the big London clubs, he found it.

''89' Prebble was enjoying himself. 'The summer of love.'

The fighting briefly stopped. Bazza began to import ecstasy tablets into the city by the thousand. After ecstasy came cocaine, an uglier drug but a much bigger mark-up. The violence kicked off again but Bazza was moving on. First a terraced house in Fratton. Then three more in an adjoining street. Then an old bed-and-breakfast ruin in central Southsea. All on drugs money and a string of mortgage frauds.

'We've got a few bits and pieces in there.' Prebble nodded towards Joyce's precious archive. 'His accounts were practically non-existent and he cut every conceivable corner but house inflation had set the market on fire and he knew he couldn't lose. It was money for nothing. Most of the building materials were thieved and he part-paid the blokes in cocaine.'

By now, his elder brother – Mark – had tired of Pompey. Mad about sailing, he'd gone to the West Indies to seek his fortune as crew on charter yachts.

'Is that important?' Faraday couldn't see the point.

'It will be.' Prebble nodded. 'Just remember the name.'

Back in Portsmouth, and by now in his mid twenties, Bazza had decided to get himself organised. Cannier and more ambitious by the year, he fell in with a young accountant. The new partner sorted out his chaotic paperwork, bought a £100 off-the-shelf company, and together they set about plotting a route to the serious money.

'The company's called Bellux Limited. It was basically a device to warehouse future developments.'

'Still exists?'

'Absolutely.'

'And the accountant?'

'They fell out a couple of years back. No one knows quite why, but

Bazza got himself a replacement within days. Woman called Amanda Gregory. Shit hot.'

There was a rustle of documentation, and seconds later a surveillance photograph appeared at Faraday's elbow, courtesy of Joyce.

'Does her shopping every Friday lunchtime, sheriff. Obliged us with this.'

Faraday studied the photograph. Amanda Gregory had been snapped beside a series 7 BMW, loading groceries into the open boot. She was a small, neat woman with a cap of black hair. The carefully cut two-piece suit had a *Save the Children* sticky on one lapel. Faraday could see the girl with the tin and the clipboard behind her, picketing the car-park entrance to Waitrose.

The smile that ghosted across Faraday's face spoke for itself.

'You're right,' Prebble said. 'This woman could be pulling megabucks from any of the biggies, PricewaterhouseCoopers, Ernst & Young, you name it. Instead, she chooses to work for Bazza. We're talking Mr Respectable here. That's just how far the guy's come.'

'And how long has all this taken?' Faraday tapped the photo.

'A decade. Max.'

Back in the early '90s, he said, Mackenzie was still an apprentice millionaire. In those days, according to Imber, the Pompey drug scene was dominated by a fellow 6.57, a scary hooligan called Marty Harrison. Bazza had known him for years and they had no problem fencing off separate chunks of the exploding drugs biz for their individual benefits. While Harrison specialised in amphetamine and happy pills for the weekend clubbers, Bazza concentrated on cocaine. Long term, it turned out to be a shrewd decision but at the time it was a nightmare.

'Why?'

'There was too much cash around. As fast as the accountant washed the stuff, Bazza would turn up with another bucket-load. One time he and his mates took a truck over to Cherbourg, bought eight grands' worth of booze for resale, and drank half of it on the way back. We've got the press cuttings if you want to see them. Riot and affray charges and letters to the local paper. That was a bit of a watershed. Bazza couldn't play the wild man any more. Not if he wanted to make it.'

Bazza's accountant, he said, had drawn a line in the sand. From now on, they had to clean up their act. One solution was more property: houses, a run-down nursing home off the seafront, plus the Craneswater house featured on the wall. Another was a boarded-up Southsea shop the accountant had spotted for sale. As a fashion outlet it had died on its feet. Bazza bought the lease for a song, put in the builders, and turned the place into a stylish cafe-bar.

'The Café Blanc.' Faraday had driven past it a million times. Sleek chrome interior, London cappuccino at Pompey prices. 'Place is always packed.'

'Exactly. From the accountant's point of view it was perfect. He could wash money straight through the till. Plus it suited Bazza's love life.'

By now, he explained, he was back on terms with Marie. His daughter Esme had turned into an attractive twelve-year-old and, after a couple of months' negotiation, Marie agreed to join him in the Craneswater mansion. A month later, they flew to Hawaii and got married. One of Bazza's wedding presents to Marie was a Mercedes coupé, bought from a Waterlooville car dealer called Mike Valentine. The other was the Café Blanc. The business, Prebble said, was hers.

'And now?'

'Still is. Along with half a dozen others.'

'They're still together?'

'So it seems.'

There was a silence. Faraday could hear Joyce busying herself with the percolator. The smell of fresh coffee reminded him briefly of happier mornings with Eadie Sykes.

'You want a break?'

'No.' Faraday shook his head. 'Press on.'

'Sure.' Prebble helped himself to the last of the biscuits before Joyce scooped the plate away. 'From where I'm sitting, the Café Blanc was the turning point. For one thing, it was a stand-alone business – earned its own profits, had a perfectly kosher set of accounts. Bazza was using it to wash the dirty money, of course he was, but you'd need to spend a lot of time proving it. Secondly, it gave Bazza a taste of what a real business could do for him. In my experience, these guys are always trying to square the circle. They want a big legit success and everything else that goes with it. At the same time, they can't tear themselves away from old habits. Money that easy is irresistible.'

'Once a criminal . . .'

'Exactly. The Café Blanc did it for Bazza. It was perfect. Trendy decor. Good vibe. Lots of profile. Plus the chance to bury all that embarrassing loot. That spelled Bazza heaven. All he needed to do now was repeat the trick.'

Another money-making opportunity, Prebble explained, arrived in the shape of his brother Mark. After nearly ten years in the Caribbean he returned home for a brief holiday. He and Bazza naturally had a lot of catching up to do and much of the conversation must have revolved around cocaine. Mark, with his working knowledge of the Caribbean, had developed some interesting contacts in Colombia. He also wanted to set up a yacht charter business of his own but needed substantial backing. Bazza, in turn, was keen to put his ever-increasing UK profits to work. Mark's dream of running a company of his own might just be the answer.

'How come?'

Prebble shot a look at Imber, then leaned forward. The fact that he hadn't once consulted the file at his elbow told Faraday a great deal about the fascination of an inquiry like *Tumbril*. Bazza Mackenzie had got under this young man's skin. No wonder Imber had put such faith in him.

'Bazza was being pressed to take some of his money offshore. The Café Blanc was turning over a decent profit and there'd be more businesses to come. He could declare these profits in the UK, no problem, but the money he was making in the cocaine biz was becoming an embarrassment. There was only so much he could put through the Café Blanc. Somehow, he had to find another hidey-hole.'

'Gibraltar.' Faraday was there already.

'Exactly. The place is perfect. Every bloke you meet knows someone who sets up front companies. Taxes are minimal and everyone keeps their mouth shut. All that . . . plus Bazza would really feel at home.'

'How do you mean?'

'Gib is Pompey with palm trees. Big naval base. Loads of pubs. Fights at the weekend when the package tours arrive. Like I just said, perfect.'

Faraday caught Imber's eye and smiled. Only last year he'd spent a couple of days in Gibraltar trying to coax a murder suspect onto the plane home. Thanks to the local police they'd scored a result, and in the back of his mind he'd always wondered about a trip back. Maybe now he'd get the chance.

'So how did Mark fit in? The brother?'

'Bazza set him up in Gibraltar. He used cocaine money to stake him on a flat and paid for a year's lease on an ocean-going yacht. The yacht was already berthed in the dockyard marina. Mark was in business within a couple of months. I've got the audit trail next door. Bazza didn't put a foot wrong.'

'And Mark would ship the cocaine over? Is that what you're saying?'

'Absolutely not. Some of Mark's contacts gave him a better deal at the Caribbean end but he'd developed delivery routes he trusted and saw no point changing any of that. Sailing the gear over in charter yachts is for the fairies. The Americans were using satellite surveillance, even then.'

Bazza, he said, had always put his faith in couriers. Local guys from Pompey were bought a new suit and a plane ticket. Colombian cocaine was available wholesale on the island of Aruba, ten miles off the coast of Venezuela. The couriers flew the cocaine back to Amsterdam, on a through ticket to Heathrow, but left the flight at Schipol. Their suitcases, stuffed with cocaine, would be retrieved by paid baggage handlers at Terminal Two.

'And it worked?' Faraday was looking at Imber. This was his territory.

'Like a dream. The gear was skimmed from time to time but you'd expect that.'

'What about Mark?' Faraday turned to Prebble.

'He was still in Gibraltar. The first year he made the charter business pay. Bazza effectively controls it so that pleased him no end.'

'It's got a name? This business?'

'Middle Passage. Mark specialised in rich dot.com kids with money to burn. He took them across to the West Indies and showed them the ropes. On the way back, they got to do it themselves. It was a neat idea.'

'But there had to be more to it.'

'Of course there was. Middle Passage, when you get down to the paperwork, is just another launderette. The company's registered to a couple of local solicitors. Behind Middle Passage, there's a front company, then another one, then a third. You have to wade through an army of nominees before you get anywhere near the name Mackenzie.'

'And it works?'

'Too right. Middle Passage is currently leasing five boats. That's a flotilla. As a legit business, it's paying the brother a fortune, but from Bazza's point of view it's even better than that. All these companies in Gibraltar enable him to recycle the money exactly as he chooses. It couldn't be easier.'

For most of the last seven years, he explained, Bazza's boys – the so-called 'smurfs' – had been hand-carrying holdalls of cash on a near-monthly basis down to Gibraltar. Paid into various accounts in amounts of less than £10,000, they attracted no attention. As the offshore nest eggs grew and grew, Bazza also began to invest in a whole range of Portsmouth businesses, from a chain of tanning salons to a stake in a taxi firm, paying with nominee-authorised transfers drawn on the Gibraltar accounts. Cash that had left Pompey in a Nike holdall returned electronically months later, newly washed and ironed.

'That simple?'

'That simple. And it doesn't stop there. I can show you a folio of properties abroad. Florida. Marbella. Dubai. Northern Cyprus. France. You name it. Plus, of course, Pompey Blau.'

'That's Mackenzie's, too?'

'Afraid so.'

Faraday shook his head, amazed at the sheer reach of Mackenzie's empire. Pompey Blau was a forecourt operation selling quality German cars from a site in North End. Over the past five years or so it had done amazing business, not least because Pompey Blau undercut every other outlet by at least 20 per cent. Faraday had lost count of the detectives in the city who were now driving around in near-new BMWs.

'The business is in his name?'

'No way. There's a guy called Mike Valentine.'

'I've heard of him.' Faraday was frowning. 'Car dealer up in Waterlooville. Tied up with Misty Gallagher's daughter. Right, Brian?'

'Right. Man his age, should know better.'

Prebble filled in the details. In the mid nineties, using money from Gibraltar, Bazza had staked Valentine's plans for the hived-off sales operation that was to become Pompey Blau. Valentine picked up decent German vehicles at the big London auctions, mainly Mercedes and BMW. Heavily discounted, they sold in days to Pompey drivers looking for a bit of class. Seventy-five per cent of the profits went back to Bazza but Mike Valentine was still a happy man. Twenty-five per cent of that kind of turnover was a great deal of money.

'It doesn't end there, either.' It was Imber again. 'Once we got into this properly, we realised that Mackenzie had built another clause into the agreement. We knew there had to be a route for shipping down the gear coming into Heathrow. Turned out it was Mike Valentine's responsibility.'

Once the cars had been bought at auction, substantial quantities of cocaine were stashed in the air-bag cavities. Protected from the possibility of routine stop searches, Valentine had been importing hundreds of thousands of pounds' worth of Mackenzie drugs into the city.

'We put all this together from the covert. We had a transmitter in his office and a Home Office warrant on his landline.'

'He was talking to Mackenzie?'

'Never. It was all done through lieutenants, people we can tie to Bazza.'

'And?'

'We let it run for a while. Like I say, none of it ever went anywhere near Mackenzie, give or take a bit of personal, so we hadn't got a prayer there. Then Willard came under pressure for some kind of result so we plotted an interception. Just to keep them on their toes.'

'When was this?'

'Just before Christmas. Headquarters were finalising the budgets for the next financial year and Willard knew we had a case to make.'

'So what happened?'

'Nothing. It was a Mercedes, nice motor. We pulled it over just south of Petersfield. Three traffic cars plus the tail from London. Bloke at the wheel had been working for Valentine for a year. Claimed to know nothing.'

'The air-bag cavities?'

'Full of air bag. Complete mystery. The intelligence was good, we knew that. The covert was still live. We knew the dates of the incoming consignment, the pick-up point, the lot. We were looking at a couple of kilos, a serious seizure. That car was in bits once the vehicle boys had finished with it. Not a trace.'

'So why did it go wrong?'

'Good question.'

'Was the covert still live afterwards?'

'Briefly. The next day Valentine was on the landline to Bazza. Old mates. Told him the whole story, how a car of his got pulled over, towed away, the lot. Never mentioned drugs once.'

'And Mackenzie?'

'Laughed like a drain.'

'Sending a message, then. For your benefit.'

'Big time. Both the transmitter and the intercept went dead within minutes. You can imagine what a Christmas bash *we* had.'

Faraday was gazing out of the window. Beyond the ferry port, a thin plume of dirty smoke was rising from the funnel of a moored frigate. A knock-back like that could slow an investigation to walking pace, he thought. No wonder Nick Hayder had kept the Spit Fort sting to himself.

'So where are we now?' he asked quietly.

'Bazza's got to where he wants to be.' It was Prebble again. 'Amanda Gregory runs the business side. She's organised it like any medium-sized enterprise. Property-wise, she's got a guy heading rental collections and another one in charge of scouting for new acquisitions. As far as cafe-bars, tanning salons, and the rest of it are concerned, that's all down to Bazza's wife. Let's call these three people line managers. They report in to Gregory, and she runs all the major decisions past Bazza. Because Bazza's not stupid, he pretty much agrees with everything she says, puts ticks in her boxes, sorts her out a profit-share at the end of the year. As a business structure, it's textbook stuff. Bazza files his accounts and pays his taxes. Give him a year or two, and he'll probably be running the Rotary Club.'

Faraday was watching an ensign unfurling on the stern of the frigate. Worse and worse, he thought.

'So where's the good news?'

'There's new legislation. Under the Proceeds of Crime Act, we'll be able to do him for money laundering. That has always been an option but until now we've had to tie him to a specific narcotics offence before the confiscation powers kick in. With the POCA, we can make a case, seize his assets, and then it's down to him to show us where they all came from.'

'And you think that's possible?'

'Definitely. And it goes way beyond Mackenzie. He's stashed millions away by buying into properties and businesses and God knows what else, and he couldn't have done any of that without the guys in the suits. You need conveyancing. You need binding contracts. You need the mortgages they never serviced. You need to get into all that legal crap. Believe me, there are solicitors in this city who should be packing their bags.'

'You're serious?'

'Absolutely. Screw Mackenzie under the Proceeds of Crime Act, nail him on a money-laundering offence, and the guys in the suits – solicitors, accountants – have some tough questions to answer. They're supposed to blow the whistle on dodgy transactions, and if they don't then they're in the shit as well. Believe me, there's nowhere left to hide.' Prebble paused. 'The way to hurt people like Bazza is to attack their money. If we can make a money-laundering charge stick and nick the money back off him, we've scored a result.'

'What would he pull for money laundering?' Faraday glanced across at Imber.

'That depends, Joe. He could be looking at fourteen years. But Martin's right. It's the money he cares about. For why? Because this bloody man's spent his whole life stealing a march on the rest of us. That's what's put him where he is. That's what's given him the big house, and the cars, and the lifestyle, and the reputation. Take that away, and you're left with a punchy little mush from the backstreets of Copnor. You hear about his daughter's wedding? The lovely Esme?'

Faraday shook his head. He ought to get out more, he thought.

Joyce was on her feet again. Another sheaf of photos. Faraday peered down at the first of the shots. An enormous group of men and women were standing in the sunshine. Mackenzie was in the middle, a short, squat figure bursting out of his suit and tails. Beside him, clamped to one arm, was the pretty blonde bride, her veil flung back, beaming at the camera. Faraday recognised the Cathedral in the background.

Joyce was bending over Faraday, doing the introductions, one technicolour nail moving lightly from face to face. Relatives. Extended family. Mates from the old days. Mike Valentine. The owner of Gunwharf's biggest nightclub. Two solicitors. Amanda Gregory. An architect. Two members of the Pompey first team. The general manager of the city's biggest hotel. A research fellow from the university's criminology department. A journalist from the sports pages of the *News*. The list went on and on, a tally of Portsmouth's finest.

There was a long silence. Prebble's fingers had strayed to the purpled blotch on his forehead. Imber was still gazing at the photograph. The two men were waiting for Faraday's reaction. Finally he glanced up at Joyce.

'No coppers?' he enquired drily.

Chapter nine

THURSDAY, 20 MARCH 2003, 10.00

It was DC Suttle's first visit to the city's CCTV control room, a windowless, slightly claustrophobic bunker in the Civic Centre. He stood behind the duty shift leader, staring up at the banks of colour monitors racked side by side while Paul Winter negotiated two cups of coffee and a generous plateful of custard creams.

'There. See what I mean?'

The shift leader was demonstrating the reach of a new zoom lens on one of the CCTV cameras in the Commercial Road shopping precinct. A lifelong member of the Seventh Day Adventist church, he'd developed an obsession with the collapse of morality in the city. Portsmouth was awash with teenage mums and here was the living proof.

Suttle found himself looking at a nubile young girl pushing a double buggy. Her skintight T-shirt stopped two inches above the waistband of her jeans and the piercings in the adolescent roundness of her belly gleamed in the chill March sunshine.

'Nice,' he murmured. 'What about her mate?'

A leftwards pan on the camera provoked another diatribe from the shift leader. If Suttle cared to come back on Friday night, any Friday night, he could watch infants like this screwing themselves stupid on the beach across from the clubs on South Parade. The pair of them couldn't be a day over fourteen. It was his taxes paying for all these bloody handouts. What kind of society encouraged schoolgirls to fall pregnant?

'Over here.'

Winter dragged Suttle towards a smaller desk by the door. Beside the mugs of coffee were three video cassettes. Winter consulted a map showing the locations of each of the city's CCTV cameras, then slipped the first of the cassettes into a replay machine. Toggling the pictures forward, he hooked a chair towards him with his foot and told Suttle to sit down. Finally, the stream of images slowed, then stopped.

'See?'

Suttle bent forward, peering at the screen. In the interests of keeping the tape budget under control, recorded video coverage was restricted to single frames grabbed every two seconds. At 02.31.47, the camera across from the town station had caught the arrival of a white Transit van. As Winter inched the sequence forward, the van did a U-turn on the approach road, and then backed towards the side entrance that led onto the station concourse. On the panel of the van, plainly visible, was the name of a local building firm.

'Mates of Bazza's,' Winter grunted. 'Bloke that runs it still turns out for his football team. Not bad for forty-three.'

'We're talking Blue Army?'

'More grey than blue but yeah.' He toggled forward again. 'Same bunch of blokes.'

A heavy-set man, jeans, leather jacket, had suddenly appeared from the passenger seat. Several frames later, with the aid of a slighter figure, he was hauling someone out of the back. Then, abruptly, they'd gone.

'This one I got from the Transport Police.'

The screen went blank as Winter loaded a second cassette. Spooling through, he kept his eye on the digital timecode. The picture showed the station concourse, grey and empty, a row of shops on the far side barred and shuttered. At 02.32.35, the same two men appeared, jumping forward frame by frame. Supported between them, his feet trailing behind, came the limp body of the youth in the back of the van. As he passed the camera, his face was plainly visible.

'What's that?' Suttle touched the screen. On the monochrome image, blotches of black masked the lower half of the youth's face.

'Blood. The big fella is Chris Talbot. Did a couple of stretches for GBH in his 6.57 days. The other one is new to me. Way too young for the 6.57.'

'More mates of Bazza's?'

'Talbot definitely. Same school, same class probably. He's been around Bazza forever. Famous scrapper. Bazza used to use him for muscle when he couldn't be arsed to do the business himself. Nice bloke once you take the wrapping off. Bright, too. Never lost a pub quiz in his life.'

Suttle was watching the sequence unfold. Once they'd got to the ticket barrier, both men let the youth slump to the concourse. While the younger of the two wiped his hands on his jeans and wandered across to a vending machine, Talbot dug in his pocket and produced a pillowslip. Bending low, he mopped the youth's face, then hauled him into a sitting position. Semi-conscious, the youth began to struggle. Two seconds later, his head had flopped sideways, the rest of his body propped against the barrier. By the time the men turned to leave, the wreckage of his face had disappeared inside the pillowslip.

'That's just in case his mates don't get it.' Winter had zoomed the picture until the ghostly white outlines of the youth's head filled the screen. 'Remember the way we found young Tracy? Bazza's returning the compliment.'

'But the Scousers didn't do it. Isn't that the story? Tracy wasn't down to them.'

'Exactly. Which might make things tricky. These kids know no fear. Getting whacked for something they didn't do won't amuse them in the least.'

Winter got to his feet, handing control of the toggle to Suttle. While Winter bent to the map again, scribbling camera designations in his notebook, Suttle played the rest of the sequence.

'Look . . .' Suttle was laughing.

Winter glanced up. On his way out of the station, Chris Talbot had paused beneath the camera, staring straight up at the lens. After a graceful bow came the raised middle finger. Then the big face split into a gap-toothed grin. Three frames later, both men had gone.

'You want to go back to the van? See what happened?'

'No.' Winter was already heading for the shift supervisor. 'This is a bit of a punt but let's see where it takes us.'

The supervisor dug around in the cupboard where he stored the recorded tapes. Last night's were on the bottom shelf, yet to be rewound. He sorted through them, checking against Winter's list, then extracted four.

'Edinburgh Road first.'

Edinburgh Road was a stone's throw from the station. Winter spooled back the tape until the time code read 02.31.00, then jabbed a finger at the screen. As the images hopscotched backwards, Suttle watched the same white van reverse towards a set of traffic lights.

'Where next?'

'My money's on Portsea.' Winter was already loading the next tape. 'The Scouse kid may have been there last night on business and gone on to Gunwharf afterwards with a wad of cash. Talbot drinks at Forty Below. Maybe they clocked him there, followed him back to a car. He'd have parked locally. No way would he pay Gunwharf prices.'

Portsea was a couple of square miles of council flats and Victorian terraced housing that lapped against the walls of the new Gunwharf development. The area scored heavily on every major index of deprivation, and offered drug dealers rich pickings.

The first of the three new tapes tracked the white van halfway down Queen Street, the spine of Portsea's bony cadaver. On the second tape, the white van disappeared into the maze of streets that stretched west towards the harbour. Winter toggled back and forth, getting his bearings. Finally, he rewound the tape, ejected it, and stood up. Suttle had learned to interpret Winter's many smiles. This one spoke of immense satisfaction.

'Southampton Row or Kent Street.' He glanced at his watch. 'Ten quid says we'll find his motor.'

It was nearly 10.15 by the time Eadie Sykes made it to the Ambrym offices. Amongst the messages waiting for her on the answerphone was a brief call from a DC Rick Stapleton. He was working out of the CID office at Southsea police station and he'd appreciate it if she could get in touch as soon as possible. He left two numbers, one a mobile, one a landline. Eadie scribbled down the numbers and then replayed the message. Stapleton sounded friendly enough, even apologetic, but a year with Faraday had taught Eadie a great deal about the CID mindset.

The master tapes from last night were still in her day sack. She turned on the editing suite she used for making copies and sorted out a couple of brand new cassettes. By the time she returned from the tiny kitchen along the corridor with a mug of coffee, the first tape had been playing for nearly five minutes.

She settled in the swivel chair she used for editing, fascinated yet again by the way she'd managed to coax a bizarre kind of truth from Daniel Kelly. She'd been lucky to find him in such a state. She knew that. Circumstances had delivered him on a plate, desperate to trade anything for that one sweet moment of oblivion, yet there was an anger and a righteousness in his defence of what he'd made of his life. He really did believe that smack was his one and only friend, his sole source of comfort in a bitterly hostile world, yet the physical results of that friendship were impossible to miss. The wildness in his eyes. The sudden fever-like shuddering he fought so hard to control. The constant itch that passed for a life. He had a rare talent for shaping a phrase but body language like this gave the lie to all his passionate rationales. Add the sequences that followed and in Eadie's view there wasn't a child on earth who wouldn't draw the obvious conclusion: surrender to smack and you'll end up wrecked.

The interview over, Eadie slipped in the second tape and reached for the phone. While the number rang, she watched Daniel in his kitchen preparing his fix. The desperation had eased. His lover had returned. He was back on home territory, back in a world he understood, locked into those moments of foreplay that guaranteed the pain would go away.

The number answered. Eadie asked to speak to the coroner. Seconds later, he was on the line.

'Martin? It's Eadie Sykes.'

Eadie reached forward, turning down the volume on the editing machine. Martin Eckersley was relatively new to the city. Eadie had met him several months ago, finding a powerful ally in her bid to raise funding for the video. Like her, he worried about the remorseless spread of hard drugs. And like her, he believed in telling kids the truth about their real-life consequences. Just now, he was playing catch-up on a suspicious overnight death in Leigh Park. Why didn't they meet for a quick bite at lunchtime? Earlier rather than later?

Eckersley occupied an office in the city centre. Eadie named a cafe-bar several doors away, promising not to waste his precious time.

'No problem. Table in the back corner? I'll be there at half twelve.'

The line went dead and Eadie looked up to find J-J standing in the open doorway. He looked drawn and pale, even gaunter than usual, and for a crazy moment she wondered whether he hadn't helped himself to one of Daniel Kelly's wraps.

J-J couldn't tear his eyes off the screen. At the third attempt, the needle found the vein. Eadie was watching him carefully, knowing that sooner or later she had to break the news. Emotionally, J-J was one of the most exposed people she'd ever met. In professional terms, she'd managed to turn that to their mutual advantage – potential interview-ees warmed to J-J's openness, his absolute lack of guile – but there'd occasionally come bleaker moments when situations had overwhelmed him. Last night had been one of them. The news that Daniel was dead would doubtless be another.

On screen, Daniel was stumbling down the hall towards the bedroom. J-J stiffened as he watched the student at the open door, gazing down at the clutter on the floor, trying to puzzle his way around the abandoned duvet. The empty syringe in his forearm was plainly visible, the pale flesh ribboned with a single scarlet thread.

Eadie waited until the sequence came to an end, then reached forward and turned off the machine. The recognised sign for someone dying is a downward movement, both hands, fingers shaped like a revolver. Instead, Eadie opted instead for a single finger across her throat. Under the circumstances, as a form of suicide, it seemed strangely appropriate.

'So what happened?' J-J was still staring at the blank screen.

'Sarah found him. After we'd gone.'

'How long after?'

'Hours after.' She paused. 'It wasn't our fault.'

Eadie got to her feet, interposing her body between J-J and the monitor, but the moment she put her arms round him she knew it was a mistake. She could feel the stiffness in him, the hostility. He wanted no part of this. Not last night. And not now. She looked up at him, wondering what else she could say, what might soften this terrible news, but J-J had already broken free.

'You want a coffee? Something to eat?'

J-J shook his head, his eyes returning to the screen.

'Where is he now? Daniel?'

'At the mortuary. St Mary's.'

He nodded, absorbing the news.

'They'll cut him up?' One bony hand touched his eye, then circled his stomach. 'Look inside?'

'Yes.'

'Then what?'

'I don't know.'

J-J collapsed into the editing chair. Then he looked up at her and for the first time in their relationship Eadie saw a new expression in his eyes. He didn't trust her. She held his gaze for a moment, stony-faced, aware of a mounting anger of her own, a small, hot spark that seemed to grow and grow.

The numbers she'd scribbled earlier were on a pad beside her day sack. She reached for the phone, turning her back on J-J, recognising the voice that answered.

'Rick Stapleton? Eadie Sykes.'

The detective took a second or two to place the name. Then he said he'd appreciate half an hour of her time. He understood she'd been involved in some kind of video shoot with a Mr Daniel Kelly. He needed to check out one or two things, maybe take a statement.

'Of course.' Eadie checked the video dubs were complete, then glanced at her watch. 'Will this morning be OK? My office?'

She gave him the Ambrym address, and agreed 11.30. By the time she put the phone down and turned round, J-J had gone.

DC Suttle found the young Scouser's car at the end of Jellicoe Place, a grim cul-de-sac off Southampton Row. A red Cavalier with rusting sills and a dented bonnet, it was parked at an angle with one rear wheel on the pavement. For more than an hour he and Winter had been phoning in registration numbers for PNC checks, working slowly through the Portsea estate. M492XBK, to Suttle's delight, had produced a double hit.

Winter was at the open end of the cul-de-sac, waiting for news on a nearby J reg Sierra.

Suttle was pointing to the Cavalier. 'Nicked last month from a car park in Birkenhead. Plus it's been flagged by Major Crimes.'

At the mention of Major Crimes, Winter abandoned his mobile conversation with the PNC clerk. Like every other detective in Portsmouth, he'd been aware of the hit and run that had hospitalised Nick Hayder. Clues to the registration had been circulated to every officer in the city, together with a heads-up on the possible make.

'The fucking Cavalier.' He whistled softly. 'Bingo.'

Suttle returned to the car and peered in through the windows, Winter beside him. The interior was a mess: two pairs of trainers, a copy of the *Daily Star*, an open box of Shopper's Choice tissues, empty cans of Stella, a discarded pizza box, a litter of CDs, and – tucked behind the driver's seat – a bag of what looked like laundry. The radio was missing from the hole in the dash and the tax disc was eight months out of date.

'Here.' Suttle was looking down at the road behind the boot.

Winter followed his pointing finger. Splatter patterns from the dark stain on the tarmac led away towards the kerb.

'Hammered the little bastard.' Winter was searching for nearby CCTV cameras. 'No wonder he was in such a state.'

Suttle was already back on his mobile. The DS on the crime squad was out on inquiries. Mention of Cathy Lamb's name drew Winter to Suttle's side.

'You're going to be talking to her? Cath?'

'Yeah.'

'Don't mention the business with the lad you tailed last night, Faraday's boy. Not yet anyway.'

'Why not?' Suttle was staring at him, bewildered.

'Just don't, that's all. Has the skipper seen your pocketbook?'

'No.'

'Good. I've just got a couple of calls to make. Then everything'll be sweet.'

'But—'

'Just do it. Call it a favour. That asking too much?' He shot Suttle a grin, then returned to the car, concentrating on the bumpers and radiator grille.

Suttle bent to the phone again. When he finally got hold of Cathy Lamb, she told him to stay with the vehicle while she raised Scenes of Crime. They'd need to go through it inch by inch to establish ownership.

Suttle mentioned the Major Crimes interest. There was a moment's silence while Cathy Lamb computed the possible implications.

'You're telling me we might be able to link this vehicle to Nick Hayder?'

'Yeah.' Suttle was eyeing Winter. 'You should see the state of the bonnet.'

'Excellent. I'll talk to Major Crimes. Keep the kids off the car.'

Cathy Lamb rang off. Winter was squatting in front of the Cavalier. Careful not to touch anything, he indicated an area beneath one of the headlights. The metalwork had been recently attacked by someone using a wire scourer, the circular gouge marks clearly visible.

'Since when did scroats like these worry about the state of their motor?' He glanced up at Suttle. 'Makes you wonder, doesn't it?'

Eadie Sykes was on the phone to the mortuary when Rick Stapleton knocked at her office door. She glanced at the proffered warrant card and waved him in, nodding towards a vacant chair while she finished her conversation. The mortuary technician's name was Jake. She'd talked to him already that morning, establishing the time lag between the blood tests and the imminent post-mortem, and now she wanted to be sure she could gain access to the mortuary at least half an hour before the first cut.

'To do what, exactly?'

'To shoot video.'

'You can't do that.'

'With permissions I can.'

'Like whose?'

'Like the next of kin. And the coroner.'

'Doesn't happen.' Eadie could picture the wag of the head. 'Not in my experience. First off, you've got to—'

'I'm afraid I've got someone here.' Eadie cut him off. 'Do you mind if I ask you one quick question? How long from start to finish? It's a question of tape, really. Hate to miss anything.'

'Home Office job, you're talking hours. This is local as far as I know. Forty-five minutes, max.'

Eadie thanked him and pocketed the phone before scribbling herself a note. Then she glanced up. Rick Stapleton was wearing a black polo neck sweater under a gorgeous leather jacket. He carried a hint of expensive aftershave and looked a great deal fitter and less careworn than other detectives she'd met. He returned her smile with interest. She liked him on sight.

'So what's Ambrym?'

'It's an island in the New Hebrides. I was born there.'

'But you're Australian, right?'

' 'Fraid so. My dad was in the government service. He taught English on the island. We stayed there until I was eleven.'

'And that's it?' Stapleton was on his feet now, inspecting a dog-eared poster Eadie had carted halfway round the world: a deep-blue lagoon framed by palm trees and shell-bursts of frangipani with a tumble of tropical clouds overhead. 'Looks good.'

'God's acre. Paradise. I wept for days when we finally bailed out.'

'And here? Southsea?'

'Paradise lost. You want coffee? My life story? Or is there some other way I can help you?'

Stapleton said no to coffee and produced a pocketbook. In the end he'd take a formal statement but first he had a couple of questions.

'You make videos. Is that right?'

'Yes.'

'And you were with a young man last night? Daniel Kelly?'

'Correct.'

'What time was that? Approximately?'

'Around half five. We were there a couple of hours max. He is – was – a junkie. We were—'

'Was?'

'I understand he's dead.'

'How do you know?'

'A friend of his, Sarah. She phoned me this morning. She was the one who gave us the initial introduction. We did an interview with him last night. About his habit.'

'How was he?'

'Brilliant. You want me to show you?'

Without waiting for an answer, Eadie leaned across and pressed the play button on the video machine. By now she was word-perfect on Daniel's attempts to get his life into some kind of focus.

'This guy was a gift.' She boosted the volume on the video. 'Just listen.'

Stapleton turned to watch but his attention soon flagged.

'The guy's strung out.' He smothered a yawn. 'What else did you tape?'

'After the interview, he shot up.'

'And you taped that?'

'Of course we did.'

'Then what?'

'He went to bed.'

'And died.'

'That was later. After we'd gone.'

'Can you prove that?'

Eadie stared at him, indignant, still aware of the murmur of Daniel's voice from the video.

'*Prove* it?'

'Yes.' Stapleton held her gaze. 'We're looking at a suspicious death here. You may have been the last to see the guy. I need to know where you went. And at what time.'

Eadie finally looked away, telling herself that this man was simply doing his job. The post-mortem would presumably establish a time of death. After leaving the flat in Old Portsmouth, she'd returned to the office to view the rushes and plan the rest of the movie.

'I was here from around eight to gone midnight.' She gestured at the pile of video cassettes beside the PC. 'I made four or five calls on my landline. They'd all show up on the billing.'

'And after that?'

'I went home.'

Stapleton nodded and made a note in his pocketbook. Then he looked up again.

'Was it smack he was using?'

'Yes.'

'How do you know?'

'I've seen it before. Plus he told me . . ' She nodded at the screen.

Stapleton paused a moment, listening to Daniel describing his days in Australia, then returned to Eadie. He wanted to know where the heroin had come from. When Eadie told him about the delivery, he pressed her for more detail.

'I haven't got any. One minute we were sitting in front of the camera, the next he was off down the stairs to sort himself out. Then he was back again. End of story.'

'Yeah.' Stapleton scribbled another note. 'End of story.' He looked up. 'The lad fixing . . . That's on this tape?'

'No. There's another one.'

'I'm afraid I'll have to seize them both. You'll get a receipt, of course, and the coroner's officer will return the tapes once the inquest is over.' He paused, eyes straying back to the screen. 'You said "we", earlier.'

'That's right. Me and the cameraman.'

'He's got a name?'

'J-J.'

'*J-J?* What sort of name's that?'

'Dunno. You'll have to ask his father. The boy's deaf.'

Mention of deafness brought Stapleton's head round. The smile was chillier this time.

'And his surname?' he said softly. 'This boy of yours?'

*

J-J rode to the top of Portsdown Hill. He'd acquired the bike only recently, his first-ever, and after a week of wobbling around the city he and the travel-worn old Ridgeback had become inseparable. He loved the freedom and reach the bike gave him. He loved the way he could thread a path through the longest rush-hour traffic jams. And most of all, as he mustered the confidence to tackle the big fold of chalk to the north of the city, he loved the way his body somehow found the strength to keep pumping up the long, long hill. The closer to the top he got, the more aware he became of the thunder of his own pulse. He could feel it in every corner of his thin frame. He could hear it in his head. For the first time in his life, he thought he understood the meaning of sound.

Today, though, was different. Halfway up the hill, exhausted, he'd got off and pushed, head down, walled off from the press of traffic on the main road north. Now and again, a juggernaut would shoulder past, a sudden buffeting and the stink of diesel, but J-J was oblivious. All he could think of, all that mattered, were the images he'd seen. First in the camera's viewfinder. Then in Eadie's office. The stuff he hadn't shot – the spoon, the syringe, the needle, Daniel Kelly's stumbling path to bed – had lodged at the very front of his brain, billboard-huge, the most public of accusations. You helped kill this sad, sad man. You helped kill him as surely as if you'd loaded a gun and handed it across. You delivered the money, arranged the delivery, took advantage of his distress, and walked away. Could any other betrayal be as damning – and as terminal – as that?

Sprawled on the grass at the top of the hill, J-J didn't know. After a while, trying to make sense of the last twenty-four hours, he propped himself on his elbows and gazed down at the city spread before him. Familiar landmarks. The gleaming spread of the harbour. The looming greyness of the naval dockyard. Beetle-sized cars, racing along the motorway that looped into the city. He'd lived with these images for longer than he could remember yet today they seemed cold and alien, a sudden glimpse of life on a distant planet. How come a couple of guys from Pennington Road had killed Daniel Kelly? And how come he'd let himself become part of all that?

The longer he thought about it, the more important he knew it was to try and make some kind of decision. Events had marooned him, washed him up in a place he hated, and it was time he took charge again. Maybe he should pack a rucksack, hop on a ferry, and have another crack at France. Or maybe he should sit down with his dad, explain the whole thing, and see where the conversation led. His dad, to his certain knowledge, would insist on the truth coming out. That J-J, his precious bloody son, had stolen up on a man standing on the edge of his own grave, tapped him on the shoulder, then given him that final nudge. Yuk.

J-J lay on his back, his eyes closed, soaking up the thin warmth of the early spring sunshine until another idea began to take shape, a stroke so bold that it hit him with an almost physical impact. A couple of years back, he'd spent some time with a young kid called Doodie. There'd been lots wrong with Doodie's world, much of it Doodie's fault, but J-J had always been amazed by the straightness of the lines this gutsy little ten-year-old had been able to draw. Given a situation like this, the last thing he'd do was lie around on Portsdown Hill feeling sorry for himself. No, if there were debts to be settled, wrongs to be righted, then actions would speak louder than words. J-J turned the phrase over in his mind, realising with a jolt of pleasure that it had governed his entire life. Actions, not words. Gesture, not language.

Pleased with himself, he thought about the idea a little more. Then he got to his feet, brushed himself down, hauled the Ridgeback upright, and set off down the hill.

Chapter ten

Faraday found himself alone at *Tumbril* HQ on Whale Island. The Mackenzie briefing over, Imber and the young accountant had driven into the city for a meeting with a senior clearing-bank executive with access to Mackenzie's five accounts, while Joyce was over at the HMS *Excellent* mess, looking for a pint of milk.

Faraday stood at the window, watching a squad of young recruits jogging past. There was a PTI behind them, rounding up the strays, and the sight of the instructor falling into step behind the worst of the laggards brought memories of his own induction course flooding back.

Twenty-five years ago, probationer PCs in Faraday's entry found themselves under the tender care of a burly prop forward who swore that rugby was the shortest cut to heaven. Faraday himself had never been keen on team games but he cycled a lot because it was cheap and knew he was as fit as anyone else in the group. Keeping up with the rest of the pack had therefore been no problem but now, watching the tail-ender redden under the lash of the PTI, he marvelled at how simple the world had then appeared.

At twenty-three, he couldn't wait to get out on the beat. The law, to his faint surprise, was a living thing, continually in the process of change, but once you understood the basic principles and memorised a hundred or so pages of detailed legislation, then applying the thrust of all those weighty clauses seemed on the face of it pretty straightforward. You were there to keep the peace, to safeguard life and property, to protect people from their own worst instincts. Little of this optimism survived his first year in uniform – policing was rarely as black and white as he'd imagined – but not once had he anticipated ending up heading an operation as complex and inward-looking as *Tumbril*. What kind of justice required an investigation to be as covert, as walled-off, as this? Of whom were the handful of senior officers in the know really frightened?

At the end of his profile of Bazza Mackenzie, the young accountant had passed Faraday a slender spiral-bound file that summarised his progress to date. With the aid of seized documentation – deposit slips, bank accounts, financial transfer instructions – he'd laid out a series of audit trails, mapping the sheer reach of Mackenzie's commercial empire. Referenced and cross-referenced, each of these audit trails dealt with a particular asset – a car, a property, a bank account, a business – proving to any jury that real ownership, behind a thousand financial transactions and a small army of relatives, friends, and professional advisers, still lay with Mackenzie. In this way item by item, page by page, Prebble was slowly building a bonfire of Mackenzie's carefully hidden assets, millions of pounds' worth of ill-gotten gains. All Faraday would have to do was provide the spark – proof positive that Mackenzie had broken the law – and the whole lot would go up in flames. That way, as Imber kept reminding everyone, we'll really hurt the guy. And not just him, either, but the handful of high-profile professional advisers who'd flagged his path to the big time.

Faraday stepped away from the window, only too aware of the pressures which had driven Nick Hayder to the brink. Pulling in a u/c officer and seeding a head-to-head with Mackenzie was undeniably clever. But the very boldness of a stroke like this smacked to Faraday of desperation. By being so successful, Mackenzie had made himself virtually impregnable. He had powerful friends. He'd established himself in legitimate business. He'd become, in one of Prebble's laconic asides, the living proof that capitalism works. Some guys built their fortunes on a string of patents. Others dreamed up a brilliant marketing idea. With Bazza Mackenzie it just happened to be cocaine. But who could prove it?

Faraday's mobile began to chirp. He didn't recognise the number. For a moment or two he was tempted to ignore it. Then he had second thoughts.

'Paul Winter. Am I interrupting anything?'

'No. How can I help you?'

'I don't want to talk about it on the phone. Lunch any good? Pie and a pint?'

'*Now?* Today?' Faraday could see the mountain of files awaiting his attention on the desk across the office.

'Yeah. Sorry about the short notice but you'll be glad you came.'

'Why?'

'It's about your boy.'

'J-J?'

'Yeah.'

'What's happened?'

'Nothing . . . yet. Still and West? Quarter to one?'

Faraday glanced at his watch. Half two he was due for yet another meeting with Willard and Imber. Until then, his time was his own.

He bent to the phone again. Three years as DI on division had taught him a great deal about Paul Winter. Rule number one was never trust the man. Rule number two was never ignore him. The Still and West was a pub in Old Portsmouth, overlooking the harbour narrows. The last time Faraday had paid a visit, the place had been full of journalists.

'Let's make it the Pembroke. I'll be there for twelve forty-five.'

Winter rang off and Faraday found himself still gazing at the number. The reference to J-J had chilled him to the bone. Given this morning's conversation with Eadie Sykes, there were a thousand and one reasons why the boy might have got himself into trouble, but how, exactly, had he crossed paths with the likes of Paul Winter?

'Sheriff . . . ?'

Faraday spun round. Joyce was back. There was a new carton of semi-skimmed on the shelf beside the electric kettle and she was already reaching for her coat.

'The Pembroke takes you through town.' She grinned at him. 'You mind giving this lady a lift?'

Faraday's Mondeo was in the car park. There was a queue of vehicles waiting for clearance at the security barrier and the saloon rolled to a halt behind a minibus full of matelots. Faraday glanced sideways at Joyce. The last thing he wanted to talk about was *Tumbril*.

'How's that husband of yours?'

'History. I binned the marriage a couple of months back.'

'Really?' The last time Faraday checked, Joyce had been married to a uniformed Inspector in the Southampton BCU, a dour Aberdonian with a roving eye and a passion for fitness routines. 'What happened?'

'One probationer too many, I guess. Plus I wasn't up to serial child molesting, not at the time. Strange thing about cancer, sheriff, it does nothing for your sense of humour. Was I harsh, do you think? Wishing him God speed?'

Her husband, she told him, had been worse than useless when tests had confirmed the oncologist's suspicions. The Royal South Hants had found her a bed within days but he'd barely managed a couple of visits over the fortnight she'd been in hospital. At the time, she'd believed his excuses about the pressure of work. Only later, thanks to a neighbour, did she discover that he'd moved the latest conquest into the marital home. Strictly as an act of compassion.

'Nineteen-year-old called Bethany. Needed somewhere quiet to study for her probationer's exams. Poor waif. But hey –' she flipped down the sun visor and studied her lip gloss in the mirror on the back '– who needs husbands?'

They were through the barrier now, and crossing the bridge beside the ferry port. Faraday wanted to know where she was living.

'Home. Just like always.'

'And Neil?'

'You tell me, honey. He phones me up, writes me letters, sends huge bunches of flowers, tries to explain what a big mistake he'd made. Me? I tell him to go to hell. Most times we get one pass at life. This lady's been given two. You think I'm gonna waste me on that bastard again? The nerve of the guy.'

She shook her head, gazing out at the traffic. Beside the roundabout at the end of the motorway into the city, a handful of students were milling around beneath a big hand-lettered placard in what looked like an impromptu demonstration. The placard read *STOP THE WAR! 6P.M. GUILDHALL SQUARE.*

'There's another shit head.' Joyce was fumbling for her lipstick.

'Who?'

'Boy George. Can you believe that man? And can you credit my dickhead countrymen for voting the guy in? Not that he even fucking won in the first place.'

Faraday smiled to himself, reaching for the car radio. This was a new Joyce, feistier than ever, her raw enjoyment of life edged by something close to anger. Maybe she was right. Maybe a glimpse of oblivion, your own life suddenly on the line, robbed voter apathy of its charms.

A pundit on Radio Four was speculating on the lengths Saddam might go to in Iraq. Oil wells were already blazing around Basra. Might he also torch the northern oilfields?

'You feel comfortable with all this?' Faraday gestured out at the students.

'The war or the protest?'

'The war.'

'Hell, no. But you know something? The problem isn't what folk like Bush get us into. It isn't even all those little kids you're going to see in the wreckage once we've bombed the bejesus out of the place. No, the real problem is the fact that us Americans actually believe all this shit. We're doing it for liberty and freedom. We're killing Iraqis to make them better human beings. Believe me, sheriff, when the world comes to an end, it'll be the Americans who pull the trigger. And you know something else? It'll be in all our best interests. You heard it first from me, Joe. Takes a Yank to know a Yank.' She applied a final dab of powder from a small compact, then snapped it shut. 'How about you?'

'I loathe it.'

'I meant your love life.'

'What?' Faraday brought the car to a halt again. The directness of this woman never ceased to amaze him. Even Eadie Sykes was a novice compared to Joyce.

'Just wondering, honey. Last time I had the pleasure of your company, you were shacked up with a Spanish lady. Am I right?'

'Yes. Sort of.'

'Still together?'

'No.'

'Someone else?'

'Yes.'

'Serious?'

'Straightforward. We laugh a lot.'

'You love her?'

'That's a big question.'

'You living together?'

'No.'

'She got a place of her own? Somewhere private?'

'Yes.'

'Is she married? Tied up with someone else?'

'Absolutely not.' He looked across at her. 'What is this?'

'Nothing, honey. Just curious, that's all. You know something else about the Big C? It gives you the right to ask the hard questions.' She paused a moment, staring out at the lunchtime shoppers dodging through the stalled traffic. 'Mind if I pop another one?'

'Not at all.'

'You're sure?'

'Absolutely.'

'OK.' She reached forward and tapped the receipt Faraday had left on the dashboard. 'How come you're having room service at the Sally Port Hotel if this relationship's so great?'

Eadie Sykes found Martin Eckersley bent over a copy of the *Independent* when she finally made it to the Café Parisien. She was ten minutes late and he was already on page 4.

She pulled up a seat and gave the proffered menu the briefest of glances.

'Three-egg omelette and fries.' She nodded at the empty cup beside the paper. 'Cappuccino to start.'

'I thought you were on a diet?'

'Never. We're talking four miles a day at the moment, and that's before I even break a sweat. Girl's got to refuel otherwise she falls over.' She grinned at him. 'How's you?'

'Busy.'

He began to tell her about the Leigh Park death, a woman in her mid forties with a history of mental disturbance and a fondness for cheap vodka. She'd been found dead in bed with an empty bottle of painkillers on the pillow and no sign of a note. Eadie let him air his worries about the possibility of interference by some other party, then leant forward, touching him lightly on the hand.

'Daniel Kelly . . . ?' she said.

Eckersley paused in mid sentence. He was a small, neat, attentive man with bright eyes behind rimless glasses and a carefully tended moustache. A lawyer by training, he'd left a profitable Birmingham practice after a couple of years as Deputy for the city's Coroner. The world of sudden death, he'd once confessed to Eadie, had put him back in touch with real life. Not as just an inquisitor, trying to establish the truth about a particular set of circumstances, but as a human being, doing his best to ease the grief of those left behind.

'I read the file this morning,' he said. 'Such as it is. One of my blokes talked to a DC first thing. How much do we know about the lad?'

The 'we? put a smile on Eadie's face. She'd known from their first meeting that she represented something new and slightly exotic in this man's life.

'He was bright, very bright. Older than your average student and pretty much alone.'

She told him about Kelly's background, the wreckage of his parents' marriage, the way he'd rafted around the world on a fat monthly allowance, a bewildered loner looking for some sense of direction.

'Or purpose.'

'Quite.'

'And the drugs?'

'Supplied that purpose.'

'You're serious?'

'I am. You should listen to him, Martin. A couple of tapes are on their way to you. A nice detective seized them this morning. Kept asking me about supply of Class A drugs. Made me feel like a criminal.'

'You were there,' Eckersley pointed out. 'In fact you were probably the last person to see him alive. That makes you a witness.'

'That's what he said but that doesn't mean I killed him, does it? The key word here is "witness". I played the recording angel. Got it all down on tape, the whole story.'

'Good stuff? Effective?'

'Unbelievable. You can judge for yourself but, believe me, the guy's amazing. What he says is pretty controversial and it might not be our take on hard drugs but that doesn't make it any less valid. More to the point, he sounds authentic. He's been there. He *is* there. Any kid watching will know that, sense that, and at the end of the day some of them just might listen. Here.' Eadie rummaged in her day sack and produced a hastily folded photocopy. 'I know you've got the world's best memory but I thought this might help.'

Eckersley studied the photocopy. Three months ago, he'd been part of the review process, helping to check out Eadie's submission to the Portsmouth Pathways Partnership for match-funding on her video project. Their first encounter had taken place in the Coroner's Office at Highland Road police station, a meeting of minds fuelled by appalling coffee. Eadie had deliberately left room for last-minute adjustments in the twenty-four-page submission document – believing that heavy-weight support could only strengthen her case – and within a week, after further exchanges on the phone, she and Eckersley had agreed the single paragraph that seemed to sum up the thrust of Eadie's video.

Eadie waited until Eckersley had finished. Then she retrieved the photocopy, looking him in the eye, and began to read the paragraph aloud.

' "The documentary maker has a duty to level the ground between the audience at risk and the real nature of the offending behaviour. The emphasis should be on reality ... on real people, real causes, real consequences. There should be no need for homilies, for finger-wagging, for lists of do's and don'ts. The case for not using drugs should make itself." '

She glanced up. 'The important word is "consequences", Martin. Like I said, the interview is knockout, but if you want the truth there's only so much that words can do. What we need now are pictures, the rest of the story, what actually *happens* in a case like this.'

'You mean the post-mortem.'

'Sure. And the funeral. And the father. And maybe you. All of that.'

'You don't think that's intrusive?'

'*Intrusive?* Dear God, of course it's intrusive. But that's precisely the issue because drugs themselves are intrusive. In fact they're so bloody intrusive they kill you. And even if that doesn't happen, even if you limp on, more or less intact, they still take your life away. If that wasn't the truth, we wouldn't be talking like this. Nor would I be spending half my life running round after bloody junkies.' She beckoned him closer, aware of listening ears at nearby tables. 'My point is simple, Martin. It's consequences again. Just ask yourself a question. How many kids are going to be shooting up if they're thinking about bodies on slabs? About Daniel Kelly getting himself sliced up? Emptied? Weighed? Whatever else happens in the mortuary? Is all that such a great advert for hard drugs?'

'Have you ever seen a post-mortem?'

'Never.'

'They're horrible.'

'Good.' Eadie held his gaze for a moment. 'Because that's the whole point.'

The waitress arrived. After some thought, Eckersley settled for a ham salad. Then he folded his newspaper and slipped it into the briefcase beside his chair.

'There's something else we ought to take on board,' he said finally. 'And that's the effect on your co-sponsors.'

'They've all signed up,' Eadie said at once. 'I've been totally frank from the start. I've told them exactly what to expect and there's absolutely nothing in this video that should take them by surprise. In fact, if anything I thought we'd have the opposite problem.'

'Meaning what?'

'Meaning I couldn't deliver what I promised. Meaning I'd end up with a mishmash of talking heads and millions of kids in thousands of classrooms all half asleep. Thanks to Dan, that isn't going to happen.'

'You're assuming I'm going to let you into the PM?'

'I'm assuming we share the same ambitions for the end result.'

'That's not necessarily the same thing.'

'Martin, I think – deep down – you know it is. You've got a problem here. I understand that. It's your jurisdiction, your call. Jesus, as far as I understand it, Daniel Kelly actually *belongs* to you until you deliver a verdict at the inquest. But let's just take the bigger picture. I can get permission from Kelly's father faxed to you this afternoon. That might relieve some of the pressure. Then there's the shoot itself. I have one-hundred-per-cent confidence in what I'm doing, in the *need* for all this stuff. I know how it will play on the screen. I know the difference it will make. It's a tricky thing to do, I know it is, but all I'm asking is an act of faith. Believe in me, Martin. And believe in what we're trying to do.'

'I'm still concerned about your co-sponsors.'

'Don't be.'

'The Police Authority? You really think they'll be up for this?'

'They'll love it. They spend half their lives trying to give people a shake.'

'The city council?'

'They might well be queasy. But does that make them right?'

'Maybe not, but you'll have to be ready for all that. And how about your private sponsors? There'll be enormous publicity, headlines in the press, letters ... Have they really signed up for this kind of controversy?'

'Most of them are in for a couple of hundred quid each. If they want to take their names off the project, they'll be more than welcome.'

'And your Mr Hughes? £7000, wasn't it?'

Eadie nodded, surprised at his grasp of the figures. Doug Hughes was Eadie's first husband, a successful independent accountant with a small clientele of local businessmen. He and Eadie had been divorced now for nearly six years but had stayed good friends. Both her flat and Ambrym's office premises were rented from her ex-husband's company, and he'd supported the video project from the start.

'The £7000 isn't his. He's simply acting as a middle man. The real donor wants to stay out of it.'

'Anonymous?'

'Absolutely. Even I haven't got a clue where the seven grand comes from.' She paused, watching the waitress approach an adjoining table with a big bowl of pasta. 'Either way, he's not going to be making any kind of fuss. Does that make things any easier?'

Eckersley didn't answer. Instead, he waited for the waitress to finish, then beckoned her over.

'Red or white wine?' He glanced across at Eadie with a sudden smile. 'My treat.'

Faraday parked his Mondeo outside the cathedral and walked the last fifty metres to the Pembroke. The pub stood on a corner on the main road out to Southsea and had won itself a reputation for reliable beer, home-cooked lunches, and an interesting clientele. Some evenings, you might find yourself drinking alongside half a dozen basses from the cathedral choir. Other nights, you'd be sharing the bar with an assortment of broken-nosed veterans from the Royal Naval field-gun crew.

DC Paul Winter was perched on a stool at the far end of the bar, engrossed in the midday edition of the *News*. The pub was busy, and to Faraday's surprise Winter didn't look out of place amongst the gathering of lunchtime drinkers, men of a certain age blunting the edges of the day with a pint or two before settling down to an afternoon of horse racing in front of the telly. Give Winter a couple of years, thought Faraday, and he might be doing this full time.

'Boss?' Winter had caught his eye and was semaphoring a drink.

'No, thanks.' Faraday barely touched the outstretched hand. 'I thought we might take a walk.'

Winter looked at him a moment, then drew his attention to the newspaper. The front page was dominated by a grainy photo showing the concourse at the town station. A couple of medics and a fireman were crouched over a body slumped beside one of the ticket barriers, while a handful of passengers waited patiently to get through. WELCOME TO POMPEY ran the headline.

'One of the punters had a digital camera in his briefcase.' Winter was buttoning his coat. 'Apparently Secretan's gone ballistic.'

'Why?'

'You don't know about this morning? One of our Scouse friends?'

'Tell me.'

Winter eased himself off the bar stool, drained the remains of his pint, and shepherded Faraday towards the door. By the time they'd reached the seafront, Faraday was up to speed.

'You're telling me the Cavalier belonged to the kid on the station?'

'Tenner says yes.'

'And the plate checks out with the Nick Hayder vehicle?'

'Scenes of Crime are all over it. They think there may be DNA residues around the offside headlamp. Won't know for certain until they've trucked it away for tests but I'll give you short odds on another yes. That puts the Scouser in the shit. Big time.'

'We're talking Nick's DNA?'

'Yes.'

'So where's the Scouse kid now?'

'Still in hospital, as far as I know. Cathy Lamb's sorting some arrangement over protection.'

'From who?'

Winter stared at him. By now they were out on the fortifications, walking briskly towards the funfair at Clarence Pier.

'Bazza Mackenzie mean anything to you, boss? Local guy? Made a bob or two out of the white stuff? Not fussed who knows it? Only a little bird tells me Bazza's not best pleased with our Scouse friends. Wants them out of town. Hence the lift to the station.'

'You can prove that?'

'Give me a couple of days,' Winter nodded, 'and the answer's yes. Not Bazza himself, of course, but a mate of his, Chris Talbot. We've got him on video, him and another fella, doing the business at the station. That's the thing about Bazza nowadays, isn't it? Bit fussy about appearances. Can't stand the sight of blood. Shame, really. He was a good scrapper once.'

Both men had come to a halt on the wooden bridge that straddled the remains of the Spur Redoubt, the outermost edge of the ancient fortifications. From here on, the Pompey garrison would have been in no-man's land, at the mercy of events, an irony not lost on Faraday.

'You mentioned J-J on the phone,' Faraday said carefully. 'What's happened?'

Winter thought about the question, his hands on the wooden rail of the bridge. To Faraday, he'd always had a certain physical presence, a bluff matey self-confidence that had served him well over the years. Winter was the DC you put into the cells at the Bridewell on a Monday morning, knowing he'd emerge with yet more recruits to his ever-swelling army of informants. And Winter, on a job that took his fancy, was a detective who had the wit and the experience to dream up an angle that would never have occurred to anyone else. In thief-taking terms, as Faraday had frequently pointed out to his exasperated bosses, the man was a priceless asset in any CID office.

Yet at the same time Winter was dangerous. He pledged his loyalty to no one and didn't care who knew it. Show him a weakness, any weakness, and he'd turn you inside out. Once, a couple of years back, he'd arrived uninvited at the Bargemaster's House, late at night, bewildered and distraught at what was happening to his dying wife. Joannie had inoperable cancer. The doctors were measuring her life in weeks. And Winter, in his rage and despair, had been utterly lost. For a couple of hours, over a bottle of Bell's, the two men had stepped out of their respective jobs and simply compared notes. Faraday knew about widowhood and had the scars to prove it. Winter, who'd never ceased to play the field when opportunities presented themselves, just couldn't contemplate a life without his precious Joannie. He'd let her down. He'd taken her for granted. And now, all too suddenly, it was far, far too late to make amends.

That night, as Winter wandered away into the dark, Faraday had known they'd got as close to each other as two needful human beings ever can. Since then, a dozen small betrayals had given the lie to those moments of kinship. Yet here he was, back on intimate territory, and Faraday wanted to know why.

Winter was describing the Crime Squad bust on Pennington Road. Everything had gone to rat shit, he said, and they'd been playing catch-up ever since.

'What's that got to do with my son?'

Winter eyed him for a moment, the look again, careful, appraising. He'd spent half his life climbing in and out of other people's heads – weighing up what they knew and what they didn't – and Faraday knew he was doing it now.

'In this business, it pays not to be surprised,' he said at last. 'No surprises. Make a note. Stick it on my tombstone.'

'And?'

'You don't know, do you?'

'Know what?'

'About your boy.'

'No.' Faraday shook his head. 'I don't.'

Winter nodded, some deep intuitive suspicion confirmed, and then gazed out to sea again. Miles away, against the low hump of the Isle of Wight, a small, brown sail.

'OK, boss,' he said. 'This is off the record. We had obs on the Pennington Road premises yesterday afternoon, high profile. We're not bothering with court any more. The plan is to run these animals out of town.'

'We?'

'Me and a young lad, Jimmy Suttle.' He glanced at Faraday. 'Country boy. Not a problem.'

'And?'

'Your lad turned up at No. 30. That's the address we did the previous night.'

'You're telling me he was there to score?'

'It wasn't a social call.'

'You arrested him?'

'No. I sent Suttle after him. It's all intelligence-led these days, isn't it? All that cobblers? Anyway, Suttle followed him halfway across the city. You'll know where he went.'

'Hampshire Terrace?'

'Spot on. Ambrym Productions. The lovely Ms Sykes. Suttle hung around for a while, then I picked him up.'

'And that was it? You didn't stop the boy? Search him?'

'No, boss. I thought –' he shrugged, hunching a little deeper into his anorak '– it was better to give you a bell.'

'Why?'

'Because I owe you.'

'Really?'

'Yeah. You're a funny bugger sometimes but I think you've got more bollocks than most of the twats I've known in your job. That make any sense?'

Faraday was conscious of a flooding warmth. With an effort, he kept the smile off his face.

'None,' he said. 'Are we done now?'

'Not quite.'

'There's more?'

'I'm afraid so.' He turned from the railing and looked Faraday in the eye. 'How come I'm the one telling you this?'

'Telling me what?'

'About your boy. After we left him, he went to Old Portsmouth. Your lady friend's making some kind of video. J-J must have taken the gear with him. They taped a student shooting up, then fucked off. Which is a shame, really.'

'Why?'

'The student died.'

For a long moment, Faraday lost his concentration. After Hampshire Terrace, he'd followed this sequence of events step by step, no surprises, matching Winter's laconic account against the images he'd seen on Eadie's rushes. He knew J-J had been behind the camera. He'd explored the criminal implications of their presence at the flat. But not for a moment had he expected the punchline.

'Died?' he said numbly.

'Inhalation of vomit. I've seen the paperwork. The gear must have been extra-special.'

'Who discovered the body?'

'An ex-girlfriend. Apparently she'd helped set up the interview in the first place.'

'When did she find out?'

'Round eleven, eleven thirty. She'd gone round to kiss him goodnight. Bit late as it turned out.'

'Do you have a name for the girlfriend?'

'Sarah somebody. Bev's picked it up from Dawn. Dawn was duty last night.'

Sarah. Faraday closed his eyes, rocking slowly on his heels, picturing Eadie retreating into her bedroom at the flat as he made his own exit for work. Sarah had been on the phone first thing. Eadie, the woman he slept with, trusted, loved even, had kept this appalling secret for half a day and said absolutely nothing. Not a phone call. Not an e-mail. Not a cautionary heads-up. Nothing.

Faraday swallowed hard, battling to get the next few hours into perspective. He knew the investigative machine by heart, every working part. A heroin overdose. Dodgy gear. A video camera tracking the prospective corpse to bed. And now evidence from two DCs on the exact provenance of the killer wrap. Open and shut case. Collusion in procuring Class A drugs. Plus a possible manslaughter charge. With his own son in the dock.

'Who's holding the file?'

'Bev Yates.'

'Does he know about –' Faraday gestured loosely at the space between them '– this?'

'No, boss.'

'OK.' Faraday nodded, stepping away. 'Then tell him.'

Chapter eleven

Faraday was still waiting for the phone to ring when Willard stepped into his office. He'd left several voice messages on all Eadie's numbers and a curt text on J-J's mobile. Neither had called back.

'We need to talk before Brian Imber gets here.' Willard shut the door. 'You've got a moment?'

'Help yourself.' Faraday nodded at the spare chair.

'I was up at HQ this morning. Had a session with Terry Alcott. He wants us to move *Tumbril* along. He's not saying so but the pressure must be coming from the top. That's the way I read it.'

Faraday was eyeing the telephone. Terry Alcott was the Assistant Chief Constable responsible for CID and Special Operations, an impressive operator with a long Met pedigree. A respected voice on several national policing bodies, he was one of the few senior officers privy to the inner workings of *Tumbril*.

'He's still onside?'

'Absolutely. But I think he's getting nervous about the funding. Wants a scalp or two, something to put on the Chief's desk. That girl in the media unit was on to me just now. She's been fielding calls from the national press about the incident on the station this morning, wanted a steer. I said talk of turf wars was totally inappropriate. This is Pompey. Not the West Midlands.'

'And you believe that?'

'Of course not. And neither does Terry Alcott. Which is why you need to have a word with Graham Wallace.'

Faraday turned the proposition over for a moment or two. Nick Hayder had been carefully developing the Spit Bank Fort sting for the best part of three months. So far, it had worked like a dream. Why let a flurry of press interest hazard the endgame?

'The next move is Mackenzie's,' he said. 'That's the way Nick planned it.'

'I realise that. What I'm asking you to do is look at the script again, have a chat with Wallace, see whether we can't put a bit more pressure on Mackenzie. One way or another we have to be seen to be on top of this, ahead of the game. That's Terry Alcott talking, not me.'

Faraday pulled a pad towards him and scribbled a note. If the media were getting excited about a Scouser shackled to a ticket barrier, what would they make of a DI's son charged with manslaughter?

'You hear about the Cavalier?' Willard had treated himself to a rare smile. 'The one that did Nick Hayder?'

'Yes.'

'Nice one, eh? Do Cathy Lamb a power of good. All we need now is the other little bastard in the car and we can put them both away. Attempted murder, possession with intent to supply, you're looking at a fair old stretch.'

'We can evidence the supply charge?'

'Scenes of Crime found half a dozen wraps in the glovebox. Whoever said Scousers were bright?' Willard chuckled, then got to his feet. 'News from the hospital, by the way. Nick's back with us again. Recovered consciousness last night.'

'How is he?'

'Groggy. Can't remember anything about the incident and not a lot before that. They'll be doing more tests this afternoon.'

'He's still in Critical Care?'

'For the time being. But the bloke I talked to thought they'd probably be transferring him to a regular ward as soon as they'd got a bed. Might pop up there this evening, see if he remembers me.' He glanced back at Faraday. 'Fancy it?'

'Of course.' Faraday was still thinking about J-J. Sooner or later he'd have to level with Willard, tell him exactly what had happened, but there seemed little point before he could raise either Eadie or his son.

'What's this, then?' Willard was pointing at one of the photos on the cork board over Faraday's desk. It showed a mottled brown bird, almost invisible against the backdrop of dead leaves and old bracken. Faraday got to his feet and joined him. He couldn't remember when Willard had last displayed the slightest interest in his private life.

'Nightjar,' he said. 'There was a family of them on the heath in the New Forest. With any luck, they'll be back in May.'

Willard nodded, scanning the rest of the photos.

'Still at it, then? You and our feathered friends?'

'Afraid so. Keeps me out of mischief.'

'Your boy still tag along? Only I remember he was pretty interested.'

'No.' Faraday shook his head. 'J-J's fled the nest, pretty much.'

'Off your hands, then?'

'I wouldn't say that.'

Willard glanced at his watch. The *Tumbril* meeting with Brian Imber was due to start in a couple of minutes. Imber might be waiting even now. The Det-Supt nodded at the pad on Faraday's desk, then reached for the door handle.

'Mum's the word, eh? About Wallace?'

The parking in the commercial heart of Southsea was a nightmare. DC Jimmy Suttle took his chances on a double yellow, pulling the unmarked squad Fiesta behind a long line of cars. Beside him, Paul Winter was peering at a property across the road: big Georgian sash windows and a glimpse of a handsome porticoed entrance behind an encircling eight-foot wall. The walls of adjoining properties, equally grand, had been defaced with graffiti. On the wall across the road, not a mark.

'Bazza HQ.' Winter helped himself to another Werther's Original. 'Told you he'd come up in the world.'

The last time he'd paid a visit, a couple of years back, the place had been a gentlemen's club, a gloomy, shadowed echo of the dying days of empire. Run-down and barely used, Bazza had bought it for cash from the trustees, meaning to restore the interior to its former glory. Back in the nineteenth century, one of Southsea's premier families had lived here, a brewer who'd made his fortune slaking Pompey thirsts. A man with political ambitions, he'd ended up as the city's mayor, bringing a gruff, broad-chested impatience to deliberations in the council chamber. Mackenzie had evidently read a pamphlet or two about the man, sensing how shrewdly he'd turned business success to other ends, and rather fancied running his own commercial empire from within the same four walls. Craneswater was fine if you wanted a decent place to live, somewhere nice for the missus and kids, but the middle of Southsea was where you'd leave your real mark.

Suttle reached for his door handle. Chris Talbot also operated from the pile across the road. There were questions he needed to answer about the Scouse lad in the back of the Transit, about the abandoned Cavalier in Portsea.

'Wait.' Suttle felt Winter's hand on his arm.

Electronically controlled gates sealed the house off from the road. As they swung back, Suttle recognised the bulky figure in a leather jacket, pausing beside a low-slung Mercedes convertible. Chris Talbot.

'What's the problem?' Suttle had the door open now. 'Either we front up now or we lose him.'

'Wait,' Winter repeated.

Another figure appeared in the driveway beside the Mercedes. She was tall and blonde with wraparound shades and the kind of tan you couldn't buy from a salon. It was hard to be sure at fifty metres, but she didn't seem to be smiling.

'The lovely Marie,' Winter murmured. 'Bazza's missus.'

Talbot opened the boot. Marie handed him a bag, then checked her watch. Time was plainly moving on.

'OK.' Winter gave Suttle the nod. 'Let's go.'

They walked across the road. Talbot saw them coming. Winter stood in the drive, blocking the exit to the road.

'Christopher,' he said amiably. 'Thought we might have a chat.'

Talbot glanced at Marie, then circled the car. His shaved head was mapped with scars and a tiny silver cross hung from one ear lobe. His eyes, screwed up against the bright sunlight, were pouched with exhaustion and his face had a slightly yellowish tint. Once, thought Suttle, this bloke might have been good-looking.

'Well?' Winter wanted an answer.

'No chance.' Talbot nodded down at the car. 'Just off. Marie fancies a run out to Chichester.'

'Riding shotgun, are we? Keeping the Indians off?' Winter glanced up at the house, aware of a watching face at an upstairs window. 'We can either do it here or at our place. Your choice. The quicker we get it sorted, the sooner you get to Laura Ashley. So what's it to be?'

There was a sudden movement behind the car. Marie had produced a set of keys. Getting into the driver's seat revealed the extent of her tan.

'Where are you going?' Talbot bent down to her window.

'Chichester, where do you bloody think? You want to talk to these guys, that's fine by me.'

'Listen, Baz said—'

'Fuck Baz.'

She gunned the engine, her face expressionless behind the windscreen and the designer shades. To Suttle's surprise, despite the language there wasn't a trace of Pompey in her accent.

Talbot bent to the driver's window again, then had second thoughts. Looking up at the house, he put his hand to his mouth. The piercing whistle opened a window. A younger face leaned out.

'Chichester, son,' Talbot yelled. 'Marie needs company.'

'See?' Winter was beaming at Suttle. 'Apaches everywhere.'

Marie and her new escort gone, Winter and Suttle followed Talbot into the house. Winter, with a memory of cobwebbed windows and threadbare moquette, paused inside the gleaming front door, already impressed. A new-looking floor lapped at the edges of the enormous hall. A big chandelier hung from an elaborate ceiling rose. Even the air itself smelled of money.

'Bazza given up on pool?' Winter gestured at the golf bag propped beside the front door.

Talbot ignored him. An elegant staircase wound up towards the first floor. Winter paused beside the second of the framed pictures. Once, this staircase would have been lined with family portraits, specially commissioned in oils, the brewer's entire dynasty gazing down on visitors below. Now, each of these huge blow-up photos captured a moment at Fratton Park: Alan Knight palming a shot over the bar, Paul Merson at full throttle down the wing, Todorov lashing the ball into the net, the crowd erupting beyond him. There was even a shot of Alan Ball, the day Pompey last made it into the top division, his arm round his beaming chairman.

'This isn't a house,' Suttle muttered. 'It's a fucking shrine.'

Talbot led them to an office at the end of the top landing. The desk looked new and there was a gentle hum from the PC. Two filing cabinets flanked the big sash window. A coffee machine was bubbling on the table beside the desk and the year planner on the wall above was already thick with appointments stretching into early summer. In early June, five days were blocked off for Wimbledon.

'This yours, then?' Winter gestured round.

'Bazza's. He's away today.'

'What's this?' It was Suttle. He'd spotted a big French tricolour carefully draped on the back of the door. It was the one splash of colour amongst the muted greens and browns.

Talbot refused to answer. Winter was looking amused.

'Go on. The boy's a Saints fan. Tell him.'

Talbot shot Winter a look then sank into the chair behind the desk and helped himself to a coffee.

'Bollocks to that. You want to talk business, go ahead. If I want a social chat I can think of better company.'

Winter was eyeing the percolator.

'Just the one sugar will be fine.'

'Help yourself.'

'I will. James?'

Suttle still wanted to know about the flag. At length, the coffees poured, Winter filled in the details. Back in the eighties, a boatload of fans had taken the early ferry to Le Havre to supply a bit of Pompey support in a cross-Channel pre-season friendly. Pre-warned about the 6.57, the French police had refused to let the blue army off the boat. Mid morning, already pissed, dozens of them jumped overboard and swam across the harbour to dry land. After a while, the gendarmes gave up and let the rest off. Big mistake.

'Why?'

'Rape and pillage. The game didn't start until the afternoon and Le Havre's full of bars. Worse still, it's full of Frenchmen. Not their fault, no offence, but the Pompey weren't having it. Trashed the place. Just trashed it. Then they all jumped in a load of cabs and went off to the game. Place called Honfleur down the coast. Used to have a nice little ground till our lot took it apart. Got the game abandoned, too. The Goths had nothing on the 6.57. Eh, Chris?'

'And this thing?' Suttle nodded at the flag.

'That was afterwards, the way I heard it. Bazza came across a bar they'd missed first time round. The name of the place was the real wind-up.'

What was it called?'

'Café de Southampton. The flag was out front, only bit to survive.'

Winter chuckled to himself, then poured more coffee. At length, Talbot yawned.

'You going to get on with this or what? Only some of us have a living to make.'

'Of course.'

Winter put his coffee to one side and produced his pocketbook. Talbot and his mate had been clocked at the station at half past two in the morning. What happened before then?

Talbot pushed the chair back from the desk and stretched his legs. Then he clasped his hands behind his neck and gazed up at the ceiling.

'You want it all?'

'Please.'

'OK. We were down in Gunwharf. Few bevvies. Quiet for a Wednesday.'

'Time?'

'Late. Forty Below chucks out at two. Must have been around then, give or take. Then we wandered back to the motor, you know, the way you do.'

'We?'

'Me and Steve Pratchett.'

'He works for Bazza?'

'He's a subbie plasterer.'

'Where do we find him?'

'Haven't a clue.'

'Doesn't he have an address?'

'Bound to.'

'Mobile?'

'Always binning them. It's a credit scam. He's always after a new model. He can't stand purple. Fuck knows.'

'So what happened?'

'The van was parked round the back of the Keppel's Head. We're driving back through Portsea, middle of the fucking night, and we see this mush hanging out of a Cavalier. At first I think he's pissed. Then we get close, right alongside like, and – shit – you should have seen the state of him.'

'Pre-damaged?'

'What?'

'Forget it. You stopped?'

'Of course we did. The bloke was spark out, blood all over his face, his T-shirt, everywhere, right beating. Then he comes round, moaning and groaning, and he must have thought it was us that did the damage because he starts thrashing around like you wouldn't believe.'

'You're kidding . . .' Winter shook his head. '*You* do the damage?'

'Exactly. Anyway, me and Steve do our best to clean him up, then we ask where he'd like us to take him.'

'Home would have been a good answer.'

'Yeah, but he doesn't say that, does he? He wants to go to the railway station. He's had enough of Pompey. He wants to get the fuck out.'

'The station's shut.'

'That's what we told him. Made no difference. There he is, bleeding all over us, and all he can talk about is the fucking timetable.' Talbot rubbed his face, then yawned again. 'In the end, we did what he wanted, took him to the station. Closest we could get was the ticket barrier. Never even said thank you.'

'And the handcuffs?'

'What handcuffs?'

'You're telling me you didn't handcuff him to the barrier?'

'No fucking way. Why would I do a thing like that?'

Winter knew there was no point pursuing the charge. While he had absolutely no doubt that handcuffs were part of the tableau, the camera angle had masked the detail.

'What about the wraps?'

'Wraps?'

'We found half a dozen wraps in the Cavalier. Smack.' Winter took a sip of coffee. 'Didn't plant them yourself, did you? Only that would have been a kindness.'

'Who to?'

'Us. We want these guys out of the city as much as you do.'

'Really?' Talbot's interest was at last engaged. 'Shame you haven't nicked them, then. You try fucking hard enough with the rest of us.'

'Is that right?' Winter sounded positively hurt. 'You're sitting here on half a million quid's worth and you're telling me we've spoiled your party?'

'Not yet. But you'd like to.'

'How does that work, then? Are we talking busts here? Street level? Half a dozen scrotes with a gram or two between them? That kind of aggro Bazza wouldn't even notice.'

'You know what I'm talking about.'

'I do?' Winter looked mystified. 'Help me out at all, Jimmy?'

Suttle shook his head. He was making notes in his pocketbook. Later, when Winter had finished, he'd take a formal statement.

Winter was brooding over this latest bend in the conversational road. He'd heard rumours about some covert operation being mounted against a major player in the city but he'd always put all this down to propaganda from the guys at headquarters who had worries about force morale. If no one had ever managed to lay a finger on Bazza Mackenzie, then it would be nice to pretend that someone was at least trying. But maybe, for once, the rumours were true.

'Tell me more –' he said at length '– then we might leave you alone.'

'You have to be joking. That's me done.'

'Worried about Bazza? Speaking out of turn?'

'Fuck off.'

'My pleasure.' Winter held his gaze for a moment, then produced a card from his wallet. 'When's the great man back?'

'Baz? Late this afternoon.'

'Good.' Winter slipped the card onto the desk. 'My mobile's on there. Tell him to bell me if he fancies it. Tonight would be good. The telly's awful.'

It took less than ten minutes for Faraday to turn the *Tumbril* meeting into a head-to-head with Willard. Brian Imber had reported back from his visit to Mackenzie's bank. Bazza, he announced with a frown, had ordered the sale of a penthouse flat in Gunwharf. The property, on a prime harbourside site, was on the market at £695,000.

'There has to be a reason,' Imber puzzled. 'Has to be.'

Faraday wanted to help out but knew he couldn't. In all probability, Mackenzie was raising cash against the purchase of Spit Bank Fort, proof positive that he'd taken Nick Hayder's carefully laid bait, but a single glance at Willard produced a tiny shake of the head. Any mention of Graham Wallace or the fort was still off-limits in front of Brian Imber. Strictly need to know. At least for now.

Willard steered the meeting onto safer ground. He wanted to know the status of Prebble's input, how far the accountant had got, how soon Willard could expect a totally reliable statement of the assets under

Mackenzie's control. Faraday knew this information was important. The moment they managed to tie Mackenzie to a specific criminal offence – proven in a court of law – was the moment the confiscation process kicked in. From that point on, it would be down to Mackenzie to justify his legal ownership of every one of those assets, a challenge – in Prebble's view – that would be beyond him. In this sense, as Imber kept reminding him, *Tumbril* had turned the investigative process on its head. First Prebble calculated how much they could nick back off the man. Then they looked for a specific charge that would stand up in court.

The latter, as far as Faraday could fathom, was the real problem. Trapping a criminal as well protected as Mackenzie was a near-impossibility, and only a detective as driven and original as Nick Hayder would even be minded to try. In the shape of Spit Bank Fort he'd come up with a big fat plum that Mackenzie just might be tempted to scrump but in Faraday's view the odds against a successful sting were stilll high, not least because *Tumbril* – despite Hayder's best efforts – was itself far from secure.

An incoming phone call drew Willard to his desk. When he returned to the conference table, Faraday brought up the pre-Christmas intercept. Mike Valentine's Mercedes had been stopped and searched en route back from London. The plan had been hatched and overseen by the *Tumbril* team, albeit with substantial input from other units. There was overwhelming evidence that the Mercedes was carrying substantial quantities of cocaine. Yet the full search found nothing.

'And your point is ... ?' Willard sounded testy. This was old ground.

'My point is someone leaked. Told Valentine. Told Mackenzie. Maybe not directly. Maybe it went through different hands. But either way it got there in the end. Hence the fact we drew a blank.'

'We know that. And it's been addressed.'

'How?'

It was a direct challenge. Willard, to his obvious irritation, couldn't duck it.

'Listen, Joe. We've always known from the start that *Tumbril* was basically an audit operation. It's paper-based, figures-based. That's how far the budget stretches and even then, believe me, we've barely got enough. The moment we want to spread our wings, mount an operation, scoop someone up, we have to widen the circle, bring in the specialists – covert, surveillance, whatever. There's no way, short of the Good Fairy, we can do anything else.'

'Of course.' Faraday nodded. 'But has anyone asked the hard

questions about the intercept? Drawn up a list of names? People who knew? People who might have –' he shrugged '– leaked?'

'I did.' It was Imber.

'And?'

'How long is a piece of string? We needed Special Ops for the covert. That's a couple of blokes, minimum. Surveillance? Maybe half a dozen more. Say ten in all. It's maths, Joe. Each of these guys has mates. Each of those mates has more mates. Suddenly you're into half the force. The miracle is, we're still reasonably watertight, at least as far as the paperwork is concerned.' He paused. 'Did *you* know about Whale Island?'

'No.'

'Well, then . . .'

Faraday accepted the point with a curt nod. He was still curious to explore exactly what had happened back before Christmas but at least he now understood Willard's determination to keep Wallace and the u/c operation under wraps. Quite how Imber would react when he discovered he'd been out of the loop was anyone's guess but that, he told himself, would be Willard's problem.

'You want to answer that?' Willard drew Faraday's attention to his mobile. Faraday glanced at the number. Cathy Lamb.

'Do you mind, sir?'

'Go ahead.'

Faraday stood up and retreated to the far end of the office. Behind him, Imber was still pressing Willard about the Gunwharf flat. Faraday paused beside the window, gazing out through a gap in the venetian blinds. From the tone of Cathy's voice, he knew at once that it was bad news. J-J, she said, had been arrested at a petrol station in North End. Word that he was wanted had been out for several hours but he'd fallen into their laps after a call from the forecourt manager. J-J had been acting suspiciously beside one of the pumps. He'd filled an empty two-litre bottle with unleaded and appeared to have no intention of paying. Control had dispatched an area car less than a minute away and after a brief chase J-J had been detained.

Faraday closed his eyes.

'Chase?'

'He legged it, Joe. And I understand there was a bit of a fracas.'

'Is he OK?'

'Upset. I've talked to the Custody Sergeant at Central and he's aware of the situation. We've taken the case over from division because of the Scouse involvement but Highland Road have volunteered Rick Stapleton and Alan Moffat to handle the interview. I understand from

Winter that you pretty much know the circumstances. Daniel Kelly? The student who died last night?'

Faraday was following a flock of racing pigeons as they wheeled over the nearby rooftops. Head north, he thought, and leave all this chaos behind you.

He bent to the phone.

'What's the charge?'

'There isn't one. Not yet. We're waiting on interview.'

'What about someone who knows sign?'

'The Custody Sergeant's phoning through the names on the qualified interpreter register. So far, he's drawn a blank.' She paused. 'It may have to be you, Joe. We can't wait forever.'

'Great.' Faraday glanced at his watch, realising there was no point prolonging the conversation. Like it or not, Willard had to know. He thanked Cathy for the call and returned to the table. Willard knew at once that something had happened.

'OK?'

'Afraid not, sir.' Faraday offered him a bleak smile. 'Know a good solicitor?'

Within the hour, Faraday was ringing the entryphone at Central police station. A uniformed PC let him in and the duty Inspector emerged from an office up the corridor. From deep in the building came the rattle of bars and a yell from someone desperate for a fag. To Faraday's relief, it didn't sound the least like J-J.

'Your boy's in the cells. I'm afraid he's still cuffed.'

'Is that necessary?'

'I'm afraid so. He's been –' the Inspector was choosing his words carefully '– less than helpful.'

Faraday nodded. He wanted to know whether Hartley Crewdson had arrived. For the time being, J-J could wait.

'We've put him in one of the interview rooms. You want tea or anything?'

'No, thanks.'

Faraday followed the Inspector to the suite of interview rooms. Hartley Crewdson was a solicitor with a successful criminal practice in the north of the city. He specialised in defence work, representing a never-ending stream of young tearaways from the Paulsgrove and Leigh Park estates. Faraday had never had personal dealings with him before but was aware of the man's reputation. Half the DCs in the city thought Crewdson was a menace. The rest viewed him as a genius, the brief who could spot the weakness in any prosecution case. If you found yourself in a really tight corner, they said, then Crewdson's was the number you called.

The Inspector knocked lightly on the door before going in. Crewdson was sitting at the interview table, leafing through a thick file. His taste in suits and ties was never less than flamboyant, and for a man in his late forties, he'd won a big following amongst the more impressionable female clerks at the magistrates court.

'Leave you to it?' The Inspector nodded at Faraday and left, closing the door behind him.

Crewdson got to his feet. Faraday accepted the proffered handshake, curious to know why Crewdson had phoned him with the offer to represent J-J.

'Paul Winter gave me a ring,' he said briefly. 'He thought you might need a bit of support.'

Faraday permitted himself a thin smile.

'Winter's right. You'll not have spoken to the lad?'

'Hardly. I was waiting for you to arrive.'

'But you've talked to the Custody Officer?'

'Yes.'

'And?'

'It's not as bad as you might think.'

'Really?'

Faraday shed his jacket and sank into one of the four chairs. According to Crewdson, the evidence against J-J was – at best – thin. Winter and Suttle had photographed him arriving at Pennington Road. There was no evidence he'd left in possession of drugs. Neither had they seen money change hands. Eadie Sykes had volunteered a statement establishing that no drugs had been present in the student's flat, and in the shape of the videotapes, she appeared to have behavioural evidence to prove it. According to Sykes, the drugs had been dropped off early in the evening. She herself had taped the fixing sequence and everything else that followed. In terms of supply, J-J was therefore home free.

'What about the business with the petrol?'

'That's a mystery. No one knows.'

'OK?' Faraday sat back. 'So what do we do now?'

'I suggest he goes no-comment.'

'Why?'

'Because that way we leave nothing to chance. The last thing we need is your boy saying anything –' he smiled '– silly. The lad's going to be upset, bound to be. We can use that later, if they try and make anything of the no-comment.'

'In court, you mean?'

'Yes.'

'You think it'll come to that?'

'No. Not if we're sensible.'

Faraday sat back a moment, trying to order his thoughts. The thrust of Crewdson's defence was obvious. J-J was about to become yet another stroppy, tight-lipped interviewee.

'That means it's down to us to make the case,' he said at last.

'Exactly.' Crewdson was smiling again. 'But it's them, Mr Faraday. Not us.'

Minutes later, the interview strategy agreed, Faraday went to find the Custody Sergeant. To his relief, it was someone he knew. The two men masked their mutual unease with a brisk exchange of nods. When Faraday enquired about someone to sit alongside J-J during the interview, the Custody Sergeant confirmed he'd drawn a blank on the two registered interpreters within the county.

'One's on holiday in Egypt. The other isn't answering her mobile.'

'You've tried out of area? West Sussex? Surrey? Dorset?'

'To be honest, no, sir. I know the ACPO guidelines favour sticking to the register but we're up against the PACE clock. The lad needs communication support, no question, but . . .'

The Sergeant spread his hands. There was a brief silence, broken by Faraday.

'You're asking me to do it?'

'I'm asking whether you'd mind, sir.'

'You think it's appropriate?'

'I think we ought to move things along.'

'Good idea.' Faraday eyed him for a moment. 'Do you mind if I see him before we start?'

'Of course not.'

The Custody Sergeant lifted a phone and summoned one of the jailers. A burly woman in a white blouse appeared moments later, and led Faraday down through the station to the cell complex at the end. Faraday had made this journey countless times before – as a probationer, as a young CID aide, as a serving DC – yet never had it occurred to him that he would, one day, be on the receiving end of all this watchful attention. The bleakness of the place had never hit him quite this way before: the harsh neon lights, the institutional greens and whites, the way that the jangle of a bunch of keys echoed around corner after corner.

J-J was in a cell towards the end of the corridor. A concrete plinth beneath the window served as a bunk, and through the hatch in the grey steel door Faraday could see his son stretched full length on the thin sponge mattress. His eyes were closed and his bony wrists lay handcuffed on the rumpled bottom of his T-shirt. Faraday had never seen anyone looking so solitary, so cut off, so alone. Already, in the stir of air as the jailer unlocked and opened the door, he could smell the harsh tang of petrol.

J-J, hearing nothing, didn't move. Faraday glanced back at the jailer. 'Mr Crewdson?'

The woman nodded and left. Faraday heard the key turn in the heavy door before she set off down the corridor. He reached out and touched J-J's face with the back of his hand. The boy's eyes opened, staring up at him, the way he might greet a total stranger. Faraday tried to coax a smile. When nothing happened, he turned his attention to J-J's wrists. The handcuffs were double locked, and the skin was raw and inflamed where the steel edges of the cuffs had chafed. J-J struggled upright on the mattress, holding his wrists in front of him the way you might carry a precious object.

'They hurt?' Faraday signed.

J-J shook his head. His face was pale and he wouldn't meet his father's gaze. When Faraday gave him a hug, he could feel a tremor running through his thin frame.

'What happened?'

Approaching footsteps paused outside the cell. A key turned in the lock and Faraday glanced back to find Hartley Crewdson stepping into the cell. The jailer was preparing to lock them in again.

'We need these cuffs off,' Faraday told her. 'He'll be fine now.'

'I'll talk to the Custody Sergeant.'

'You do that.'

Crewdson, a tall man, was looking down at J-J. He must have been in this situation a thousand times, Faraday thought. Another youth colliding head-on with the judicial system. Another plea before the magistrates.

Faraday did the introductions. J-J offered the faintest of nods but his father was unsure whether he really understood what was about to happen.

'You're going to be interviewed,' he explained. 'Two policemen, two detectives. They'll be asking you what happened. All you need tell them is your name and date of birth. Everything else . . .' He glanced at Crewdson for support. 'Just shake your head.'

'That's right.' It was Crewdson. 'We know already what really happened and there are ways we can prove it. The detectives you'll be talking to may push you to make mistakes. As long as you say nothing, that can't happen. Everything's going to be fine. Just do what we say. OK?'

J-J was staring at his father as Faraday translated Crewdson's assurances into sign. Then his gaze transferred to the lawyer. This stranger might have been trying to explain the rules of a particularly complicated game. J-J's face was quite blank.

'You understand what we're saying?' Faraday signed.

J-J's slow nod put a smile on Crewdson's face. He reached out and patted J-J on the shoulder, then turned back to the door, calling for the jailer through the open hatch. J-J watched his every movement, something new in his eyes, and Faraday's heart began to sink again.

The interview started forty minutes later. Rick Stapleton had driven across from Highland Road, bringing another detective – Alan Moffat – with him. Faraday had been in charge of both DCs for three years on division, and once again he tried to defuse the awkwardness of the situation, this time with a brisk handshake. Stapleton was a lean thirty-three-year-old, openly gay, a detective whom Faraday had always rated extremely highly. Moffat, a slightly older man, had served on the Force Surveillance Unit before returning to the grind of volume crime. Neither man returned Faraday's smile.

The bare, white-walled room was equipped with both audio and video facilities. Central had been chosen to pilot video recordings of all interviews, and two cameras mounted high on the wall offered coverage of the table that dominated the room.

Stapleton and Moffat sat on one side of the table, J-J and his father on the other. Hartley Crewdson fetched a spare chair from an adjoining room, and stationed himself to J-J's left.

Stapleton raised an eyebrow and glanced at Faraday.

'OK?'

Faraday nodded, watching Moffat as he cued the video recorders. The audio machines were on the table, backed against the wall. Moffat sat down again, leaving Stapleton to reach for the printed checklist and go through the preliminary announcements that preface every inter-view. Stapleton introduced himself and Moffat, confirmed the time and place, established that the interview was being recorded, and then turned to J-J.

'Please give your full name and date of birth.'

Faraday signed the request. J-J looked confused for a moment, then shrugged. Surely his dad knew the answer? There was a brief silence before Faraday supplied the details. Stapleton glanced at Moffat. This was new territory.

'Your lad's supposed to speak for himself.' He frowned. 'If you see what I mean.'

Stapleton returned to his script. After explaining what would happen to the recorded tapes and CDs, he glanced quickly up, looking at J-J, before ducking his head again.

'You do not have to say anything,' he read. 'But it may harm your defence if you do not mention when questioned something which you may later rely on in court. Anything you do say may be given in evidence.' He paused, then looked at Faraday. 'You want to tell him all that?'

'I just did.'

'And he understands?'

'Of course he does.'

'Good. So let's start with yesterday. As I understand it, you've been involved in the production of a video. Would you like to tell us something about that?'

Faraday hesitated a moment, then passed on the question. A shake of J-J's head would have been enough for 'No comment.' Instead, J-J bent towards the table, eyeballing Rick Stapleton, inviting the detective into his life, offering him a long account of exactly how he'd first met Eadie, how he'd shot black and white stills for her Dunkirk documentary, how she'd taught him to use a video camera, and how his involvement in Ambrym had slowly extended into a research responsibility for her new drugs project. The work, he signed, had been brilliant. Hard, but brilliant. He'd met loads of people. And Eadie had been right. Everyone should know about this stuff.

'Who's Eadie?'

'My dad's girlfriend.'

'And the research was down to you?'

'Yes. I had to find the people we were going to tape.' He extended his arm and mimed a syringe. 'The users.'

For Faraday, struggling to keep up with the blizzard of sign, this experience was quickly becoming surreal. This was the last year of J-J's life going onto the CDs and audio cassettes. Whatever happened to 'No comment.'?

When Stapleton paused to scribble himself a note, Faraday shot a look at Crewdson. The solicitor was gazing at J-J, appalled.

Stapleton took up the running again. When did J-J first meet Daniel Kelly?

'Couple of days ago. There was a girl called Sarah. I think she really wanted to be part of the video, help us make it. She thought it was a cool idea. She knew Daniel and told me about him.'

'You met him?'

'Yes.'

'What was he like?'

'Lost.'

'Lost?'

'Confused. Sick.' J-J clawed at his heart and pulled a face. Faraday hunted for the right word. 'Wounded,' he managed at last.

'Did he have friends?' Stapleton didn't take his eyes off J-J's face.

'I don't think so. Only Sarah.'

'What about family?'

'His mum's in Australia. He never sees his dad.'

'Would you say he was vulnerable?'

'Definitely.'

'An easy target?'

Crewdson leaned forward, reaching towards J-J, trying to still those busy hands.

'This is totally inappropriate,' he told Stapleton. 'You're leading my client on.'

'You think so?' Stapleton's eyes were stony. 'I'd say we were simply establishing the facts. Mr Faraday?'

On the point of supporting Crewdson's protest, Faraday realised that the question was directed at J-J. When he signed it to his son, J-J merely shrugged.

'I haven't got a problem,' he signed back, looking at Stapleton. 'Ask me whatever you want.'

Faraday hesitated. The temptation now was to treat these answers with a certain degree of latitude, if only for J-J's sake.

'My son would prefer if you kept to the point,' he muttered at last. 'He's happy to help with the facts.'

'OK.' Stapleton's gaze lingered on Faraday for a moment or two, then he returned to J-J. 'Let's be clear about the situation here, Mr Faraday. Your job was to go and persuade Kelly to be in this video. Kelly was a mess. That's why you were there, that's why you went to see him in the first place. Do you really think he was in any fit state to make a sensible decision? Be honest.'

There was a brief pause while J-J thought about the question. Finally, he shook his head.

'The second time I saw him he was in a terrible state.' The clawing motion again, then the syringe. 'He needed heroin. He hadn't got any.'

'The second time you saw him?'

'Yesterday. Before we did the interview.'

'Did he *want* to do the interview?'

'I –' J-J was frowning '– don't know.'

Once again, Faraday was tempted to embellish the answer. J-J's despairing shrug, though, spoke for itself. Stapleton looked down at his notes, taking his time.

'But the interview happened, didn't it?' he enquired at last.

'Yes.'

'So why did Kelly say yes? What made the difference?'

Hartley Crewdson intervened for the second time. In his opinion, this line of questioning was definitely prejudicial, planting suggestions in J-J's path, luring him into self-incrimination. Faraday was looking at the ceiling. Twenty-five years of policing told him the solicitor hadn't got a prayer.

Stapleton barely spared Crewdson a glance. Instead, he once again asked Faraday to pass the protest on to his son. What did J-J think?

J-J signed that he was OK with Stapleton's questions. He was here to explain exactly what had happened. Absolutely no problem.

'So answer the question. Why did Kelly agree to do the interview?'

J-J signed that he'd agreed to buy drugs for Kelly. Faraday turned to Stapleton.

'He says Kelly asked him a favour.'

'What favour?'

Faraday glanced back at J-J, watching him mime a syringe in his arm again, realising that his fatherly attempts to shield his son from these remorseless questions were doomed. One way or another, J-J was determined to share the truth about yesterday's events. What might happen as a consequence didn't appear to trouble him in the least.

Stapleton was looking at Faraday. He wanted clarification on the last answer. Faraday sat back in his chair, suddenly aware of what guilt must feel like. Any more of this and he'd be facing a charge himself. Perverting the course of justice.

'He's telling you that Kelly asked him to buy drugs.'

'That's not what you said just now.'

'I know. You wanted a clarification. I've just supplied it. OK?'

For the first time, Stapleton permitted himself a small, tight-lipped smile. It was, Faraday realised at once, a warning.

'Ask your son whether he agreed to buy the drugs.'

Faraday signed the question. J-J nodded, slowing the signing, spelling it out, trying to cut his father out of the loop.

'Did Kelly tell you where to go?'

'Yes.'

'He gave you money?'

'Yes.'

'Where was the address?'

Lip-reading the question, J-J hand-signed Pennington Road. Faraday obliged with a translation.

'Number?'

'30.'

'And you bought the drugs?'

'They took the money off me.'

'Who's "they"?'

'Two guys.'

'Names?'

'One was called Terry.'

'How much money did they take off you?'

'£90.'

'And gave you the drugs?'

'No.'

'Why not?'

'I don't know.'

'That's robbery. Why didn't you come to us?'

There was a silence while J-J tried to think of an answer. Faraday glanced across at Crewdson. To his surprise, the solicitor motioned for him not to intervene. Alan Moffat stirred, taking over from Stapleton. After he'd established that J-J had returned to Hampshire Terrace without the drugs, he asked about Eadie Sykes.

'She didn't know about the drugs,' J-J signed.

'But she knew about the state of Kelly?'

'Yes.'

'And she still went ahead with the interview?'

'Yes.'

'Were you happy with that?'

There was a long moment of silence. Then J-J shook his head.

'Why not?' It was Stapleton this time.

'Because I thought it was cruel.'

'Cruel how?'

'Taking advantage.'

Stapleton nodded and scribbled himself a note before looking up again.

'What state was Kelly in by the time you did the interview?'

'Terrible, worse. You can see it on the tape.'

'But still no drugs?'

'No, they came later.'

'How?'

'Somebody came round. There must have been a buzz on the phone. I don't know.'

'Were these the same people you'd met earlier?'

'I don't know. I never saw them.'

Unprompted, through Faraday, J-J described what happened next. Eadie had taken over the camera. Daniel had injected himself, then stumbled away to bed.

'Like a drunk,' J-J signed. 'Like a zombie.'

Stapleton leaned towards him. 'And you had no part in any of that?'

'None.'

'Why not?'

'I thought it was wrong.'

'And what do you think now? Now that Daniel's dead?'

'I still think it was wrong.'

'You think you were responsible for him dying?'

'No. He'd have died anyway.'

'So why was it wrong?'

'Because we robbed him.'

'*Robbed* him?'

Stapleton looked at Faraday to check the translation. Faraday confirmed it with a nod, resigned now to letting the interview run its course. Stapleton returned to J-J.

'Robbed him how? Robbed him of what?'

J-J took his time. He was staring at his father. Finally, he cupped a shape with his hands and then made a tiny turning motion with his body.

Faraday paused for a moment, reflecting on the gesture. Then he looked at Stapleton.

'I think he means Kelly's entire life,' he said quietly. 'By putting it on tape and taking it away, they stole it.'

The interview ended at 17.05. Between them, Stapleton and Moffat went back over J-J's account, confirming details, asking for extra information, making it plain that J-J had to realise how important it was to be absolutely sure he hadn't missed anything out. Finally, almost as an afterthought, they enquired about the incident at the petrol station. Just what had J-J intended to do with two litres of Supergreen unleaded?

Faraday, bracing himself for the next revelation, had dutifully signed the question. This time, to his relief, J-J simply shook his head.

'You don't know or you won't tell us?'

Another shake of the head. Stapleton looked to Faraday for help.

'He means, "No comment,"' Faraday said.

Afterwards, J-J was returned to his cell, scarcely sparing his father a backward glance. Faraday and Crewdson were shown into the Duty Inspector's empty office while Stapleton and Moffat conferred with the Custody Sergeant. The next half-hour, as Faraday knew only too well, would probably decide J-J's fate.

'What do you think?'

Crewdson had opened a window and lit a small cheroot.

'I think I might have been wrong.' He expelled a thin blue plume of smoke. 'Your boy was sensational. In a court of law he'd win a round of applause.'

'I'm not with you.'

'He confirmed everything they already know. Sure, he tried to score for Kelly but he did it with the best of intentions. There's no question that he was physically involved in supply, but every indication that he was appalled by what followed. There's something else, too.'

'What's that?'

'You fucked around with a couple of the answers . . .' He paused. 'Didn't you?'

Faraday nodded, aware of the hot blush of colour rising in his face. 'Instinct,' he muttered. 'Couldn't help myself.'

Crewdson gazed at him a moment, then stepped across. Faraday felt oddly grateful for the hand on his shoulder.

'I'm not blaming you for a moment,' Crewdson said softly. 'Any father would have done the same. It's just nice the whole interview's on video.'

Faraday stared at the solicitor. The last hour or so had upset him more than he'd thought possible. Why the broad grin?

'You're telling me all that was inadmissible?' he said at last.

'Totally. They had no right to put you in that situation, total conflict of interest. Believe me, that interview won't get anywhere near a courtroom.' He gave Faraday's shoulder a final pat. 'They won't see it that way, of course, but then policemen never do.'

The summons to the Custody Sergeant came shortly afterwards. Faraday followed Crewdson through to the Charge Room. They passed Stapleton and Moffat in the corridor. The two DCs were on their way out to the car park. Neither said a word.

The Custody Sergeant was standing at his desk, sorting through the paperwork from the arrest and interview. He acknowledged their presence with a nod, then reached for a pen, glanced up at the clock on the wall, and began to write. Finally, he closed the folder and capped the pen.

'I've had a word with DCs Stapleton and Yates.' He tapped the file. 'I've also been through statements from DCs Winter and Suttle. Given the lad's cooperation, there's no point in remanding him. Under the circumstances, we're bailing him for two weeks, pending further inquiries. He needs to be back here on the fifth of April.' He produced another form for signature. 'Would you mind, Mr Faraday?'

Chapter twelve

The last place DC Jimmy Suttle would have chosen for a discreet meet was the top floor of the Southsea branch of Debenhams. The Debs cafeteria was for bored housewives with oodles of kids or OAPs in search of a cheap snack. What on earth was a vision like Trudy Gallagher doing in a place like this?

'It's Blue Cross Day. They're giving stuff away. What makes you so choosy? Are you rich, or something? Look . . .' She reached down for her bag and produced a collection of boxed underwear. Two pairs of black lace knickers. A scarlet bikini for the summer. Three silk thongs in case she ever met the man of her dreams. 'Under forty quid the lot. Happy now?'

'Very.' Suttle was thinking of the body they'd found in the upstairs room at Bystock Road. Black lace would be perfect. 'What about blokes' stuff?'

'Take your choice. 501s. Maine. Adidas. Stuff they rip you off on any other place.'

'You think I should take a stroll, then? While you finish that lot?' He nodded at her bowl: three scoops of ice cream with a dressing of maple syrup.

'No.' She shook her head. 'Stay here.'

She ducked her head to hide her smile and loaded her spoon with melting ice cream. She'd phoned Suttle on the mobile number he'd given her at Gunwharf, the first time they'd met. She wanted to talk to him about something but it had to be private, one on one. If he turned up with that tosser Paul Winter, there was no way they'd even start a conversation.

Suttle, amused by her dismissal of Winter, had invented a pressing appointment at his dentist and left Winter pursuing house-to-house inquiries in Portsea. He'd heard him on the phone to the Crime Squad DS, telling him there was no way anyone with half a brain in Portsea would ever testify against one of Bazza's lieutenants, but it seemed that

DI Lamb was under the cosh for a result and was insisting on giving the house-to-house a punt. Winter, he knew, hadn't been fooled by his line about the dentist but was evidently happy to cut his young oppo a little slack. 'Whoever she is,' he'd grunted, 'give her one from me.'

Trudy had abandoned the ice cream. The smoking tables were on the other side of the cafeteria, beside the loo. Suttle pulled out a chair for Trudy, catching a swirl of perfume as she sat down. His last girlfriend had also been mad about Ralph Lauren, though a £36 atomiser for Christmas had done nothing to rescue the relationship.

'Where did you learn stuff like that?' Trudy shook out two Marlboro Lites and laid one beside his half-drained glass of 7 UP.

'Stuff like what?'

'Manners.'

'Comes naturally. I was born polite.'

'Naturally bollocks. How come you're in a job like this, nice bloke like you?'

'The money's good. Plus you get to meet interesting people.'

'Like who?'

'Like you, for starters.'

'I didn't come here to be chatted up.'

'Yes you did. Light?' He cupped a match in his hand, keeping it close, and felt the soft brush of her hair as she leant forward over the table. Moments later, behind a cloud of blue smoke, she started to laugh.

'You know something? You're really nice. I mean it. Most blokes in this city haven't got a clue. They treat you like you're something out of a zoo. Give your cage a rattle. Give you a poke to see if you're still breathing. Bet you're really gentle, aren't you?'

'Yeah.' Suttle nodded. 'I am.'

'I like that in a man, I really do. Not enough of it around.'

'What?'

'Gentle.' She paused while a middle-aged woman in an ankle-length coat swept past en route to the loo.

Suttle caught a gust of air freshener as she pushed at the door, then Trudy was beckoning him closer.

'It's about Dave Pullen,' she muttered. 'I've done something really daft and I'm scared shitless about what's going to happen. There are ten million people I could talk to about it but they're all pretty fucking clueless.'

'So why me?'

'I just told you. You're nice. Plus you've probably got a brain.'

'I'm also a cop.'

'Yeah, but that's not your fault.'

'Thanks.'

'I'm serious. If I wanted a cop I could talk to Uncle Paul. I know he's a twat sometimes but he knows what he's about when it comes to doing the business.'

'Who says?'

'My mum. And she should know.'

Suttle nodded. There were snares here, he knew it, traps of his own baiting. Just looking at this girl, he sensed she was genuine. Not only did she fancy him but she wanted his advice. Was that asking too much? He thought not.

'Tell me about Dave Pullen,' he said quietly. 'Pretend I don't know.'

'Know what?'

'That he was the guy who hurt you the other night.'

'How the fuck did you know that?'

'I listened when we were down at Gunwharf. And I watched you.'

'Listened? Well, there's a first. Not too many girls get listened to in this town.' She frowned at him. 'What made you think it was them Scouse kids, then?'

'Guesswork. You sort out what you know, find a pattern, then try and make everything else fit. Sometimes it works.' He shrugged. 'Sometimes it doesn't.'

'Too right. The Scouse kids were OK.'

'Wrong, my love. The Scouse kids are shit.'

'So what does that make Dave Pullen?'

'He's shit as well. And ugly with it. So what does that make you?'

'You want the truth? It makes me a pathetic little slapper who's completely fucking lost it. You know what I've done about Dave? You really want to find out just how fucking stupid I am?'

'Tell me.'

'There's a guy called Bazza Mackenzie.' She paused. 'Yeah?'

'Yeah.'

'OK. So Bazza and my mum go back years. He's been screwing her since I can remember. He's like family, looked after me and my mum really well. Lately they've been having a bit of a problem but that doesn't make any difference to me. If I need someone to talk to, *really* talk to, then I know he'll always be there for me.'

'So you told him about Dave?'

'I did, yeah.'

'And you're worried what'll happen next?'

'I *know* what'll happen next. Bazza will kill him. And that's if he's lucky.'

'Does that bother you?'

'Of course it does. Dave's got his bad side, just like all of us. If I never see him again there won't be a happier girl in the world, but you can't be with a bloke for a couple of months and not feel something for him. He's a dickhead. He can be really horrible sometimes. But I shouldn't have gone shouting my mouth off the way I did. Because it's going to be my fault, isn't it? When Bazza breaks his legs?'

The loo door opened. Another blast of air freshener. Suttle waited until the woman had gone, then leant forward across the table.

'One thing I don't understand.'

'What's that?'

'Why Dave Pullen in the first place?'

Trudy gave the question some thought. Then she glanced at her watch and crushed the remains of her cigarette in the ashtray.

'Do you really live in Petersfield?'

'Near there, yes.'

'Own place?'

'Rented cottage. Shared with another guy.'

'Cool.' She reached down for her bag. 'I know some great pubs out that way.'

By the time Eadie Sykes got to Guildhall Square, the demo had already begun. She was no judge of crowds but the briefest headcount in the area closest to the Guildhall steps suggested a grand total of maybe a thousand. From his perch halfway up the steps, a thin, intense-looking man in jeans and T-shirt was using a portable megaphone to offer his thoughts on stopping the war. He himself, it seemed, had volunteered to go to Baghdad as a human shield, prepared to hazard his own flesh and blood against the fury of the fascist warlords. Reference to Bush's billion-dollar killing machine sparked yells of approval from the small army of school kids at the front of the crowd, and the human shield volunteer drew a wider round of applause as he ended his speech with a call for solidarity.

Eadie watched as the megaphone passed to a huge, bear-like man with a full beard. He beamed down at the mass of protestors, battling with the rising swell of chants, trying to impose some kind of order on the chaos below. The demo was to form up behind the wall of placards. The route would take them past the railway station and through the Commercial Road shopping precinct. With luck, he said, they'd stop the rush-hour traffic at the other end. The plan was to rally at the gates of HMS *Excellent* on Whale Island, but with so many police around there were no guarantees they'd make it that far.

Eadie knew what he meant. She'd been in touch with the demo organisers earlier, a mobile number handed out by the Stop The War Coalition, and her offer to tape the proceedings had been snapped up.

There were plans to pool video footage from all over the country, to edit maybe a half-hour documentary interweaving the people's protest with news footage from the opening hours of the war itself. That way, the voice at the other end had explained, there might be a chance of shaming the government into pulling back from this madness. Even now, he had said, with British troops pouring into Iraq, there had to be someone left in government with just a shred of conscience.

Eadie herself rather doubted it. For whatever reason, it had become clear that this was Tony Blair's war, the consequence of a deal struck months ago with the neo-cons in Washington. Quite why a centre-left Prime Minister should ally himself with a bunch of ultra-rich fascists was beyond her, but it was already clear that the forces of law and order were preparing themselves for a spot of serious containment. The man with the loudspeaker was right. The milling crowd of demonstrators was already boxed in by a line of yellow-clad policemen and there were rumours of dozens of police vans lying in wait outside the square.

Eadie raised the little Sony and began to hunt for images. A wide shot from the top of the Guildhall steps established the scale of the demo. A brief interview with the man nursing the loudspeaker provoked an eloquent if despairing tirade against New Labour's latest sell-out. Then, down amongst the crowd itself, she concentrated on the shots she knew would make an impact: a child in a *Capitalism Sucks* T-shirt, two gays with a placard reading *Screw Boy George*, a pensioner in a wheelchair trying to coax some sense from his hearing aid.

Surfing these faces, storing them away on tape, gave her an almost physical buzz, a sense of kinship at once intimate and detached. Using her skills this way, she told herself, was as practical a contribution as she could ever hope to make. The next hour or so, as events developed, might yield pictures that would make a real difference. It was, in a way, a grander, more public version of what she was trying to achieve with the drugs project. Attitudes had to be changed. People deserved the truth. It was time for the nation to wake up.

Working her way towards the front of the demo, she felt the column of protesters begin to shuffle forward. At the exit from the square, she ducked out of the crowd and stationed herself beside one of the council buildings, letting the river of faces flow through her viewfinder. Then, spotting a gap, she rejoined the march, picking up the chant, '*Hell no, we won't go! We won't fight for Texaco!*', looking for cutaways that would put the event in its proper context. The police were everywhere. She filmed them in twos, threes, arms crossed, watchful, waiting, tiny earpieces feeding them the bigger picture. Then, quite suddenly, came something new on the tiny fold-out screen. A police cameraman. Taping her.

Nick Hayder's bed was curtained off when Faraday finally made it to Critical Care. He'd driven to the hospital after a detour to take J-J home. The ride to the Bargemaster's House had been tense. J-J was white-faced, utterly beyond reach, and by the time he dropped the boy off Faraday had the feeling that he, rather than his son, was somehow the accused. Trying to break the ice, he asked J-J what he'd really meant to do with the petrol, and the matter-of-factness of his reply had chilled him to the bone.

'I was going to burn their house down,' he signed. 'The guys with the drugs.'

Had he been joking? Was this simply a gesture, a piece of wishful thinking in the face of events which had clearly overwhelmed him? Or was there something more profound brewing inside his deaf son, a violence that he'd never detected before? In truth, Faraday hadn't got a clue. All he knew for sure was that these same events, plus everything else, were beginning to swamp his own little boat.

The manager in charge of the Critical Care unit told him that Mr Hayder had been stabilised. Fully conscious, he was now breathing for himself and there were no indications of post-ventilator chest infection. It would be a while before he began to recover any kind of reliable memory of recent events, and there was a chance that Tuesday night had gone forever, but thankfully there was no sign of lasting neurological damage.

When Faraday enquired about the pelvic injury, the prognosis was less cheerful. Within a day or so, Nick would be transferred to an ortho-paedic ward. An external metal frame would be surgically attached to stabilise the wreckage of his pelvis, and the bones would take at least three months to knit. The process, she said, was extremely painful, and it would be a while before Mr Hayder was on his feet again.

With the care team still busy around Nick's bed, Faraday wandered down the corridor. A windowless, rather depressing room at the end had been specially set aside for relatives, and he slipped inside. Chairs faced each other across a low table. The table was littered with empty plastic cups, and there was a nest of panda bears heaped in a far corner. Faraday studied the bears for a moment or two, his mind quite blank, then turned his attention to one of the Edward Hopper prints on the wall.

'Joe?'

A slim, blonde woman was standing at the open door. It was Maggie, Nick Hayder's partner.

Faraday stepped across and gave her a hug. The last time he'd seen her was at least a month back, and even then the strain of the relationship had been beginning to show. There were worse things in life than getting involved with a serving DI, he thought. But not many.

'How is he?'

'Pretty well, considering. I've been amazed.'

'All that running.'

'You're right. That what the doctors say.'

He gazed at her a moment. She had a round, dimpled face, a lightly freckled complexion, and eyes the colour of cornflowers. He'd once seen her at a CID midsummer ball just weeks after she'd first met Nick, and she'd turned every head in the room.

She mumbled something about a heavy day at school and sank into one of the chairs. Faraday offered to fetch her a coffee from the machine outside but she shook her head.

'You think he's up to reading?' Faraday nodded at the Tesco bag she'd left beside the chair. Amongst the grapes and a bunch of bananas, was a Scott Turow thriller.

'He says he is, but you know Nick. He'd tell me anything if he thought it would make me happy.' She was gazing up at Faraday and something in her face told him she wanted to talk. He closed the door and sat down beside her.

'So how's it been?'

'You want the truth? It's been a bit of a relief. That sounds terrible, doesn't it, but at least I know where he is.'

'Meaning you didn't before?'

'Oh no.' She shook her head. 'I always knew where to find him, that dreadful place he had, and most nights when he had any time he'd come round anyway, but that wasn't the point. He just wasn't *there*. He just wasn't the bloke I thought I knew. Something had gone, Joe. It was like meeting a stranger. Even Euan noticed.'

Euan was Maggie's boy, a studious, bespectacled fourteen-year-old whose flirtation with soft drugs had helped drive a wedge between Nick and his mum.

'How is he?'

'Glad to get his house back. Nick couldn't cope with him.' She offered Faraday a weary smile. 'As you probably know.'

'It must be tough.'

'It was.'

'But for Nick, too.'

'Yeah?'

The question hung in the air between them. For the first time, Faraday realised she was no longer wearing the ring Nick had bought her, a big opal mounted on a simple silver band they'd found in a backstreet jeweller's on Corfu.

Faraday got to his feet and began to clear up the mess on the table. He wanted to enter a plea in Nick's defence, tell her just a little about the kind of pressures the job had brought to bear, somehow convince her that there were reasons for the gap that had opened between them, but another glance at her face told him there'd be no point. In a sense, Maggie was right. If you were after a decent relationship then you'd be better off finding someone who'd know where to draw the line when it came to monsters like *Tumbril*. She wanted someone warm and funny in her life, the old Nick she'd met on a blind date, not the haunted ten-miler who ended every impossible day by chasing his own demons.

The door opened. It was the unit manager Faraday had met earlier. The doctors had finished with Mr Hayder and they were welcome to come down to the ward.

Faraday looked at Maggie. She shook her head.

'You go, Joe. I'm sure he's seen enough of me.'

Hayder spotted Faraday the moment he appeared at the end of the ward. Lacerations down his cheek and jaw had scabbed, giving his smile an awkward, lopsided look. He lifted an arm in salute and tried to struggle upright in bed. Faraday eased him back onto the pillow, then took the proffered hand and gave it a squeeze. For a long moment, Hayder wouldn't let go.

'Geoff Willard, isn't it?' He was frowning in concentration. 'How's life at the top?'

For a moment, Faraday thought the worst. Then he realised Hayder was spoofing.

'Very funny,' he said. 'How are you?'

'How am I?' Hayder gestured vaguely at the cardiac monitors attached to his chest and the loops of plastic tubing dripping fluids into both arms. Damage to his jaw had slowed his speech to a mumble but he was still game for a conversation. 'I'm trussed up like a bloody turkey.' He paused for breath. 'Apart from that, I've never been better. You?'

Faraday was grinning. It said a great deal about a copper's day, he thought, when only a visit to Critical Care could put a smile on your face.

'I'm fine,' he said. 'Maggie's outside.'

'Ask her in. Make it a party.'

'She's being discreet. Thinks we need time alone. She's brought you some grapes, too, which makes me a bit of a sad bugger.'

'No flowers?'

'Afraid not.'

'Thank Christ for that. When I first came round, I thought I'd had it. This place looks like a funeral parlour, all those bouquets.'

The thought provoked a wince. Laughing evidently hurt. Faraday took his hand again.

'You look better than I expected,' he said.

'Bollocks, Joe. I look shit.'

'Do you feel shit? Seriously?'

'Seriously . . . ?' His face screwed up again, another spasm of pain. Nick Hayder had never carried an ounce of spare flesh but now he looked thinner than ever. At length, he managed to catch his breath. 'You know what I do to pass the time in this place?'

'Tell me.'

'I go for runs in my head. They all think I'm having a little doze. This morning I did a six-miler, out to the Hayling ferry.'

Faraday gave his hand another squeeze. He could feel the bones between his fingers.

'Willard sends his best. He wanted to be here but something came up.' He paused. 'Does *Tumbril* mean anything to you?'

'*Tumbril*?'

'Yes.'

'How the fuck . . . ?'

Hayder was staring at him, appalled. For a moment Faraday thought it was another wind-up, then realised that the reaction was genuine. Whatever else had happened to his brain, he was still as paranoid as ever.

'I've taken *Tumbril* over,' Faraday said quietly. 'Thought you might like to know.'

'Really? No kidding?'

'Really. As of yesterday morning.'

'Poor you.' He closed his eyes and winced again. 'It's a bastard.'

Faraday waited for the pain to pass. A nurse was eyeing Hayder from the other side of the ward. At length Hayder signalled Faraday to carry on.

'No way.' Faraday shook his head. 'You need rest, mate. Not all this nonsense.'

'Tell me.' He meant it.

Faraday hesitated, then shrugged.

'OK.' He said, 'I've got a desk on Whale Island and half a million documents to read by the weekend. Listen to Willard and you'd think it's a breeze.'

'Willard's an ally, big time.' The mumble had sunk to a whisper. 'He's protection. Without him, you're fucked.'

Faraday nodded, wondering quite how far to take this conversation. Hayder was struggling again. At last, he settled down.

'You know what the real problem's been?' His voice seemed suddenly stronger. 'Other people.'

'In the job, you mean?'

'Yeah. Compared to our lot, Mackenzie's a doddle. Criminals I can cope with. Coppers I can't.'

'Bent coppers?'

'Coppers with gripes. Coppers not getting enough at home. Coppers who think they should be running the bloody force. Something like *Tumbril* gives them the chance to have a grizzle.' He nodded. 'Big time.'

'So how come I never knew about it?'

'Because you were too busy doing a proper job.' He squeezed his eyes shut a moment. 'Pass me that drinks thing?'

There was a plastic cup with a straw on the bedside cabinet. Faraday held it while Hayder took a sip. Then his head was back on the pillow again, a thin film of sweat across his forehead.

'TCU are really pissed off.' Come what may, Hayder was going to complete this conversation. 'They think we've stolen their baby, and you know what? They're fucking right.'

'TCU? You mean Harry Wayte's lot?'

'Yeah.'

'You want to give me names?'

'I haven't got names. It's a team thing. They're good blokes really but they hate competition.'

'And you think that's –' Faraday hunted for the word '– unhelpful?'

'I think it's a pain in the arse.' He paused for breath, turning his head on the pillow. 'You see that pretty one over there?' His eyes led Faraday to the nurse he'd noticed earlier. She was closer now, dispensing tablets from the nearby drugs trolley. 'She's the one who normally sorts me out. Her name's Julie. She can't wait to put me in bloody nappies. Eh, Jules?'

Faraday watched the nurse return his smile. Already, he was aware that he'd pushed Nick Hayder way too far. Another ten minutes of *Tumbril*, and he'd be back on the critical list.

'Listen, Nick.' He bent down towards the pillow. 'Just one more thing.'

'Go on.'

'What happened to put you in here?'

Hayder gazed up at him.

'Haven't a clue, mate,' he whispered at last.

'You can't remember anything? No incident? No details? No recall at all?'

'Nothing.' A tiny, painful shake of the head. 'I thought you might know.'

Suttle took Trudy Gallagher to a pub in Buriton, a picturesque commuter village tucked beneath the northern folds of the South Downs. Thursday night in early spring, the pub was nearly empty. Suttle and Trudy settled themselves in a corner next to the blazing log fire. A couple of pints and four Bacardi Breezers developed into a meal, and Trudy insisted on buying a bottle of champagne to go with it. By now, to Suttle's delight, she was well pissed.

'We celebrating?' Suttle poured her a second glass. 'Or what?'

'Yeah.' Trudy eyed him over the candle. 'Or at least I am.'

'Why's that, then?'

'You don't want to know . . .' She ducked her head and started to giggle.

'Try me.'

'No way. You'll think I'm completely dumb. Real wuss. Let's talk about you. Winter said you're married.'

'He lies.'

'Have been married?'

'No way. Who'd want a wife at my age?'

'What about your mum and dad?'

Suttle blinked. Trudy was drunker than he'd thought.

'What about them?'

'They still married?'

'Yeah. My dad's dotty about her. Always has been. He's like a kid when she's around. Can't keep his hands to himself.'

'Must be nice. Having parents like that.'

'I never really thought about it.' Suttle speared a chip. 'You?'

'It's just been me and Mum.'

'Always?'

'Since I can remember, yeah.'

'What about your dad?'

'I never knew him. Mum's had loads of blokes but no one who'd own up.'

'To what?'

'Me.' She pulled a face and reached for her glass. 'Here's to us.'

The barmaid collected the empty plates and handed Suttle the menu. Instead of dessert, Trudy settled for a rum and Coke, insisting on another pint for Suttle. Steak and kidney pudding seemed to have soaked up a little of the alcohol, and when Suttle asked about who she was seeing just now she took the question seriously.

'It's been mad.' She put her head on one side and began to twist a curl of hair around her finger. 'Last year or so, I've been like living with this older guy. His name's Mike. I've known him for years, friend of my mum's. My mum and I have never really, you know, got on, and there came a point where I had to move out, just had to. Mike knew about all that. He was round our place all the time. Then he just phoned up one day and said come and live with me.'

'Just like that?'

'Yeah. I didn't know what to say, not at first. He was married once, years ago, but he's been divorced for ages and he's got a really nice place up in Waterlooville – jacuzzi, double garage, big garden, the lot. So . . .' She shrugged. 'I said yes.'

Suttle had heard this story from Winter, not in such detail but enough to suggest that Mike Valentine wasn't just lucky in the motor trade.

'You moved in with him? Like . . . properly?'

'You mean did I shag him?' She shook her head. 'No.'

'Did that upset him?'

'Not at all. In fact, the one who was upset was me. After a time I really got to like him. More than that, actually. I fancied the pants off him. He had real style, know what I mean? And he was funny, too. Not only that but he was really kind. Looked after me. I liked that.'

'Did you –' Suttle shrugged '– make any moves?'

'Loads. I was so uncool about it. He could have helped himself any time, night or day. I was the only girl in Waterlooville sunbathing naked in April. Anything. Anything to turn him on.'

'But it didn't happen?'

'Not once. Then I decided he was gay because it made me feel better, only that wasn't true either because it turned out he was shagging my mum.'

'When did that happen?'

'Fuck knows. I only found out a couple of months ago. I called round home to pick up a CD and they were at it in the bedroom. I couldn't believe it, just couldn't believe it. That's why I went crying my eyes out to Dave Pullen. The older man again, see? Thought he might be able to help, give me advice. Fat fucking chance.'

Suttle nodded, remembering Trudy with Winter in the Gumbo Parlour at Gunwharf. No wonder she'd been so lippy about her mother.

'So where are you living now?'

'Back home.'

'With your *mum*? After all that?'

'Yeah.'

'How come?'

'Can't say.' Her face had suddenly brightened again. 'Except that it's fine now.'

'Just like that?'

'Yeah.' She snapped her fingers. 'Just like that. You get yourself in a state, get really worked up, then you realise you'd got it all completely wrong. Me? Total wuss.'

The drinks arrived. Trudy diluted the rum with a splash of Coke and held the glass under her nose. Then she looked up.

'You know how people talk about life? How it can be so funny sometimes? Only I'm just learning.' She tipped the glass to her lips and took a tiny sip. 'Something else, too.'

'What's that?'

'You're really, really nice.' She paused, then looked at her watch. 'Amount you've drunk, there's no way you're driving me home.'

'You want a cab?'

'No.' She reached for his hand across the table. 'I want you. Where's this place of yours?'

'Across the green. Last cottage on the left.'

'And your mate?'

'In London all week. Training course.'

'Cool.' She leaned forward and kissed him on the lips. 'Think you can manage to fuck me?'

By eight o'clock, the demo was beginning to break up. The column of protesters had surged through the shopping precinct in Commercial Road, picking up support en route and finally emerging at the roundabout that funnelled rush-hour traffic onto the motorway. Keen to keep the demonstration on the move, the police had stopped three lanes of cars, hurrying the column on towards Whale Island. To the delight of the veterans at the head of the march, the forest of placards had stirred the odd toot of support from waiting drivers, but Eadie – hunting for pictures amongst the blank-faced commuters – was only too aware that the bulk of these people simply wanted to get home. Portsmouth, after all, was a naval city – martial by instinct – and once the fighting had started, a protest like this smacked of treason. Our boys and girls were in harm's way. Now was the time to get behind them.

Whale Island was a mile north, beyond the continental Ferry Port. The protesters swung along, bellowing slogans, punching the air. George Bush was a madman. Blair was a poodle. The Americans had blood on their hands. By now, Eadie knew she'd done the event justice. She had maybe half an hour of recorded material, more if you included the handful of snatched interviews, but the moment the column rounded the final bend before the causeway that fed naval traffic onto Whale Island, her heart leapt. A line of helmeted police blocked the path forward. Behind them, half a dozen waiting Transit vans, mesh over the windows, heavy metal visors to protect the windscreens. Overhead, the steady drone of the police spotter plane, wing dipped, flying a wide circle as the demonstration came to a halt.

Eadie hurried along the flank of the column, incurring the wrath of a uniformed sergeant who warned her to stay in line. At the front, police and protesters eyed each other over ten metres of tyre-blackened asphalt. The man with the beard was locked in negotiation with the senior officer in charge. Eadie did her best to get close enough to pick up the dialogue but another officer waved her away. Behind her, the chanting was beginning to flag. Finally, the man with the beard turned to the press of bodies and switched on the loudspeaker. There were to be a couple of brief speeches. Then, in what he called a display of solidarity for the Iraqi people, they'd return to the Guildhall Square.

There were murmurs from the crowd. One student yelled an obscenity. Eadie caught a smirk on the face of a watching PC. Elsewhere in the world a situation like this would be seconds away from kicking off. Instead, as the first of the speeches got under way, Eadie knew it was all over. There'd be more rants against the evils of American imperialism, more calls for Blair's head, but in essence the demonstration – this column of good intentions – had hit the buffers. The police, in the shape of a couple of hundred men, had flung down the gauntlet, knowing full well that they'd won.

Won? Half an hour later, as the police chivvied the last of the stragglers back towards the city centre, Eadie fumbled for her mobile. A couple of hundred metres away, she could still see the security barrier and gatehouse that barred the entry to Whale Island and HMS *Excellent*. Bathed in a pool of orange light, it seemed to symbolise everything that the Brits – in their very orderliness – refused to confront.

She paused for a moment, ignoring the attentions of a police Alsatian. When she dialled Faraday's mobile, she got no further than the answering service. When she tried again, knowing he'd check the caller's number, she heard the same recorded voice. Finally, knowing she had to get the last couple of hours off her chest, she sent a text to J-J: *Plse tel yr dad to call me. Luv. E. XXX* She waited a moment, wondering if they were both at home. Then, when nothing happened, she took a final look at the gatehouse. On the evening breeze, very faint, came the sound of laughter.

Paul Winter was half an hour into his DVD of *The Dambusters* when his mobile began to ring. The lone figure of Barnes Wallis was wandering away over the Reculver mudflats, trying to work out why his bomb wouldn't bounce properly. Winter propped the tumbler of Laphroaig on his lap and reached for his mobile.

'Paul Winter.'

A voice he didn't immediately recognise asked him what he was doing. It was a light voice, Pompey accent. Winter studied the caller number. No clues there.

'Who is this?'

'Bazza Mackenzie. Just wondered whether you fancied a chat.'

'Now?'

'Whenever. Tonight would be good for me. You know Craneswater at all? Sandown Road. Green floodlights. Number thirteen. Can't miss it.' The line went dead and Winter was left staring at the television. Barnes Wallis was back at his drawing board, designing a bigger bomb.

Chapter thirteen

Winter took a taxi to Southsea. The driver dropped him halfway down Sandown Road, scribbling a phone number for the return fare. Across the street, a substantial two-storey house was bathed in a lurid shade of green, an effect which gave the place a strangely unearthly look, as if it had just touched down from another planet. If you wanted to announce your arrival in this quietly prosperous enclave, thought Winter, then this was definitely the way to do it.

The driver shot Winter a look and then handed him the receipt.

'You should come by here on Mondays,' he said. 'Pink's even worse.'

Winter watched the taxi disappear down the street. The house was protected by a sturdy brick wall, well over head height, with a timber trellis on top. Sliding steel gates barred a drive-in entrance, and there was another access door further down the street. The door, which was locked, looked new.

Winter fingered the button on the entryphone, buzzed twice.

'Who is it?' A woman's voice.

'Paul Winter.'

'Wait a moment.'

There was a longish silence. Through the entryphone, from somewhere in the depths of the house, a dog began to bark.

'He says to come in.'

The door opened automatically, swinging inwards with a soft, electronic whine. For a moment Winter was tempted to applaud, then he spotted the CCTV camera, mounted on a pole beside the brick path that led towards the house. The floodlights with their green gels were set in tiny traps, recessed into the surrounding lawn, and Winter began to feel slightly nauseous. At first he put it down to the third glass of Laphroaig but a glance at the backs of his hands – flesh the colour of putty – told him otherwise. A couple of minutes out here, and you'd think you'd strayed into the fun fair. The Chamber of Horrors, maybe. Or the Ghost Train.

The camera tracked Winter as he headed down the path. The front door opened, and Winter found himself face to face with Mackenzie's wife.

'How was Chichester?' he said pleasantly. 'Buy anything nice?'

Marie stepped aside to let him in, saying nothing. She was wearing a dressing gown belted at the waist. Barefoot, she smelled of the shower.

The interior of the house had been recently gutted, walls torn down to create an enormous open space. A glass conservatory had been added, deepening the living area, and the linen blinds glowed aquarium-green against the wash of the lights outside. A crescent of leather sofa faced a widescreen TV. The TV was tuned to a news channel, shots of heavy armour churning through the desert. A plate of salad on the low table beside the sofa had barely been touched.

'He's in the den. Said to go through. Second on the left.'

Marie nodded at a door in the far corner of the room. The door was heavy, new again, and swung closed the moment Winter stepped through. A carpeted hall was flanked with more doors. After the yawning emptiness of the living area, it felt suddenly intimate. Decent watercolours – harbour scenes – on the walls. A golf putter and half a dozen yellow balls littering the long run of carpet.

'In here.' The summons came from an open door on the left. Winter stepped into a softly-lit room dominated by a big, antique desk. Tiny television monitors were racked on the wall beside the desk and Winter recognised the path to the front gate on one of them.

'Expecting company, Baz?'

Mackenzie ignored the dig. He'd bought the latest motion-sensitive software. Anything that moved in the garden, he'd be the first to know. At two grand off the internet, he regarded this latest toy as a steal.

'You should be here when we get a bit of wind in the trees.' He nodded at the monitor screens. 'Whole lot goes bonkers.'

Winter unbuttoned his coat and sank into one of the two armchairs. The last time he'd seen Bazza Mackenzie was a couple of years back at a CID boxing do on South Parade pier. They'd shared a bottle of champagne while two young prospects from Leigh Park belted each other senseless.

'Lost a bit of weight, Baz. Working out?'

'Stress, mate, and too many bloody salads. Marie started going to a health farm last year. Worst three grand I ever spent. You know why we moved here?'

'Tell me.'

'It's at least a mile to the nearest decent chippy. She measured it in the Merc then phoned me up and told me to put the deposit down. You'd think it would be views, wouldn't you? And the beach? And all these posh neighbours? Forget it. We live in a chip-free zone. Welcome to paradise.'

Winter laughed. Unlike many other detectives, he'd always had a sneaking regard for Bazza Mackenzie. The man had a lightness of touch, a wit, an alertness, that went some way to explaining his astonishing commercial success. You could see it in his face, in his eyes. He watched you, watched everything, ready with a quip or an offer or a put-down, restless, voracious, easily bored.

In the wrong mood, as dozens could testify, Bazza Mackenzie could be genuinely terrifying. Nothing daunted him, least of all the prospect of physical injury, and Winter had seen the photographic evidence of the damage he could do to men twice his size. But catch him in the right mood and you couldn't have a nicer conversation. Bazza, as Winter had recently told Suttle, had a heart the size of a planet. Whatever he did, for whatever reason, he was in there one thousand per cent, total commitment.

'What's this, then? New chums?'

Winter was inspecting a gaudy mess of colour snaps pinned to a cork wallboard, one image overlapping with the next, briefly-caught moments in the cheerful chaos of Mackenzie's social life. One of the latest photos featured four middle-aged men posing on a putting green. They all looked pleased with themselves but it was Mackenzie who was holding the flag.

'Austen Bridger, isn't it?' Winter was peering at a bulky, scarlet-faced figure in slacks and a Pringle sweater.

'That's right. Plays off seven. Unbeatable on his day. Look at this, though. Here . . .' Mackenzie dug around in a drawer, then produced a scorecard and insisted Winter take a look. 'Three birdies and an eagle. Cost him dinner at Mon Plaisir, that did. Foie gras, turbot, Chablis, the lot. Marie gave me serious grief for weeks after.'

He retrieved the scorecard and gazed at it while Winter's eyes returned to the cork board. Austen Bridger was a solicitor with a booming out-of-town practice in a new suite of offices in Port Solent. He specialised in property and development deals, high-end stuff, and had the executive toys to prove it. Away from the golf course, he sailed a £350,000 racing yacht which regularly featured in the columns of the News. Another winner.

Mackenzie was on his feet now, ash-grey track-suit and newish-looking Reeboks. He began to poke through the photos on the cork board, hunting for a particular shot.

'Here.' He unpinned it. 'Dubai at Christmas. Can't do too much for you out there. Marie loved it. See that ramp thing in the background?'

Winter was looking at a beach shot. Mackenzie and his wife were posed against the brilliant blue of the sea. Marie was an inch or two taller than her husband and for a middle-aged woman, bikini-clad, she was in remarkable nick.

'What ramp thing?'

'There. Look.' Mackenzie tapped the photograph. 'It's for water skiing. Day one you get to stand up. Day two you go tearing off round the bay. Day three they tell you about jumping and ramps and stuff, and day four you get to cack yourself. Amazing experience. You ever done it?'

'Never.'

'Brilliant. Some blokes do it backwards. *Backwards*, can you believe that? Can't wait, mate. Still on the Scotch, are you?'

Without waiting for an answer, he went across to a filing cabinet and produced a bottle of Glenfiddich from the top drawer. A glass came from a table in the corner. It was down to Winter to pour.

'You?' Winter was looking at the single glass.

'Not for me.'

'Why not?'

'Given up.'

'You're serious?'

'Yeah, just for now. I'm nosey, if you want the truth. I've spent so much time pissed, all this is a bit of a novelty.' He waved a hand around, a gesture that seemed to have no geographical limit, then he settled back behind the desk, a man with important news to impart. 'You know something about this city, something really weird? It's about the way you look at it. As a nipper, you just do your thing, head down, get on with it. A little bit older, you follow your dick. A bit older still, you maybe get married, all that stuff. But you know your place, right? Because everything's bigger than you are. Then, if you're lucky, you wake up one morning and there it is, there for the taking.'

'What?'

'The city. Pompey. And you know why? Because this place is tiny. Get to know maybe a coupla dozen guys, the *right* coupla dozen, and there's nothing you can't do. Nothing. We're not talking bent, we're just talking deals, one bloke to another. And you know something else? It's easy. Easier than you can ever believe. Suss how it's done, make the right friends, and you start wondering why every other bastard isn't doing it too.'

'So what does that make you?'

'Lucky.' He reached for a paper clip and began to unbend it as he elaborated on this new world of limitless opportunities. How one deal led to another. How business could breed some genuine friendships. How wrong he'd been about some of the middle-class blokes he'd always had down as wankers. Fact was, a lot of them were hard bastards, knew how to live with risk, knew how to party. Collars and ties, in the end, were nothing but camouflage.

'Know what I mean?'

Winter nodded, his eyes returning to the cork board. Then he took a long swallow of Glenfiddich, the drift of this sudden outburst of Mackenzie's slowly slipping into focus. The city, he was saying, had become his plaything, the train set of his dreams. He could alter the layout, mess with the signalling, change the points, play God.

A smile warmed Winter's face. Bazza Mackenzie, he thought. The Bent Controller.

Mackenzie was on his feet again, restless. He'd found another photo, framed this time: a young bride on her wedding day, beaming out at the world.

'You hear about my Esme? Pregnant. As of last week. That makes me a grandfather. Sweet, eh?'

'Must be. I wouldn't know.'

'Shit, I forgot.' He paused, looking down at Winter, then patted him on the shoulder the way you might comfort a sick dog. 'Sorry about your missus, mate. A while back, wasn't it?'

'Two years ago next September.' Winter gazed at his glass for a moment, wondering how Bazza had got to know about Joannie. Then his head came up again. 'You must be proud of her.'

'Who?'

'Esme. Not just the baby, everything else.'

'Yeah, definitely. The girl's done well. Most of that's down to Marie if you want the truth, but that doesn't stop me being silly about her, does it? She called up tonight, matter of fact. She'll be through with uni this year and she's looking for chambers to take her on. Turns out some shit-hot briefs in town have offered her a pupillage if her degree turns out OK. Couldn't wait to tell us.'

'And the baby?'

'Fuck knows. I'm putting it down for Winchester the moment it appears.'

'The nick?'

'The school.' Mackenzie barked with laughter. 'Marie's idea. Put a bit of class back in the family. Women these days, do it all, don't they?'

Winter was thinking about Misty Gallagher. Her role in Mackenzie's life was common knowledge amongst a certain slice of Portsmouth life. So where did she figure on the cork board?

Mackenzie dismissed the question with a shrug.

'Silly girl, Mist. Can't take a joke. Shame, really.' He looked morose for a moment, then visibly brightened. 'Don't want a nice harbourside apartment, do you? Yours for seven hundred grand.'

'You've put it on the market?' Winter feigned amazement.

'Yeah. Wait a week, and you'll be looking at seven fifty. View like that, they'll be queuing for it.'

'And Trudy?'

'Trude'll be OK. She's a survivor, that girl. Has to be, living with Mist.'

'I thought she was tucked up with Mike Valentine?'

'No way. Mike's got a bob or two, saw her right, but he's old, isn't he? Trude's a kid. Doesn't want some wrinkly like Mike.'

'Or us.'

'Yeah.'

'Or Dave Pullen.'

Mackenzie didn't answer. The temperature in the room seemed to plunge. After all the joshing, all the catching-up, Winter had bent to Mackenzie's train set and thrown the points.

Mackenzie was staring at Winter. In certain moods, he had the blackest eyes.

'Is that what this is about, then? Mr Dave fucking Pullen?'

'Partly, yes.'

'Well don't worry about that arse-wipe. He's taken care of.'

'Since when?' Winter was genuinely surprised.

'Since –' Mackenzie glanced at his Rolex '– about an hour ago. What else do you want to know?'

Winter was eyeing the bottle. Glenfiddich wasn't quite his favourite malt but under circumstances like these it would certainly do. He splashed a generous measure into his glass and swirled it round. With people like Mackenzie, it sometimes paid to keep them waiting.

'My bosses have got this thing about law and disorder,' he said at last. 'Keeping it private, keeping it out of sight, is one thing. What Chris Talbot did at the railway station was something else.'

'Like what?

'Like stupid. And like unnecessary.'

'Says you.'

'Says my bosses. And they've got a point, too. If you can't run a business without pulling those kinds of strokes, then maybe you ought to let someone else have a go.'

Mackenzie hated criticism. With the sole exception of his wife, people never talked to him like this. He'd visibly stiffened behind the desk. All the chumminess, all the little flurries of wit, had gone. Winter, aware that this conversation had to deliver some kind of truce, tried to coax a smile.

'Think of me as the poor fucker in no-man's-land,' he began. 'I'm waiving the book of rules. I'm here to tell you to cool it. Call off the dogs, ignore the Scousers, and it'll be business as usual.'

'Rules bollocks.' Mackenzie was angry now. 'If your bosses are so fucking keen on business as usual, then how come they're trying to put me away? Talking to the bank? To my accountant? Sticking blokes across the road in clapped-out Fiestas?' He paused for long enough to let Winter raise an eyebrow. 'You think I don't know about all that shit? Operation *Tumbril?* Three men and a dog banged up on Whale Island? You go back and tell them they haven't got a prayer. Not a fucking prayer. And you know why? Because I can afford the kind of advice they'd only ever dream about. And you know something else?' He jabbed a finger at the photos on the cork board. 'That advice is kosher, legit, paid-for. Problem with you blokes is you're either skint or looking the wrong way when the big deals go down.' He was on the edge of his chair now, leaning forward across the desk. 'A little word in your ear, my friend. Watch the press.'

'The local press?'

'Absolutely. Give it a couple of days and we might be able to put this conversation in perspective. Big announcement. Major acquisition. Hundreds of grand.' He nodded, belligerent, proud of himself. 'You know what really pisses me off about you lot? A bloke comes along and works his arse off for this city, pours in millions, one-man fucking regeneration agency for that poxy Osborne Road, and what does he get for his troubles? Operation fucking *Tumbril.* How's that for gratitude, then? No wonder this city's halfway down the khazi.'

Winter tried to hide his smile. Not only did Mackenzie believe all this stuff but most of it was probably true. Add a recently purchased kitchen equipment shop to his cafe-bars and tanning salons, and this man was transforming Osborne Road. Drugs money or otherwise, the heart of Southsea would be shabbier without the likes of Bazza Mackenzie.

'Just think about it,' Winter said quietly. 'That's all we're saying.'

'What's this "we", then? They ask you to come here?'

'They?'

'Those fucking bosses of yours.'

'Of course they didn't. It's called initiative. Went out the window years ago.'

'And if they knew you were here?'

'Major bollocking. Either that, or another form to fill in. Listen, Baz, I'm just telling you, marking your card. Chasing Scouse kids round the city just isn't worth the hassle. Some people hate the sight of blood. You'd be amazed.'

'That's not the point. What else am I supposed to do? Dial treble nine? Come running to you lot? My line of work, it's just that.'

'Just what?'

'Business. Blokes try and muscle in, we give them a hiding. Same with Pullen. Twat like him messes with Trude, he knows exactly what to expect. That's the thing about us.' The laugh again, abrupt, challenging. 'We're dead straight. What you see is what you get.'

Mackenzie nodded towards the door. The gesture was Winter's cue to leave. Back on his feet, he drained the last of the malt and buttoned his coat. Mackenzie came round the desk. Close to, Winter suspected he'd begun to use blond tint on his hair.

'Another thing about young Trude.' Mackenzie wasn't smiling.

'Yeah?'

'Don't even think about it, OK?'

'Me?'

'Any of you guys.'

Winter nodded, giving the threat due respect, then paused beside the door.

'One thing I need to know, Baz.' He nodded at the curtained window.

'What's that?'

'Why green gels?'

'Ah . . .' Mackenzie touched him lightly on the shoulder. 'Colour of envy, mate.'

Trudy lay on her side, her head supported on her elbow, her hair tumbling over Suttle's face.

'Going to sleep on me?'

'Yeah.'

'You were brilliant. You're allowed.'

'Thanks.'

'I mean it.' She wetted her forefinger and traced a love heart across his naked chest. 'What about me, then. OK, was I?'

'I've had worse.'

'Bastard.' She leaned over him and retrieved a copy of *FHM* from the carpet beside the bed. 'What's this, then?'

Suttle opened one eye and found himself looking at a familiar photospread of Jennifer Lopez.

'Forget it,' he mumbled. 'You'd fuck her out of sight.'

'You mean that?'

'Definitely. Except she's the one with the money.' He snatched at the magazine, then tossed it across the tiny bedroom. 'There's half a bottle of white in the fridge, if you fancy it.'

'You get it.'

'You're closest.'

There was a stir of cold air as she pulled back the covers. Suttle heard the soft pad of her footsteps on the stairs and the distinctive click as she opened the fridge door. Seconds later, she was back in beside him. The way her flesh goosepimpled reminded him of the night they'd found her trussed to the bed in Bystock Road.

'You first.' She'd only found one glass.

'No, you.'

He watched her sipping the wine and realised he hadn't been so happy for months. It can't be this simple, he kept telling himself. This easy.

She offered him the glass. When he reached out for it, she shook her head and dipped a finger before slipping it into his mouth. He sucked it for a moment, then asked for more. She smiled at him in the half darkness and Suttle caught the chink of glass as she lodged the glass beside the bottle on the cluttered bedside table.

'I meant more wine.'

'I know you did.'

'You're outrageous.'

'Yeah?' She was straddling him now, her breath warm on his face. 'Tell me something.'

'What?'

'Just say I had lots of money. Pots of it.'

'And?'

'Would you come away with me? Seriously, would you?'

'Come away where?'

'Dunno.' She nuzzled his cheek for a moment and then began to lick his ear. 'Wherever you like, really. Abroad? America? Thailand? Oz? Don't care.'

'You mean for a holiday?'

'Whatever.'

'Not a holiday?'

'Doesn't matter. Just you and me.'

Suttle gazed up at her for a moment and then tried to struggle free, but Trudy was stronger than she looked.

'I've got you.' She began to giggle. 'And you still haven't answered the question.'

Faraday was on the way to Eadie Sykes's apartment when his mobile began to chirp. It was Willard. Faraday pulled the Mondeo into a parking space on the seafront and killed the engine.

'You called,' Willard grunted. 'If it's about that boy of yours, forget it.'

'Forget what, sir?'

'Whatever you were going to tell me. As I understood it, no charges have been laid. Police bail pending further inquiries. Am I right?'

'Yes, but the point is—'

'Wrong, Joe. There is no point. Nothing has changed unless you're telling me you want out, and even then you'd have to have a bloody good excuse.' He paused. 'As I understand it, there's fuck-all evidence against the boy, not when it comes to a serious charge. Anything else?'

Faraday stared into the darkness beyond the promenade. A late car ferry was heading out towards the Isle of Wight, leaving a long, white tail of churning water. Just how could he voice the thousand and one questions J-J had left in his own wake? About gullibility? About other people taking advantage? And – most important of all – about the sudden gap that had opened up between father and son? None of these issues was of the remotest relevance to *Tumbril*, and Willard doubtless knew it.

'Nothing else, sir.'

'Good. Heard from Wallace yet?'

'No. I left a message.'

'Bell me when he rings. Doesn't matter how late.'

'Of course.'

Minutes later, he let himself into Eadie's apartment building. Up on the third floor, the door to her flat was open, and Faraday caught the breathless tones of the BBC newscaster while he was still on the stairs. Coalition forces were attacking the Iraqi port of Umm Qasr. Preliminary reports from the advancing columns of armour suggested that the city's defenders were on the point of surrender. Tony Blair, meanwhile, had returned from an EU summit to stiffen the nation's resolve.

Faraday walked into the flat. Eadie was stretched on the sofa, engrossed in the news report, the remains of a takeout curry on a tray on her lap. After a while, Faraday moved into her eyeline.

'Hi.' She barely looked up.

'Hi.' Faraday stared down at her. He'd rarely felt angrier. 'Are we going to talk or shall I come back later?'

'Give me a minute, OK?' She nodded at the screen. 'Then you can get it all off your chest.'

'No.' Faraday shook his head and reached for the zapper. When he couldn't find the mute button, he turned the whole set off. Eadie was about to react, then had second thoughts. There were a couple of tinnies in the fridge. Maybe, for the sake of his blood pressure, a cold Stella might be wise.

Faraday ignored the suggestion.

'You knew,' he said thickly. 'You knew this morning and you didn't tell me.'

'Knew what?'

'That the kid was dead.'

'Ah . . . young Daniel.' She nodded. 'My apologies. Mea fucking culpa.'

'So is that it?' Faraday couldn't believe his ears. 'You step into this kid's life, drag my son with you, tape the lad while he kills himself, and leave him to die? Endgame? Finito? Too bad?'

'You're being dramatic.'

'*Dramatic?* The boy's dead, Eadie. That's big time. We cops sometimes call it murder. In fact, this afternoon they very nearly did.'

'They?'

'Yes, they. Thanks to you, I've just spent a couple of hours trying to keep my son out of the remand wing at Winchester prison. That might mean nothing to you but I'm telling you now it made a very big hole in my day.'

'I know.'

'You *know?* How do you know?'

'J-J told me. There's not a lot you can get into a text but I caught the drift.'

'What did he say?'

'He said you tried to shut him up. You and a lawyer.'

'He's right. We did.'

'And he said he thought that was bullshit. So he went right ahead and told them the way it had been.'

'That's right, too. Completely reckless.'

'Really?' She raised an eyebrow. 'So how come he's still a free man?'

'Christ knows. I've left guys in the cells for thirty-six hours on less evidence. That could have been J-J. Easily. Thanks to you.'

There was a long silence. A lone car whined past outside. Finally, Eadie put her tray to one side.

'I thought this was about Daniel Kelly?' she muttered. 'Or is he division two compared to J-J?'

'That's cheap.'

'Sure, and you're being irrational. Listen Joe, you're right. The kid's dead. It happened to happen last night. Equally, it could have happened last week, or last month, or tomorrow, or fuck knows when. All I know is the thing was inevitable. He was a funeral on legs. I hate to say it but we're not talking big surprise here.'

'And that makes it OK? When you've supplied the gear?'

'I didn't supply the gear.'

187

'No, but J-J did, or helped to, at least. And you know why? Because otherwise you wouldn't have got your precious bloody interview. That's called pressure. And in the end the pressure came from you.'

'OK.' Eadie conceded the point with a nod. 'So I believe in what I do. Does that put me in the wrong? When the kid would have scored in any case?'

'You don't know that.'

'You don't? You think I'm making all this stuff up? You want to see the way he looked? The state of him? Be my guest. We'll run the rushes again. Evidence, Joe. Pictures you can't fucking dispute. If J-J hadn't run the errand for him, he'd have found someone else. It's called money, my love, and it'll buy you anything.'

'Don't patronise me.'

'I'm not. I'm pointing out the facts of life. You don't believe me? OK, so here's something else for that poor aching head of yours. What tells me we've taken the right decision, done the right thing, are those.'

'What?'

'Those.' She was pointing at the pile of video cassettes beside the TV. 'I've told you. Poor bloody Daniel Kelly was a basket case. He'd lost it. He didn't care any more. But the way things turned out we might at least be able to rescue something from the wreckage, offer some kind of hope for the future. Not Daniel's but maybe other kids', lots of other kids'. When you've calmed down you're going to ask me whether I regret what happened last night but I'm telling you now the answer is no.' She looked up at him, weary now. 'Can't you see that?'

'No, I can't. But that's not the point.'

'It isn't?'

'No. The point is that you didn't tell me.'

'You're right.' She nodded. 'I didn't. I knew, and you were in the flat when I took the call, and I didn't pass the message on.'

'Exactly.' He took a deep breath. 'So explain to me why.'

'You're sounding like a cop.'

'That's because I am a cop. It's what I do. But that makes it complicated, doesn't it? Because I'm also a father. And I'm also . . .' he began to founder, gesturing at the space between them '. . . part of whatever this is.'

'Really?'

'Yeah, really.'

'So what is this?'

'Oh, for fuck's sake—'

'No, seriously, if it all boils down to this morning, then we ought to get down to basics, strip the thing off a little. OK, I should have told you. For a thousand reasons, I owed you that news. But, hey, hands up,

I didn't pass it on. And why didn't I pass it on? Because I knew that it would lead to this. Not tonight but this morning. And to tell you the truth, the absolute truth, I had more important things to sort out.'

'Like what?'

'You don't want to know.'

'Try me.'

'There's no point.'

'No *point*? See? You're doing it again.'

'Doing what?'

'Keeping it all to yourself. Keeping me at arm's length. We're supposed to be having a relationship here. I know it's old fashioned but that involves just a little bit of trust. I've been here before, my love. If you won't tell me about Daniel Kelly, and about whatever else, then I just might start thinking.'

'You do that.'

'Yeah . . . ?' Faraday gazed down at her for a long moment, then turned away. The view from the window, for once, made absolutely no sense at all. Random lights. Lots of darkness. Then he sensed a movement behind him, felt a hand on his shoulder.

'Listen, Joe . . .' For once in her life, Eadie sounded unsure of herself.

'Listen what?'

'Haven't we had good times?'

'Of course we have.'

'And isn't that important?'

'Yes.' Faraday nodded. 'But good times are the easy bit. I'm just asking you to be honest with me.'

'I'm sorry. I apologise.'

Eadie slipped between him and the view, suddenly contrite. For a moment Faraday wasn't at all sure if this wasn't tactical, another puzzling little bend in their road, but when she nodded back towards the sofa he allowed himself to sit down. Some of the anger had boiled away and he was grateful when she returned with a Stella from the fridge.

'Drink this.' She pulled the tag on the can. 'Then I'll tell you.'

'Tell me what?'

'About tomorrow.'

'More glad tidings?' He shot her the beginnings of a smile.

'Afraid so. Two big gulps now. Attaboy.'

She waited until he'd poured the lager and taken a long pull. Then she told him about the post-mortem she'd arranged to tape. Kelly's father had faxed his permission and the coroner was onside. There was no guarantee she'd ever use the footage but it wasn't the kind of sequence you could ever reconstruct.

Faraday absorbed the news. A lifetime of post-mortems had left him more or less indifferent to dead flesh. The sight of Daniel Kelly weaving his way to his grave had been far, far worse.

Eadie was eyeing him with obvious caution.

'You don't want to shout at me?'

'No.'

'Thank God for Stella.' She leaned across and kissed him. 'You want the remains of the curry? Only J-J's left most of his.'

'J-J?'

'Yes.'

'He's been here?'

'He's in the spare bedroom. Asleep.'

'You're serious?'

Eadie thought about the question for a moment or two, then frowned.

'Tall bloke? Skinny? Bit quiet?'

She got to her feet and returned to the kitchen, leaving Faraday to absorb this latest revelation. He heard the pop of the gas as she fired up the oven, ready to warm the curry. Moments later, she was back with three poppadoms and a bowl of onion chutney. She gave a poppadom to Faraday, and then took his hand.

'J-J was adamant. No way was he sleeping at home.' She glanced briefly towards the bedroom. 'You two guys have some talking to do.'

Chapter fourteen

Faraday was still asleep when the call came in. He'd left his mobile next door, lodged in a corner of the sofa, and it was Eadie who shook him gently awake.

'Yours.' She blew in his ear. 'Might be important.'

Naked, Faraday made his way into the lounge. A pale grey light washed through the big picture windows and he could see a lid of cloud clamped over the Isle of Wight. Dimly, he remembered that his son was asleep in the spare bedroom. Unless, of course, something else had happened.

'DI Faraday.' He didn't recognise the number. 'Major Crimes.'

'It's Graham Wallace.'

'Yeah?' Faraday rubbed his eyes. 'Something come up?'

Wallace began to describe a call he'd just taken from someone he described as 'our mate'. He wanted a meet within the next couple of days. Wallace had promised to get back to him as soon as he'd checked his diary and now needed some advice. Faraday was still wrestling with the implications of this sudden development when he looked up to find Eadie standing beside the sofa. She was wearing an unfastened cotton wrap and wanted to know whether it was too early for tea. Faraday said yes to the tea and took the mobile back to the bedroom.

By the time Eadie joined him, the conversation was over and Faraday was sitting on the edge of the bed, deep in thought. Eadie looked down at him, the tray in her hands.

'Something you're going to share with me?' she enquired drily.

Paul Winter had been up since dawn. Nights when he couldn't sleep – and there were more and more of them – he'd taken to prowling round the bungalow, chasing his insomnia from room to room, often pausing in the tidy little lounge to reach for one of Joannie's well-thumbed paperbacks, giving the first page or two the chance to ease him back to sleep. On occasions, to his surprise, it worked. Half a chapter of Jeffrey

Archer had the coshing power of Nembutal. But lately even the bludgeon of Archer's prose had left him alert and fretful, turning on the radio, pulling back the curtains, scouring the late winter baldness of the back garden for signs of what the coming day might bring.

The postman arrived earlier than usual, a cascade of junk mail through the letter box. Nursing his second mug of tea, Winter stooped to the mat. He wasn't sure what demographic these people used when they drew up their hit lists of likely punters but lately he'd become slightly depressed by the flood of geriatric appeals. Help the Aged. Saga Insurance. Motability. Forty-five, Winter told himself, was the prime of a man's life, but the sight of yet another warning about prostate cancer had begun to make him wonder. How come these envelope-stuffers knew he was feeling so washed-up?

The biggest of this morning's missives was a novelty: Guide Dogs for the Blind. He returned to the kitchen, meaning to bin the lot, then had second thoughts. The last couple of months, he'd thought seriously about getting himself a dog. The couple next door had one. There was a pretty redhead with the tightest jeans imaginable who walked a greyhound on the top of Portsdown Hill. Saturdays at Asda, shoppers on foot lashed their poodles to a special bar beside the trolley park. He'd watched these people and their pets, idly puzzling about what a dog brought to their lives, and he'd concluded that the right choice of animal – nothing mad – could offer the perfect antidote to his increasing sense of solitariness. At three in the morning, it might be nice to have something to talk to.

Winter perched himself on the kitchen stool and shook out the contents of the envelope. A folksy collection of black and white photographs caught his eye, domestic snaps featuring Labradors and their unsighted owners. A mere £5 a week, according to the copy beneath, could make all the difference when it came to training another of these miracle wowsers. Was that too high a price when someone's life might be transformed?

Winter returned to the biggest of the photos, a shot of an eager-looking Labrador threading a portly gent in a long raincoat through a busy shopping centre. Without the dog, this man would be banged up at home, dependent on the Tesco phone delivery service. Thanks to Rover, and trillions of caring donors, he could toddle off to the shops any time he liked.

Winter nodded to himself, amused. Half close his eyes, and he could be the man in the picture, someone so helpless, so out of touch, that only a guide dog could map his path through life. Maybe that's what he really needed, thought Winter. Maybe he'd got so old, so preoccupied, so blind, that something as tasty as *Tumbril* had passed him by.

Last night, sitting in Mackenzie's den, he hadn't let on about his own ignorance of this covert operation, but the more he'd thought about it afterwards, the more annoyed he'd felt about his own failure to clock whatever was going on. There was always the possibility, of course, that Mackenzie had got it wrong. Serious villains were famously paranoid and they often mistook a casual passing interest for a full-scale operation, booted and spurred. But on the evidence of last night, he rather suspected that Mackenzie wasn't kidding himself. Christ, he even had a code name.

Operation *Tumbril*? Winter shook his head. His entire CID career had been dedicated to sensing the likely passage of events. Keep your ear to the ground, learn to tune out all the rubbish, and a footfall half a world away could tell you everything you needed to know. Yet here he was, dumb as the next detective, totally unaware that someone way above him had emptied the piggy bank, rolled up their sleeves, and decided to take on Bazza Mackenzie.

The thought, even this late in the day, put a smile on his face. Given the success of Mackenzie's recent makeover – drug baron turned millionaire businessman – the case would be a real bastard to make. Any serious bid to hurt him would doubtless revolve around disman-tling Bazza's vast commercial empire but Mackenzie wasn't joking when he talked about the people he paid to advise him, and they'd have drawn up a survival kit for bent millionaires.

Rule one was stay away from drugs: no possession, no supply, absolutely no involvement with the distribution chain. The money-laundering legislation seemed to be getting more powerful by the month, but even under the latest set of rules Winter thought you still had to prove some kind of drugs-related offence. In view of the mountain of goodies he stood to lose, the last thing Mackenzie would therefore risk was a criminal charge. That way, he'd hand the *Tumbril* boys the victory of their dreams. So how would they do it? And why now, when Bazza seemed so armour-clad?

Winter helped himself to more tea. Bazza's terse mention of Whale Island was intriguing. On one level it made perfect sense to ring-fence an operation like this, to bury it away from canteen chatter, yet on another level the strategy plainly hadn't worked. And if Bazza himself knew about *Tumbril*, then who else was reading the files? Winter reached for the sugar bowl. The implication, of course, was that Bazza numbered coppers on his payroll, tame porkers – uniformed or otherwise – with their snouts in Bazza's trough. That in itself would be no surprise – Winter knew a number of DCs who'd gone to the same school, drank in the same pubs, and would doubtless regard the odd titbit from Bazza's table as a gesture of mateship – but what gave last night's revelation a real edge was the fact that *Tumbril* was far from common knowledge. For once in their lives, the bosses had managed to keep a secret. So who was keeping Bazza in the loop?

This single question floated Winter through the next hour of his day. He thought about it in the bath. He drew up a mental list of candidates over breakfast. Finally, sitting on the john, he realised that there were cleverer ways of carving a piece of *Tumbril* for himself. He was looking at the wrong target. It wasn't Whale Island or the covert ops team that mattered. It was Bazza himself.

He'd left his mobile on the window sill. Reaching up, he dialled a number from memory. She took a while to answer and sounded badly hung-over.

'Mist.' Winter was smiling. 'We need to talk.'

DC Jimmy Suttle never made promises he intended to break. Half past eight in the morning found him dropping Trudy off at the entrance to Gunwharf. She was due for an appointment at her GP's surgery and needed to get home to sort herself out. Leaning in through the car window, she gave Suttle a lingering kiss and told him to forget everything she'd said about Dave Pullen.

'Yeah?'

Suttle checked his image in the rear-view mirror and engaged gear. He'd phone her later about tonight. Maybe they could drive into Southsea for a curry or something. Then he was gone.

Minutes later, he found himself a parking space in Ashburton Road. There was a squad meeting at Kingston Crescent scheduled for 9.15 and DI Lamb was merciless about latecomers but he still had forty minutes to get one or two things off his chest. A succession of CID colleagues, older and wiser, had warned him about the perils of mixing your private and professional lives. Unless you had some kind of death wish, letting the job fuck the inside of your head was the last thing you ever did. Standing on the pavement, staring up at Pullen's top-floor flat, Suttle permitted himself a grim smile. They were wrong.

At the top of the fire escape, he tried Pullen's door. It was locked. He knocked twice, yelled Pullen's name, gave the handle a shake, and toyed briefly with kicking it in. Back on the pavement, aware of twitching curtains in the flats opposite, he walked round the corner and rang the top bell. Two days ago, the name space alongside had been empty. Now, in fat black capitals, *DAVE PULLEN*.

A third try with the bell produced nothing from the adjoining speakerphone. Checking his watch, Suttle rang the ground-floor flat. At length, there came a small querulous voice through the speakerphone. Suttle introduced himself, offering his warrant card a minute or so later when the door finally opened. The woman must have been eighty. The cardigan was matted with ancient soup stains and when Suttle repeated that he was CID, she thought he'd come about the recent spate of doorstep milk thefts.

'Both bottles went last week.' She peered up at him. 'I'd buy from the shops if I could get there.'

Suttle left her in the cavernous hall. Three flights up, he paused on the top landing. Pullen's was one of only two apartments. To Suttle's surprise, the door to the flat was open. Even at ten paces, there was a perceptible smell of shit. He paused by the door, called Pullen's name. The smell was much stronger now. He called again, hesitated a second or two, then pushed inside.

The gloom of the tiny lobby had an almost physical texture, thickened by the stench. From memory, Pullen's living room lay beyond the door on the right. Suttle nudged it open with his foot, alert now, aware of the thud of his own pulse. Situations like these, it was wise to have back-up, at the very least a message left with someone who'd know where to come looking. Like this, totally solo, he was horribly exposed. Another rule broken.

'Pullen?'

Suttle looked round the chaos of the living room. The curtains were closed against the grey March morning. There was a copy of yesterday's *News* folded across the back of a chair and the collection of football magazines he recognised from his last visit. Pullen must have tripped over them because they were scattered everywhere, big cover-page faces of Beckham and Thierry Henry peering up from odd corners of the room.

On a work surface in the tiny kitchenette, Suttle found a half-eaten kebab and chips in a nest of stained newsprint. Beside it, an open can of Tennant's Super. He studied it a moment, aware that this abandoned room was beginning to resemble a crime scene. There were things he should do here, steps he should take. Any more freelancing, and he was in danger of tainting the evidence.

'Pullen? Where the fuck are you?'

He heard a faint moan. Motionless in the half-darkness, Suttle strained every nerve to pick up the faintest movement. It happened again, louder this time. Somewhere close, he thought. And definitely human.

Back in the hall, the first door he tried opened into a narrow bathroom. The rail for the shower curtain was hanging from the ceiling and the washer had gone on one of the taps in the hand basin. He stepped back into the hall again and pushed lightly at the sole remaining door. It was open already, a foot or two ajar, but the moment he stirred the air inside, the smell enveloped him, the hot, meaty stench of shit.

This time, the window was draped with a blanket. Daylight leaked in around the edges and in the semi-darkness Suttle could just make out a figure on a bed. He fumbled against the inside wall until his fingers found the switch. He snapped on the light, bracing himself for whatever might happen next. Almost expecting some kind of physical attack, he found himself looking at a naked male body spreadeagled on the bare springs of the bed frame. Wrists and arms had been cable-tied to the edges of the frame and the flesh was red-raw where the trussed body had tried to struggle free. A conclusive ID was difficult because the head was covered in a grubby pillowslip but there was no problem guessing a name. Déjà-vu, Suttle thought. Dave Pullen. Had to be.

He stepped forward, meaning to remove the pillowslip, but then stopped. Beneath the bed, visible through the bare springs, was one of the football magazines, open at a double-page spread of a team in red shirts with the Carlsberg logo scrolled across their chests. The photo had been positioned at ground zero, directly beneath Pullen's arse. Michael Owen, in the front row, had taken a direct hit. Another heroic curl of turd had obliterated the bottom half of Emil Heskey. A third, a huge dump, had splatted across most of the back row. Half the Liverpool team wiped out by the contents of Pullen's flabby bowels. No wonder the place stank.

Suttle at last removed the pillowslip. Pullen stared up at him, his eyes huge in his parchment face. A length of gaffer tape sealed his mouth and it gave Suttle immense pleasure to tear it off. Pullen yelped in pain, then swallowed hard and began to lick his lips.

'Thank fuck,' he kept saying. 'Thank fuck.'

'Thank fuck for what?'

'You. Jesus . . .' He closed his eyes and shook his head. 'Just get me out of here.'

The mattress and a duvet had been thrown against the far wall. Suttle retrieved the duvet and draped it over Pullen's naked body. As he did so, he noticed a line of DIY tools neatly arranged on the carpet beside the bed. With the electric drill came a roll of extension cable and a plug. The Stanley knife looked brand new and there was a generous selection of blades. Help yourself time.

'What's this, then? DIY?'

'Don't ask.'

'I just did. So tell me. What happened?'

Pullen shook his head. It had been a game, one too many bevvies. He didn't want to talk about it.

'Whose game?'

'No way.' Another shake of the head, more emphatic this time.
'Tell me.'

'Fucking no way.'

'Was it the Scousers?'

'The *Scousers*? Shit, no. That's the whole fucking point.' His eyes had gone down to the tools beside the bed.

'What point? Whose point?'

'No, please, just get these fucking ties off me. Then maybe we'll talk.'

Suttle gazed down at him. A couple of nights ago this man had taken a billiard cue to Trudy Gallagher. In bed last night, on the promise that Suttle could keep a secret, she'd spelled it out for him, blow by blow. Pullen had said he was doing her a favour. He'd told her a smacking would mend her ways. This morning, outraged, Suttle had decided to administer a little correctional punishment of his own. Now this.

Pullen had started up again about the cable ties. He was stiff as fuck. He needed a wash. He had loads of stuff to sort out but absolutely no interest in making any kind of statement, official or otherwise. Wasn't that right up Suttle's street? Wasn't he doing him a favour, sparing him all that paperwork?

Dimly, Suttle was beginning to put it all together: the newly scrawled name on the speakerphone downstairs, the open door, the carefully recreated tableau in the bedroom, the hostage offered up and waiting, the shiny blades beside the bed, the open invitation to a spot of help-yourself revenge.

'Aren't you going to do anything, then? Just standing there?'

'Afraid not, Dave.' Suttle made a show of checking his watch. 'I've got an important meeting at nine. All kinds of shit if I'm late. Listen –' he began to back towards the door, away from the reeking magazine '– if I get a moment later, I'll try and pop back, OK?'

'Fuck you.'

'Yeah, and fuck you too.' Suttle smiled at him. 'Bye then, and, hey . . .' He raised a derisive thumb. 'Good luck.'

He left the room, pulling the door to behind him. A pace or two down the hall, Pullen began to yell. Anything, he said. He'd do anything to get these fucking ties off. Just name it. Anything. Suttle paused, let him plead a little longer, then returned to the bedroom. Breathe through your mouth, and the smell wasn't quite so bad.

'Anything, Dave?'

'Yeah . . . Fuck you . . . Yeah.'

'So did Bazza do this to you?' He beamed down at the bed. 'Or is that too much to ask?'

The post-mortem on Daniel Kelly was scheduled to start shortly after nine, the first on the morning's mortuary list. Eadie Sykes had driven up to St Mary's hospital half an hour earlier, keen to steal a little of the pathologist's time. She'd never attended a post-mortem in her life but she'd taped several surgical operations and knew the importance of a proper briefing. Miss the crucial cut and the impact of the sequence disappeared.

To her surprise, the pathologist was a woman. Martin Eckersley had mentioned a couple of names over lunch yesterday, promising to phone once permission came through from Kelly's father, but both had been male.

'Pauline Schreck.' She was a small, neat woman with dancing eyes and a light, dry handshake. 'My colleagues send their apologies. I'm the closest you'll find to a locum.'

'Bodies R Us?'

'Something like that.'

She led the way into a small, bare office and offered Eadie a seat. Eadie produced a copy of the fax from Kelly's father. The pathologist barely spared it a glance.

'I've seen it,' she said. 'You wouldn't be here otherwise. So tell me . . . How can I help you?'

Eadie explained a little about the video. What she needed was graphic coverage of the post-mortem procedure, nothing spared. The more clinical and explicit the footage, the better it would serve the video she had in mind.

The pathologist nodded. She had no problem with any of that. The body in the fridge had become a parcel and it was her job to unpack it. Vital organs – brain, heart, lungs, liver, stomach, spleen, kidneys, bladder – came out for inspection. Various fluids went off to an address in Kent for analysis. Afterwards, the mortuary boys would sew Mr Kelly back together again.

'End of story?'

'From my point of view, yes. It's a procedure, just like proper surgery. There are techniques you pick up, like tying off the stomach at either end to preserve the contents, but you learn it stage by stage. The only difference is that Mr Kelly isn't going to get better.' She nodded down at Eadie's file. 'You've got a spare sheet of paper in there?'

Eadie obliged with the back of a flyer from the Stop the War Coalition. The pathologist sketched the outline of a body and then talked Eadie through the sequence of cuts: the long central-line incision from the Adam's apple to the pubis, rib-shears to remove the breast plate and get at the tongue and neck organs, a smaller scalpel to draw a line from ear to ear across the top of the hairline.

'Why the hairline?'

'We have to take a look at the brain.' She tapped the diagram with her pencil. 'Sorry to disappoint you but that's more or less it.'

'And the stuff you take out? The organs?'

'We weigh them, measure them, then seal the lot in a plastic bag and pop them back in the body.'

'Whereabouts in the body?'

'Here.' She patted her own stomach. 'Abdominal cavity. Sealing the bag's important. We also pack the neck and mouth with tissues. Leakage is the last thing we need.'

'And that's it?'

'Afraid so. I'd love to tell you otherwise but it's not rocket science. Death is rarely complicated. Medically, we're talking the full stop at the end of the sentence. No more.'

Eadie made a note of the quote. It had a chill matter-of-factness perfectly in keeping with the effect she had in mind. After the chaos of Daniel Kelly's final months and the hand-wringing over his death, it all boiled down to this grey March morning in a provincial mortuary with a schedule of bodies to dismember and a pile of forms to fill in. The full stop at the end of the sentence. Perfect.

Eadie glanced up.

'Would you mind me doing an interview? Just briefly.'

'With me?'

'Yes.'

'About what?'

'Daniel Kelly.' Eadie gestured down at the pencilled body shape. 'And this.'

'Of course I'd mind.' The pathologist was laughing now. 'How on earth can I talk about someone I never knew?'

Suttle rang Winter on his mobile. He was standing on the pavement outside Pullen's apartment block with line of sight to the communal entrance. Pullen himself was still upstairs, cable-tied to his bed frame.

Winter was at his desk in the Crime Squad office at Kingston Crescent. The 9.15 meeting, he said, had been cancelled. Cathy Lamb had been summoned to a council of war in Secretan's office, along with every other major player on the drugs containment scene. With the News evidently planning a major feature spread on the erupting turf war, the time had come for some hard analysis.

'Hard analysis?' Suttle was lost.

'Damage limitation. Pathways forward. All that managerial bollocks.' Winter stifled a yawn. 'Where are you, then?'

Suttle briefly described what had happened to Dave Pullen. Mackenzie, it turned out, had got word that the state of Trudy Gallagher was down to Pullen and not the Scousers at all. Far from suffering at the hands of a bunch of Liverpool toerags, she'd in fact been smacked around by her so-called boyfriend.

'We'd sussed that already,' Winter pointed out.

'Yeah, but Mackenzie hadn't. He'd believed Pullen. That's why he ordered the Scouse kid to be sorted. Now it turns out that Pullen was lying all along, just to protect his arse, because he knew Mackenzie would go ballistic if he thought he'd laid a finger on the girl. And he's right.'

'So what did Bazza do?'

'You won't believe this.' Suttle began to laugh, then told Winter about the little tableau he'd discovered in the wreckage of Pullen's bedroom. 'Kippered,' he said finally. 'Totally fucking kebabbed.'

'But why the Stanley knives?'

'Because Mackenzie's put the word out to the Scousers that Pullen's there for the taking. Directions. Address. The lot. The guy's caused them no end of grief so his front door's open and the rest is down to them. That's why Pullen's been cacking himself. Literally.'

Suttle's description of the mess beneath the bed drew a low whistle down the phone. Even Winter had heard of Michael Owen.

'And you're telling me he's still up there? Still on offer?'

'Yeah.'

'And he's really expecting a visit?'

'Yeah. You can smell it in the next street.'

'But they'd be mad, wouldn't they? Half the city looking for them? Attempted murder charge in the offing?'

'They *are* mad. That's the whole point.'

There was a moment's silence. Pullen could imagine Winter at his desk, computing the possibilities. Suttle cleared his throat. Time for a suggestion of my own, he thought.

'Why don't we just leave him there? Mount surveillance? Wait until they turn up?'

'And then nick them?'

'Yeah. Bloody sight easier than racing around after a bunch of lunatics.'

Suttle heard Winter chuckling. Then the older man put his finger on the obvious problem.

'We'd get crucified in court,' he said. 'Imagine what a half-decent brief would make of this. Hazarding a victim's life. Exposing him to further injury.'

'But he's not a victim. What he did to Trudy adds up to GBH.'

'Can we prove that?'

'Yeah.'

'How?'

'She told me.'

'Who told you?'

'Trudy.'

'Trudy Gallagher *told* you? When?'

'Yesterday.'

'When yesterday?'

'Last night.'

'Ah . . .' Winter was beginning to chuckle again. 'Then I think we have a real problem.'

Faraday was summoned to Willard's office minutes before the big troubleshooting meeting with Secretan. He'd put a call through to the Det-Supt first thing, as soon as he'd spoken to Graham Wallace, and now – a couple of hours later – Willard had reached a firm decision.

'We run with it,' he said briskly. 'We have no option.'

'I already told Wallace that.'

'You did?'

'Yes, sir, subject to your approval. Wallace says Mackenzie's definitely up for some kind of negotiation though he's still waiting for him to come back with a time and a place.'

'You think he's going to fuck us about? Switch locations at the last moment? Throw the covert?'

'I'd imagine so. Wouldn't you?'

'Yeah.' Willard was gazing at a newly arrived e-mail on his PC. 'I suppose I would.' He scribbled a note to himself and then turned back to Faraday. 'So we're talking the weekend?'

'Saturday or Sunday.'

'Can't Wallace pin him down? Try and box a meeting off?'

'I'm suggesting Sunday. It's busier in Southsea, more cover. Wallace took the point, said he'd plead a prior engagement for tomorrow.'

'But you're telling me it might still be tomorrow? Regardless?'

'I'd put money on Sunday, but yes, tomorrow's still a possibility. I've talked to Wallace's handler at Special Ops. Wallace is happy to wear a wire.'

'Recorder/transmitter?'

'Yes.'

'Fine, but we'll need to record at our end as well. If Wallace gets shaken down, they'll find the recorder and we lose the lot. As long as he's been transmitting, at least we've got a fallback. People with nothing to hide don't shake business partners down. Plays really badly in court.'

'Fine.' Faraday nodded. 'I'll tell Wallace that.'

'You don't sound convinced, Joe.'

'I'm not, sir. We're hanging this guy out to dry. Mackenzie could turn up mob-handed. What happens if it all gets silly?'

'We deal with it.'

'How?'

Faraday's challenge hung in the air between them. This was the crux of the issue, and Willard knew it. Enlist half a dozen blokes to supply back-up and they'd give themselves an enormous problem. There had to be time for proper briefings salted with the kind of information that any Pompey cop could turn into the target's name. From that point on, no matter how briefly, *Tumbril* itself might be at risk. Something similar had already happened on the aborted vehicle stop before Christmas, with Valentine taunting them afterwards on the covert. Spreading the word about *Tumbril* might trigger another disaster.

Willard was gazing out of the window, deep in thought. At length, he appeared to make some kind of decision.

'We handle it ourselves, Joe.'

'Ourselves?'

'Yeah.' He nodded. 'You, me, and the handler from Special Ops.'

Minutes later, Willard and Faraday descended a floor to Secretan's office. Most of the key players had already gathered, familiar faces around the Chief Superintendent's conference table, and Faraday slipped into the empty chair beside Cathy Lamb. She was busy sorting out a trayful of coffees but she still found time to enquire about J-J.

'How is he?'

'Fled the nest. Decamped.'

'Really?' Cathy stopped pouring. 'When?'

'Last night. He seems to have moved in with Eadie.'

'That's two of you, then.'

'Yeah.' Faraday offered her a bleak smile. 'For now.'

While Cathy began to hand round the coffees, Faraday pushed J-J to the back of his mind and tried to take stock of the assembled company. He and Willard were representing the Major Crimes Team. Len Curzon, the DI in charge of the city's divisional detectives, had driven over from Highland Road, while Cathy Lamb would be inputting contributions from the newly formed Portsmouth Crime Squad.

One surprise to Faraday was the presence of Harry Wayte, the DI from the Tactical Crime Unit. His was a similar mission statement to Cathy Lamb's: get out there, talk to the bad guys, anticipate their every move, then turn all that intelligence into arrests. The current buzzword for this style of policing was 'pro-active', a description which gave the higher echelons of management a certain degree of comfort. The belief, no matter how fanciful, that you weren't solely at the mercy of events, played wonderfully with the more gullible politicians.

Harry Wayte, across the table, caught Faraday's eye. Faraday, who hadn't seen him for a while, was shocked by how much older he looked. Since his days as a Chief Petty Officer in the navy, Harry had made no secret of his fondness for decent Scotch. In the job, over the years, he'd won himself a reputation as a good solid cop and weathered more than his share of crises but the booze had never been a problem. Now though, with his watery blue eyes and vein-mapped face, he looked truly wrecked.

'All right, Harry?'

'Never better, Joe. You?'

'You want the short answer? My boy's in deep shit. The job's a bastard. And I haven't seen anything interesting with wings since the weekend before last. Apart from that –' Faraday spread his hands wide '– life's a peach.'

'I heard about your boy.'

'Really?'

'Yeah, along with every other copper I know. Funny how bad news gets round quickest, isn't it? Drink later? Upstairs at lunchtime? It's my birthday.'

Faraday nodded a yes, then Secretan and the DCI who acted as Crime Manager for the city stepped into the room and the buzz around the table began to die. Faraday had never seen the Chief Superintendent in action before but was already impressed by the framed colour shots on the wall above Secretan's desk. He'd heard from others that this man kept a regular date with some of the UK's more challenging mountains, week-long expeditions to the Cuillins and some of the tougher Welsh peaks, but if these rain-soaked, fog-shrouded walls of sheer granite were scalps on his belt then he already had Faraday's undivided attention. Finding a perch halfway up a mountain for some serious birding was one thing; conquering monsters like the Cuillins, quite another.

Secretan began with a brief update on what he called the developing situation. He spoke with a soft, West Country burr which did nothing to mask his irritation at the recent turn of events. After a period of relative calm, outsiders had decided to rock Pompey's little boat. Some of them, as everyone knew, came from Merseyside. Attempts at repatriation had so far failed completely. Others, according to Met Intelligence, were expected any day from Brixton and other areas of south London. These guys, largely West Indian, were driven by the prospects of selling into a largish and quickly expanding market. The size of the policing challenge, said Secretan, was best expressed in simple figures. The price of an ounce of cocaine in London was currently £1700. In Portsmouth, dealers would expect a 10 per cent premium. Supply and demand. Obvious.

There was a murmur of agreement around the table. None of this was news, but Secretan, in his understated way, had summed it up rather well. He turned to Willard. They were all busy men, and time was precious, but it was important to avoid investigative chaos – one inquiry overlapping with another – and to this end he'd asked the Det-Supt to establish a clear demarcation in terms of ongoing operations. The last thing anyone needed just now was dozens of blokes getting in each other's way.

Willard nodded. Faraday knew already that he rated Secretan, a rare accolade from someone as driven and unforgiving as Willard, and Faraday sensed at once that the two men were in virtual lockstep.

'We'll start with Nick Hayder,' he said. 'We've had a decent squad on what happened to Nick, and there's no question in my mind that it was drugs related. What Nick was doing there that night is still a mystery, and to be frank we might never get to the bottom of it. It might have been pure chance, though knowing Nick I doubt it. Either way, a senior police officer is seriously injured, seriously ill, and that's totally unacceptable. Thanks to some quality detective work from Cathy Lamb's squad, we've had a bit of a breakthrough. Cathy?'

Cathy Lamb took up the story. A couple of her guys had traced a stolen Cavalier. Early indications from forensic tests on the vehicle suggested that the car might well have been used to run down Nick Hayder. A Merseyside youth hospitalised in a separate incident had been DNA-tied to the car and was now under armed guard in the QA hospital.

'For whose benefit?' It was Secretan.

'Ours,' Cathy conceded at once. 'And his, too.'

'So are we suggesting the boy in hospital is down for Nick Hayder?'

'Yes, sir. But a witness who saw the car arrive puts another youth in the front. And we've yet to find him.'

'Leads?'

'A few. Nothing that excites me.'

Secretan nodded at the DCI by his side, who made a note. Then he looked across at Willard.

'So who's driving the Hayder inquiry? Major Crimes? Cathy's squad?'

'Cathy. Under my supervision.'

'You're SIO?'

'Correct. But the troops on the ground are Cathy's.'

'Fine. So where does that leave the Major Crimes Team? As far as this discussion is concerned?'

It was a pertinent question and Faraday bent forward to be sure of catching Willard's answer. In reality, of course, *Tumbril* was a Major Crimes operation, albeit at arm's length.

'Nowhere, sir.' Willard was looking down the table at Secretan. 'If you want a list of ongoing operations, I'll happily supply one. Some are drug related but none of them need to be part of this debate.'

Faraday smiled to himself. It was a consummate response, the perfect finesse, and Faraday wondered whether Willard would make a note of it for later use. In two years on the Major Crimes Team he'd never had Willard down as much of a politician but now he began to wonder.

Secretan had returned to Cathy Lamb. At his prompting, she confirmed the beginnings of a serious turf war. Getting some kind of result against two of the Scousers would doubtless thin their ranks but every last shred of incoming intelligence suggested that the certainty of fat profits spoke louder than anything else. Her guys had their thumbs in the dyke but the market, in the end, would swamp their best efforts at containment. If not the Scousers, then the West Indians. If not them, then any number of a dozen other tribes. Albanians? Turks? Chinese? Russians? In this game, said Cathy, you could take your pick.

Down the table, a figure stirred. It was Harry Wayte.

'Cathy's right,' he said softly. 'We got word this morning of a major cocaine shipment down from town. Hand on my heart, I can't attest it. Ask me where it's gone, I can't tell you. But demand is through the roof. And where there's demand, there's supply.' He paused. 'I know I sound prehistoric but this used to be a city I understood. We knew what we were in for. Weekends could be lively and drugs were part of all that, no question, but we knew the major players, talked to them, kept the lid on. Now, it's all turning to rat shit. One day soon, we're going to be wishing the locals had stayed in charge.'

Willard was leaning forward. He wanted to know about this latest cocaine shipment. What was the strength of the intelligence? Who'd sourced it? Secretan extended a cautionary hand. They could discuss all that in a moment or two. For now, he was keen for Harry Wayte to continue.

Harry shrugged.

'There's nothing more to say, sir. Except it's sometimes better the devil you know.'

'You mean Mackenzie?'

'Of course. To stay in the game nowadays, blokes like him have to up the violence. That's why it's all kicked off. But it didn't used to be that way. Not when they had the city to themselves.'

'And you think that's a shame?'

'I think it made our job easier.'

'Even when they were turning over millions of quids' worth? Flaunting it?'

'Yes. Because that's the price you pay for peace and quiet. Look at us now. We wouldn't be here, around this table, unless all that had broken down. You're asking me what to do about it? To be frank, I haven't a clue. Worse still, I don't think anyone else has. We're chasing our tails. I'm sorry, but it's true.'

Heads around the table had turned to Secretan. To Faraday's surprise, he seemed completely at peace at the direction this meeting had suddenly taken. Where many men in his position would have dismissed Harry Wayte out of hand, there was absolutely no sense that his authority was being challenged. On the contrary, he seemed to view Harry's contribution as genuinely worthwhile.

'Geoff?' He was looking at Willard. 'What's your take on this?'

'Me?' Willard gazed at his empty notepad a moment, then looked up at Harry Wayte. 'I think you're talking absolute bollocks.'

Chapter fifteen

The mortuary at St Mary's Hospital occupies a remote corner of the sprawling inner-city site. Mid morning, sunshine spills onto the oblong of patched tarmac reserved for staff cars and undertakers' vans. Eadie Sykes emerged from a side door and leaned back against the brickwork, grateful for the thin warmth.

No briefing, she now knew, could have prepared her for the realities of the post-mortem. Expecting some kind of variation on the operations she'd attended, she'd found herself in a butcher's shop. Her close-ups of the scalpel slicing through Kelly's waxy flesh, of the bile-green and vivid yellows of his dripping intestines, of the splintering crunch as the steel rib shears chopped through bone, had been bad enough. But what had followed once the belly and chest cavities had been exposed was – to Eadie – deeply shocking.

She'd often told herself she had a rare tolerance for life's uglier surprises. She could cope with the aftermath of motorway pile-ups and hard-core footage from combat zones. But the very deadness of what she'd just witnessed, the knowledge that any of us might one day become the carefully emptied carcass on the stainless steel slab, filled her with dread.

The air-conditioning vents were on the roof above her head and a breath of wind brought with it the sickly sweet smell of the next post-mortem. People like Pauline Schreck live with this smell every day of their working lives, she thought. Even in your sleep, a smell like that would never leave you. She shuddered, heading for her car. She stored the camera in the boot and retrieved her mobile from the glovebox. Amongst the stored messages was a number she didn't immediately recognise.

Eager to get out of this place as quickly as she could, she reversed the Suzuki into a tight turn and threaded her way back through the maze of buildings. Only when she'd emerged onto the main road, waiting for the lights to change, did she key the message tape.

A male voice, northern accent, wished her a very good morning. He'd driven down late last night. He was staying at the Marriott Hotel and he'd appreciate half an hour of her time. Might there be room in her schedule for a coffee? Mid morning? Say half ten? Eadie glanced at her watch. The Marriott was fifteen minutes away, up at the top of the city. Daniel Kelly's father was the last person she trusted herself to meet just now but she knew how important the contact might be.

When the lights changed, she hesitated for a second. Then she turned left, heading north.

Jimmy Suttle waited in his car while Winter took a look for himself. A minute later, he was back in the street. Disgust was something Suttle could recognise at twenty metres.

'Man's an animal.' Winter pulled the car door shut behind him and dug in his pocket for a Werther's Original. 'I told him I'd call the RSPCA. Put him out of his misery.'

'What did he say?'

'Sod all. I think he's losing the will to live.'

'So what do we do?'

'Untie him. Clean him up. Get him out of there. If Cath wants to put in an OP, some kind of ambush, there's nothing to stop her. The Scousers won't know Pullen's gone.'

'OK.' Suttle tried to mask his disappointment. He nodded at the flats across the road. 'You want me to give you a hand?'

'Yeah . . . but there's something we ought to discuss first.'

'What's that, then?'

'It's about young Trudy . . .' Winter pushed back the passenger seat and made himself comfortable. 'You want to share anything with me?'

'Like what?'

'Like whether or not she was the bird you met yesterday.'

'I told you already.'

'Wrong, son. You told me you met her last night. I'm asking you whether she was the reason you bailed out of the house-to-house. A yes would be fine. For starters.'

It began to dawn on Suttle that Winter was serious. Not just serious, but something else too. Pissed off? He wasn't sure.

'OK.' he said carefully. 'She asked for a meet.'

'*She* asked?'

'That's right. Phoned up. Fixed a time and a place. Like you do.'

'Any idea why?'

'She fancies me.'

'Naturally. Any other reason?'

'She wanted to talk about –' Suttle nodded across the road '– him upstairs.'

He explained about how she'd gone to Bazza on the spur of the moment, told him everything, and how worried she was about the consequences.

'I'm not surprised.' Winter nodded down at the mobile. 'Give her a ring. Invite her round for a look. Might do our friend the world of good.' He paused. 'What else?'

'Nothing else.'

'Except you shagged her.'

'I did, yeah.'

'Ever think that might not have been such a great idea? No, you didn't, did you. Just went right ahead, helped yourself. Look at me, son.' Reluctantly, Suttle's head came round. Winter might have been his father. 'Keen, was she?'

'Very.'

'Got tonight planned? The weekend? Somewhere nice? Only if I were you, I'd be thinking abroad, somewhere remote. Patagonia's nice this time of year.'

'What's the problem?' Suttle tried to defend himself. 'It just happened. These things do. We had a couple of drinks, got it on. No harm in that, is there?'

'Plenty, my friend. In case no one else has ever mentioned it, let me have the honour. Screwing the customers is a really crap move, and you're talking to someone who knows. Getting emotionally involved is even worse.'

'Who said I'm emotionally involved?'

'You went round to Pullen's first thing.' Winter nodded at the building across the road. 'Social visit, was it? Chance to compare notes? Or had you something else in mind?'

There was a long silence. Suttle was doing his best to hide his embarrassment.

'She's a kid,' he said at last. 'Christ knows what she was doing with a dosser like Pullen.'

'Or Valentine, indeed.'

'No.' Suttle shook his head. 'That was different. Turns out the thing with Valentine was platonic. They never got it on, much to her disgust.'

'She told you that?' Winter didn't bother to hide his surprise.

'Yeah, and I believe her, too.'

'So what was in it for him?'

'Dunno. Maybe he felt sorry for her. Maybe he just liked her, liked her being there, having her around. Ignore the attitude and she can be really sweet, yeah . . .' He nodded. 'Really sweet.'

'Maybe Valentine's gay? Or maybe he's just lost it?'

'No way.' Another shake of the head. 'Trude says he's been shagging her mum.'

'Misty? Valentine's shagging Misty?' Winter was grinning now.

'Yeah.'

'Still?'

'Yeah. As far as I know.'

'Excellent.' Winter celebrated with another Werther's, his earlier hunch confirmed. 'So where does that leave you?'

Suttle laughed. 'Pretty sorted, if you really want to know.'

'And Trude?'

'She's talking about going away. It's probably fantasy but she seems to mean it. Mentioned it twice last night.'

'Poor you. Just when things were getting—'

'No, no.' Suttle grinned at him. 'She wants me to go with her.'

'Where?'

'Fuck knows.'

'How?'

'Dunno. She says she's due money.'

'Lots of money?'

'No idea.'

'Are we talking holiday here?'

'Maybe.'

'Something longer?'

'Possibly.'

'And?'

'Well . . . it's a joke, obviously. She's a nice girl and everything but there's no way.'

'Thank Christ for that.'

'I'm not with you.'

'No, and you won't be if you carry on like this.' Winter turned to face him. 'Listen, son. You're a bright lad, you cope OK, Christ, I even like you, but you're from way out of town and believe me that makes a difference. There's an etiquette here, things you just don't do in this city, and one of them is Trudy Gallagher. Why? Because Bazza regards her as a daughter, always has done, kith and kin, his own flesh and blood, and the last person he wants screwing the arse off her is anyone in the job. He'd take that personally, believe me.'

'You're telling me Trude is Bazza's daughter? Only that would be news to Trude.'

'I'm telling you nothing. I'm simply the messenger.'

'He *told* you?'

'Good as.'

'When?'

Winter looked at him a moment, then shook his head. He'd said his piece and now was the time to get back upstairs and sort Dave Pullen. First, though, he ought to update Cathy Lamb.

He extended a hand. Suttle shook it. Winter gave a despairing sigh. 'The mobile, dickhead.'

Faraday was back in his office in the MCT suite when Gisela Mendel rang. He recognised her voice at once, the clipped German accent, and reached for the pad by the phone.

'It's about the sale on the fort,' she said at once. 'Your Mr Mackenzie has been on to me again.'

'And?'

'He says we need to set up a meeting for next week. He wants to bring his solicitor and says I ought to bring mine.'

'What about other bidders?'

'He doesn't seem to think that'll be a problem.'

'Really?' Faraday was calculating the time line. Mackenzie wanted to have a sort-out with Wallace over the weekend. Whatever he had in mind would presumably clear his path for a solo run at Spit Bank Fort. If Willard and Faraday were looking for proof of Mackenzie's confidence, then this was surely it.

'Last time we met, you mentioned a change of circumstances,' Faraday said carefully. 'Personal circumstances.'

'That's right. My husband's started divorce proceedings.'

'Which means the sale's for real?'

'I'm afraid so.'

'Do you have a figure in mind?'

'Yes.'

'Which you'll table next week?'

'Obviously.'

'Do you mind telling me what that figure might be?'

There was a long silence. When Gisela finally answered, her voice had hardened.

'This is difficult, Mr Faraday. Until now, as you know, it's been make-believe. I'm not asking for extra information, I don't want to know why I'm playing these games, all I'm saying is the rules have changed. I have to sell the place for real. I have to turn it into money. Of course I'd love £1,200,000 but no one's going to part with that kind of sum, not for Spit Bank. It would be nice if they did but it isn't going to happen. Frankly, given my husband's decision, I'm largely in Mr Mackenzie's hands.'

'You'll take what he offers?'

'I'll haggle, obviously, but . . . yes, I have no choice.'

Faraday sat back. Not once had he thought beyond Mackenzie's impending meet with Wallace. That was the crux of *Tumbril*, the hinge on the investigative door, the single square on which they'd piled all their chips. What if the operation fell apart? What if – by the end of next week – Mackenzie had picked up this little piece of Pompey for a song?

'Have you told Mr Willard any of this?'

'No, I tried but he was engaged.'

'Fine, leave it to me.' Faraday paused again, struck by another thought. 'What happens if Mackenzie's unable to bid?'

'I don't understand.'

'What if –' Faraday knew already that this was a conversation he should never have started '– he suddenly loses interest?'

'Why on earth should he do that?'

'I've no idea, but tell me. Imagine the situation. No Mackenzie. And no one else.'

There was another silence, longer this time.

'Are you serious?' she said at last.

Daniel Kelly's father was waiting in the coffee shop at the Marriott Hotel. Eadie spotted him at a corner table the moment she walked in, a smaller man than she'd imagined, dark suit, scarlet tie, enormous blue-rimmed glasses. He folded a copy of *Variety* and got to his feet. He had a warm handshake, if slightly damp.

He signalled to a distant waitress. Eadie noticed curls of bacon rind on the edge of his empty plate.

'Late breakfast. You want something to eat?'

Eadie gagged at the suggestion.

'Coffee's fine,' she said.

The waitress collected Kelly's plate and departed. The subsequent silence might have been awkward had Eadie not decided that this man deserved the truth.

'Your son was a mess,' she said quietly. 'A mess when he was alive, and a mess afterwards. I'm not sure you understand quite how bad that mess was.'

Kelly rocked back in his chair. In certain moods, Eadie Sykes could have an almost physical impact.

'You said as much on the phone,' he managed at last.

'I know. I just think it's worth repeating. I don't normally feel sorry for people but in Daniel's case I'm going to make an exception. You failed him. I guess we all failed him. Poor little bastard.'

'Is that why you're here? Give me a good slagging?'

'Not at all. I came because you left a message on my mobile. I suppose I'm just trying to be helpful. Fill in the missing bits.'

'Sure, fine, you go ahead then. But you really think I haven't been through all this? How much I didn't know? How much I should have known? How it doesn't help to have a stranger barge into your life and tell you your son's just OD'd?'

'Are you talking about me?'

'No, I'm talking about the police. Nice enough guy, not his fault, just doing his job. But it doesn't help, does it? Knock on the door? Seven o'clock in the morning? No reason to suspect your world's about to collapse?' He paused, reached for his empty cup, then changed his mind. There were tiny spots of colour high on his cheek. 'Daniel's mother was an alcoholic,' he said suddenly. 'Did you know that?'

'Was?'

'Is. These days I often think of her as dead.'

Eadie looked away for a moment, wondering how far to push this conversation. Anger was a force over which she had little control. She owed this man nothing. What the hell.

'Do you have any other family?' she inquired.

'No.'

'Two down, then. None to go.'

'I beg your pardon?'

'You heard what I said.'

The waitress returned with the coffee pot. Kelly avoided Eadie's gaze while she poured. Then he changed the subject.

'You mentioned some kind of interview . . .'

'That's right.'

'Are you still interested? Only –' He gestured at the Filofax beside his cup '– I need to know.'

'Schedule it in?'

'Whatever. Listen. I'm trying to help here. I'm looking at a ton of stuff to do, things to sort out – Daniel's flat, undertakers, a funeral – and I have to be back home by tonight. I listened to you on the phone. Tell you the truth, I admire what you're doing, and I don't blame you for being so . . .' He frowned. 'Uptight. You're right. I'm a tramp compared to my son. I sold out years ago. He never did. Not once.'

'Sold out?'

'All this showbiz shit.' He touched the magazine. 'Believe it or not, I represent A-class celebs by the drawerful, names you wouldn't believe. Sport, soaps, movies – Manchester's the place to be. And you know what it is with these people? They're all into drugs big time, billy, coke, smack, you name it. Show them serious money and they stick it straight up their nose. That's a fact. So tell me. How come they get away with it when Daniel . . . ?'

'Maybe they don't. Ever thought of that?'

'Yeah? Then how come they're still alive and kicking? Still walking around? Still rich and famous?'

'Because people like you look after them, do their deals.'

'Exactly. And you think that makes me feel any better? Sitting here with someone like yourself?'

Eadie brooded for a moment. There were images she simply had to offload. She looked up.

'You said Daniel never sold out?'

'That's right.'

'And you believe that? You think that's really the case?'

'I do.'

'Then you're wrong, Mr Kelly. I never knew Daniel, not properly. What little I picked up came from a friend of his, a girl called Sarah.'

'He mentioned her.'

'I bet he did. My guess is that Sarah was the only thing that stood between Daniel and the fucking grave. That doesn't make it her fault, don't get me wrong, but when I say that Daniel sold out, what I'm really saying is this. The boy was obviously bright. He had a brain. He had prospects, hopes, ambitions. He wanted to write a fucking *novel* for Christ's sakes. But what did he do before he picked the pen up? He looked for company, for love, just like the rest of us. And when it wasn't there, he found the next best thing and stuck it in his arm. Friends are supposed to prevent that. And so are family.'

'Daniel didn't have any family. He had me.'

'I know. And here you are, taking him to the crematorium.'

Eadie sat back, oblivious to the waitress at her elbow. The last thing she wanted just now was another cup of coffee.

Kelly was lighting a small cheroot. Hands like his son's, Eadie thought. Short, stubby fingers, nails bitten to the quick.

'Tell me something,' Kelly murmured.

'Go ahead.'

'Why are you so angry?'

'Angry?' It was a reasonable question. 'Because I was there this morning, Mr Kelly, and because I saw what happened. Have you ever been to a post-mortem? It's grotesque, truly fucking bizarre. First off, it's not too bad. There has to be a way of getting at all that plumbing so – hey – they cut you open. And then there's all that stuff they have to get at inside the ribcage, but that's no big surprise either. The right tools, it's a stroll in the park, crunch-crunch, all done. But then comes the head, and at that point, believe me, it gets personal. You know how they do it? They cut you from here to here.' Eadie traced a line across her head from ear to ear. 'Then they peel your whole fucking face off so it's just hanging there. Then the scalp comes off too, backwards, all one piece, just like in the Westerns. You think that's bad? Just wait. They have this saw. It's called an oscillating saw. They run it right round your head and you're trying to keep the thing in focus in the viewfinder and you're wondering what the smell is, the new smell, and then you realise it's burning bone. Bad shit, Mr Kelly, but worse when the lid comes off the cookie jar, and you're standing about a foot from the body, and you're suddenly looking at somebody's brain. Know what happens then? It's help-yourself time. Out comes the brain and they take it across to the place by the window where they've put the rest of him and then they start cutting right through it, grey stuff, gloopy, wobbling around, slice after slice.' She paused to catch her breath, then nodded. 'Daniel's brain, Mr Kelly. Daniel's memories. Hopes. Fears. Dreams. Everything he never got a chance to say. Everything he never told you. Just lying there in slices. Yuk.'

Kelly had abandoned the cheroot. His hands were shaking. When he finally looked up, there were tears in his eyes.

'Have you finished?'

'No. I haven't.' Eadie was looking for a Kleenex. 'You still owe Daniel, big time.' She blew her nose. 'And I've got a camera in the car.'

Faraday was late getting to Harry Wayte's birthday drinks. The social club was on the top floor at Kingston Crescent, a generous space with half a dozen tables and views across the rooftops towards the distant chalk fold of Portsdown Hill.

Harry was propped at the bar, a pint of lager at his elbow, entertaining a tight ring of well-wishers with a war story or two. The dawn drugs bust, middle of winter, when they chased a naked dealer halfway round Emsworth in the snow. The covert op when they arranged for the transmitting mike to be secreted in a new sofa, only to have the wife send it back because she couldn't stand the colour. Each of these yarns raised a collective chuckle, prompting other stories, and Harry stood in the middle of it, a big smile on his scarlet face, floating contentedly down this river of memories. There were worse things in life, Faraday thought, than being someone like this, a good solid cop, nearly thirty years of service, with the knowledge that he'd locked up far more than his share of quality villains.

Faraday ordered himself a half of Guinness, raising his glass in salute when Harry caught his eye. Moments later, Harry abandoned his audience and took Faraday by the arm. The crescent of banquette by the window was empty. Harry was already drunk.

'Back there, son.'

'Where, Harry?'

'Downstairs. That poxy drugs meeting. No offence.'

'*Offence?* What are you on about?'

'What I said.' He frowned. 'I know it's not P fucking C but sometimes you just get up to here with all the bullshit. Know what I mean?'

Faraday nodded. He knew exactly what Harry Wayte meant. Drugs were everywhere, an indelible stain. They turned families inside out. They'd put Nick Hayder under the wheels of a car. They'd sent J-J on an errand that might still land him up in a prison cell. Small wonder guys like Harry, guys in the know, lost patience with management-speak.

Faraday patted him on the arm.

'Right or wrong, Harry. It needed saying.'

'You mean that?'

'Yeah.' He raised his glass again. 'Happy birthday.'

'Cheers. Here's to the next one. Same day, same place, eh?'

'I thought you were retiring?'

'I am. I've put my thirty in. September the twenty-third. Can't wait.' He beckoned Faraday closer. 'Seriously, Joe, you've been there, you've been around. What's your take? Think we're coping? Scousers? Yardies? Kids running round with Glocks and sledgehammers?' He went on, his finger in Faraday's face, painting an ever more lurid picture of urban chaos, a widescreen horror flick scored for psychotic adolescents with limitless ammunition. 'It'll happen.' He tapped the side of his cratered nose. 'Believe me, Joe. And soon.'

'You really think so?'

'I know so. It won't be my problem, except I fucking live here, but it might be yours.' He gave Faraday a nudge, slopping his drink in the process. 'And you know something else?'

'What's that, Harry?'

'We should legalise the fucking lot. Forget Class A, Class B, all that shit. Just make it all legit and then tax the arse off it. Clean gear and a million new hospitals. You heard it here first.'

'You think that would work?'

'I think two things, Joe. Number one, it would take out every scumbag dealer in this fucking scumbag city – bosh – just like that. And number two, there's no way it'll ever happen. So ... how do you explain that little poser? Because every other bloke you know's got a finger in the pie. It's big business, Joe. It's an industry. Legalise gear, and half the country – half the planet – are looking for a new job. Am I right?'

Faraday ducked the question. Most weeks now, correspondents to the letters page of *Police Review* magazine were banging the same drum, and lately there were signs that a lobby within ACPO – some of the country's top police officers – were beginning to despair of the current approach, but Faraday had yet to make up his mind. Friday nights in the city, largely fuelled by alcohol, were bad enough already. What would happen if you legalised everything else?

Harry Wayte was still demanding an answer.

'Haven't got one, Harry. The script says nick the bad guys, so that's what I try and do.'

'But that's the point, Joe. Nicking the bad guys drugs-wise solves fuck all because the bad guys are everywhere. Put one away and another half-dozen turn up to take his place. It's numbers, Joe. It's Custer's last stand. Dien Bien Phu. We're fighting the wrong war.'

It seemed to Faraday that Harry Wayte meant it. His passion for military history – like his passion for model boats – was well known, and if nothing else then his sheer length of service gave him the right to question the larger assumptions. Part of the problem nowadays was that old campaigners like Harry Wayte were too easily dismissed. Not everything in life responded to pie charts and SWOT analysis.

Faraday stole a glance at his watch.

'I'm with you, Harry,' he said.

'Like how?'

'Like it's a bastard.'

Faraday glanced up to find Willard looming over him. He wasn't smiling. When Harry struggled to his feet and offered to buy a drink, Willard ignored him.

'A word, Joe.' Willard nodded towards the stairs. 'If you can spare the time.'

Willard shut the door to his office. He'd been talking to Gisela Mendel and he wanted to know what the fuck was going on.

'She's tellling me she's going to be left high and dry,' he said. 'Now who put that idea into her head?'

'High and dry how?'

'A fort on her hands and no one to sell it to.'

'I've no idea, sir.'

'She said she'd been talking to you.'

'That's true.'

'And she said you asked what would happen if Mackenzie wasn't around any more.'

'That's not quite the way I put it.'

'It wasn't? Well it didn't take too long for her to suss that's what you meant. This is u/c, Joe. This is a six-figure investment, God knows how much resource, and you've just blown the whole fucking caboodle. So far, she's been good as gold, completely onside. She knows we're up to something. She knows Mackenzie's hot for it. And she knows Wallace is a plant. But that's all she knows. Or used to.'

'I'm not hearing you,' Faraday said softly.

'Too fucking right, you're not.'

'No.' Faraday shook his head, taking a tiny step closer. 'You don't understand. From where I'm sitting, it goes like this. You or Hayder or whoever sets up the sting. The fort is the bait in the trap. Mackenzie takes the bait. Is the fort really up for sale? No. Does our German friend have to pretend it is? Yes. Does it occur to her that we might have a professional interest in Mackenzie? Yes. Might she therefore draw one or two conclusions? Yes . . . unless she's very, very stupid.' He paused. '*Is* she very very stupid?'

'How would I know?'

'I've no idea. Except her husband's suddenly suing for divorce.'

'What the fuck's that supposed to mean?'

'It means the game has changed. It means she doesn't want to play any more, not by our rules anyway. Show her a buyer – Mackenzie – and she'll sell, for real. That says liability to me. That says she's got every interest in keeping Mackenzie a free man.' He paused. 'How well do you know her? Only now might be the time for a serious word or two.'

Willard turned away. Standing by the window, he cracked open the venetian blinds with his fingers, peered down into the car park beneath.

'Wallace has been on again,' he said at length. 'Mackenzie's come up with a time and place for Sunday. Wallace wants a face-to-face to talk it through.'

'Both of us?'

'Just you, Joe. McDonald's off the motorway, two thirty. He'll probably have his handler with him.' Willard was still staring down through the venetian blinds. 'OK?'

Chapter sixteen

Eadie Sykes, driving back from the Marriott, felt strangely light-headed. After the darkness of the post-mortem and a conversation she should never have inflicted on someone in Kelly's position, she'd ended up with the interview of her dreams: a full-frontal glimpse of a father racked by guilt, determined to share his grief and anger with as wide an audience as possible. Deaths like Danny's, he'd muttered at the end, gave you nowhere to hide. No one should ever have been that alone.

Afterwards, in the privacy of his hotel room, she'd given the man a hug and apologised. She should never have been so direct, so brutal. Down there in the coffee shop, he'd had every right to walk away.

Kelly had given her a strange smile.

'If I knew you better, I'd say you did it on purpose,' he'd told her. 'You'd make a great lawyer.'

'You really believe that?'

'Yes.' He'd nodded. 'I do.'

Now, driving back through the city, Eadie wondered if what he'd said was true. Manipulation was part of the game, she knew it was, but this morning – for once – she felt she'd lost control completely. There were times when she saw no point fighting the truth and the sight of Kelly in the coffee shop had been one of them. The fact that some kind of relationship had survived was a bonus she'd no right to expect, as were the contents of the digital cassette she'd tucked in her bag.

Back at the Ambrym offices and feeling infinitely more cheerful, she found J-J hunched over the PC. Beneath a day's growth of beard, he looked pale and withdrawn. His eyes had a watchfulness, an intensity, that she'd never seen before, and when she tried to coax him into the beginnings of a conversation, he plainly wasn't interested. Normally, J-J could fill a room with his warmth and enthusiasm, almost deafen you with his animation and his exploding bubbles of sign. Today, though, he was practically invisible.

Last night at the flat, before Joe came round, they'd had a long set-to about the Daniel Kelly project. Deeply uncomfortable with his own role in the student's death, J-J wanted nothing more to do with the production. He'd been OK with the research and the reading, more than happy to make friends with the people they were trying to help, but what had happened in the taping session had shocked him. There were ways you didn't push people, he'd signed, short cuts you shouldn't take. Eadie, in his view, had ignored all that and he was ashamed to have been part of what followed. The same had happened at the police station. It was a game they were playing. There were weird rules and lots of stuff you weren't supposed to talk about, and no one seemed to realise that someone had just died. That his dad, of all people, should be part of this pantomime he'd found inexplicable. He was, once again, ashamed.

Eadie, who had limited room in her life for the concept of shame, had defended herself and Faraday with some vigour. In J-J's world, she told him in an elaborate mime, he'd never make an omelette because he could never steel himself to break an egg. Sometimes the hard thing to do was the right thing to do. J-J, who loved omelettes, was mystified. What did eggs have to do with Daniel Kelly?

At this point, thankfully, J-J had started to laugh. Eadie cemented an uneasy truce with an offer to phone for a takeout curry and they'd been expecting the delivery when the speakerphone buzzed. Instead of the driver from the Indian Cottage, a small, rotund emissary from the Stop the War Coalition came puffing up the stairs. He understood Eadie had been taping video sequences from the evening's demo. He'd also been told that she had access to broadcast-quality editing software. Eadie said yes to both questions and found herself listening to a proposal she found instantly irresistible.

Comrades in London, said the man, were recording broadcast feeds from Al Jazeera, the Qatar-based Arab news station. Twenty-four hours into the war, their footage from areas under bombardment in Baghdad and Basra was already graphic. This kind of material would never find its way into Western news coverage, not least because it might shame the watching audience into doing something about this obscene adventure. The Stop the War Coalition were therefore wondering about the possibility of somehow showcasing the worst that Al Jazeera might be able to supply.

Eadie had got there before him.

'Three elements.' She'd tallied them on her fingers. 'The Arab footage. UK protest sequences. And all that jerk-off stuff we're seeing on BBCNews 24.'

'Jerk-off stuff?'

'Cruise missile launches. Guys loading bombs onto airplanes. Carrier battlegroups. Tank commanders riding into battle. Apache gunships.'

'*Top Gun?*'

'Exactly.'

The activist had liked that a lot. A call to London confirmed that the first whack of Al Jazeera footage could be FedEx'd next day. BBCNews 24 pictures could presumably be recorded off-air. For now, Eadie would have to make do with her own tapes of the Pompey demo but extra footage would soon be available from other protests elsewhere in the country.

Eadie said there was no need to use Federal Express. She had a broadband link that could carry incoming video.

'What about money?'

'Forget it.'

'No charge?'

'Not a penny.'

'Copyright?'

'Ignore it. We're at war.'

'And you've got someone to sort all this out?'

'Indeed.' Eadie shot J-J a look. 'I know just the guy.'

Now, fifteen hours later, J-J was sieving Eadie's rushes from last night's demo for the best shots. She leaned over his shoulder while he quickly played the highlights: kids bursting out of HMV in the shopping precinct to join the march, two old ladies clapping as the column of protesters swept past, a pit bull pissing on a discarded placard featuring George Bush.

As the images came and went, Eadie realised that J-J had a real talent for cutting to the meat of an event like this. Maybe it was the fact that he was never distracted by the soundtrack. Maybe the media gurus were right when they insisted that TV and film had an overwhelmingly visual logic. Whatever the explanation it didn't matter because Eadie could sense already that footage like this, intercut with the other material, could play to any audience in the world. This was the true Esperanto of moral outrage, a torrent of visceral images that would relocate the business of war to where it truly belonged. No longer a pain-free crusade peddled to the voters on the back of half-baked intelligence, but real babies, everyone's flesh and blood, blown apart in the name of freedom.

J-J got to the end of the out-takes from the demo. Some of Eadie's passion seemed to have rubbed off on him and he grinned up at her when she gave him a hug. Funny, she thought. Show J-J a real-life tragedy unfolding in front of his eyes, and he doesn't want to know.

Multiply that single death a thousand-fold, and he can't wait to get stuck in.

'Al Jazeera?' she signed.

'Nothing yet.' He fingered his watch, then shrugged.

Early afternoon, the McDonald's on the turn-off beside the M27 was packed. Faraday spotted Wallace and his handler in the far corner by the window. Wallace had commandeered a four-seat table and was tucking into a treble cheeseburger with a brimming cone of fries.

The handler was a DS, Terry McNaughton, who had served under Faraday for six busy months at Highland Road, a tall, relaxed-looking thirty-year-old with a smile that could open any door. Two years later, he'd swapped the Top Man suits for jeans and a dark blue button-down shirt.

The moment he saw Faraday, he got to his feet and left the table. Wallace followed, abandoning the burger but hanging on to the fries.

'Let's do it in the car.' McNaughton nodded towards the exit doors. 'This is mad.'

McNaughton's Golf was parked next to the fence. Faraday got into the back, making space for himself amongst a litter of scuba magazines. A travel brochure caught his eye, a specialist company he'd never heard of.

'Galapagos, boss.' McNaughton had twisted himself round in the driver's seat. 'Three weeks in May for two and a half grand. Ten days diving guaranteed. Turtle heaven.' He paused. 'You OK, sir?'

'Me?' Faraday looked at him in surprise.

'Yeah . . . It's just you look . . .' He shook his head, embarrassed now. 'Forget it.' He glanced across at Wallace. 'Yer man here's got some news.'

Wallace offered Faraday a chip.

'He phoned up this morning, first thing, Mackenzie. Gave me the name of a hotel, the Solent Palace.'

'When?'

'Sunday. He wants to buy me lunch. Thinks I'm coming down from London.'

'Time?'

'Half twelve in the Vanguard Bar.'

'But you're definitely eating as well?'

'That's what he's saying. Apparently there's a two-for-one offer on all month. It's a carvery. He thinks I'll love it. Real food, mush. None of yer nouvelle muck.' The Pompey accent drew a grin from McNaughton.

Faraday made a note. The Solent Palace was one of the bigger hotels on the seafront, a Victorian pile in red brick with sensational views across the Common towards the Isle of Wight. The last time Faraday had been there was a year or so back, a formal dinner for a visiting police chief and his team from Caen. The food had been appalling, though the French, to their credit, hadn't turned a hair.

'The restaurant's at the front on the first floor,' Faraday said. 'How do we want to play this?'

'That's down to you, your call.' Wallace finished the last chip and wiped his fingers on a towel he'd found in the footwell. 'This car's a doss, Terry. What do you do, kip in it?'

'Only when my luck's in.' He was still looking at Faraday. 'What are we doing for back-up, sir?'

'There isn't any. Or not much.'

'You're serious?' McNaughton was responsible for Wallace's physical safety.

'Yes.' Faraday nodded. 'My boss is paranoid about security. Doesn't want to risk it.'

'Risk what?'

'Compromising the operation. He thinks we're half-blown already and he's probably right.'

'Tomorrow, you mean? The meet with Mackenzie?'

'No. The rest of it. Apparently, my lot plotted a hard stop back before Christmas. Should have netted a load of cocaine but they found nothing. That's why he's kept tomorrow so tight.'

'Thank fuck for that.'

'Exactly. The downside is back-up. I gather he's thinking himself, me, and you.'

'In the hotel?'

'Probably not. I'll recce the place tomorrow, but there's no way Mackenzie would have chosen it unless he knew the management, which means there's no way we can install cameras. Mackenzie's plugged in everywhere, as you know.' Faraday was drawing a diagram on his notepad. 'My guess is a couple of cars across the road, line of sight from the restaurant, say a hundred metres max if we get there early.'

'He wants a transmitter?'

'Plus a recorder. Both ends.'

'That's no problem. We've got a dinky little Nagra in on appro, recorder/transmitter, all one unit. Plus a receiver/recorder for one of the cars, plus the Olympus for stills, and we've cracked it.' He frowned. 'Doesn't solve the back-up, though.'

'Don't worry.' Wallace was watching a pretty young mother steering her infant daughter towards a nearby sports car. 'Worst that can happen, he shakes me down. I'm Jack the Lad, never go anywhere without a wire.'

'You think he'll buy that?'

'Haven't a clue, but you just keep talking, don't you?' The young mum was bending over the sports car, strapping her daughter into a child seat. 'What happens if he changes his mind about the hotel? Rings me with another r/v couple of minutes before the off?'

'You bell us.'

'And what if we meet at this place and he carts me off elsewhere?'

'We follow. And you keep talking.'

'OK.' He shrugged. 'Sounds sweet to me.'

The mother was climbing into the sports car now, smoothing down her skirt as she shot Wallace a smile. Faraday wanted to know what else Mackenzie had said on the phone.

'He was fine. Just said he wasn't fucking me around.'

'What did that mean?'

'He meant it was worth my while to make the trip down. Offered to show me the sights, too, if I was arsed.'

'What sights?' McNaughton started to laugh.

'He didn't say.' Wallace ignored McNaughton. 'As far as I'm concerned, the story's simple. I've got a thousand deals on the go and the last thing I'm up for is half the afternoon poking round the *Victory*. He knows that. I've told him. Baz, I said, it's a quick bite and you have your say. Then I'm back to town. That's one good reason we'll be staying at the hotel. If he starts to fuck around, I'm out of there.'

'It's Baz, is it?'

'Yeah, has been the last couple of calls. Old mates, we are. Same game.'

'You mean that?' Faraday at last felt his spirits begin to rise.

'Too right. The bloke's sharp as a tack. You can tell. Funny, too. He doesn't buy all the tosh about shopping developments in the Gulf for a moment, probably never has. As far as he's concerned, I'm the opposition. And we're not just talking Spit Bank.'

'You think he'll come across with an offer?'

'Yes.'

'Money?'

'Maybe, though I doubt it. These blokes hate parting with dosh. If there's a better way, he'll find it.'

'Threats?'

'No, he'll like to think he's classier than that.'

'What then?'

'Dunno.' He flashed Faraday a sudden smile. 'Stay tuned, eh?'

*

It was Cathy Lamb's decision to evacuate Dave Pullen to what she called 'a place of safety'. Between them, Winter and Suttle cut through the cable ties, threw Pullen a T-shirt and a pair of filthy jeans, and pushed him towards the bathroom to clean himself up. As soon as two other members of the squad had driven down from Kingston Crescent to babysit the flat in case the Scousers turned up, Winter and Suttle would escort Pullen to Central police station where, Winter explained, the Custody Sergeant had volunteered an empty cell.

The two DCs turned up shortly after two. Winter briefed them in the curtained lounge. Shortly afterwards, as he and Suttle stepped out into the gloom of the upstairs landing with Pullen, Winter heard a yell from one of the DCs. Five seconds in Pullen's bedroom had wrecked his entire afternoon.

'There's bleach in the kitchen cupboard,' Winter shouted back. 'We might be some time.'

Out on the street, it dawned on Pullen that Winter meant it about Central.

'No way,' he said, starting to struggle free.

Winter gave him a look, told him it was in his own best interests. Until the Scousers were off the plot, he should resign himself to a little protective custody. When Pullen refused to get in the car, Winter arrested him.

'Why?'

'Suspicion of kidnap and assault. Bloody do as you're told.' He told Suttle to fetch the handcuffs from the glovebox, then bundled Pullen into the back of the car and locked the doors.

Central police station lies beside the city's magistrates court. Winter found a space in the public car park, turned off the engine, then wound down his window an inch.

'How much of a wash did you have then, Dave?' He was eyeing Pullen in the rear-view mirror. 'Only some of our blokes in the station are really particular.'

'Fuck off.'

A gaggle of university students sauntered past, kicking at a stray can. Suttle watched them, saying nothing, aware that he hadn't a clue what might happen next. In situations like these, as he was beginning to discover, Winter made up the rules as he went along.

Winter found the release catch on the driver's seat and pushed it back, making himself more comfortable. Pullen yelped as the bottom of the seat caught him on the ankles, then he twisted sideways in the back.

'That fucking hurt.'

'Yeah?' Winter reached up, adjusting the mirror until he found

Pullen's ravaged face again. 'Here's the deal, Dave.' He nodded towards the nearby police station. 'Either we take you in there, do the paperwork, book you in, sort you out a lawyer, all that crap, or we have a little chat out here, just the three of us.'

'I done nothing.'

'Wrong, Dave. You done Trudy.'

'Who says?'

'Trude does. As you well know.'

'How's that, then?'

'Because Bazza would have told you. Not face to face, maybe, but good as. Do I have to spell this out, Dave? Or do we think Bazza's mates came round to your place to talk football?'

Pullen brooded for a moment.

'You got no proof,' he said at last.

'Wrong again, Dave. We've got a statement.'

'Who from?'

'Young Trudy. Am I right, James?'

Suttle nodded. He was beginning to get the drift.

'Dead right, mate.' Suttle glanced over his shoulder at Pullen. 'No more freebies from Trude, Dave. You've put her off billiards for life.'

'What she say, then?'

'She said she was having a little chat with some Scouse lads down Gunwharf. She said you got the hump and dragged her off. She said you smacked her around a bit in the car, then took a billiard cue to her once there was no way she could do anything about it. She also said you were pissed out of your head, but I think we're starting to take that for granted.'

'OK, Dave?' It was Winter again. 'Are we getting there now?'

Pullen said nothing. He'd shifted again, trying to get comfortable, and his head was back against the seat. At length, he closed his eyes and mumbled something incomprehensible. Winter waited until the yellow eyes opened again, then gave him a smile.

'Like I said, Dave. We can either put you through a couple of interviews and bang you up for the weekend pending a kidnap charge, or . . .' He fingered the steering wheel.

'Or what? What's the deal?'

'You tell us one or two things about Bazza.'

'Like what?'

'Like why he's so touchy about young Trude.'

'No way.'

'Really?' Winter kept eye contact in the mirror for a moment or two. Then he sighed. 'Kidnap's a serious offence, Dave. We can put you in front of the magistrates on Monday and I'll give you odds they'll refuse bail. You know the remand wing at Winchester? Bazza's mates practically run the place. I'd give it a couple of days, max.'

'Couple of days how?'

'Use your imagination, Dave. You know those big urns they use for boiling water in the canteen? They put sugar in, sticks better when they want to make a point. But then I expect you'd know that already, the time you've done.'

Pullen shook his head, not wanting to listen. A dustbin lorry growled past, two pink balloons attached to the back. Finally Pullen stirred. He appeared to have come to some kind of conclusion.

'What's in it for me, then?'

'We take you up to the QA for a proper check, then we find you a nice hotel for a couple of nights. Stick a bottle of Scotch in the fridge.'

'And after that?'

'You go back home. Get the Hoover out. If the Scousers come round at all, they'll do it in the next twenty-four hours.'

'You're serious about staking the place out?'

' 'Fraid so, Dave. Part of our Safer City Initiative. So . . . tell me about Bazza. Pretend we know nothing.'

'Bazza and Trude?'

'That's right.'

Pullen nodded, still not quite convinced, then a resigned shake of the head told Winter he was home and dry. Thanks to Cathy Lamb, there was a room already booked in the Travel Inn on the seafront. All Pullen had to do now was earn it.

'Trude's Bazza's daughter,' he mumbled.

'How do you know?'

'Bazza told me. Years ago.'

'So why doesn't Trude know?'

'He's never got round to telling her. Thinks it might get complicated. He loves her and everything, looks out for her, but he doesn't want any legal hassle. Having a kid of his own, like.'

'You mean Esme?'

'Yeah.'

'And the missus? Marie? Does she know about Trudy?'

'Haven't a clue.'

'And Trude?' It was Suttle this time. 'Where's she in all this?'

'Trude's off the planet. She's got a list of dads as long as your arm. Mother like Mist, you takes your pick. That's why I felt sorry for her.'

'Trude? You felt *sorry* for her? Fuck, I'd hate to be someone you didn't like.'

'You don't understand, son.'

'You're fucking right, I don't understand. You're an arsehole, Pullen.

227

Maybe it's time you picked on someone your own size. How about me for starters?' Suttle lunged at him, ignoring Winter's restraining hand. Pullen had retreated to the far corner of the back seat.

'See, Dave?' Winter was laughing. 'See the effect you have on people? My mate here, Jimmy, thinks you cocked it up with Trude. And I'll tell you something else: Bazza does too. Only thing that puzzles me is why Baz ever let you near his precious daughter in the first place. Is he blind or something? Doesn't he know you're a scumbag?'

'We were good mates, me and Baz.'

'Yeah, I remember. Same team, wasn't it? Only that was when you could still put one foot in front of the other.'

'I was fucking useful.'

'I know you were, Dave. I even watched you a couple of Sundays when I'd got nothing better to do. You were in a different class. Play your cards right, knock the charlie and all that booze on the head, and you could have turned pro. But it didn't happen, did it, Dave? And you know what that makes you? One sad bastard. You're right, couple of years ago Bazza thought the world of you. Now he's thrown you to the dogs.'

'Yeah.' Suttle nodded. 'And about fucking time too.'

Pullen didn't want to know. He was squirming around in the back, trying to ease the bite of the handcuffs. Winter watched him for a moment or two, not bothering to hide his disgust. Then he readjusted his seat and began to toy with the car keys.

'One last question, Dave. What's with Bazza and Valentine?'

'They're mates.'

'I know that. I meant with Trudy. Did Bazza know Trude was living with Valentine?'

'Of course he did.'

'And he thought Valentine was shagging her?'

'No way.'

'No *way*? How does that work?'

Pullen's eyes found Winter's in the mirror, the look of a man who knows he's gone too far but can't do much about it.

'He warned him off,' he said at last. 'Told him he'd break his legs if he laid a finger on her.'

'That personal?'

'Yeah.' Pullen closed his eyes again. 'You know fucking Bazza.'

Willard sat at his desk in the Major Crimes suite, waiting for Prebble to pick up his extension. According to Joyce, who'd answered Willard's call to *Tumbril* HQ, the young accountant was busy putting another thousand documents through the photocopier. She'd given him a shout and told him the chief was on the line, top priority. He responded well to pressure, she said, and would doubtless be back in seconds.

Willard, who'd taken a while to tune in to Joyce's sense of humour, scribbled himself a note about an extension to Prebble's contract. Once they had Mackenzie in the bag, the accountant would be working flat out preparing the paperwork for the CPS file. Willard also foresaw endless conferences with the Assset Recovery Agency, the new government body charged with stripping major criminals of their ill-gotten gains. This would be *Tumbril*'s real harvest, the seizure of millions of pounds' worth of property, business holdings, cars and sundry other goodies which Mackenzie had accumulated over the last decade. Prebble had spent the best part of a year sorting out the artful chaos Mackenzie had created around himself, and it would be Willard's pleasure to watch dusk fall on the city's biggest criminal. Up like a rocket, he thought. Down like a stick.

'Apologies, Mr Willard.' It was Prebble. 'Ran out of toner.'

'How's it going?'

'Fine.'

Willard had already rung this morning, telling Prebble that he'd need a headline summary of Mackenzie's major investments by the middle of next week. Now, he advanced the deadline.

'Monday morning,' he said. 'On my desk.'

Prebble's silence suggested this might be a problem. When he asked why, the accountant had a question of his own.

'What are you going to use this stuff for?' he enquired. 'Only it might help me to know.'

'Why?'

'Because there's ways I can dress the thing up.'

'I don't want it dressed up. I just want a simple breakdown – what the guy's worth, where it comes from, what he's into.'

'Like a wiring diagram?'

'Yeah.' Willard liked that idea. 'Exactly.'

'You're going to use it for some kind of presentation?'

'It doesn't matter what I'm going to use it for. It just has to be clear. If we can follow the links, see how it all ties up, so much the better. You know what I mean? We discussed it this morning.'

'Of course, sir.'

'Monday morning,' Willard repeated. 'OK?'

He put the phone down and sat back in his chair for a moment. Prebble had been right to talk about a presentation. If Sunday furnished the appropriate evidence – ideally some kind of drugs-related inducement – then Willard would be using the recordings and Prebble's asset analysis to lock in his own boss for the next stages of the operation.

To secure a result when *Tumbril* finally got to court, Mackenzie had to be seen to be behaving as a major drug dealer. Given a fair wind, that evidence might come from Sunday. Alternatively, Mackenzie might insist on a subsequent meeting for the physical exchange of drugs or money. Either way, the tapes, photos, and first-person testimony from Wallace would be all the more persuasive with the backing of Prebble's impressive research. The accountant was mapping every corner of Mackenzie's empire, vital reconnaissance if the asset recovery boys were to conduct a slash-and-burn raid of their own.

Willard pushed at the desk with his foot, letting the bulk of his body slowly revolve the chair. The last couple of months he'd put on a pound or two that he regretted, but he'd begun to invest in made-to-measure suits, cleverly cut, and knew that the extra weight remained a secret between him and his bathroom mirror.

He steepled his fingers and gazed out at the rain. Beyond next week, lay the press briefings and the headlines, those glorious moments when *Tumbril* could at last break surface and give a decent account of itself. Already, Willard was mentally preparing a briefing for the headquarters media unit, an outline account of the violence and intimidation that had smoothed Mackenzie's path to a fortune. This, he'd insist, was the reality that lay beneath the glitzy cafe-bars and the fuck-you lifestyle. The guys on the media unit would shape it into a press release, and Willard smiled at the thought of the subsequent off-the-record conversations he himself would be having with favoured local hacks. Then would be the time to gently muse about bent solicitors and corrupt accountants, about the raft of middle-class expertise on which Mackenzie and his tribe had floated to glory. These people knew who they were, he'd say, and they too should start thinking hard about explaining themselves in front of a judge and jury. Time to make them sweat, he thought. Time to make the bastards understand that not everyone was for sale.

He revolved full circle on the chair and found himself looking at the phone again. Checking his watch, he dialled a number from memory. This time in the afternoon, she was normally up in the living quarters on the fort, sorting out the day's ration of paperwork. Faraday had been right. There were wrinkles here that needed straightening out.

The phone answered on the second ring.

'Gisela?'

Eadie spent the afternoon at the Ambrym offices, sorting out the rushes on her drug project. With J-J already hard at work on the PC, she decamped next door to a small, bare room with a card table, a folding director's chair, and a view of the tiny backyard they used for parking. J-J had brought in a sleeping bag in anticipation of working through the night, and she unzipped it with his blessing and hung it over the window to mask the light before setting up her laptop and starting work.

She'd already been through the interview with Daniel Kelly, selecting the pieces she knew played best, and now she did the same with this morning's interview at the Marriott Hotel, filleting the tape for the moments when Daniel's father met the harder questions head on. The Adobe Premiere editing software supplied on-screen bins into which she could tuck the choicer morsels, and as the afternoon wore on she realised that even in rough-cut form – way over length – the impact of the video was going to be enormous.

After a break for coffee and a doughnut from the Café Parisien down the road, she steeled herself for a look at the footage from the mortuary. Already this felt like history – something she'd done weeks ago – and she marvelled at how dispassionate and professional she seemed to have remained. From time to time she could hear her own voice on the soundtrack asking the pathologist or her assistant exactly what was going to happen next, and there was no trace of the bile she'd tasted in her own throat.

Turning away from the laptop as the mortuary assistant began to pack the inside of Daniel's skull with paper tissues, she sensed again that she was putting together something unique. The interviews were extraordinarily powerful. Add footage like this plus shots of Daniel shooting up, and she could already write the headlines.

Excited now, she dug in her bag for her mobile. Her ex-husband Doug had recently been nice enough to enquire how the project was going. Not only had he leased her these offices but he'd negotiated by far the largest of the private donations which had enabled her to seek match-funding. She'd still no idea where the £7000 had come from but she was deeply grateful. The least she owed Doug was a call.

While she dialled his number, she tried to calculate how quickly she could come up with a rough cut. She could make a decent start tonight. Tomorrow, she was committed to shooting more demo footage in London. A mass protest had been widely advertised and the *Guardian* was anticipating at least 100,000 on the streets. With luck, though, she could be back by early evening.

Doug answered the moment the call rang through. It seemed he was on a friend's yacht. The wind was crap and it was starting to rain. Eadie got to her feet and peeked out through the window. Doug was right. Big fat drops were darkening the flagstones below.

'Listen,' she said. 'What are you doing tomorrow afternoon?'

'Why?'

'I'll have something to show you.' She grinned in anticipation. 'Knock your socks off.'

It was nearly five by the time Faraday got to Whale Island. To his surprise, he found Prebble still at his desk. As far as he could gather, the accountant never left later than four. Rush-hour trains back to London were a nightmare.

'Hi.' Prebble didn't look up from his laptop. 'Maybe you should have a look at this.'

'What is it?'

'Little present for Mr W. He wants the easy-read version for Monday.'

'Version of what?'

'Here.'

Prebble sat back for a moment, gesturing at the screen. A small mountain of documents covered the rest of the desk, some of them decorated with coffee stains. Conveyancing forms. Property leases. Trustee deeds. Invoices from motor auctions. Photocopied financial information – mainly stock market prices torn from newspapers, certain stocks highlighted in yellow.

Faraday turned his attention to the screen. Under 'European Properties', Mackenzie evidently owned or had an interest in a farmhouse in Northern Cyprus, an apartment block in Marbella, a vineyard in the Lot valley, and miscellaneous premises in Gibraltar.

'This is for when?'

'Monday.'

'Ah . . .' Faraday permitted himself a smile.

Prebble began to scroll down but an incoming call took Faraday away. Apologising for the interruption, he stepped across the office towards the open door that led to Joyce's precious archive.

'Gotcha.' It was Eadie.

'Good to hear you.'

'You, too. Listen. What time are you back tonight? Only—'

'I wasn't coming back. Not early.'

'No?'

'No. I thought we might go to the movies.'

'The *movies*? Is this Joe Faraday I'm hearing?'

'There's an Afghani film on. A woman director *and* subtitles. Thought it might appeal. Then maybe something to eat afterwards.'

'Joe, that's sweet . . .'

'But you can't make it?'

'Afraid not. Listen, there's a guy coming round to the flat to sort the boiler. I fixed for seven. Another cold bath and I'll fucking die.'

'Where's J-J?'

'Next door. Working his arse off.'

Wearily, Faraday agreed that he'd try and deal with the engineer. Across the office, in some haste, Prebble was packing up. By the time he'd reached for his coat and shouldered the laptop, Eadie had gone. Faraday watched Prebble heading for the door, wondering vaguely what other bits of Europe Mackenzie had bought.

The silence was broken by a stir of movement from the archive. It was Joyce.

'Couldn't help overhearing.' She grinned at him. 'Me? I just love all that Afghani feminist shit.'

Chapter seventeen

FRIDAY, 21 MARCH 2003, 18.50

Dusk was falling by the time Winter made it to Gunwharf. He left his Subaru in the underground car park and took the escalator to the plaza at the centre of the shopping complex. From here it was a five-minute walk across the central basin to the residential side of the new development. He'd been up to the harbourside apartment on a number of other occasions, sometimes social, mostly not, and had always been amused by how easy it was for a looker like Misty Gallagher to land on her feet. Screw the right men in this city, he thought, and you end up with a state-of-the-art kitchen and a £700,000 view.

A public footpath skirted the waterfront edges of Arethusa House. Winter paused by the rail, gazing out. He'd heard newcomers to the city prattling on about other great views. Portsmouth Harbour, they told each other, was like Hong Kong, San Francisco – full of mystery and romance and the promise of exotic foreign landfalls. Half close your eyes, they said, and you might already be at sea. To Winter, this was tosh, the kind of drivel you might expect from estate agents or the tourist board. Pompey Harbour was what it had always been: busy, purposeful, a working space. Warships eased away from their dock-yard berths and disappeared to sea. Ferries came and went. Fishing boats butted out against the tide. And, a couple of times a month, yachts ghosted in to one or other of the commercial marinas, laden with drugs. Legal or otherwise, this was where Pompey made a living.

Winter turned, looking up at the carefully stepped face of Arethusa House. Misty's apartment was at the top, a penthouse that Bazza had snapped up before it even got on the market. The curtains were partly drawn against the gathering dusk but the lights were on and from time to time Winter caught a shadowed movement inside. He'd been careful not to phone ahead and he knew she might have company, but there was a reasonable chance, this time of night, that she'd be up there alone.

She answered the buzzer on the entryphone at the second ring.

'Mist? It's Paul . . .'

'What do you want? I'm busy.'

'Just a chat, love. You got any Scotch?'

A moment or two later, Winter heard the door release engage. A lift from the lobby took him up to the top floor. The way the lift opened directly into Misty's apartment never failed to impress him.

She was standing in the big lounge surrounded by cardboard boxes, and Winter didn't need the half-empty bottle of Bacardi on the glass-fronted cabinet to tell him that she was drunk again. Her eyes were swimming and when she tried to move she had trouble staying upright.

'See?' The gesture took in the entire room. 'You didn't believe me, did you?'

'Believe you how, Mist?'

'Chucking us out. Two weeks he's giving us. Two weeks last . . .' She frowned, trying to remember.

Winter stepped into the room. The nearest cardboard box, bigger than the rest, had become a refuge for Misty's collection of stuffed animals. Winter counted two panda bears, a chimpanzee, a wallaby, and a sorry-looking tiger with a tear across its ribcage.

'Trude around?'

'She's out. Some bloke she's just met.'

'Who's that, then?'

'Fuck knows. You think she'd tell me?' She took a tiny step backwards, then collapsed onto the sofa. She was wearing a creased pair of white trousers, tight across the arse, and a see-through top in mauve that left absolutely nothing to the imagination. To get to forty and not need a bra, thought Winter, was truly remarkable.

'Next door.' She was waving vaguely towards the kitchen. 'Usual place.'

Winter helped himself to Scotch, topping the glass with ice cubes from the fridge. The big freezer compartment, he noted, was practically empty.

'Where next then, Mist?' He settled companionably beside her on the sofa. She smelled, unaccountably, of cigars.

'Dunno.' She shrugged. 'Victoria Park? The beach? What would he care?' She peered towards the window and her precious view. 'You ever seen that big house of his? Bloke I know says he and Marie have dinner parties, black tie, the works. Invite half fucking Craneswater and spend the evening talking about Waitrose and their kids' bloody education. Who'd ever have thought it, eh? Bazza getting it on with knobbers like that?'

'Gossip, Mist. Pay no attention.'

'I never did, until this. Now look at us. Out on the fucking street.'

'Yeah?'

She caught the tiny rise in his voice, the inflection that told her he didn't believe a word. She gazed at him, outraged.

'Haven't got a clue, have you? Blokes are all the same. It's the women that keep it together, women who sort everything out. Men? When it suits them, they help themselves. Loved it once, didn't he? Couldn't keep him off me. "Forget the fucking bedroom. Right here, Mist. Right here on the sofa, right here across the back of the chair. Who's got time to bother with the bedroom?" Fuck and forget. Gotta go now. Bang. Away. Gone.'

Winter swallowed a mouthful of the Scotch, surveying the chaos around him. Beside another cardboard box, a litter of unironed clothes and an enormous pile of CDs. Coldplay. White Stripes. Blur.

'What about Trude, then? Is that the two of you kipping on the beach?'

'Trude'll cope. Trude always fucking copes.'

'I hear she's back with you.'

'Yeah. For all the good it'll do her.'

'What about Valentine, then?'

'What about him?'

'Never worked out? Him and Trude?'

'Haven't a clue.' She ducked her head, more cautious now, her brain beginning to catch up with the lazy drumbeat of Winter's questions. 'Why don't you ask her?'

'Maybe I have.'

'Yeah?' Misty's head came up. 'How's that, then?'

'She got beaten up. I think I mentioned it. We get to ask questions about incidents like that, Mist. It's part of the job description.'

'And?'

'She was on the rebound. From Valentine. Because Valentine wouldn't fuck her. Strange, eh? Good-looking girl like Trude? Wouldn't make sense, would it? Unless Valentine was otherwise engaged?'

Misty shook her head, said nothing. When Winter got up to fetch the bottle of Bacardi, she first covered the empty glass with her hand, then shrugged, letting Winter pour. Her whole body had gone slack. Whatever trench she'd dug, whatever position she was defending, had just been overrun. At length, she fumbled for a cigarette.

'What else did she tell you?'

'Not much. She's a strong kid.'

'Fucking right. Catch her in the right mood, she can be nice, too.'

'I'll drink to that.' Winter touched glasses and then sat back, making himself comfortable. 'So who's her dad, then?'

The question, this sudden bend in the road, caught Misty by surprise. Even now, half a bottle of Bacardi down, there were places she didn't want to go.

'What makes you think I know?' she managed at last. 'And even if I did, what makes you think I'd tell you?'

It was a reasonable point. Winter tipped his head back, staring up at the ceiling.

'Bazza thinks she's his,' he murmured at last. 'Doesn't he?'

Misty nodded, said nothing.

'Did he think that from the start? Way back?'

'Might have done.'

'And was he right?'

Winter became aware of Misty gazing at him. Some of the fog seemed to have cleared. She looked almost sober.

'You've got to understand one thing about Bazza,' she said quietly.

'What's that?'

'He can be fucking crazy. A madman.'

'You mean *go* fucking crazy?'

'Yeah. You might never have seen it but it's true. Press the wrong button and he goes apeshit, truly fucking bonkers. A mate of his once told me it was his strength, made him what he was, gave him everything – the business, the cars, Marie, all this . . .' She gestured round. 'I don't know whether that's true or not but the bonkers bit is spot on. When Bazza flips, you don't want to be around. Believe me. I've been there. I know.'

'So does that make him Trude's dad?'

Misty looked away. When Winter asked the question again, she gave a tiny shrug.

'You're telling me you don't know?'

'I didn't. Not for years I didn't.'

'But now?'

'Now I do know.'

'And Trude?'

'Yeah.' She nodded, wistful. 'She knows too. We did one of them DNA tests. Hundred and fifty quid. You do a couple of swabs, the inside of your mouth, and send them off. Couple of days later . . .' She smiled to herself. 'Bingo!'

'You said a couple of swabs.'

'That's right.'

'Trude and who else?'

'Listen, you've got to promise me something.' Misty's nails began to trace a pattern on the back of Winter's hand. 'You're right about Bazza. He's always thought Trudy was his from day one. He's never

237

said so, not to Trude, only to me, but I know that's what he thinks. That's why we stuck together for so long. That's how come we got this place. OK, part of it was so me and Baz could still keep getting it on but there was Trudy as well. She's part of his life. He loves her like a daughter. I know he does.'

'Sure.' Winter held eye contact. 'So Bazza needs a bit of protection? A bit of TLC? Is that what you're saying?'

'Protection from what?'

'The truth. About young Trude.'

'Fucking right.' Misty nodded. 'And not just Bazza, either. If it ever crossed his mind . . .' She shook her head, then shuddered.

Winter squeezed her arm. 'It's Valentine, isn't it?'

There was a long silence, then, from the harbour, three long blasts from an outbound ferry.

'Yes.' Misty's eyes were swimming. 'Trude belongs to Mike.'

'And that's why he never touched her.'

'Yes.'

'Because he knew?

'Because he thought he knew. We only did the test last week. Trude and I had had a set-to over Mike. She'd come in unexpected and caught us at it. In the end, there was no way I couldn't tell her. The test was her idea.'

'She's happy about it?'

'Over the fucking moon. Not just a mum and a dad but a mum and a dad who are still –' she nodded towards the bedroom '– getting it on.'

'And Bazza?'

'Hasn't got a clue. Never had. You want to know how long I've been with Mike? Off and on?' She reached for the nearby box of tissues. 'Eighteen years.'

Trudy wanted to know why Jimmy Suttle wasn't drinking alcohol. The car in the nearby parking lot was a reasonable excuse but the rest of it made her laugh. Whoever played squash on a Friday night?

'Me, for starters.'

They were sitting in a busy waterside pub in Port Solent, a marina complex tucked into the north-east corner of Portsmouth Harbour. Trudy had taken a cab up from Gunwharf and was bitterly disappointed that their evening would go no further.

'What about afterwards?' she said again. 'I can watch you, go for a walk or something. Then we can go on some place. Like last night.'

'Can't do it, Trude.'

'You're meeting someone.'

'You're right. His name's Richard. I beat him last time so tonight we've got a tenner on it. We play. We go to the pub. We get pisssed.'

'I'll come, too.'

'You can't, love. It's a blokes' thing.'

'Oh yeah? So what does that make me? Some fucking slapper you shag when you're in the mood?'

'I never said that.'

'No, but that's what you think, ain't it? I had you down for someone half decent last night, I really did. That must make me fucking brain dead. How come you blokes are all the same?'

'We're not all the same. It's Friday night. We've had the game fixed all week. And that's all there is to it.'

'So where does that leave me?'

She stared at him a moment. Suttle leaned forward to kiss her but she turned her head away. Two lads at the next table exchanged grins.

'Listen, Trude—'

'Fuck off. I hate you.'

'No, you don't.'

'I do. You come over all sincere, all nice, you get what you want and now look what happens.'

'Last night was your idea.'

'Oh yeah? Twist your arm did I? Or was that someone else fucking the arse off me?'

'Listen, maybe—'

'Forget it.'

'What?'

'I said forget it.' Trudy was reaching down for her bag. She knew the cab number by heart. She began to stab the numbers in, then paused. 'You know what you're missing, don't you?'

'What?'

'I'm off next week. Going away.' She gave him a cold smile. 'Play your cards right, and we could have done it all night again.'

'When?'

'Tonight, dimlo. Except squash with your little friend's more important. Maybe it's right what they say about the Filth. All fucking queens together. Still –' she shrugged. '– see if I fucking care.'

Suttle reached across and snatched at the mobile.

'Tomorrow night,' he said. 'I promise.'

She looked at him, then laughed.

'Tomorrow night what?'

'Anything. Anything you like.'

She studied him a moment. 'Gunwharf? Forty Below? Somewhere nice afterwards?'

Forty Below was the happening nightclub. Kids Trude's age couldn't get enough of it. Neither could some of Bazza's chums.

Suttle gave the proposition a moment's thought, then nodded.

'Deal?' She grinned at him, retrieved the mobile, blew him a kiss, then started on the number again.

Faraday sat in the flickering darkness, understanding nothing. A woman in a burka was making some kind of journey. She needed to find her cousin in Kabul. En route across the parched landscape, she skirted a number of lives, stopped now and again for lengthy conversations, pondered the problems of contemporary Afghanistan. Kids were everywhere. Many of the men had lost limbs to landmines. In a sequence that held Faraday spellbound, hundreds of Afghanis hopped madly across the desert as a tangle of prosthetic legs descended from the heavens on a parachute. It was a strange way, Faraday thought, to frame one of the world's undoubted tragedies – crazy, surreal, funny – but then he sank back into the puzzling chaos of his own life, and conceded that this young film-maker might have a point. Surreal was pretty close.

He awoke, some time later, to find the house lights on and Joyce bent over him.

'You OK, sheriff? Only I think they want us to go.'

Outside, it had started to rain. The film was showing at an art-house cinema in a marina development in Southampton. They'd driven across from Portsmouth, Faraday relieved to get out of the city. Beside his car he paused to fumble for his car keys. Joyce again, a hand on his arm this time. She nodded across the car park towards a distant restaurant. Rain had slicked the tousle of dark curls against her head.

'On me,' she said briefly.

'What do you think?' It was a sign that Eadie Sykes had come to know well. An outstretched hand, palm up, a tiny interrogative twist of the wrist.

She reached for the PC mouse over J-J's shoulder and took the sequence back to the start. A line of placards she recognised from last night's demo was swaying towards the camera. Late shoppers in the precinct were pausing to take a look. On the soundtrack, denied J-J, came the bellowed chant, 'Esso, Mobil, BP, Shell, take your war and go to hell!'

The head of the march broke like a wave around the camera, and as it did so, a slow mix dissolved the protesters into another scene. Eadie bent towards the screen, watching a crowd of Arabs gathered around the back of an ambulance. It was night-time. In the background, beyond the chaos of the street, a building appeared to be on fire. Paramedics, desperate men fighting their way through the crowd, wrestled a small body into the back of the ambulance.

Then, without warning, the camera was panning across a bare, tiled interior. Dozens of men and women lay on the floor, jigsawed haphazardly together. One or two were unconscious. The rest gazed numbly into the middle distance, or stared up at the camera, uncomprehending. There was blood everywhere, open wounds, makeshift bandages, the stooping presence of a nurse with a bottle of fluid in one hand and an i/v line in the other. Then came a stir of movement in a far corner, and the camera tilted up and probed the gloom, hunting for another image.

A young baby lay sprawled on its mother's bloodsoaked lap. As she became aware of the presence of the camera, she gently rolled the tiny body over. The back of the baby's head had disappeared. The image trembled for a moment, the cameraman twitching with the focus as he closed the shot around the tiny corpse.

Faces again, Pompey faces, fists punching the air as the column of protesters swept across a dual carriageway. Behind the wheel of a car, stalled in the waiting queue, a young man in a suit was reading the back page of the *News*, oblivious to everything.

'Incredible.'

Eadie stepped back from the PC and gave J-J's shoulder a squeeze. The first instalment of Al-Jazeera footage had come in half an hour ago, pumped down from London on the broadband link. Poking his head around Eadie's door, J-J had signalled its arrival, but she'd been too busy with pictures of her own to spare the time for a look. Now, as J-J played her the rest of the news coverage, she realised how priceless the footage would be. This was the Arab view of the war, tens of millions of men and women on the receiving end of Bush's hi-tech onslaught. Against Apache gunships and cruise missiles, these people were practically defenceless. All they could do was hang on and pray. The Americans and the British had promised them a bloodless war, liberation without tears, and here it was.

J-J was on his feet, stretching his arms back to ease the cramps. He planned to work through the evening, dossing down in the sleeping bag when he got too tired. What he wanted was five minutes of tightly cut footage, something for Eadie to take to London and give to the Stop the War people, something to let them glimpse the possibilities of this kind of document. Eadie nodded, thumbs up. In a couple of days, she'd find the time to sort out a series of sound bites from Bush and Blair – White House press conferences, House of Commons speeches – all the drivel about WMD and the imminent threat, all the fervent pledges that the allies had embarked on a moral crusade. 'Sometimes the tough decision are the right decisions,' she remembered Blair saying. Just how comforting was that when your baby had just been blown apart?

Joyce had been to the restaurant before. Friday night, the place was packed but the waiter she knew found her a reserved table at the back. The people who'd booked it were half an hour late. Too bad if they still showed up.

'They do scrummy chicken tagine.' Joyce surrendered her dripping raincoat. 'Dunno how you feel about North Africa, but the couscous is to die for. Sheriff?'

Faraday was still on his feet, gazing around at the sea of faces. Young couples, foursomes, conversations spiced with laughter and the chink of raised glasses. It seemed unreal, like the film he'd just watched, mysterious, inexplicable, remote. He shook his head the way you might try and adjust a badly tuned TV. This sense of detachment, of drift, was beginning to bother him.

'Sheriff?'

He turned his attention to Joyce and at last sat down. She was offering him a bowl of small, deep-fried objects in a nest of mint leaves. He wondered what they were.

'Call me Joe,' he muttered. 'Do you mind?'

He tried one of the balls. It tasted spicy.

'Falafel,' Joyce said helpfully. 'I can't believe you've never eaten this stuff. Sorry about the movie.'

'It was good. Unusual.'

'Yeah? So why did you go to sleep on me?'

Faraday said he didn't know. More to the point, while he'd never admit it, he didn't much care. More and more, these last couple of days, life was passing him by, a piece of theatre for which he'd neglected to buy a ticket. This sense of detachment could be rather wonderful, a sense that nothing really much mattered, but other times – like now – he felt a stir of something that felt close to panic. What was he doing here? Why wasn't he at Eadie's place, sorting out the central heating? What in God's name was *happening* to him?

'You want red or white?' Joyce was consulting the wine list.

'Neither. Water will be fine.'

'I can get you a cab back. Leave the car here.'

'Water.' It sounded peremptory, almost an order, not at all the way he'd meant it. Joyce had abandoned the wine list. She looked genuinely concerned.

'Joe? What's the matter?'

'Nothing. I'm sorry.'

242

'Tell me, honey. Pretend I know nothing about all this shit. Pretend I'm someone you just met. This is Casablanca, OK? We're in the same hotel. I'm happily married. You're shacked up with someone luscious. No pressure. Just conversation.'

'All what shit?'

'*Tumbril*. The office. Our little glee club. I know it's Friday night, Joe, but *Tumbril*'s like rheumatism, isn't it? Gets in your bones. Won't let go.'

'You find that?'

'All the time. Constant damn ache. Doesn't respond to medication. You don't believe me? Then take a trip to the QA. That lovely Nick would back me to the hilt if he could only remember.'

'You've been up there?'

'Lunchtime. Guy's away with the fairies.'

'That wasn't *Tumbril*'s fault.'

'No?' She leaned forward across the table, V-necked cashmere sweater, enormous breasts bursting for attention. 'You should have seen him the past couple of weeks. Whoever ran him over did him a favour. The way I read it, Nick was a nervous breakdown waiting to happen, the real thing, totally blown away. Couldn't concentrate, couldn't hold a conversation, couldn't make a decision. Talk to him most days, you had to check he was still sentient.' She paused, her hand closing over Faraday's. 'Am I getting through here?'

For the first time, Faraday sensed something he recognised, something familiar in the torrent of noise he kept trying to tune out.

'That's what his partner says. You know Maggie?'

'Sure.' Joyce helped herself to a falafel. 'Pretty girl. Teacher. Met her twice. Mad as a coot. Goes with the job.' She looked up at him. 'So how come they saddled you with *Tumbril*? Only from where I'm standing, it wasn't an act of kindness.'

'You think I'm making a mess of it?'

'Other way round, sheriff.'

'It's that obvious?'

'Didn't I just say so?' She gave his hand a squeeze, then reached for her napkin. 'Tell me about that boy of yours. Blew it, I hear.'

'Who told you that?'

'Doesn't matter. Our job, Joe, there's no such thing as secrets. My favourite DI's son goes AWOL, launches a new career, becomes a drug baron, the world knows about it within seconds. We thrive on this stuff. We love it. Marty Prebble says it's ironic. Marty's big on irony.' She paused. 'So how is he?'

Faraday considered the question. The last day and a half he'd thought of little else.

243

'You want the truth? I haven't a clue. We've met a couple of times, bumped into each other, but he won't talk to me, won't communicate, won't even look at me.'

'Talking's tough, isn't it? Guy like him?'

'You know what I mean. You met the lad a while back. Nothing's changed since then. Normally, he's all over you. Now . . .' Faraday shrugged, wishing he'd said yes to the wine. 'He's just not there any more.'

'Not at home, not opening the door. Not to you, at least.'

'That's right.' Faraday gazed at her, surprised and hurt by the stab of the metaphor. 'Definitely not to me.'

'What about your lady friend? Is she any use?'

'She's closer to him than I am. Has been for months.'

'Sounds like robbery. Arrest her.'

Despite himself, Faraday laughed. When Joyce pushed a little further, he found himself telling her about Eadie, about Ambrym, about the protest march they'd been on back in February, about her commitment to her video work, about the sense of possibility she'd brought to his life.

'Possibility how? I don't get it.'

'She's different. It's hard to explain. She just comes at everything with this incredible –' he frowned, trying to pin it down '– conviction.'

'She knows who she is.'

'Exactly.'

'And you don't.'

'Is that a question?'

'No, my love, it's one of those folksy little home truths. You won't mind me sharing it with you because it happens to be true. Matter of fact, it's something I've thought ever since we first met. Remember what happened after Vanessa? How hard you found it to cope with this big Yankee dame that stepped into your life? I used to sit and watch you some days, and wonder what you were doing in a job like this. Don't get me wrong, Joe. You were a damn fine cop, still are – and I should know because I was married to the other sort – but sometimes damn fine isn't enough. You know what I'm talking about?'

'No.'

'You're vulnerable, Joe, and it shows. That's why women like me want to mother you. Is your Eadie like that?'

'No. But that's the point. That's what I love about her. She's got it cracked, Joyce. She knows exactly what she wants to do. She gets angry, not at me, not personally, but at bits of the bigger picture, and instead of sitting around and moaning like we all do she gets out there and *does* something about it.'

'Megalomaniac, then. No wonder you're a basket case.'

'You don't understand.'

'You're serious? You really think I don't? When I'm sitting here? Looking at you? Seeing a man I admire in deep, deep shit? I might be a little crazy, Joe, and I guess I might be just a shade megalomaniac myself, but I recognise what I see. You're lost, honey. And this Eadie is a woman who should be coping with that.' She extended a perfect nail, accusatory. 'So where is she tonight? Why isn't she here instead of little me?'

'She's busy.'

'Yeah. And I bet she's always busy. But you know something, Joe? Busyness is a pile of shit, no matter how many films you make. Why? Because you'll never change the world. Boy George, your guy Blair, these people are in there for what they can get. Vote them out, you're dealing with another bunch of bastards. Same with drugs, matter of fact. *Tumbril*'s a dandy idea. Spend a couple of trillion pounds, sort out all that paperwork, and maybe we get to put Bazza Mackenzie away. But you really think that'll make the slightest bit of difference? Out on the street where it really matters? My sweet arse.'

'So what do you do?'

'About the drugs thing?'

'About –' Faraday gestured helplessly at the space between them '– everything.'

'How we should be with each other? Men and women? Fathers and sons? How we can best get through?'

'Yes.'

'Geez, I don't know.' She reached for a bread roll and tore it apart. 'I guess in the end it's personal. I've got a few ideas on the subject, mainly about levelling with folks, being yourself, sparing a little time, taking a risk or two. Your Eadie? Does she read it that way? You tell me.'

'She takes huge risks. That's what she's best at. That's what I'm trying to tell you.'

'And that makes you feel good?'

'Feeling good's irrelevant. She does what she has to do. I admire her for that.'

'Sure. And where are you in all this? You singular? You plural? She doesn't care, Joe. Else you wouldn't be sitting here with me.'

'That's unfair. You've never met her.'

'I don't have to. Looking at you is all I need.' She let the point sink in. Then she beckoned him towards her, the way you might share a secret with a child. 'You're a good man, Joe Faraday. You're honest. You care. You put yourself on the line. And that's from someone who's got no time for irony.'

Faraday sat back a moment, warmed by her generosity. Then he looked at the faces around him, listened to the swirl of conversation – people getting on with their lives, people coping, people at ease – and he felt the tide of panic beginning to rise again.

'That's all fine,' he muttered. 'But it's not enough, is it?'

Chapter eighteen

The early-morning train to London was full of Pompey fans. They drifted from carriage to carriage, toting bacon baps and cans of Stella, still sober. From time to time, buried in her copy of the *Guardian*, Eadie caught the name 'Preston North End'. Couple more points, acccording to a fat boy in a Burberry coat, and it's ours for the fucking taking.

'What's ours for the fucking taking?' Eadie enquired of the elderly woman sitting beside her.

'The football, dear,' the woman whispered. 'Even my Len's getting excited.'

Minutes later, for the second time, Eadie tried to phone Faraday. Last night, a little to her surprise, he hadn't returned to the flat, but on reflection that wasn't so unusual. Saturday mornings, he often left early for a birding expedition and slept at the Bargemaster's House, not wanting to disturb her.

Faraday's mobile still wasn't taking calls. On the off chance, she tried the landline at the Bargemaster's House just in case he'd opted for a lie-in. The last couple of days she'd noticed a tension in him, a tightness that conversation simply seemed to compound. She'd been meaning to ask him about it, to make the kind of time she sensed he needed, but events – as ever – had ganged up against her.

There was no answer from the Bargemaster's House and Eadie glanced at her watch as the train slowed for Woking station. She'd been right first time. By now, Joe had probably been on the road for hours, with his waxed cotton jacket, packets of dried soup, and Thermos full of hot water. She'd never met anyone so organised, so single-minded, so self-sufficient. Pass on a rumour of something exotic, some bird he hadn't seen for a year or two, and he'd be gone all day. Sorted, she thought, with a tiny stab of relief.

Faraday sat in front of his first-floor study window, his binoculars

247

abandoned, the pad on which he tallied each morning's birds untouched. Way out on the harbour, high tide, a raft of something grey was floating gently south. They were probably brent geese, he thought, but he couldn't be bothered to check. That ceaseless urge to seek and find, to classify and record, to keep his finger on the pulse of life beyond this window, had left him. His curiosity had gone. Even the ringing of the phone downstairs had failed to rouse him.

He gazed numbly at the view and wondered about going back to bed. Unable to sleep, he'd been sitting by the window since before dawn. Last night, against his better judgement, he'd allowed Joyce to invite him in when he'd dropped her off at home. She lived in a featureless modern semi on an estate to the east of Southampton, every trace of her errant husband carefully erased.

She'd slipped a Peggy Lee album into the CD player and then bustled through to the kitchen to brew coffee, leaving Faraday in the tiny box-like lounge-diner surrounded by little colonies of Beanie Babies. How anyone could live with this shade of fuschia was beyond him and his heart had sunk when she'd thundered up the stairs to the bedroom. Minutes later, in a turquoise dressing gown, she was back down again, raiding her ex-husband's store of duty-free booze. Cheerfully shameless, she offered him a choice of five liqueurs to go with the coffee and said it might be best to put his Mondeo on the hardstanding in front of the garage.

Faraday said no to everything, swallowed the coffee, and headed for the door. On the front step, not the least upset, she gave him a big hug and told him to get a good night's sleep. He'd smiled at her and said he'd do his best. He drove up the road to turn round, and as he passed the house again he could see her through the net curtains in the lounge, a huge swirl of turquoise, dancing alone to the music.

Now, he wandered downstairs and put the kettle on, forcing himself to plan the day. If he had the energy, he'd put a coat on and walk the three miles to the bird reserve at Farlington Marshes. Contributors to the *Birdline* website had been talking of short-eared owls and he knew the sight of one of those daylight hunters might cheer him up. Back by mid morning, he'd be in good time to drive down to the Solent Palace Hotel. Maybe he'd treat himself to lunch, find out if the food had improved, pretend he was Graham Wallace, check out the sight lines from the restaurant and the exits to the car park, and all the other stuff that setting up a meet like this involved. The thought filled him with gloom, not because he'd lost faith in the operation but because the very prospect of having to make any kind of decision seemed hopelessly daunting.

The kettle began to boil and he stepped across to switch it off. The teapot lay on the nearby tray. J-J had been the last to use it and a couple of ancient tea bags were still visible inside. Faraday froze for a moment, staring down in bewilderment. His brain appeared to have locked solid. Try as he might, he couldn't work out what to do next.

Paul Winter was the first customer of the morning at Pompey Blau. He parked his precious Subaru and sauntered across the road towards the forecourt. A £2.99 breakfast at a cafe round the corner had improved an already promising day and the sight of a line of gleaming BMWs lifted his spirits still further. He hadn't felt so cheerful for years.

A small hut at the back of the forecourt housed the sales operation. This, thought Winter, was Pompey at its best. Half a million quid's worth of German engineering on display and some dosser's garden shed to tidy up the paperwork.

A youth in a baseball cap and a Saints football top lounged behind the desk. A Saturday copy of the *Sun* was open at the football page.

'Brave lad.' Winter nodded at the shirt, 'You got a death wish or something?'

Without saying a word, the youth twisted round in the chair. Scrolled across the back of the shirt, *Scummers Suck.*

'Nice one. Mike Valentine around?'

'No.'

'Any idea where I can find him?'

'No, mush.'

'Seen him at all recently, have you?'

The youth shook his head. His eyes hadn't left the paper. Winter planted himself in front of the desk, then bent low, his mouth an inch from the youth's ear.

'What if I want to buy one of those nice cars?' he whispered.

The youth at last lifted his head.

'You can't.'

'*Can't?* How does that work? I thought this was a garage?'

'They're all sold.'

'*All* of them? Why doesn't it say so?'

'Run out of stickies, mate. And my writing's crap.' He'd gone back to the paper. 'Valentine's probably at Waterlooville. Why don't you try there?'

Waterlooville was fifteen minutes up the motorway. Once a quiet country town, it had recently sprawled outwards in a rash of trading estates and executive housing developments that threatened to engulf the surrounding countryside.

Mike Valentine Autos occupied a corner site on the trading estate to the west of the town centre. Winter left the Subaru at the kerbside and strolled across to the big, glass-fronted offices beside the showroom. A crescent of blue sofa was littered with motoring magazines and a water cooler bubbled on a stand in the corner. A banner hung on the wall behind the empty reception desk. *More For Less*, it read. *Driving Is Believing*.

Winter lingered beside the desk for a moment or two. Twenty-five years in the job had given him a talent for reading documents upside down, but he had to double-check before he believed the figure on the sales invoice. A two-year-old Beemer for £9500? Couldn't be done.

There were dozens more invoices underneath. He stepped round the desk and began to flick through them. A 2002-reg series 5 for £14,950. A Mercedes S for £11,750. No wonder everyone he knew in the job was beating a path to Mike Valentine's door. This wasn't a sales operation, it was a charity.

'Can I help you?'

A woman had appeared from a room at the back. She was young, tall and blonde with a spray-on top and low-slung jeans to showcase her belly piercing. Winter offered a cheerful grin. If her name wasn't Sharon, it should have been.

'Mike Valentine?'

'Not here today.' She was looking down at the invoices. 'You from the VAT or something?'

'Just curious. Friend told me this was the place to come for a bargain.'

'You wanna *car*?' She seemed astonished.

'That's right. Prices like these, who wouldn't?'

'Yeah?' She frowned, then started picking at a nail. 'You'll have to talk to Mike, then. There's no one else now.'

'Why's that then?'

'Dunno.' She shrugged. 'You'll have to ask him.'

'Fine. Love to. Where is he?'

'Out.'

'Out where?'

'London.'

'What about the cars next door?'

'Most of them are gone, sold. Bloke came in this morning and cancelled on the blue series 3 convertible. You can have a look at that, if you want.'

'Through there?' Winter nodded across at the door that led into the showroom. 'You got a service history or anything?'

'Try the workshop at the back. There's a bloke called Barry.' She sank into the chair behind the desk and dug around in the drawer for a nail file. The conversation was evidently over.

Winter headed for the showroom. Amongst half a dozen cars was the blue convertible. Winter made a cursory inspection, gave one of the front wheels a kick, noticed the distinctive *Play Up Pompey* sticker on the back, then headed out into the sunshine again.

The workshop, invisible from the road, was a breeze-block construction with folding metal doors. Two CCTV cameras looked down on the apron of oil-stained tarmac at the front and a prominent sign threatened illegal parkers with clamping. One of the two doors was open, and Winter stepped into the gloom, peering round.

The workshop was bigger than he'd expected. A couple of inspection pits occupied one side and a powered chain hoist hung from one of the overhead girders. Like every other detective in the area, Winter had picked up the gossip after Valentine had survived a carefully plotted road stop on the A3 shortly before Christmas. Judging by the resources they'd thrown at the job – surveillance, traffic cars, spotter plane – you'd have expected something substantial in the way of a result, yet even the wreckers in Scenes of Crime had failed to find even a trace of anything naughty.

The fact that Valentine was tied in with Bazza Mackenzie was common knowledge, but Christmas was the first time that Winter had given the partnership serious thought. Maybe the guys who'd set up the intercept were right, he thought. Maybe Valentine's lads really did run shitloads of cocaine down from London. If so, then a workshop like this would be exactly the kind of unloading facility they'd need.

Except for a tidy-looking BMW X5, the garage was empty. Winter sauntered across and took a look. Someone had been working on the vehicle only recently because there was dirty oil in a plastic bowl between the front wheels. The tyres were new, too, tiny whiskers of rubber curling up from the tread. Curious, Winter peered inside. The BMW's documentation lay pouched in a plastic wallet on the dashboard. On the passenger seat, was a new-looking Michelin European road map. Winter returned to the front of the vehicle, making a mental note of the registration, then he noticed the tiny black triangles of black tape patched carefully onto the headlights. They, too, looked new. Preparations for a trip abroad, he thought.

He heard a door bang, then footsteps. Turning round, Winter found himself looking at a small, thin figure in stained green overalls. The face, for a second, looked familiar: receding hair, bony skull, small deeply recessed eyes. He'd seen this man recently, maybe in one of the Custody Suite photos that decorated the cork board in the CID squad office at Highland Road.

'What's this, then?' The man was wiping his hands on a tangle of oily rag. A good night's sleep would do wonders for his complexion.

Winter explained about the blue convertible, wanted more details. The mechanic told him the car was a dog.

'Got shunted up the arse in a motorway pile-up. Twisted chassis. Fuck all we can do about it.'

'Shame.' Winter nodded back towards the showroom. 'What about the rest of them?'

'Couple of decent motors. The series 7 is a steal. That kind of price, you could clean up if you had the patience. Private sale after, ad in the paper, fifteen grand easy.'

'So what are you asking?'

'Eleven three. And it's gone, in case you're wondering.'

Winter nodded, plunging his hands in his pockets. He could detect bitterness in seconds and this man had plenty.

'How come everything goes so fast?' he enquired.

'Always has done. Pile 'em high, sell 'em for fuck all. Shift enough motors, do it quick, and no one has time to spot how it's done. Same with them magicians, ain't it?' He made a shuffling motion with his hands, invisible cards in some pavement scam, then cleared his throat and turned his head to spit into the gloom.

'No motors left, then? Except the bent Beemer?'

'That's right, mate, all gone.'

'So when should I come back?'

'Wouldn't bother if I were you. He's selling up.'

'Who's selling up?'

'My boss. Selling up and shipping out. Couple of weeks, this place'll be doing bathrooms. Great, if you fancy selling fucking khazis for the rest of your life.'

The Solent Palace Hotel occupied a prime site on the seafront. Look one way, and the long line of Ladies Mile tracked across the Common towards Southsea Castle. Look the other, and the sweep of the promenade took the eye west towards the busy mouth of Portsmouth Harbour. From the upper floors, on a clear day, you could see fifteen miles across the Isle of Wight to the low, blue hump of Tennyson Down. Faraday, who'd once spent half a morning in a top-floor bedroom trying to get to the bottom of an alleged rape, remembered being transfixed by the view. Tennyson Down was the landscape of his youth, miles and miles of close-cropped turf that still spoke to him across the years. Just now, he could think of nothing sweeter than to be back there, perched on the cliff top, listening to a skylark belting its head off, invisible against the sun.

The hotel restaurant on the first floor was a long, sunny room with tall picture windows over-curtained in heavy brocade. At a couple of minutes before noon, it was virtually empty. An elderly couple at a nearby table were puzzling over the *Daily Telegraph* crossword. In a far corner, a waiter was polishing glasses.

Faraday found himself a table by the window. He could feel the sun through the glass and he swapped chairs so the thin warmth bathed his face. He closed his eyes a moment, forcing himself to relax. There was something about the feel of this place that reminded him of a convalescent home. Its very emptiness should have been peopled with casualties, he thought, and amongst those broken bodies he was tempted to number himself. He felt exhausted, physically knocked-about, a front-line survivor evacuated from some far-flung war, and when he opened his eyes again he half expected a nurse to turn up with a wheelchair, ready to give him a breath or two of fresh air.

'What can I get you, sir?' It was the waiter.

Faraday looked at him, vaguely surprised.

'Lunch?'

'The menu's there, sir. I'll be back in two ticks.'

Faraday studied the menu, presented again with the impossibility of making any kind of choice. Lightly poached salmon on a bed of watercress? Breast of chicken, Italian-style? He hadn't a clue.

He put the menu to one side and gazed out of the window. Tomorrow's business, he'd decided, could pretty much look after itself. If Willard was really determined to keep this latest episode in the *Tumbril* story so tight – even Brian Imber didn't know – then there was precious little that Faraday could make in the way of prior arrangements. He'd already acquired RIPA authority for the operation, which would protect the covertly gathered evidence in court. Tomorrow, God willing, Wallace and Mackenzie would turn up, and Mackenzie would make a choice of table. Faraday and Willard, meanwhile, would be parked across the road, eagerly tuned in to whatever followed. Faraday got to his feet and took a precautionary peek round the curtain, confirming that even now, on a busy Saturday, there were still parking spaces across the road. Tomorrow, McNaughton, Wallace's handler, would grab another of them, and the rest was down to the miracle of radio waves.

Faraday resumed his seat, wondering just how much political capital Willard had invested in tomorrow's outcome. The other night, in hospital, Nick Hayder had described the Det-Supt as a key ally, vital protection against marauding predators from higher up the force food chain. Faraday knew this was true, and was grateful for the knowledge that Willard's fierce loyalty would be unwavering if it came to resisting boarders. Nonetheless, Faraday had been less than comfortable to find himself in the crossfire at Secretan's council of war, and the more he thought about the drugs issue, the less certain he became of his own position.

Did Harry Wayte have a point when he banged the table about wholesale legalisation? Was Eadie Sykes right to break every rule in the book in the battle for hearts and minds? Would J-J – his own son, for God's sake – become an unwitting victim in the ongoing war? To each of these questions, Faraday had no answer, and in policing terms he knew that made him next to useless.

The likes of Willard and Brian Imber didn't have a moment's self-doubt when it came to *Tumbril*. Bazza Mackenzie had grown fat and all too visible, thanks to his dealings in the cocaine trade, and in their view he'd deserve everything that a judge and jury, convinced by hard-won evidence, could throw at him. The fact that other men, almost certainly outsiders, would fill his boots within weeks was irrelevant. Justice, he could hear Willard saying, was best served by taking on the bad guys and putting them away.

So far, so good. But what of the Brixton Yardies queuing up at Pompey's door, just itching for a crack at the market? What of the Scouse lunatics, with their Stanley knives and their cut-price wraps? And what, rather closer to home, of the envy and resentments that rumours of a covert operation like *Tumbril* were inevitably stirring up amongst other coppers? Brian Imber had already warned him about the old-stagers, seasoned detectives like Harry Wayte. But how would Imber himself feel once he realised that he too had been kept in the dark about tomorrow's little adventure?

'Have you made a choice, sir?' The waiter had returned, pad in hand.

'Yes.' Faraday was still gazing out at the sunshine. 'I think I'll have a large Scotch.'

A call to the PNC clerk at Kingston Crescent had given Winter all the details he needed on the BMW in Valentine's workshop, Unsurprisingly, DVLA at Swansea was giving Valentine himself as the vehicle's owner, a fact that might indicate a temporary transfer of ownership ahead of commercial sale. On the other hand, the Beemer had been registered in Valentine's name for more than a year, which suggested to Winter that it might be his personal set of wheels.

A second call, this time to the force control room, supplied phone numbers and addresses for three Valentines in the Waterlooville area. Only one of them was a Mr M. Valentine, and on the strength of this information Winter drove round for a look. Number 4 Avondale Gardens turned out to be an executive-style four-bedroomed house in a select crescent on the nicer side of town. There was a *For Sale* notice in the front garden and no sign of life inside.

Winter phoned Valentine's number to be on the safe side, then called the estate agency. He was down from London with an hour or two to spare. He was desperate for a cash buy and rather liked the look of number four. Any chance of a quick tour? The woman at the other end said she was up to her eyes but thought one of the other sales staff might be able to help. Minutes later, she rang back. Interest in the property, she warned him, was keen, but there was still room for what she termed 'a competitive bid'.

Bored with coverage of the big London anti-war demo, Winter turned off the car radio and gazed at the house. If Valentine was indeed doing a runner, then he certainly wasn't covering his tracks. Winding up his garage business and putting his home on the market was a public declaration that he was moving on, and it was inconceivable that Bazza Mackenzie didn't know. In Winter's view, it was odds-on that Misty Gallagher and probably Trudy were going with him, and it was at this point that the likely passage of events was trickier to call.

Misty, last night, had been adamant that Bazza had never caught a whisper of her on/off liaison with Valentine. Only too conscious of the likely consequences of him finding out, she and Mike been ultra-careful to shield the relationship from prying eyes. They were all friends, obviously; Valentine, Bazza and Misty were often in company together. But never, she insisted, had Baz ever suspected that she and Valentine sometimes met to get it on, or even disappeared together for extended weekends in a variety of secluded West Country hotels. As far as Bazza was concerned, Posh Mike, as he called Valentine, was simply a mate and a business partner.

And what of Trudy? Once again, Misty had shaken her head. Baz had long ago made up his mind that Trudy was his. Misty had never bothered to put him right in this belief – largely because it guaranteed her a generous monthly allowance – and supposition on Bazza's part had become fact. The moment he discovered that Trudy belonged to someone else, not just someone else but posh fucking Mike Valentine, then the shit would truly hit the fan.

Was this why they were all getting out? To escape the terrifying prospect of Bazza's wrath?

The woman from the estate agency drove a white Toyota. At the newly painted front door, hunting for the key, she mentioned the price again. Nothing was set in stone. A couple of thousand over the odds, and she was sure the vendors would snap an offer up.

'You've got the name of the owner?'

'Valentine, I think.' The woman flicked quickly through the file. 'yes. A Mr Michael Valentine.'

Winter followed her into the property. The wooden parquet flooring was beginning to fade from the sunshine and Winter caught the lingering scent of cigars. The door to the lounge was open, sunshine jigsawed on the carpet, and Winter found himself looking at a big room furnished by someone with a bit of taste. While the agent enthused about the recently upgraded central heating system and state of the art intruder alarms, Winter toured the room, inspecting a set of fine watercolours that looked original. One of the things about Valentine that had always attracted Misty was the man's education. He'd been a St Joseph's boy, she'd said, briefly a classmate of Bazza's until Baz got expelled. He spoke French. He knew his way round a decent menu. He went to the theatre. He even read books.

The agent, obviously pressed for time, was already leading the way into the kitchen, but Winter lingered beside a glass-fronted cabinet that held a much-thumbed collection of novels. Winter's taste didn't run much beyond Tom Clancy and Clive Cussler but the names on these shelves impressed him. A complete set of D.H. Lawrence. A bound edition of *Middlemarch*. A long line of Graham Greene novels. Misty was right. After the gale-force excitements of Bazza Mackenzie, an evening with Mike Valentine would have been an altogether gentler experience.

Winter was examining a roll-top writing bureau in the corner when he heard the trill of a mobile. The agent stuck her head round the kitchen door and apologised for having take the call. Winter shot her a smile, said it was no problem, and waited until she was back inside the kitchen before opening the bureau. To his disappointment, it had already been cleared. He tried the drawers beneath. They were all empty. About to explore the dining room next door, he remembered the phone in the hall. It was a stylish unit he'd spotted recently in a catalogue. It contained an answering machine.

Stepping back into the hall, he lifted the phone and keyed the message button. There were three messages waiting. The first was Misty. She was running late. She'd be at Waterloo for twelve o'clock, usual place. If he was serious about staying over in London, it was no problem from her point of view as long as they could go to the Lanesborough again. The next caller, a man, left a name and a number and rang off.

Winter glanced up. The agent was still on her mobile – he could hear her laughing. He bent to the phone again, waiting for the last of the messages. A woman this time, calling from a travel agency. Mr Valentine's tickets for the ferry crossing had come through. She'd managed to get him a nice outside cabin with full en suite, four bunks as requested. He could pick up the tickets himself or she could have them sent round. Mr Valentine was to remember to be at the ferry port half an hour before embarkation. The phone went dead, leaving Winter gazing at yet another watercolour.

Faraday had decided to level with Willard. The Det-Supt, after all, deserved the truth. There were reputations on the line here, and a ton of money, and if Faraday felt he couldn't deliver then it was only fair to say so.

Willard lived in Old Portsmouth. Faraday had never been to the house before but Willard had described it on a number of occasions, a converted bakery in Warblington Street, and Faraday knew exactly where it was. Glad of the smack of fresh air, he set out from the hotel and made his way towards Old Portsmouth. For a man who rarely drank at lunchtime, he was pleasantly surprised at how mellow the third Scotch had made him feel. For the first time in days, he risked a smile.

The route to Willard's house passed the Anglican cathedral. Across the road from the cathedral was a pub, the Dolphin, that Faraday had always rather liked. Inside, it had a timbered, low-ceilinged, shadowy feel, unspoiled by piped music or this month's makeover. Years ago, he'd asked the publican about the history of the place, how far back it went, and the assurance that Nelson might have paused here before embarking to hunt for the French came as no surprise. In the clamour that passed for today's society, the Dolphin somehow represented peace.

The pub was empty. Faraday had bought a copy of the *Guardian* from the newsagent's on the corner, and now he found himself a chair beside the fire. The first pint, London Pride, slipped down beautifully. Faraday thumbed through the news section of the paper, trying to piece together the chaos of the allied advance into Iraq. Had Umm Qasr surrendered or not? Would Basra be the next plum on Saddam's tree? After the second pint, Faraday didn't care. Folding the newspaper, he made his way back onto the street,

Crossing the road, resuming his journey, he became aware of the unaccompanied chant of a choir. It was coming from the cathedral, a sound like none other he'd ever heard. Even here, out in the sunshine, it had a bare, haunting quality that spoke of something indefinably precious. The door on the western corner of the cathedral was open. He stepped inside, glad at once that he'd done so. On the dais beneath the organ loft, a dozen or so men were involved in some kind of rehearsal. The choirmaster stood before them, a portly man in a red check shirt. He conducted with one hand, fluid circular gestures, beautifully expressive, and the music rose and fell as he did so.

Faraday slipped into a chair at the back of the nave, engulfed by the music. He'd always loved this cathedral. Domestic in scale, it had never set out to intimidate or impress. On the contrary, with its honeyed stone and softly lit recesses, it offered the most intimate of welcomes.

Faraday let his head sink back against the ribbed stone of the nearby pillar. The chant, it seemed to him, had slowed. Closing his eyes, he began to drift away, feeling the sudden warmth of the sun on his face, catching a glimpse of something big, a lammergeier perhaps, soaring on a thermal high in the Pyrenees. The flight of the bird, circling and circling, perfectly matched the music. Away beyond the frieze of peaks, the sun was beginning to dip towards the horizon. Later, he thought, he'd retrace his steps, clamber down towards the valley, find a bodega in the village below, treat himself to chorizo sausage and Catalan bean stew and a decent bottle of Rioja. He'd maybe risk his broken Spanish on a local or two, try and share his day in the mountains, then – in the warm darkness – he'd beat a path to bed.

His mouth dry from the alcohol, he began to snore. After a while, the chanting stopped. Then, from deep sleep, Faraday found himself shaken awake. A figure in a black cassock was standing over him. It was a face he recognised, a face from years back. He reached up, touched the man's hand, grateful for this small miracle.

'Nigel?' he queried.

The march had been a disappointment. After the unforgettable turnout in February, one and a half million people bringing central London to a halt, Eadie had known at once that this march was infinitely smaller. The faces had changed, as well. Gone were the ranks of middle England, the civil servants in from Haslemere, the young mums up from the shires. Instead, Eadie found herself taping placards from an organisation called Sex Workers of the World Unite. She knew that bizarre lobby groups like these would be a gift to waverers tempted to close ranks behind the troops in the front line. *Weep with the widows of Iraq* might touch a nerve or two, but the public mood was undeniably changing.

As a speaker from the Socialist Workers' Party seized the microphone on the platform in front of the crowd, Eadie hunted one last time for images that would give J-J the ammunition he needed. A young black vicar with a child on his shoulders. Two Muslim women, their eyes letter-boxed in black. Distant spectators hanging over a balcony on a hotel overlooking Park Lane. Cold and hungry after the sunshine of the early afternoon, Eadie finally lodged the camera in her day sack and got out her mobile. Three calls to Joe had so far failed to raise a response. She tried again.

Nothing.

Chapter nineteen

Winter was surprised to find Cathy Lamb at her desk on a Saturday. The DI's hideaway lay next door to the bigger squad office, and Winter glimpsed her through the open door as he walked past.

'Paul.' She called him back. 'What are you doing in?'

Winter tried to fend her off with a grouch about paperwork. Unless he caught up on the backlog he'd be chained to his desk for most of next week. She didn't buy it for a second.

'The day you bin a Saturday for paperwork is the day pigs fly.' She snorted. 'What's going on?'

Winter, playing willing, took a seat in front of her desk. Cathy Lamb was a sturdy, big-boned woman with a slightly butch attitude to fashion and make-up. Winter had known her for years and had always taken a lively interest in her career. As his skipper on division at Southsea, she'd been tough but shrewd, allowing him the benefit of the doubt as long as the scalps he took outweighed his transgressions. As DI, shackled to a desk, she was less forgiving.

'You know a bloke called Barry?' Winter said lightly. 'Rat-faced? Mid thirties? Qualified motor mechanic?'

'Can't say I do. Does he have a surname?'

'Yeah. That's why I asked. I've seen this bloke somewhere before but I can't place him.'

'Why the interest?'

'He's working for Mike Valentine.'

'The car dealer? Bazza's mate?'

'Yeah. Except that Valentine's selling up, getting out.'

'Who said?'

'Me. I was up there this morning.'

'Why?'

Winter had seen this question coming since he launched the conversation.

'Why is he getting out?' he queried. 'Or why was I up there?'

'The latter.'

'I need a car, Cath, something half decent. The Subaru's been great but you know how it is . . .' He made a gesture of resignation. 'Nothing lasts forever.'

'But why Valentine?'

'Because he's cheap. In fact he's giving the bloody things away. Fire sale.'

'But no fire.'

'Exactly.'

He held Cathy's gaze. He knew she didn't believe the story about the car for a moment but there was something else going on in there.

'There's street talk about a big cocaine shipment,' she said at last. 'Have you picked that up at all?'

'No.' Winter's interest began to quicken. 'How big?'

'Couple of kilos, minimum.'

Winter was impressed. Two kilos of cocaine, cut and bagged, could net you £120,000.

'When was this?'

'No one knows, not for sure.'

'But recently?'

'This week.'

'And we don't know whose name's on the label?'

'No . . . but it has to be something to do with Mackenzie. Not hands-on, of course, but I bet he's staking it, that kind of weight.' She leaned forward. 'If you were overrun with Scousers and Jamaicans and God knows who else, and everything else had failed, what would you do?'

Winter thought about the question for a moment or two, then grinned.

'Flood the market,' he said. 'Bring the price down.'

'Exactly. Couple of kilos of cocaine? It's Blue Cross Day.' She nodded. 'Has to be linked to Mackenzie. Has to be.'

Winter was thinking about the workshop behind the showroom, the guy Barry gobbing into the gloom, clearly pissed off.

'Bazza's gear's supposed to come down in Valentine's cars.' Winter was beginning to enjoy himself. 'Did you hear that?'

'That's what everyone says. You're telling me it's true?'

'I've no idea. Except you'd need a mechanic to get at it at this end.' Winter got to his feet. 'You here for a bit, Cath?'

'Why's that?'

'I just need to make a phone call. Back in a jiff.'

Winter called the CID room at Highland Road, catching Dawn Ellis as she put the finishing touches to a CPS file on a serial shoplifter. As duty

DC on lates all week, she'd come in early to keep herself out of the shops.

'My Visa statement arrived this morning,' she told Winter. 'Overdrawn just doesn't do me justice.'

'Have you still got that cork board over the kettle? The one with the mug shots?'

'Yeah.' She sounded bemused. 'Why?'

'There's a bloke called Barry. Looks like a child molester. Thin hair. Scary eyes.' He paused. 'Do us a favour?'

'Barry Leggat.' She didn't need to go across to the board. 'Came out a couple of months ago. Did two years for ringing bent motors.'

'Local?'

'Leigh Park. Supposed to be shacked up with a woman called Jackie something or other. She's scary, too. You want the address?'

Winter grunted a yes and waited while she thumbed through a couple of files. Oakmount Road. House with a whole family of gnomes in the front garden.

'Anything else I can do you for?' Dawn laughed. 'Cappuccino? Carrot cake? Nut cutlet?'

She rang off, leaving Winter gazing at the address. Moments later, he was back in Cathy Lamb's office.

'Just an idea, Cath. Are you up for this?'

'Go on.' She was looking wary again.

Winter explained about the workshop at the back of Valentine's showroom. Barry Leggat, he suspected, might be the guy to unpack the goodies once the cars had driven down from London. He'd undoubtedly earn a drink or two in the process and, with Valentine bailing out, that source of income would suddenly dry up. If that was the case, and the last consignment had been as huge as street talk suggested, then what would be the harm in helping himself to an ounce or two on the side?

'What are you suggesting?'

'We get a warrant on his house. Do it ASAP. If we find any gear, he might be up for a longer conversation.'

'A warrant on what grounds?'

'Good point.' Winter gazed at the ceiling a moment. He needed an informant, someone with credible information. 'Dave Pullen.' He smiled. 'I saved his arse this morning, and he knows it. Plus he's not best mates with Valentine.'

'He'll stand the intelligence up?'

'Enough for the magistrate, no problem.'

Cathy still wasn't convinced.

'What about this Leggat?' she said. 'You think he'd be silly enough to stash the cocaine at home? Assuming you've got this right?'

'He's just done two years, Cath.' Winter was looking wounded. 'Bright guys in this world never get caught.'

Faraday was happy to accept Nigel Phillimore's offer of afternoon tea. Mortified by his conduct in the cathedral but still cocooned by three hours of drinking, he accompanied Phillimore up the High Street to the narrow little house that came with the post of Canon.

He and Phillimore had met a couple of years back. Faraday was investigating the death of a fourteen-year-old from Old Portsmouth, and had been surprised to unearth a relationship between the dead girl's mother and this man of the cloth. The inquiry had led to a couple of lengthy conversations in Phillimore's house, both of which had stuck in Faraday's mind not simply because they'd been evidentially so vital but because he'd rarely met anyone so open and sympathetic. This man, he'd thought at the time, offers something extraordinary: the gift of immediate and unconditional friendship. For a detective used to a culture built on instinctive suspicion, he was a very rare bird indeed.

Phillimore's house, when he pushed the door open and stood aside, even smelled the same: a certain brand of joss stick, exotic, pungent, that brought the memory of their previous encounters flooding back. Faraday made his way along the narrow hall, reaching for support when the drink threatened to get the better of him, recognising the framed colour photos of Angola hanging on the wall. Phillimore had taken them himself, years ago during a Fair Trade visit, and Faraday remembered him talking about the country with a quiet intensity that was all the more arresting for being so unforced.

Upstairs, too, little seemed to have changed. The cosy sitting room warmed by bookshelves and a threadbare oriental carpet looked out onto the High Street, and Faraday recognised the Chinese bowl of pot-pourri on the window sill. He settled himself in a battered armchair beside the window as Phillimore enquired about his taste in tea. He had Earl Grey, Lapsang, or a new discovery he'd made only last week, Munnar Premium. Faraday beamed at him, telling him it didn't matter. Medium height, with a slight stoop, Phillimore had put on a little weight since they'd last met but the smile on his face was just the same. It was a face made for kinship and laughter. Just sitting here, Faraday felt immediately brighter.

'Your cat?' he asked.

'On loan. I've been away for a while. Only got back last night.'

He disappeared into the kitchen while Faraday inspected the postcards pinned to corners of the bookshelves. On this evidence,

Phillimore had friends in Salzburg, Bombay, Paris, and a cityscape that looked like Rio. Someone in Pompey who dared to look outwards.

Minutes later, he was back with a tray of tea. Another journey yielded a lemon cake and a plate of macaroons.

'This one turned up at lunchtime from a woman in the choir.' His knife was hovering over the cake. 'Go away for a couple of weeks and you forget how spoiled we are.'

He cut two generous slices and passed one to Faraday. He'd been off on a three-week jaunt to Kerala. That part of India had always fascinated him, the *idea* of the place, and he'd been glad to discover that communism could indeed go hand in hand with equality and a certain levelling of outcomes.

'Communism?' Faraday was lost.

'The provincial government is communist, and I have to say that it shows. Superb education. Terrific command of English. And the nicest people in the world.' He paused, slipping effortlessly from one theme to another. 'Do you mind me saying something?'

'Not at all.'

'You look exhausted.'

'Drunk, I'm afraid.'

'No,' Phillimore was stirring his tea. 'It's more than that.' He glanced up. 'What did you think of the choir?'

'I thought they were superb.'

'They're Estonian. They come from Tallinn. They're singing tomorrow night, half past seven. You should come. And I mean that.'

'I will.'

'Good. Last time I seem to remember it was you asking all the questions.' He smiled. 'So how's it been?'

Faraday gazed at him for a long moment. It was an innocent enough enquiry, a near-stranger expressing a passing interest in his well-being, but there was something in his tone of voice, in the tilt of his head, that spoke of genuine concern. This man really cares, Faraday thought.

'It's been bloody,' he said quietly. 'If you really want to know.'

'Bloody . . . how?'

'Bloody awful. Just –' he spread his hands hopelessly '– bloody.'

He told Phillimore a little about the last two years, the wash-up after the fourteen-year-old's death, his subsequent transfer into Major Crimes, the caseload he'd been dealing with since.

'Was it a promotion, Major Crimes?'

'They put it that way, yes.'

'And you? What do you think?'

'I think they're right. In my business we talk about the quality of a crime. You get to concentrate on one thing at a time – a rape, a murder, sometimes both. After divisional CID, believe me, that's a relief.'

'You felt spoiled?' Phillimore was smiling again.

'Definitely. But it's a compliment, too. It means they trust you. Some of this stuff is tough, high profile. You can't afford to let them down.'

'The relatives?'

'Of course. And your bosses, too.'

'Which matters most?'

It was a good question and Faraday conceded as much by ducking his head and reaching for a slice of cake. Eadie Sykes, he knew, would say Daniel Kelly. What did Faraday himself think?

'Each case is different,' he said at last. 'Just now I have to tell you I don't know.'

'Do you want to talk about it?'

'I'm afraid I can't. Operationally –' he shot Phillimore a bleak smile '– it's impossible.'

'Are you sure that's the problem?'

'I'm not with you.'

'This operation . . . inquiry . . . investigation . . . whatever it is. We all hide behind our jobs. Are you sure it's not something else?'

Faraday looked startled. This man's judgement was faultless. But how could he begin to disentangle J-J, and Eadie Sykes, and the wreckage of his private life from the monster that was *Tumbril*?

'Policemen have a knack of taking their work home,' he began lamely.

'So do we. And it's not always helpful, is it?'

'No, not at all. But what do you do about it?'

'You find a relationship, and then stick to it. In my case, it happens to be God. Whether that makes me lucky is for other people to judge. Most of us have to make do with each other.'

'I've tried that.'

'And?'

'It's falling apart.'

'Because of the job?'

'Partly, yes. There's –' he shrugged '– a conflict of interest. Interests plural, if you want the truth. My partner thinks she can change the world. My son thinks the same. I admire them for trying but I know they'll fail.'

'Why?'

'Because I'm a policeman. I know what people are like. Criminals. Bosses. Colleagues. I see it every day. On the other hand . . .' He frowned, trying to concentrate, trying to tease out the essence of what he wanted to say. 'I'm the first to get behind my partner, my son. It's vital someone has a go. Even if they fail.'

Briefly, he explained about Eadie's commitment to Ambrym, the trust she'd vested in J-J, the drugs video they were making – tough, uncompromising, brutally realistic.

'Has it occurred to you they may not fail?'

'They will. I know they will. Drugs are like rain, like gravity. Whatever we do, they'll still be there. That's the way of the world. Blood and treasure. Greed. Power. Taking advantage. That's why people like me have a job to go to every morning.'

'You should be glad, thankful.'

'I know. And most of the time I am.'

'So where's the problem?'

'The problem is I'm piggy in the middle.' Faraday laughed, suddenly struck by the phrase.

'And that's uncomfortable?'

'Impossible sometimes. It turns you into someone you're not. You can feel it happening, feel it inside you. Next thing you know, you're sitting in the Dolphin, ordering that second pint, losing your grip.'

'And grip's important?'

'Grip's essential. From where I sit, grip's everything. No grip, no job.'

'OK.' Phillimore conceded the point. 'And if it comes to no job?'

'No nothing.' Faraday blinked, astonished by this small truth. Did the job matter to him that much? Was it true what people said about coppers? Once a policeman, always a policeman?

'No nothing,' he repeated. 'Maybe it's that simple.'

Winter was in his car outside the duty magistrate's Old Portsmouth flat when he finally got hold of Jimmy Suttle. Getting the search warrant had been harder than he'd anticipated. Even with the intelligence from Dave Pullen, the magistrate had pointed out the lack of hard evidence against Barry Leggat, and it was only Winter's insistence that a search of these premises might have a significant impact on the current explosion of drug abuse that had finally won the woman's grudging approval. Anything, she'd said, to stem the flood of increasingly young druggies through her courtroom.

Now, Winter wanted Suttle's full attention.

'The address is 17 Oakmount Road,' he said. 'I've got to organise a dog. There's a lay-by round the corner. Meet you there for seven.'

'Can't do it.'

'*What?*' Winter was staring at the mobile.

'I promised Trude I'd meet her for nine. We're going to Forty Below.

Why don't you tap up one of the married blokes? They'll jump at the overtime.'

Winter was about to give Suttle an earful about the wisdom of appearing with Trudy Gallagher on Bazza's turf, then paused, struck by another thought.

'You going to be there for long?'

'Where?'

'Forty Below.'

'Haven't a clue. Depends on Trude. Couple of hours at least. Why?'

Winter didn't answer. The warrant lay beside him on the passenger seat. A decent search might take a couple of hours, with a good dog maybe less. If they scored a result, he'd have to haul Leggat down to the Bridewell and book him in. The paperwork would take another half-hour, max, and if they'd lifted a decent quantity of gear he wouldn't need to start interviewing until the following day. Misty Gallagher was in London. That left him plenty of time to get down to Forty Below and have a word or two with young Jimmy before the lad dragged Trudy off to bed.

'You still there?' It was Suttle.

'Yeah.' Winter nodded. 'Forget the search.'

Faraday was up in the seafront apartment, watching television, by the time Eadie made it back from London. She'd taken a cab from the station and now, exhausted, she bent over him on the long sofa. She gave him a kiss on the cheek, then pulled back.

'You've been drinking,' she said.

'That's right.'

'You're pissed.' She was looking at the bottle of South African red on the floor by his foot.

'Right again.'

'Why?' The smile of amusement on her face made Faraday reach up for her. She sank briefly down beside him.

'Come to apologise.' His smile widened into a grin.

'Who has?'

'Me.'

'Why?'

'I'll tell you about it.' He nodded towards the screen. 'How was the demo?'

'Average. You eaten at all? Only I'm starving.'

Faraday nodded, watching her as she left the sofa and headed for the kitchen. He turned back to the TV, watching the now nightly bombardment of Baghdad. A minute or two later, Eadie was back standing beside the sofa, an enormous sandwich in her hand. She

267

wolfed it down, telling Faraday about the Al Jazeera footage between mouthfuls. J-J was lashed to the PC at Ambrym, knocking the stuff together. He should be proud of the boy. Natural eye for the telling cut.

'Al Jazeera?'

Eadie looked down at him, then began to laugh. Events had moved so fast these last couple of days, she'd forgotten to tell him about the invitation from the Stop the War people. She and J-J were putting together a video to bring the world to its senses. Knock-out stuff.

'Really?'

'Yeah.'

'And your drugs thing?'

'Rough cut ready by tomorrow. I'll tell you the rest when you're sober.' She glanced at her watch, then nodded down at the bottle. 'I wouldn't stay up if I were you. It's going to be a late one.'

Faraday gazed up at her, lost again.

'You're off? Already?'

''Fraid so.' She bent to the sofa and kissed him briefly on the cheek. 'Paracetamol's in the bathroom cabinet. See you in the morning.'

It was dusk by the time Winter was ready to launch the search of Leggat's house. Cathy Lamb had detailed one of the older of the squad's DCs, Danny French, to make the rendezvous in Leigh Park, and a dog handler had turned up in a white Escort van. The dog's name, he said was Pepys, a German shepherd. He was new to the game and occasionally overeager.

They drove in convoy to Leggat's address. Number 17 was an ex-council house that had been given the full makeover. The double-glazing units looked brand new and the front door was protected by a gleaming porch in white UPVC. Dawn, to Winter's amusement, hadn't been kidding about the gnomes. He stood outside the house, counting them, while the dog handler readied Pepys for the search.

'All right?'

The porch was a couple of steps from the front gate. Winter rang twice and waited. From a corner of the tiny front garden came the trickle of a water feature. The most distant of the gnomes, according to French, was incontinent. At length the door opened.

'Mrs Leggat?' Winter showed her his warrant card.

'What's this about?' She was staring at the panting dog.

Winter produced the search warrant and began to explain but she cut him short.

'I'm not having that thing in here. Not with Treacle around.'

Treacle was her cat, an enormous tom which was standing in the hall, its back arched, hissing. Winter suggested Treacle take a walk in the garden. Cat or no cat, they were coming in.

The woman looked at him a moment, then turned and shooed the cat towards a door at the back. She was a big woman who didn't suit jeans.

Winter and French stepped inside. They'd call the dog in later.

'Barry around?'

'He's in the bath.'

'Get him out of there, will you? Tell him not to flush the loo or empty the bath. Second thoughts, I'll do it.'

The expression on the woman's face sent Winter up the narrow stairs. The house was spotless. Winter's taste didn't run to Regency wallpaper or Tiffany lamps but the place was plainly cherished. The bathroom door was at the end of the upstairs landing. Winter could hear the splash of water and the blare of a radio with the volume turned up. Guests on some phone-in programme were discussing the Portsmouth game. Preston had been rubbish, the caller was saying. Pompey should have hammered them.

Winter pushed inside and plucked a towel from the rail behind the door. Leggat was sitting in the bath, washing his hair.

'Out.' Winter threw the towel at him and nodded at the open door. 'Now.'

'Who the fuck are you?' Leggat had shampoo in his eyes. It was several seconds before he recognised the face looking down at him.

'DC Winter. We met this morning.'

'You're Filth?' Leggat looked astonished, then outraged. 'How come—'

Winter hauled him upright in the bath.

'We'll start upstairs,' he said briskly. 'Best if you're there too.'

Back on the landing, the woman barred the way to the bedroom at the front. She was even bigger than Winter had thought.

'Mrs . . . ?' Winter smiled at her.

'Comfort. And it's Ms.' She was looking at Leggat. 'If this is what I think it is . . .' The warning was all the more effective for being unspoken. Leggat, dripping suds onto the carpet, wound the towel round his waist and began to protest.

'We've got a warrant.' Winter cut him short. 'I showed your missus.'

'Missus?' It was the woman again. 'Since when have I been your missus?'

'Don't fucking ask me. I was just having a bath.'

Winter took him by the elbow and steered him round the woman as she stepped back, trying to avoid physical contact.

'It's the one at the end,' she said, 'if you're looking for his room.'

Leggat's bedroom must have recently belonged to a teenage girl. There were luminous stars on the ceiling and no one had bothered to remove the torn-out photos of Robbie Williams and Jude Law Blu-tacked to the wallpaper. After the rest of the house, thought Winter, this room was a doss.

'Do you want to help us out here?' Winter was looking at Leggat. 'Only it'd be nice to leave the floorboards in one piece.'

'You bloody dare.' The woman was standing in the open doorway.

'Try me.' Winter nodded beyond her. French had appeared on the landing. He was a tall man, an ex-para, and he carried the crowbar with a certain authority.

Leggat had found himself a pullover and a pair of tracksuit bottoms. He sat down on the bed, refusing to say another word. After the spasm of anger in the bathroom, he looked defeated.

'Try the wardrobe.' The woman had folded her enormous arms. 'He's always poking around in there.'

Winter stepped across to the MFI wardrobe in the corner. Various bits of clothing were stacked on the shelves down one side. A velvet suit hanging at the front of the rack had suffered at the hands of the dry cleaners.

'Drawer at the bottom. Where he keeps his toys.' The woman again.

Winter knelt on the carpet. The drawer was a tight fit and the whole wardrobe rocked as he wrestled it open. Inside, to his surprise, he found half a dozen model railway engines, die-cast self-assemblies in metal, nestled on a carefully fitted oblong of green baize. Each of the steam engines was mounted on a single length of track. OO gauge, thought Winter, lifting one out.

'You make these?'

Leggat nodded. He'd found a spent match from somewhere and was cleaning the dirt from under his nails.

'Merchant Navy class.' Winter turned the model over. 'Beautifully painted, really nice. They got motors inside?'

'No.'

'Just for show, then?'

'Yeah.'

French had joined Winter in front of the wardrobe.

'Look.' He'd found a set of jeweller's tools in a plastic wallet.

Winter glanced at the proffered screwdriver then turned the engine over. Underneath, a line of four tiny screws held the body to the chassis. Look hard, and you could see the tiny scratch marks around the head of each of the screws. Winter held the engine to his ear and then gave it a shake. Nothing.

He glanced across at Leggat again.

'Must have packed it really tight.' Winter held out the screwdriver. 'Best if you do the honours.'

At nine o'clock, Faraday rang for a cab. Half a pint of coffee and a couple of minutes under the cold shower in Eadie's bathroom had restored more than his balance. When the cab arrived, he left the TV and lights on, pulled the door shut, and made his way downstairs. On the journey across to the Bargemaster's House he sat in silence in the back, nodding along to the cabbie's choice of music. Neil Young, he thought. Nice.

Home at last, he closed the front door behind him and checked the phone for messages, then shortened the response time to three rings. In the kitchen, with a comforting briskness, he cleared up the last of J-J's debris, binning the remains of a bacon sandwich before preparing himself a cheese omelette. Realising how hungry he was, he cut four thick slices of bread and dropped two into the toaster. There was a jar of lime pickle in the fridge, a tin of baked beans in the cupboard over the sink, and half a bagful of wilting rocket in the vegetable rack. Sitting in the lounge with the curtains back, he demolished the meal in minutes. Out on the blackness of the harbour, he watched the lights of a fishing boat, or perhaps a yacht, pushing slowly out towards the harbour narrows and the open sea.

When the phone went, he ignored it. He made himself a pot of tea and added an extra spoonful of sugar to the waiting mug. Full now, and surprisingly content, he switched on the radio and surfed the pre-sets until he found a concert. Berlioz. *Romeo and Juliet*. He laughed at the irony, genuinely amused, and wrestled his favourite chair closer to the view. Settling back, he kicked off his shoes and rested his feet on the low table where he normally kept his birding magazines.

Already, the events of the day seemed to have happened to someone else. Too much introspection, he thought. Too much time wasted demanding more from life than anyone could reasonably expect. Truth was, blokes like him – coppers, detectives – couldn't afford the luxury of thinking too hard, worrying too much, not if they wanted to get through in one piece. The little insight that Nigel Phillimore had unearthed was spot on. Grip was more important than anything else.

He raised his second mug of tea in a private tribute to the cleric, recognising how skilfully he'd handled their teatime encounter. The best counsellors, like the best detectives, never bullied you with too many questions. Instead, like a good helmsman, they supplied a thought here and there, tiny adjustments on the tiller, until you suddenly found yourself voicing a truth you'd failed to notice under all the other crap. Grip, he thought again.

Later, the concert over, he checked the phone. It was Willard. He wanted to know that they were set for tomorrow. 'No surprises' was one of his trademark expressions.

With a glance at his watch, Faraday called him back, glad he'd never made it to Willard's Old Portsmouth house. Bothering him with today's nonsense would have been a real imposition.

'That you, Joe?' Willard had evidently been asleep.

'Just returning your call, sir.'

'Anything happened?'

'Nothing.'

'We're OK, then? Tomorrow at twelve?'

'I'll be there.'

'Anything else?'

'No, sir.'

'Thank Christ for that.'

Willard rang off, leaving Faraday at the foot of the stairs. He stood motionless for a full minute, listening to the house breathing around him. The wind had got up again, and he could hear the slap-slap of halyards from the nearby dinghy park. At length, from out on the harbour, came the peeping of a flock of oystercatchers squabbling over a late supper. Birds with attitude, Faraday told himself, and a certain sense of purpose. He smiled at the thought, then began to climb the stairs.

Forty Below was bursting by the time Winter made it to Gunwharf. Booking Leggat into the Bridewell had taken longer than he'd anticipated. The queue for the Custody Sergeant was already five deep by half past eight, and even the discovery of a sizeable stash of uncut Colombian – the contents of four Merchant Navy-class engines, each sealed in its plastic evidence bag – failed to shift the backlog.

Winter had mopped up the time with a second call to Cathy Lamb. She was mystified by his request that she talk to P&O in the morning, but wrote down the name he mentioned. Thanks to her husband Pete, she had a direct line to a woman called Penny who ran the ferry company's PR department. She and Pete both sailed Lasers from the Lee-on-the Solent club and if anyone could confirm the number of a pre-booked outside cabin in the name of Valentine then it would be her.

'What next?' Cathy had enquired.

'Going home, boss. Long day.'

Now, eyeing the mass of clubbers queuing for Forty Below, Winter calculated his chances of talking himself in on a freebie. Entry was £15, an outrageous sum, but the last thing he wanted to use was his warrant card. A portly middle-aged gent in an M&S suit was clue enough. Why should he make it really easy for the bastards?

At the door, he found himself suddenly engulfed by a party of middle-aged swingers fresh from a birthday celebration in a nearby restaurant. They'd pre-booked entry to the club's VIP suite and, for the second time that night, Winter knew that his luck was in.

'Cheers, mate.' Winter patted the doorman on the shoulder, briefly pretending he was as pissed as the rest of them. 'Happy days, eh?'

Inside, the noise was deafening. Winter stuck with his new friends until he was well clear of the door, then peeled off. The club was cavernous, the size of an aircraft hangar. Bodies whirled around each other, a blur of arms and legs, and Winter found himself raked by regular bursts of strobe lighting, a splatter of mauves and greens. Half an hour of this, he thought, and you'd be begging for mercy.

A dispute over a spilled drink brought the music to a brief halt. Security waded in, sorting out a drunken youth with a gelled Mohican and marching him towards the door. Then the DJ bent to his decks again, announcing something even louder, with a pumping bass that brought whoops of approval.

By now, Winter was methodically searching the room, a dozen dancers at a time, hunting for Suttle. He found Trudy first. She was over towards the long brushed-metal crescent of the bar, dancing with a girl her own age, arms up, fingers splayed, eyes closed. Winter edged slowly round her, eyes scanning left and right, at last recognising the slender figure of Suttle as he threaded a path through the dancers towards Trudy.

Winter intercepted him. Suttle, for a second, hadn't a clue who he was.

'My shout.' Winter was easing him towards the bar. 'What do you want?'

'What are you doing here?'

'Favour.'

'What?'

'Favour!' Winter yelled.

He abandoned the bar and indicated the nearby lavatories. Suttle shot him a look but came just the same. It was quieter here, with a mill of youths gelling-up at the mirrors over the line of hand basins. Beside the contraceptive machine at the door, Winter broke the bad news.

'Young Trudy,' he said. 'I need her key.'

'What key?'

'The key to that flat across the road, Misty's place.'

Suttle stared at him, bemused.

'So why ask me?'

'I want you to nick it out of her bag.'

'You're mad. You must be off your head. Why would I do that?'

'Because I just asked you.'

It began to dawn on Suttle that Winter was serious.

'Why do you need it?'

'Can't tell you. Not yet.' Winter breathed in to let an enormous youth in a Liverpool shirt through. 'Let's say it's for Trudy's sake. And yours.'

'*Mine?* How's that, then?'

'Just get the key, son.' Winter checked his watch. 'Give me forty-five minutes. Then I'll have it back here. OK?'

'No, it's not fucking OK. In fact it's well out of order. You can't just—'

Winter caught his arm and squeezed hard.

'I nicked a guy with twelve grands' worth of charlie an hour ago,' he murmured. 'Just do what I ask, OK?'

Mention of the cocaine seizure confused Suttle still further. Was he at work or was this really Saturday night?

'All right,' he said at last. 'Stay here.'

He was back within minutes. Trudy's bunch of keys was attached to a small fluffy teddy bear, candy pink. Winter slipped them in his pocket, then checked his watch again.

'Half eleven, OK?'

Outside the club, Winter made for the bridge that led to the residential part of the development. In front of Arethusa House, he paused for a second to peer up at Misty's flat. The curtains were pulled back on the big picture windows and there was no sign of lights inside.

At the main door to the block, he stopped to examine Trudy's keys. The third one he tried released the lock. On the other side of the lobby, the lift was waiting, the door already open. Better and better, Winter thought.

On the top floor, the lift whispered to a halt and Winter found himself stepping into Misty's apartment. This time, he recognised the lingering scent of cigars. Valentine had been here.

Winter crossed the darkened lounge, body-checking around the piles of cardboard boxes, and pulled the curtains across the window. With a knife from a kitchen drawer, he returned to the lift and wedged the door open. Anyone coming up would have to use the stairs.

Back in the apartment, he put the lights on, adjusted the dimmer switch, then hesitated a moment, uncertain where to start. He knew what he wanted but he couldn't see himself finding it in any of these cardboard boxes. Where, he wondered, would Misty keep her documentation, the paper trail that would flag her path out of Pompey?

He went through to the bedroom, dropped the ruched curtains, and turned on another set of lights. The huge bed was unmade: dark blue sheets, an abandoned silk nightgown, a packet of Marlboro Lites, and a Barbara Taylor Bradford paperback open on the pillow.

Winter began to search, starting with the dressing table beneath the window. The first drawer he opened was full of cosmetics and a playful selection of sex toys. The next one down was brimming with tights and thongs. No sign of anything on paper.

Winter turned away and started on the wardrobe, a huge French-looking antique with a full-length mirror facing the bed. He opened the door and began to rummage amongst the jumble of shoes at the bottom, inserting his hand into a pair of thigh-length boots, getting down on his hands to inspect the void beneath. Again, nothing.

Dozens of dresses hung from the rail at the top of the wardrobe. A leather jacket at the back looked briefly promising but all Winter could find in the pockets was a twenty-pence piece, a ticket stub for a Pompey game, and a wafer of spearmint chewing gum. Finally, he circled the bed, feeling under the mattress, just in case.

On the point of abandoning the bedroom and starting on the lounge, he paused. The stool in front of the dressing table looked sturdy enough and he carried it across to the wardrobe before steadying it with one hand and clambering up. The wardrobe was topped with a scroll-like flourish of decorative oak, a wooden pediment that took the wardrobe within inches of the ceiling. Behind the pediment, invisible from below, might be some kind of hidey-hole.

Winter reached up, feeling around, fighting to keep his balance. His fingers snagged a shape. It felt like leather. He tried to get a purchase on the object, inch it towards him. Finally, he found a handle. He knew now that it was some kind of briefcase. With an effort, his forearm wedged against the ceiling, he managed to lift it clear of the pediment. It looked new, ox-blood red, and it felt heavy. Good sign.

The phone began to ring in the lounge. Winter, still on the stool, froze. The answering machine kicked in, then came a voice, Pompey accent, male, light, distinctive. 'Mist,' the voice said. 'Mate just told me Trude's letting herself down. Silly girl. Keeping company like that.' The phone went abruptly dead. Winter gazed towards the open door. No doubt about it. Bazza.

Winter stepped carefully off the stool and went across to the window. Easing back the curtain, he could see the Gunwharf waterfront. One of the white public order Transits from Central had just driven onto the plaza, the winking blue light mirrored in a thousand panes of glass. Uniforms were piling out of the back, mob-handed, trying to contain the clubbers spilling out of Forty Below. Moments later, another blue light, an ambulance this time.

Winter watched as the drama unfolded. The blokes from the Transit dealt with a couple of fights. Youths milled around, watching, drinking, laughing, giving anything in uniform the finger. Then the paramedics returned to the ambulance, pushing a body on a trolley. The youths crowded round, calling to their mates. Opening the back of the ambulance, the paramedics hoisted the trolley and slipped it in. Winter was too far away to be sure of a positive ID but experience told him never to discount coincidence. Bazza's mates had spotted Trudy. And Suttle had paid the price.

Winter retreated from the window, laid the briefcase on the bed and opened it. Inside, on top of a mass of brown A4 envelopes, were two passports, a driving licence, an E111 form, and a copy of the *Rough Guide to Croatia*. Beside it, in a Thomas Cook wallet, a thick wad of foreign currency. Winter began to sort through the envelopes. Bank details. Money transfer forms. Car documentation. Towards the bottom of the pile, he found a brand new envelope labelled with a big T circled in red. He felt inside and extracted four copies of an official-looking document. At the top, thickly embossed, it read 'Confirmation of Paternity'. Beneath, typed, the results of the test Misty had described. Trudy Gallagher was indeed Mike Valentine's daughter, and here was the proof.

Winter read the certificate again. Then he removed one of the copies, folded it carefully, and slipped it into his jacket pocket. The remaining three he returned to the envelope. With the briefcase back on top of the wardrobe, he replaced the stool, turned off the light and pulled open the curtains. He did the same next door, then made for the lift. Back outside on the waterfront, he looked across towards the plaza. The ambulance had gone and the uniforms were doing their best to shepherd everyone back inside the nightclub.

Winter turned and gazed up at the darkened apartment a moment, then stepped across to the rail. The black waters of the harbour lapped at the pilings below and Trudy's bunch of keys made the softest plop as he dropped them into the darkness. The kitchen knife he'd used to wedge the lift door followed, but he made no move to leave.

After a while, he looked up at the apartment for a second time. Why Croatia?

Chapter twenty

Broad stripes of sunshine on the wall beside the bedroom window. A curtain stirred by a feather of wind from the harbour. Scents of bladderwrack and crusting mud, of tarry rope and – very faintly – rotting fish. Underscoring it all, the squawk of black-headed gulls busy contesting booty from the morning's high tide.

Faraday turned over, reaching for the radio. Another noise, much closer. Footsteps within the house. He lay back a moment, then swung his legs out of bed. Naked except for the dressing gown he kept behind the door, he stepped onto the upstairs landing in time to see a tall, gawky figure disappearing into the bathroom. Then came the slide of the bolt as the mystery intruder locked himself in, and a sudden gush of water. J-J.

Downstairs, Faraday found a pile of dirty clothes heaped around the washing machine on the kitchen floor and a mug of cooling tea on the low cupboard in the lounge where he kept his CDs. The TV was on, with the sound wound down, and he spotted the red record light winking on the VHS player beneath.

He paused a moment, then found the zapper and turned up the sound. Half a dozen British servicemen had been killed in some kind of mid-air collision. Baghdad had suffered its fourth consecutive night of heavy air raids. Coalition forces were facing stiffening resistance.

Faraday sipped at the tea while a studio pundit explored the implications of these latest developments, then the coverage switched to the home front. Yesterday's demonstration in London, said the newscaster, had failed to measure up to last month's protests. British public opinion was hardening in support of the war while the rest of Europe waved a collective fist at Washington and Westminster. Shots of Blair followed, getting out of a low-slung Jaguar in Downing Street. He looked tired but purposeful, ignoring the press pack across the road. The black front door opened as he strode across the pavement. Then he was gone.

Faraday finished the rest of the tea, then turned the TV off. This was an arm's-length war, he'd decided, an increasingly surreal adventure delivered to every household in the country by the channel of our choice. That pictures like these should sully an otherwise pleasant spring weekend was beyond his comprehension. A month ago, a million and a half people had cared enough to fill thousands of coaches and bring London to a halt. Millions more had begged the government not to go to war. Yet here we all were, tucked up with BBCNews 24 or Skynews or CNN, watching a sovereign nation doing its best to defend itself. This was breaking and entering on an international scale. In a court of law, Bush and Blair would be looking at a five-year stretch. Minimum.

Faraday retreated to the kitchen, hearing the gurgle of water overhead as J-J emptied the bath. Moments later, came the clatter of footsteps on the stairs and a moment's pause. Then J-J was at the kitchen door. When he got really angry, his mouth tightened to a thin line. Just now, it was practically invisible.

He wanted know why Faraday had turned the TV off.

'Tea?' Faraday signed peaceably.

'I put it on specially. We need the pictures.'

'I'm sure you do. Would you like more tea?'

'You turned it off. Deliberately.'

'Why would I do that?'

'Because you don't care.'

'Really?' Faraday's amused smile drove J-J back into the lounge. He turned the television back on, this time with the sound up. When he swung round to retrieve the towel he'd thrown onto the sofa, he found his father propped against the open kitchen door, watching him.

'The VHS was still recording,' Faraday pointed out. 'I left that on.'

J-J faltered for a second, too angry to make room in his head for the obvious conclusion. Only the TV had been switched off. As far as his precious pictures had been concerned, he'd lost nothing. At length, dismissing the offer of tea, he told his father he might have to go to London for a while. Eadie had found a place where he could carry on cutting the war footage. Better Soho, he signed, than Hampshire Terrace.

Faraday shrugged. So be it. J-J was eyeing the laundry on the kitchen floor. His father blocked the path to the washing machine.

'How long do you think this thing'll last?' Faraday nodded towards the television.

'Months. The Iraqis are fighting back.'

'And you?'

'I'll be doing what I can.' He made a scissors motion with his fingers.

'Editing pictures?'

'Of course.'

'Fine.' Faraday patted him on the shoulder. 'Just remember you're on police bail. OK? I know it's boring but you'd be amazed how angry we can get if you don't turn up.'

Paul Winter treated himself to another splash of aftershave before he got out of the Subaru. He'd checked by phone with the Custody Sergeant before driving down to Central police station. Leggat would be honking.

Winter was sharing the interview with Danny French, the DC who'd accompanied him on the search of Leggat's house. Winter found him in the tiny kitchen, wrestling the lid from a catering-sized tin of Nescafé. His missus was giving him serious grief about Sunday lunch at his mother-in-law's place in Gosport. The old bat had bought a shoulder of pork specially. With luck, the interviews might stretch the whole day.

'Coffee?'

'Black.' Winter checked his watch. 'Two sugars.'

'How's that boy Suttle?'

'Dunno, mate. I'll be finding out later.'

'Beaten up, wasn't he? Gunwharf?'

'Yeah. You know the thing about kids these days?' Winter reached for the coffee. 'Never bloody listen.'

The duty solicitor turned out to be a paralegal from one of the city's biggest partnerships. She was a local girl, no university degree but an implacable determination to battle her way through to full qualification. Winter had come across her a number of times before and had been impressed.

She was waiting in the corridor beside the new AFIS fingerprint terminal: neat charcoal-grey suit, nice legs, hint of a tan from somewhere exotic. Leggat was already in one of the interview rooms, waiting for them all to appear.

'You know he's in the shit, don't you? Seven ounces is practically full flag. We're not talking personal here.'

'My client—'

'Yeah, but seriously.'

'I know, Mr Winter, and so does he.' She smiled. 'Seriously.'

'OK.' Winter shrugged, then shot French a look. 'You might be in luck, Danny.'

'Come again?'

'That lunch.'

They all went into the interview room. Leggat was sitting at the table, facing the door. Already he'd adopted the resigned defensiveness – body slouched, eyes blank – that badges a man for prison.

'Morning.' Winter pulled back a chair and sat down. 'Lovely day out there.'

Leggat didn't move, didn't answer. French loaded the video and audio recorders before Winter helped himself to the PACE cue card and went through the preliminaries. Then, with a glance at French, he leaned forward. On the training courses, this phase of the interview was termed 'open account', offering the interviewee the chance to establish exactly what had happened. Fat chance.

'Tell us about those lovely little engines, Barry. Pretend we know nothing.'

Leggat was still gazing into the middle distance. His eyes were bloodshot and he needed a shave.

'Car boot,' he mumbled at last. 'Couple of Sundays ago.'

'Which car boot?' Winter didn't bother to hide his disbelief.

'Don't really remember. Could have been Havant. Wecock Farm. Pompey. Clarence Field. I goes to 'em all.'

'I bet. So how much did you pay for them?'

'Fiver each. He wanted a tenner but I wasn't having it.'

'Who's "he"?'

'Bloke I got 'em off.'

'Does he have a name?'

'Expect so. Everyone's got a name, ain't they?'

'But you can't remember?'

'Never asked.'

'What did he look like?'

'Nothing at all, really. Ordinary-looking, know what I mean?'

'Age?'

'Hard to tell. Getting on? Forty? Dunno.'

'What else was he selling?'

'Stuff. Rubbish, most of it.'

'You'd know him again?'

'Course.'

'But you haven't seen him since, this bloke? Whoever he might be? Whatever else he might have been selling? Wherever the car boot was? Is that fair? Am I on the right lines?'

'Yeah.' Leggat yawned. 'Spot on.'

Winter leaned back while French came at Leggat from a different angle. A seizure of this size, he warned, they'd check every car boot in the area, take photos of the engines with them, throw serious resources at checking out Leggat's alibi. If it turned out he was lying, he might be giving himself some serious problems a month or two down the road.

'Is that right?' Leggat didn't appear to be bothered.

'Yeah.' French nodded. 'Like a couple of years over the tariff. Not that you're going to be short of bird.'

'Listen, Barry.' It was Winter again. 'Let's just pretend for a moment that we buy the car boot. It went the way you said it went. You spotted the engines, bought them, took them home. Then what?'

'I puts them in the wardrobe.'

'And you left them there?'

'Yeah. I looks at them from time to time, you know, like you do.'

'You didn't tamper with them? Take them apart?'

'Never. Why should I?'

'Why the little tools, then? The jeweller's kit?'

'My watch broke.'

'And you mended it?'

'Yeah.'

'So where is it?'

'The watch? I threw it away.'

'Why's that, Barry?'

'It bust again.'

'What a surprise.'

'Not really. I'm crap at repairs.'

'But you're a mechanic. You repair stuff all the time. It's your living, Barry. It's the label on your box. Mechanic. Repairman.'

'That's big stuff. Watches ain't Beemers.'

'OK.' Winter was the soul of patience. 'So let's get this straight. You go to the car boot. You spend twenty quid on four model engines. We come along a couple of weeks later and, guess what? We're looking at twenty grand's worth of cocaine. Is that it?'

'Yeah, more or less.'

'What's more or less about it?'

'You missed out the bit about me lending them to a friend.'

'When was that?'

'Last week.'

'And who is this friend?'

'Calls himself John. Don't know his surname.'

'Where does he live, this John?'

'Dunno. He's gone abroad somewhere. Met him down the pub.'

'And talked about model engines? Like you do?'

'Yeah, he's a model nut himself. I let him have them for a couple of days. Favour really.'

'What did he do? Stroke them? Talk to them? Take them apart and stuff them full of cocaine? You're talking nonsense, Barry. You're taking the piss. If I had a pen, I wouldn't even write this down. How thick do you think we are?'

The paralegal intervened. In her view, it was no part of Winter's job to put oppressive questions like this.

French ignored her. Leggat's wind-up had found its mark.

'We just sent those little tools away,' French said. 'The whole lot, wallet, screwdrivers, everything. Forensics these days, they can find flakes of paint you can't even see. So why don't you help yourself, Barry? Before the lab boys do it for you?'

'Help myself how?'

'By telling us where the cocaine came from.'

Leggat shrugged. This kind of pressure didn't alarm him in the slightest. Winter took up the running again. One of the surprises at Leggat's house had been the complete absence of any sign of dealing: no readied paper wraps, no scales, no deal list, no money stash. Even the directory on his mobile phone had been limited to a handful of friends and family. Now, Winter wanted to know how long Valentine had employed him.

'Six weeks, give or take.' Leggat shrugged.

'You know him well?'

'Known him years, Mike.'

'And he trusts you?'

'Trusts me how?'

'Trusts you to unload all that charlie he's been shipping down. I'm just curious, that's all. Does he know you've been skimming it? Or is it some kind of deal you've got with the guy? Charlie in lieu of overtime? Only from where we're sitting, Barry, you've done rather nicely. Bit of a pension, in fact. Seven ounces.'

The word 'pension' at last stirred a response from Leggat. For the first time, he looked almost animated. When the paralegal voiced her objections to this new line of questioning, Leggat put a restraining hand on her arm.

'Pension?' he repeated. 'You're talking to the wrong bloke.'

'Care to give us a name?'

'Fuck, no.' He sat back, amused. 'You think I'm that stupid?'

Eadie Sykes had been at Ambrym for a couple of hours, working on the drugs video, before she keyed the final edit in the rough cut.

Last night, working late, she'd pushed herself to within sight of the end. Just occasionally, she thought, there comes a moment in the editing process when the story acquires a life of its own, when decisions about the next talking head or the next action sequence take themselves, when your own role becomes somehow secondary to the onward thrust of the story. At that point, strangely, you find yourself surfing on a wave of the video's own making, your sole responsibility limited to pressing the right keys in the right order. This experience, a gleeful creative surrender, had only happened to her once before. On that occasion, a video about the Allied evacuation from Crete in 1941, she'd come close to winning an award. This time, she sensed there'd be no such disappointment.

She went across to the window, opened it wide, and took a deep lungful of air. Fifty metres down the road, a man in his back garden was piling winter debris onto a bonfire. Excitement, she thought, tastes faintly of woodsmoke.

She returned to the laptop and sat motionless for the best part of thirty minutes, trying to pretend she'd never seen these images, heard these voices, before. Deliberately, she'd opted for letting Daniel's story unfold against the events that had surrounded his death. By the time he was describing his first encounter with heroin, therefore, we already knew that the little wraps of brown powder would finally kill him. As his love affair with smack deepened, sudden cuts to the post-mortem offered a very different perspective, a brutal bass note that underlined the depth of his self-deception.

In a particularly striking passage, he talked with real passion about an early fix. He'd gone short for days. He'd kept himself going on toast and shots of neat vodka. Then, thanks to a new friend, he'd managed to fill his works with a particularly pure teenth, and talked of that sudden rush of unconditional sweetness that had stripped the world of its pain and its menace. It had, he testified, been a glimpse of eternity, an experience that he'd cherish for the rest of his life.

The first time Eadie had heard this story, she'd almost been tempted to try smack for herself. Now, as she watched the glint of the pathologist's scalpel as she readied Daniel's stomach for the dissecting bowl, Eadie felt only revulsion.

Towards the end of the video she'd left space for Daniel Kelly's funeral, but the closing sequence – a carefully assembled reprise of his final steps from the kitchen of the Old Portsmouth flat to the bed where he'd die – was unbearably poignant. By now, his story should have held few surprises. We knew Daniel was bright. We'd grasped his despair, his sense of lostness. We understood how money and heroin had offered him the promise of salvation. And we knew just how false that dawn turned out to be. Yet watching him lurch down the darkened hall, Eadie at last understood how big a lie this tormented young man had sold himself. He'd surrendered his life to the guys in Pennington Road. And that same life had bubbled away through the mouthful of vomit that had finally choked him.

Eadie was still debating where to run the end credits when her mobile began to trill. She recognised the number.

'Doug.' She was grinning. 'Come over any time. Have you eaten?'

'No.'

'Just as well.'

Willard, for once in his life, had skipped breakfast. Now, a couple of minutes before noon, he sat behind the wheel of his Jaguar watching Faraday demolish an egg and cress baguette.

They were parked on Clarence Parade seventy metres from the Solent Palace Hotel. Behind them, the big green expanse of Southsea Common was hosting a spring fly-me festival, dozens of kites bobbing and soaring against the blue of the sky. Screw up your eyes, thought Faraday, and those shapes dancing in the wind could be exotic species of bird life, intruders from some far-flung continent briefly tethered to the grass below. One in particular had caught his eye. The way it danced up and down, trailing a long, black tail, reminded him of choughs he'd seen in Spain, rising on the hot columns of air bubbling out of the narrow mountain gorges.

'He's late.' Willard was looking at his watch. 'Wallace should be here by now.'

McNaughton, Wallace's Special Ops handler, was sitting in his Golf three bays further along Clarence Parade, buried in a copy of the *Mail on Sunday*. Minutes earlier, he'd slipped into the Jaguar's back seat, briefing them on the little Nagra receiver/recorder, pre-tuned to Wallace's wavelength. No need to hit record until Wallace and Mackenzie met inside the hotel.

Faraday was back with the kites again, wondering whether Willard welcomed this brief return to front-line service. It was rare for a Det-Supt to involve himself quite so intimately with a covert operation, though under the circumstances Faraday agreed he had little choice. One clue to the difficulties of an investigation like *Tumbril* was the degree of paranoia it brought with it. The day when you couldn't trust word leaking beyond an inner circle of just four people – Faraday, McNaughton, Wallace and Willard himself – was the day when policing was in trouble.

Faraday put his baguette to one side and wiped his fingers on a tissue from Willard's glovebox. Gisela Mendel's situation still bothered him. A suspicion that she might lose the buyer she'd secured for Spit Bank, he suggested, might breach the walls they'd built round *Tumbril*.

Willard disagreed. 'I talked to her last night. Sorted a couple of things out.'

'Like what?'

'Like where today might lead.'

'You *told* her?'

'Not at all. I just said our friend might be off the plot for a while.'

'So you did tell her.'

'No, I simply said there was every chance he'd be looking for pastures new. As far as she's concerned, we're chasing him out of town.'

'So no sale on the fort.'

'Exactly, not to Mackenzie, anyway. I said, you know, we'd give her every practical assistance finding a replacement buyer but it wouldn't be him.'

'How did she react?'

'No problem. She's a good girl, totally onside, very sensible, very sound. . .' He let the sentence trail away, nodding to himself.

Faraday was wondering which direction Wallace might appear from. According to McNaughton, he'd be driving the trademark Porsche Carrera. Lucky bastard.

'How come the divorce?' Faraday mused.

'Haven't a clue, Joe. What makes you think I'd know?'

'No idea, sir. Just thought you might have talked, that's all.' Faraday caught a glimpse of something low and silver peeling off a distant roundabout. Half a minute later, a Toyota MR2 roared past, a middle-aged woman at the wheel.

Faraday glanced across at Willard. For once, he was looking glum.

'Do you mind me asking you something personal, sir?'

'About Gisela?'

'About the job. About *Tumbril*.'

'Not at all.' Willard permitted himself a small, mirthless smile. 'Do I think it's been a bastard? Yes. Do I think it's been worth it? Ask me again in half an hour and I'll tell you.' He shot Faraday a look. 'Does that cover it?'

'Pretty much. Except I still can't get a handle on locking ourselves away like this.' He gazed out at the Edwardian bulk of the hotel across the road. 'Rock and a hard place? Would that be fair?'

'Rocks, plural.' Willard's bark of laughter took Faraday by surprise. 'And places so bloody hard you'd never go that way again. Not if you had a brain in your head. Have you been up to see Nick Hayder recently?'

'No.'

'He's starting to sort out the last couple of months. He's still clueless about Tuesday and probably always will be but *Tumbril*'s come back with a vengeance – and you know what he said to me? "Thank Christ for hospitals." Do you believe that? From Nick? That man's not a

285

quitter, never has been. Neither, thank God, are you. But stuff like this . . .' He shook his head. 'You don't know who to trust.'

'Does that make Mackenzie clever?'

'Not at all. But the guy's got reach, pull. We've known that for years. That's what drugs buys you. Set up an operation on his scale and you can put anyone in your pocket. But that's the irony, isn't it? If he wasn't that powerful, we wouldn't be here. But because he *is* that powerful, the job's close to impossible. If this falls through . . .' He left the thought unvoiced.

There was a long silence. From the kite flyers on the Common, a whoop of delight.

'What about headquarters?' Faraday queried at last.

'Always dubious. I don't blame them in a way. The Home Office don't want policing, not the way we used to understand it, they want miracles. Here's half a pound of marge. Here's a couple of thousand loaves of sliced white. See what you can do.' He fingered the leather steering wheel. '*Tumbril*'s living on borrowed time. Has been for a while.'

'But you think . . . ?'

'I think nothing, Joe. I'm a copper, a detective. Show me Mackenzie, tell me to take him down, and that's what I'll do.'

'But I thought it was your idea? Your initiative?'

'Wrong. It was Nick's. And look what happened to him.'

Abruptly, there came a crackle from the Nagra and then the sound of Wallace's voice. He was half a mile down the road, putting in a test call to McNaughton. McNaughton confirmed reception and wished him good luck. When Faraday checked along the line of parked cars, McNaughton was still buried in his paper, acknowledging Faraday's glance with a barely perceptible nod.

Willard's finger had found the window controls.

'Hot in here,' he muttered.

Winter sat in Cathy Lamb's office at Kingston Crescent, trying to work out how much a man like Mike Valentine would need to start a new life.

'Say he clears two hundred grand on his house after the mortgage. And say he cashes in the business for another £200,000. Make it half a million including all the other bits and pieces. It's still not enough, is it? Not if you like a bit of style in your life.'

'Where's he going?'

'No idea. Except Le Havre's first stop.'

'You're absolutely sure?'

286

'Positive. I got it from the travel agent he's using. How did you make out with P&O?'

'I'm waiting on a call back. They've promised me something by this afternoon.' She paused. 'You're really telling me he's taking the cocaine with him? Why would he take the risk?'

'What risk? He's going against the flow, Cath. He's swimming upstream. How many people re-export the stuff? The last thing French customs expect is a load of charlie off the Pompey boat. And once he's through Le Havre, he's home free. The kind of weight he's probably carrying, he could set himself up anywhere. It's what they always say, Cath. The best scams are the simplest.'

Cathy smiled. She'd come straight from her allotment in Alverstoke: patched jeans, sweat-stained T-shirt, and dirt under her nails from a morning's weeding. She'd also brought a bag of assorted veg in case Winter fancied real food but so far he didn't seem interested.

'So what are we saying here?' She reached for a pad. 'The guy's off tomorrow night? We let him get on the ferry? Impound the Beemer aboard? Turn him round the other end and bring him back? Only I don't understand why we don't spare ourselves the grief and do it here and now.'

'He may not have stashed the cocaine yet.'

'Sure. Tomorrow then, en route to the Ferry Port. *At* the Ferry Port. Whatever.'

'No, Cath.' Winter was emphatic. 'Just say I've got it right. The guy's carrying hundreds of grand's worth of gear. He's tied in with Mackenzie. You know it. I know it. Everyone knows it. That makes it dodgy, Cath, from his point of view.'

'You're telling me he's nicking it? From Mackenzie?'

'Yeah.'

'You think he's got some kind of death wish?'

'No idea. But if we let him get on the boat, a tenner says we'll find out.'

Cathy nodded, beginning to sense the direction Winter was headed. 'You mean we do the cabin?'

'Exactly. We talk to P&O, get the cabin number, put a couple of techies on the crossing tonight. Get them to wire it up, video as well. We block off the cabins either side, make ourselves at home tomorrow night and see what happens. The guy might just have bailed out with hundreds of grands' worth of someone else's charlie. It'll be party time.'

'What if Mackenzie knows about it? What happens if it's part of some bigger scam?'

'Same difference. Either way, he's going to be mouthing off. I'm talking evidence, Cath. This way, we might get to hurt Mackenzie as well.'

Cathy said nothing, thinking it through.

'What makes you so sure Valentine's got company?'

'It's a four-berth cabin. On his tod, he'd have gone for a two-berth.'

'So who is he travelling with?'

'Haven't a clue, Cath.'

'And you really think this is for keeps? Valentine's not coming back?'

'Yeah.' Winter nodded. 'That's exactly what I think.'

Cathy was still wondering whether to give Winter the benefit of the doubt. She'd been in this situation with him dozens of times on division and she knew it paid to listen. It also paid not to ask too many questions. Winter's MO was unlike any other and he shared his secrets with nobody.

'We'll need a RIPA.' She was thinking aloud now. 'And someone needs to talk to Special Ops. Then there's P&O. Those are conversations for Willard, not me.'

'Willard will take it over. Be nice to keep it to ourselves. Put the squad on the map.'

'There's no way, Paul. Willard has to know. I can't authorise this. It's way beyond my pay grade.'

'OK.' Winter accepted the logic. 'You've told Willard about Leggat yet?'

'No.' Cathy nodded at her phone. 'I tried just now but he's not answering. I need to brief him about Jimmy Suttle, too. You heard about last night? Gunwharf?'

Winter held her gaze for a moment, then nodded.

'They told me at Central this morning.' He looked pained. 'Bit of a scuffle, wasn't it?'

Chapter twenty-one

'Look, Joe.' Willard couldn't believe his luck. 'Second window along. Perfect.'

He was right. Mackenzie had arrived at the Solent Palace fifteen minutes ago, dropped off by his wife. After a drink with Wallace in the Vanguard Bar on the other side of the building, largely inaudible on the radio link, the pair of them had now moved into the first-floor restaurant. At Mackenzie's insistence, they'd taken a table in the window. Just a snatch of conversation as they sat down together was enough to confirm the rapport they'd established. They were old mates already, Faraday thought. The Graham and Bazza Show.

Faraday watched them settling in the window, clearly visible, and wondered whether it was the same table he'd occupied only yesterday. Nice views of the kite festival plus three guys in two cars listening to your every word. Bizarre. Faraday stole a look at McNaughton in the nearby Golf. Sooner or later, when he judged it safe, he'd be snapping a couple of close-up shots on the telephoto for the CPS file. U/c officer charms full flag level three. The incontrovertible proof.

Bazza was asking Wallace where he lived. When Wallace said he had a little place in Chiswick, it turned out Bazza's cousin lived a couple of streets away.

'Thin girl. Dyes her hair pink. Does everything at a thousand miles an hour. Drinks in a pub called the Waterman. Can't miss her –' he laughed '– even on a dark night.'

Wallace said he'd keep his eyes open. These days, he did most of his socialising in town.

'Clients?' Mackenzie enquired.

'Yeah. My girlfriend works for the Saudi military attaché. Big place in South Ken. She's got a pad of her own round the corner in Queen's Gate Gardens. Huge rooms. No offence, mate, but it puts this place to shame.'

'Yeah? What's her name?'

'Sam, but everyone calls her Boysie. Never found out why.'

'She in business with you as well? Or strictly pleasure?'

'Both. But mainly pleasure.'

'Well connected, is she? All those Arabs? Bring you lots of trade?'

'Trade?' Faraday caught the subtle lift in Wallace's voice. Willard, entranced, had his eyes closed. The u/c officer, it was already apparent, was playing a blinder.

'Call it business, then.' It was Bazza again. 'I'm just being nosey.'

'About what exactly?'

'What line you're in. Only, business these days, you know, you read the label on the tin and it turns out to mean fuck all. You with me, Gray?'

'Not really, no.'

'OK. So you develop stuff abroad. Shopping centres, wasn't it?'

'Bricks and mortar. Anything that turns a profit. Customer wants a Formula One circuit and he's got the money to fund it, I'll find the people who can make it happen.'

'Middleman, then. Mr Ten Per Cent.'

'Fifteen. Else I don't get out of bed.'

'You serious?' Mackenzie sounded genuinely impressed. 'That's fifteen per cent of what?'

'The development budget.' Wallace laughed. 'Lovely phrase.'

'So what are we talking?'

'Last deal? High fives.'

'Five figures?'

'Yeah. You remember the place down in Gloucestershire I mentioned on the phone? The Tudor place the guy wants to turn into a health spa? So far I've made a couple of phone calls, sorted the people he should talk to, sent him the invoice. Fourteen grand says I'm one happy bunny.'

'And him? The bloke himself?'

'Over the moon.'

Faraday glanced over at Willard. They both knew that Mackenzie had already made a check call to this particular client, a plant who'd been happy to blow Wallace's little fiction. Not that you'd know it, listening to Mackenzie.

'And are there more like him?' he asked.

'Enough, if you know where to look. Some sectors, the economy is hammering along. That's why the Arabs are buying everything up. Property, land, business, franchises, you name it. France and Germany are dead in the water. Here? Fucking El Dorado.'

'What else do they buy?'

'Not with you, mate.'

'What else do you help them with? Bricks and mortar, great. The odd business, no problem. But you've got to have a laugh from time to time . . . or am I missing something here?'

'Girlies, you mean?'

'Sure . . . and everything that goes with them.'

Faraday still had his eye on the two men in the window. It was hard to be sure at this distance but he sensed an over-reluctance on Wallace's part to be tempted down the path that Mackenzie was trying to flag. In this curious charade it was important not to be hasty but Wallace was taking coyness just a bit too far.

Mackenzie had evidently decided to dispense with the foreplay. Time was moving on.

'Something tells me you're full of shit, mate,' he said amiably.

'Yeah? How's that?'

'The bloke in Gloucestershire for starters. That's all bollocks. And I should know because I phoned him.'

'You did?'

'Yeah. And he's barely heard of you. Couple of calls the back end of last year, you fishing for work . . . Told you to fuck off, didn't he?'

'Not exactly.'

'Yeah, all but though.' Faraday saw the smaller of the figures in the window leaning forward over the table. 'So what *do* you do?'

Faraday heard the muffled sound of someone laughing. Wallace or Mackenzie? He didn't know.

'You're not the Old Bill, are you?' Wallace enquired at last. 'Only I've been had this way before.'

There was a long silence. Willard was grinning now and even Faraday managed a smile. Masterstroke, he thought, the perfect double bluff. Then came the laughter again, louder this time. Mackenzie.

'No, I'm not the Old Bill. Though you can never be sure, can you? Clever bastards sometimes.'

'Too right.'

'You're not convinced, are you?'

'I'm thinking about it.'

'You wanna bin the meal? Call it quits? Only—'

'No. It's a long way to drive for a glass of fizzy water and a wind-up.'

'Who says it's a wind-up? You know why I've asked you down, Gray. We talked about it on the phone. Me? I'm just a nosey mush who's wondering what it might take to sort that fucking fort out there.'

'You want a clear run.'

'You got it.'

'And you think I'm complicating things.'

'I think two things, my friend. Number one, I think you're bidding a

291

silly price. And number two, if you're bidding a silly price, that must mean you've got money to burn. Does it come from all those shopping developments? All those Tudor manor houses? Does it bollocks. Something tells me it's much simpler. Them Arabs practically live on cocaine. As I'm sure you've sussed.'

'Cocaine?' Wallace sounded as if he was barely familiar with the word. 'You really think . . . ?'

'Yeah, I really do. And Graham, nice bloke though you are, that could be a problem.'

'Why?'

'Because—' When Mackenzie broke off, Faraday heard Willard softly cursing. His eyes were better than Faraday's.

'Bloody waiter,' he muttered. 'Would you believe it?'

Mackenzie wanted steak and kidney pudding. Wallace settled for tiger prawns à la Creole. Willard could barely contain himself. This is developing into a radio soap, Faraday thought, one cliffhanger after the next.

Wallace, subtle as ever, had changed the subject. He wanted to know what Mackenzie was going to do with the fort.

'Why?'

'Because it might make a difference.'

'A difference how?'

'Dunno.' Faraday could visualise Wallace's shrug. 'Maybe we could cut some kind of deal, share costs and profits. That way we'd limit each other's exposure.' He paused. 'Casino, isn't it?'

'Who told you that?'

'Gisela Mendel.'

'What else did she tell you?'

'She told me you were the most un-English bloke she'd ever met.'

'How's that, then?'

'She told me you made her laugh a lot. She also said you spoke your mind. Play your cards right, I got the definite impression . . .'

Faraday stole a look at Willard. He wasn't impressed.

'You've met her at all? Face to face?' It was Mackenzie.

'Yeah.'

'She's a looker, isn't she? Plus she's not stupid.'

'How do you mean?'

'There's plenty she's not telling us, you feel it from the start. Know what I mean?'

'Sure.' Wallace was on the same wavelength. 'Bit like this.'

The comment seemed to surprise even Mackenzie. Faraday's admiration for Wallace's nerve was boundless.

'Yeah,' Mackenzie admitted. 'Bit like this.'

Someone else approached the table, an old mate of Mackenzie's. While the two of them bantered about yesterday's game at Preston, Faraday was watching a big black Toyota SUV. It had cruised past twice now, once one way, once the other. Two men inside, both wearing baseball caps.

'Get on with it.' Listening to the wire, Willard was getting impatient.

At last, Mackenzie's mate departed. Wallace enquired about Pompey's prospects if they made it to the Premiership and for a moment Faraday sensed that the heat had gone out of the conversation. Then Mackenzie stoked the fire again.

'This hotel of yours,' he said. 'Helicopter pad. Transfers down from Heathrow. Casino. High rollers. Something tells me you're washing dirty money.'

'Shit.' It was Wallace's turn to laugh. 'I thought for a moment you were going to accuse me of ripping off your own idea.'

'Maybe I am.'

'Same idea? Too much dosh? High-class laundry?'

There came a silence. Very suddenly, no warning, they'd arrived at the crunch. Waiting for an answer from Mackenzie, Willard's knuckles had tightened on the steering wheel. A yes would be a giant step towards court. At length, Faraday caught a low chuckle from Mackenzie.

'No,' he said softly. 'I meant the chopper pad. It's a neat idea. I might get my guys to scope it out. You up for wine, mate, or are we sticking on the fizzy water?'

Wallace settled for a bottle of Sancerre. When he offered to split the tab, Mackenzie told him to forget it.

'No need,' he said.

'Why's that?'

'I'm buying the place.'

'This place? The hotel?'

'Sure. Funny that.' The chuckle became a laugh. 'I thought someone might have told you.'

Doug Hughes had stood throughout the viewing. He was a tall, loose-limbed man with a boyish, unlined face and an affection for yachtie leisure gear from the expensive end of the market. During their eleven-year marriage, he'd often been mistaken for Eadie Sykes's kid brother.

'That was incredible,' he said. 'I've never seen anything like that in my life.'

'I should hope not. That's the whole point.'

'And you've got permission for all this?' He waved a hand at the laptop. 'None of it's ripped off?'

'Do me a favour, Doug. Nice girl like me?'

'So how did you swing it? The morgue stuff for instance?'

'Charm. And not taking no for an answer. Helps to be an Aussie sometimes, skin that thick.' She held her finger and thumb inches apart. Hughes was still staring at the tiny screen.

'So what happens next?'

'I tape the funeral and add some other footage – stills maybe, stuff I can get from Daniel's dad. Good, wasn't he?'

'Incredible. Just perfect. No actor in the world could do that.'

'Sure. Catch 'em in the right mood, treat 'em rough, never fails.'

'Don't cheapen yourself.'

'I'm not, I'm just telling you. In this game, as long as you know where you're going, and why . . .'

'Yes?'

'Nothing. It's means and ends, my love. Always was, always will be.' She reached for the PC. Once the video was complete, she had a list of people she needed to see it. That list included the mystery backer her ex-husband had tapped up for £7000. He should, at the very least, see what he'd got for his money

'Does he have a name, this guy?' She enquired.

'Of course he does.' Hughes was watching Eadie as she extracted the VHS. 'This video's still going to schools?'

'Sure. And colleges, and youth groups, and anyone else who wants it.'

'For money or for free?'

'Depends. Why do you ask?'

'Because my generous friend –' he smiled '– might have a view.'

With the arrival of the food, the mood had changed. Mackenzie and Wallace appeared to have agreed to explore some kind of partnership deal. There'd been no further mention of cocaine or the need to launder profits. As far as both men were concerned, this had the makings of a straightforward business lunch.

Willard, Faraday knew, was disappointed. Mackenzie and Wallace were barely a glass of wine down and there was plenty of scope for excitements to come, but the feeling persisted that the key moment had passed. Wallace had cleverly led Mackenzie towards the very edge of self-incrimination yet – when the words were on his lips – Bazza had stepped back from the brink. Now, as the sturdy little figure in the window called for more horseradish for his steak and kidney, Wallace had returned to football.

'Ever think of buying into the club?' he asked. 'Only the way things are going . . .'

'You're right, mate. Premiership come August, for definite.'

'Not worth a punt?'

'Tried it once, really fancied it. Part of my life, Fratton Park.'

'And?'

'I bid for eleven per cent. They wouldn't have me.'

'Why not?'

'Dunno. Never said. Thanks, mate.' Faraday caught a muttered comment from the waiter as the horseradish arrived, then Mackenzie was talking about the club again. Back in his 6.57 days, he'd have died for Pompey. Nearly did, couple of times.

'6.57?'

'Hard-core fans. Head cases. Paulsgrove boys. The skinheads from the Havelock. Mushes from all over. We took the first train out on away games, anywhere for a fight, bang right up for it. We were Pompey and we didn't give a fuck. The Millwall at Waterloo. The Chelsea, Leeds, Cardiff Soul Crew, Brummie Zulus. We'd take anyone on, steam straight in, didn't matter who, and you know what? We never went tooled up once. Too pissed most of the time, just forgot. One Derby game we ended up in a race riot. Those blokes would have eaten us, given half a chance.'

'What happened?'

'We had it with them, gave them the fucking large one. Situation like that, really tasty, some blokes just cack themselves. You can smell it, fear. Know what I mean?'

It was an innocent enough question, just a ripple in the conversational tide, but Faraday detected an edge in Mackenzie's voice that hadn't been there before. Willard had caught it too. The sun was hot through the windows. He was beginning to sweat.

Wallace remained as relaxed and untroubled as ever. The 6.57 sounded like a good laugh. Maybe every town should have one.

'Yeah, but that's the point, isn't it? This isn't just any old town and we were't just any old firm. Live here, grow up here, be part of the place, and you'd understand that. It's special, Pompey. And something else, mate, it's fucking mine. OK?'

Willard and Faraday exchanged glances. The transformation, all too sudden, was complete. For whatever reason, a smirk, a misplaced gesture, Wallace appeared to have lit a fuse under Mackenzie. His voice had hardened. In the window, he was halfway across the table, his meal ignored. This had ceased to be a peaceable business negotiation, a matey head-to-head over a pile of Victorian granite. From here on in, Mackenzie had a very different agenda.

'You know what, mate? People like you make me fucking ill. You think it's a piece of piss, don't you? You think I'm shit, small time, just some punchy little mush from the backstreets of Copnor. You think you can fanny down here and just turn me over. Well, it ain't gonna fucking happen. Not now and not ever. You understand that? Not *ever*. And for why? Because I'm not as fucking thick and not as fucking small time as you all seem to think.'

All seem to think? Willard rolled his eyes.

'We're talking about a fort,' Wallace was saying, 'Not World War Three.'

'Fort, bollocks. I'll tell you what we're talking about. We're talking about fucking *Tumbril*. We're talking about a bunch of guys who spend the best part of a year sitting on their fat arses over in Whale Island, trying to stitch me up. That costs millions. Must do. And you know who pays your wages, Mr Undercover Man? You know who pays for all that fancy clobber under your shirt? Plus the geezers listening in, wherever they are? People like me, blokes who go out every day and work their fucking socks off. You cunts should be out on the street, sorting out the kids, nicking the paedos, making this city safe at night. Not wasting your time with this kind of crap.'

Faraday was thinking hard about back-up. Wallace had clearly been blown. Any minute now, given the likelihood of Mackenzie's mates in the offing, this could turn into a bloodbath. Faraday glanced across at McNaughton. With his responsibility for Wallace, he plainly had the same idea.

Faraday reached for the door handle. Mackenzie was ranting now, accusing Wallace of harassment. The kind of stuff he'd had to put up with over the last year, Filth sniffing round his accounts, getting up his lawyer's arse, most blokes he knew would have taken a swing. Couple of times he'd been tempted himself. Like now.

'Where are you going?' Willard's hand was on Faraday's arm, restraining him.

'In there.' Faraday nodded across towards the hotel.

'Forget it.'

'*What?*'

'I said forget it. The last thing he'll do is land himself in the shit. This is for our benefit, Joe. He's talking to us.'

Willard slumped back in the driving seat, his head against the plump leather. The black Toyota was back again. It coasted to a stop in front of the Jaguar, hemming them in. Two men got out. The older one was wearing jeans and leather jacket. He stood beside the driver's door, staring down at Willard. Willard ignored him.

Faraday got out of the car.

'What is it?'

'Starter motor's stuffed.' The man in the leather jacket nodded towards the Toyota. 'Thought you gents might give us a push. Favour, like. Seeing you've got nothing better to do.'

Faraday looked at him a moment, aware of McNaughton emerging from the nearby Golf. Then he ducked his head back into the Jaguar. Willard had his eyes closed.

'Tell him to fuck off,' he said softly.

It was Paul Winter's second visit to the QA in a week. To his relief, there was a different face behind the reception desk in A & E. Winter produced his warrant card and asked after a lad called Jimmy Suttle.

'Brought in last night,' he explained. 'Fracas down at Gunwharf.'

The receptionist scrolled back through the log, locating Suttle between two walk-ins after a domestic upset in Stamshaw, and a youth who'd put his mate's scooter through a garden fence.

'We treated him in minor injuries,' the woman said. 'Discharged at 03.44.'

'By himself, was he?'

'Doesn't say.'

'Where did he go?'

'Home, I expect.'

'Downside Cottage?' Winter had reached in and swivelled the PC for a better view. 'Buriton?'

It was nearly two by the time Winter drove out to Buriton. Suttle's Astra was parked outside an end-terrace house a quarter of a mile beyond the pub. A side entrance led down a narrow path. Body-checking past a brimming dustbin, Winter pushed at a wooden door at the end. Already, he could hear music and the sound of girlie laughter. His heart sank. Trudy.

She was sitting on a big rug spread over a tiny patch of threadbare lawn. The sky was cloudless – a perfect spring day – and Suttle was stretched out on the rug, his head in Trudy's lap. A bottle of vodka was flanked by two glasses. The music came from a ghetto blaster at Suttle's feet and Winter spotted the remains of a deep-pan pizza in the nearby flower bed. A blackbird was pecking greedily at a smear of cheese.

'Brought you these, son.' Winter offered Suttle a brown bag. 'What happened?'

'It's worse than it looks,' Suttle said at once. 'They only called the ambulance because I whacked my head when I went over.' Suttle's left eye, swollen and purple, had nearly closed. There were marks across his forehead, too, and a scarlet weal across his cheek.

'So what happened?' Winter said again.

'Fucking Chris Talbot, that's what happened.' It was Trudy. 'Bloke was well out of order.'

'You piss him off somehow?' Winter was still looking at Suttle.

'Yeah, he did. By being with me. That's typical of this city, that is. They ought to put Talbot in a zoo.' Trudy was reaching for the bottle. 'Drink?'

Winter declined the vodka. The sun was warmer than he'd anticipated. He took his jacket off and settled on a corner of the rug. Suttle was up on one elbow now.

'You want a chair? Only—'

'This is fine. You going to take it further?'

'No.' Suttle shook his head. 'Wouldn't give him the satisfaction.'

'Witnesses?'

'Against Talbot?' Trudy started to laugh. 'Do me a favour. You guys are supposed to be cluey. Who's going to grass up someone like that?'

Suttle was looking at the bag Winter had brought.

'What's in there.'

'Grapes. I thought you needed a bit of TLC.'

'That's me.' Trudy started to laugh again. 'I'm TLC, aren't I, Jimmy? You know what time we got up? Tell him, lover.'

The state of Suttle's face couldn't hide his embarrassment. When he asked Trudy to put the kettle on, she got reluctantly to her feet and disappeared into the house.

Suttle turned on Winter.

'What fucking happened to you, then?'

'I was on my way back.'

'So where are the keys?'

'Bit of an accident. I locked them in the apartment by mistake.'

'Great. I could have used you in there. Turned out the bloke had been watching me from the off. Trudy—' He broke off and shook his head.

'Trudy what?'

'Had a real go. Borrowed one of her mate's heels and tried to bury it in Talbot's head. If he hadn't been still battering me, it would have been funny.'

Winter was looking at the back of the house. Through the downstairs window, he could see Trudy drifting around the kitchen, looking for the tea bags.

'Still keen is she?'

'Keen? Shit, you should have been up there a couple of hours ago.' He nodded at the bedroom window. 'She's more knackering than taking on Talbot. Her version of convalescence could put you in hospital.'

'Lucky boy.'

'You think so? She was going away next week. Know what's happened now?'

'Tell me.'

'She's cancelled. Can't leave me in this state, she's saying. Has to move in and look after me.' He paused. 'What's the matter?'

'Nothing.' Winter was watching Trudy as she tottered into the garden with a tray of tea. 'I'd enjoy it, if I were you.'

'While it lasts, you mean?'

'Yeah.' Winter cleared a space on the rug. 'That's exactly what I mean.'

Faraday had never seen Willard so angry. It wasn't just the collapse of *Tumbril*. Nor was it the fact that the Spit Bank sting had gone so spectacularly wrong, nor that a year's work had gone down the khazi, nor that he'd be personally held responsible for the waste of hundreds of thousands of pounds' worth of precious resources. No, it was the humiliation. Find yourself trapped in your own car, obliged to listen to the rantings of Bazza Mackenzie, and you'd be looking for blood.

'Where are they?'

'Brian Imber's taken a couple of his boys to London. Joyce isn't answering her mobile. Prebble's gone to Milan for the weekend.'

'Keep trying. I want them all in here ASAP.'

'It's Sunday,' Faraday pointed out. 'And they weren't invited in the first place.'

'Sure, but that's a bit academic, isn't it? I'm no mathematician, Joe, but I can count. Leave Hayder out of this and there's five of us in *Tumbril*, five of us that matter. I've listened to the end of that fucking tape twice now and it's obvious.'

'Obvious how?'

'Mackenzie knows. He knows everything. He's probably known since we moved into Whale Island. In fact I wouldn't be surprised if the little fucker knew before we even dreamed the operation up. This is madness, Joe. Unless we get on top of this, we'll all end up in St James.'

St James was the local psychiatric hospital, a sprawling Victorian pile half a mile inland from the Bargemaster's House.

Grip, thought Faraday. 'We're really talking about the covert,' he said slowly. 'And I make that four, not five.'

'Four?' Willard was looking blank.

'You, sir. Me. Wallace. And McNaughton.' He paused. 'Plus Gisela Mendel.'

'Gisela's straight,' Willard said at once.

'So is McNaughton. So is Wallace. So am I. Gisela wants to offload the fort for real. That says motive to me.' He offered Willard a chilly smile. 'Just a thought, sir, that's all.'

Willard's phone began to ring. It was Cathy Lamb. She was downstairs. She needed to talk to Willard urgently.

'Come up,' he grunted. 'Join the party.'

It took Cathy less than a minute to appear at the door. The sight of Faraday seemed to take her by surprise. She nodded at him, then apologised to Willard for her gardening gear.

'Been on the allotment,' she explained.

'Don't blame you. I can think of worse ways of spending a Sunday. What's the problem?'

Cathy explained about the arrest of Barry Leggat. Winter had pulled him last night with a decent stash of cocaine. Leggat worked for Valentine and Winter had cause to believe that the car dealer was getting out with the rest of the coke.

'Whose coke?'

'Winter doesn't know. He thinks there's probably a connection to Mackenzie but he doesn't know how.'

'Evidence?'

Cathy summarised it. Most of it was either guesswork or circumstantial. Beyond dispute was the fact that Valentine was selling his house, disposing of his business, and had booked a ticket on tomorrow night's sailing to Le Havre. P&O had finally come back and confirmed a ticket for a vehicle and a four-berth cabin in the name of Mr M. Valentine.

'They've got a number for the cabin?'

'Yes, sir.'

'You think they might be up for a spot of covert? Only we're good at that.' To Cathy's relief, Willard appeared to be ahead of the game.

'Don't know, sir. I thought you might make the call. That's why I'm here.'

'Fine. Get me a name and phone number.'

'It's the divisional manager. He's at home at the moment but he's expecting a call.'

'No problem.' He offered her a thin smile. 'It'll be a pleasure.'

Cathy disappeared downstairs again to phone the number through. Willard stared at Faraday.

'You think Mackenzie's taking the piss again?' He frowned. 'Or is Winter onto something?'

Chapter twenty-two

Paul Winter had been trying to raise Harry Wayte for the last couple of days. Early Sunday evening, he finally got through.

'Been away,' Wayte explained. 'To what do I owe this pleasure?'

'Just wondered whether you'd fancy a pint.'

'Why?'

Winter had known Harry Wayte for years and had always admired him. There was a bluntness and impatience about the man that had made him one of the more effective DIs. At one point Winter had almost sorted himself a transfer to Wayte's Tactical Crime Unit, but Harry had a nose for artists like Winter and the vacancy had finally gone to a younger DC. Winter had been disappointed at the time but Wayte – for him – was still a light in the darkness. Spend an hour or so with Harry, and you felt you were talking to a real copper.

'One or two things to discuss,' Winter said lightly.

'It's Sunday. Why can't it wait?'

'Because next week's a bastard.' Winter glanced at his watch. 'You still living up in Havant?'

Wayte told him a meet was out of the question. He was off to Fort Nelson this evening for a get-together with some friends. It was a regular thing, happened every month, and even the likes of Paul Winter wouldn't break the pattern.

Wayte paused. 'What's it about, then?' he queried.

'Mike Valentine.'

There was a long silence. Then Wayte was back on the phone. The meeting at Nelson started at half seven, bunch of guys from the Palmerston Forts Society. First half-hour or so was boring as fuck but this evening they were watching a little play of some kind, an entertainment, and guests were welcome. Why didn't Winter come up, watch the play, then afterwards they could talk?

'Delighted. Half seven, then.'

*

301

Faraday had decided to walk to the cathedral. From the Bargemaster's House to Old Portsmouth was a serious trek – with the detour down to the seafront, at least five miles – but he knew he needed the fresh air. *Tumbril* had blown up in their faces, an event as violent and unexpected as any car bomb, and his head was still ringing from the explosion.

Willard had spent most of the afternoon with Terry Alcott, the Assistant Chief Constable in charge of CID and Special Operations. Alcott had a place in the Meon Valley, and had evidently abandoned his day's fishing to survey the smoking ruins of *Tumbril*.

Willard had phoned Faraday just after four with a series of preliminary decisions. He wanted full statements on the lunchtime meet from Wallace, McNaughton and Faraday himself. The offices on Whale Island were to be sealed and guarded, absolutely no one permitted entry. Faraday was to make the arrangements with the MoD police, and further ensure that the *Tumbril* team – Imber, Prebble and Joyce – were to be turned away at the guardhouse when they appeared tomorrow morning at Whale Island. Willard wanted all three in his office at Kingston Crescent for half nine.

On the phone, Willard had been businesslike, almost abrupt. Whatever happened next, the consequences of the lunchtime meet at the Solent Palace were brutally clear. This investigation was no longer about Bazza Mackenzie but about *Tumbril* itself.

To his own surprise, Faraday felt almost relieved. From the start, less than a week ago, he'd been bounced into this sealed-off world where nothing was quite what it seemed. Every conversation, Faraday realised, had been governed by an uneasy sense of who knew what. Every phone call became another piece of the jigsaw to be locked away and assessed before anyone else took a look. Most investigations, in Faraday's experience, relied above all on teamwork. Without the support of the blokes around you, any major inquiry was dead in the water. But *Tumbril* turned that kind of automatic, instinctive kinship on its head. In the course of four short days, trust had become a currency to be spent with extraordinary care.

Faraday had hated it. On one level, he'd understood why Willard had fenced *Tumbril* off, and then built firewalls within the operation itself. 'Need to know' was rule one for every security service in the world, and there were decent coppers, people like Nick Hayder, who thrived on it. Yet to Faraday, this kind of MO – tight-fisted, calculating, cold – fed a paranoia that ended up tainting everything. You didn't know who to confide in, who to bounce ideas off. Your hands were shackled by the constant anxiety that a misplaced word or gesture might blow an entire year's work. These were pressures that it took someone very special to withstand, and Faraday now understood why even Nick Hayder – in the weeks before his accident – had begun to buckle.

What would happen next? Lawyers at the Crown Prosecution Service would clearly have a view, and that would probably govern the immediate days ahead, but beyond the CPS lay deeper family issues that the force itself would have to confront. Willard was right. *Tumbril* had been comprehensively blown. Someone within the tight inner circle had been feeding Mackenzie information. Maybe for money. Maybe for advantage. Maybe in revenge for some private slight. Whatever the motive, it represented the deepest possible wound to an organisation that relied on at least a measure of mutual trust.

Some form of internal inquiry, Faraday thought, was the likeliest outcome. A senior officer from the Professional Standards Department would probably be tasked to piece together the debris that was *Tumbril*, and deduce who, exactly, had lit the fuse. But that exercise, in itself, was fraught with fresh problems. Rumours of *Tumbril's* existence had already ruffled feathers, CID especially, and confirmation of this ultra-covert operation would further sour those who already regarded themselves as pariahs, untrusted by senior management.

Tumbril's post-mortem would probably last for months. People would start talking. A corporate itch would become an open sore. How come these guys get half a million to squirrel themselves away when we have problems with a night's overtime? And how come such clever fuckers let everything turn to rat shit? Faraday could imagine the gleeful, embittered exchanges in divisional CID offices across the force. Even fellow DIs, foot soldiers in the war against volume crime, would probably have a dig.

The prospect, all too likely, filled Faraday with gloom, and as the light drained from the Solent, he paused in the lengthening shadows of the funfair to take stock. To date, his contribution to *Tumbril* had been less than distinguished. Maybe now, he thought, was the time for some serious detective work.

Fort Nelson straddled the crest of Portsdown Hill, one of a series of low, red-brick fortifications that ringed the great Victorian arsenal of Portsmouth dockyard. From up here on top of the hill, the geographical facts that had shaped Pompey's turbulent past were easy to grasp. The busy spread of the city below was mapped in a thousand street lights and the southward jut of the island was defined by the blackness of the encroaching sea. Getting out of his car and gazing out, Winter could visualise the three offshore forts that had sealed Spithead and the harbour approaches from the threat of French invasion. If you ever needed an explanation for Pompey's insularity, for the city's determination to turn its back on the world, then here it was. A place apart, thought Winter. The perfect excuse for a lifetime on the piss and centuries of recreational inbreeding.

He found Harry Wayte inside the Artillery Hall, a cavernous showcase for hundreds of years of military hardware. The DI was standing beside an impressive-looking field piece, deep in conversation with an elderly man in a Barbour jacket. The hardwood of the cannon and its limber was inlaid with decorative brass. Winter was still reading the accompanying panel when Harry at last stepped over.

'Souvenir from the Sikh Wars.' He nodded at the gun. 'Where would we be without India?'

'Still eating crap food.' Winter extended a hand. 'Why haven't I been here before?'

'You tell me. There's a little tour after the play. I'd take it if I were you.'

A modest audience was already seated at the far end of the hall. Harry Wayte showed Winter to a reserved row of seats at the front. It was chilly in the hall and Winter was wondering about nipping back to the car park for his coat when a young actor stepped onto the semicircle of scuffed boards that served as a makeshift stage. Dressed in knee breeches and a collarless shirt, he sank into a solitary chair, gazed round, and then produced a letter.

'Where's the rest of them?' Winter had beckoned Harry closer.

'It's a monologue. Just him.'

'He's talking to himself?'

'That's right.' Harry smiled. 'Ring any bells?'

The piece lasted about half an hour. Winter, whose appetite for drama rarely extended beyond repeats of *Heartbeat*, found himself curiously sucked in. It was 1870. The lad was part of Fort Nelson's garrison, a clerk at a Southsea bank and a part-time volunteer soldier. Three weeks in high summer found him up here on guard duty, protecting Portsmouth against a French threat that was fast disappearing under the fury of a Prussian invasion.

News of this sudden conflagration had reached Fort Nelson through the pages of the *Illustrated London News*, and young Trooper Press had read the battlefield dispatches with immense envy. The French, he wrote to his fiancée, were defending the motherland with their usual vim, pressing home counter-attack after counter-attack with cavalry, the sabre and the bayonet. The Prussians, it had to be said, were doing rather well in their grey, methodical way but the whole world applauded the fearless French cuirassiers with their dash and their madcap courage. Better this style of warfare, he concluded, than living like a mole for weeks on end, poking your nose out occasionally to check whether any spare Froggies had made it over the Channel.

Twice during the performance, Winter stole a look at Harry Wayte. The DI seemed entranced by this little drama, nodding his head from time to time as if in agreement. A lengthy aside about the relentless advance of the Prussian Guard at St-Privat brought a particular smile to his ravaged face. 'The Prussian is trained to be a little shooted as he goes forward,' mused Trooper Press. 'He develops a keen appreciation for bullet music.'

'Bullet music?' The performance was over and Winter was on his feet, stamping the warmth back into his legs.

'Contemporary reference,' Harry explained, 'lifted straight from dispatches. St-Privat was curtains for the French. The Krauts were in Paris within weeks.'

Winter, surprised, admitted his ignorance. As far as he was aware, the Germans had stayed put until 1914.

'Wrong, mate. 1870 was the dress rehearsal. The French got a seeing-to, and forty-odd years later the pickle heads were on the march again. Trooper Press was lucky to be on the right side of the Channel. His kind of attitude, he'd have been a sitting duck for the Prussians. Times change, Paul.' He gestured towards a nearby World War One howitzer. 'The technology moved on and we *all* dug in. You want to have a look at the rest of the fort?' He indicated a group of guests mustering by the door. 'Only I could do with a couple of minutes with my mates before we find a pub.'

With some reluctance, Winter agreed to join the tour. A couple of dozen members of the audience trooped after a guide, criss-crossing the fort, filing through narrow subterranean tunnels, pausing to step into a magazine while the guide explained the importance of guarding against accidental explosions. A single stray spark, he said, and the whole place could go up. With tons and tons of gunpowder in these roomy, brick-lined vaults, there'd be bits of Trooper Press all over the city.

Thoughtful now, Winter followed the tour upwards until they emerged into the cold night air. Minutes later, they paused on the ramparts. The guide wanted to know whether anyone had any questions.

Winter raised his hand. He could see the bulky shapes of cannon nearby.

'Why do all these guns point north?' he enquired.

'Because that's where the threat might come from. You have to guard against landings further up the coast. A couple of days' march and the city's there for the taking.' The guide smiled, tapping his nose.

'That's the funny thing about Pompey. It's threats from the mainland we have to worry about.'

Winter was staring into the windy darkness, at last beginning to understand.

'Too fucking right,' he murmured.

Faraday sat at the back of the cathedral, letting the bare, unaccompanied plainchant wash over him. Sung in Estonian, he hadn't got a clue about the liturgical significance of what he was hearing, whether the world was heading for heaven or hell, but just now it didn't seem to matter. Better, he thought grimly, to keep his options wide open and discount absolutely nothing.

Earlier, in conversation with Willard, he'd drawn a ring around the five names that were privy to Tumbril's inner secret. Four of them were coppers – Willard, Wallace, McNaughton and Faraday himself – and it was an index of just how sloppy he'd become that his attention had automatically been drawn to the outsider.

Gisela Mendel, it was true, had every reason for cementing a relationship with Mackenzie. The latter's eagerness to buy the fort was, Faraday assumed, genuine, and if Gisela had realised that Wallace was simply a plant, there to entrap her one and only buyer, then she'd have been sorely tempted to mark Mackenzie's card. Willard, on the other hand, would have been mad not to have anticipated – and countered – this development. So what, exactly, was the real nature of his relationship with the woman? Was he as dotty about her as Faraday's first glimpse of them together had suggested? Had Willard, indeed, been the cue for her marriage to collapse?

This line of inquiry, Faraday knew, led to some very deep waters indeed. At best, Willard was guilty of letting Gisela get too close to the bid to entrap Mackenzie. That would argue for naivety on his part and calculating self-interest on hers. At worst, unthinkably, Willard might himself be tied into Mackenzie through Gisela Mendel. Mackenzie would presumably pay a sizeable premium not only to secure the fort but also buy his own escape from the attentions of Operation *Tumbril*. What sweeter bung than, say, £100,000 into the back pocket of his chief tormentor?

Faraday smiled at the thought, easing his position on the hard cathedral seating, sensing already that this piece of investigative speculation was a non-starter. Willard was the all-time control freak. He couldn't make a cup of tea without taking sole charge of the kitchen. Accept money from the likes of Mackenzie, and he'd hand the man a loaded gun. Why would Willard surrender the rest of his life to the man he'd sworn to put behind bars?

Dismissing the thought, Faraday returned to yesterday's crucial meet at the Solent Palace Hotel. At Willard's insistence, he'd listened again to the recording, concentrating on the moment when the conversation across the table in the window had so suddenly taken a turn for the worse. Buried in what followed could be a clue, a tiny smudge of chalk on a tree, something that might flag the investigative path forward. He'd listened to the recording three times in all, hearing the anger in Mackenzie's voice, the resentment bred by his knowledge of the trap closing around him, his belief – all too real – that his hands-on days of wheeling and dealing in cocaine were history and that he deserved a little credit for the transformation he'd wrought in his own – and Pompey's – fortunes. It was, in the end, a question of status. The butterfly had emerged from the chrysalis, a maggot no longer. King of the City, indeed.

Faraday felt a tiny jolt of recognition. He straightened on the chair, forcing himself back through his memory of the recording, trying to identify that one phrase that Mackenzie had let slip. It was there. He knew it was. He could sense its rhythm in his head, the tell-tale metre, the ripple of incandescent anger that gave Mackenzie away. Something chippy. Something about his roots. Something about Copnor. Then, as the final passage of plainsong began to fade, Faraday had it. *Punchy little mush from the backstreets of Copnor.* That's what he'd said.

As the audience began to applaud and the singers took a bow, Faraday sat back, astonished at the implications of his discovery. *Punchy little mush from the backstreets of Copnor.* Just so.

Moments later came the lightest of taps on his shoulder. Faraday twisted round in his chair. Nigel Phillimore was standing behind him. There was to be a modest reception for the Estonians in the Sally Port Hotel tomorrow evening. The choir was off back to Tallinn and the cathedral was saying thank you. If Faraday wanted to be part of that farewell, he was more than welcome to come along. Seven o'clock would be fine.

Faraday gazed up at him, aware that the details had barely registered.

'Of course.' He smiled. 'I'll do my very best.'

A couple of miles east of Fort Nelson, commanding an even better view of the city, was a hilltop pub called The Churchillian. Winter and Harry Wayte had driven there in convoy. Now they sat together at a table by the window, nearly a pint down, still discussing Pompey's role in the defence of the realm.

'Blood and treasure,' Wayte grunted. 'When the trumpets sounded and the drums beat, you couldn't find a richer city in the kingdom. The minute the war was over, they were all back on the turnpike, riding hard for London. That's why Pompey blokes grab it while they can. That's why the kids are off their heads most of the time. It's in the genes, mate.' He nodded. 'Blood and treasure.'

'Whose blood?'

'Ours.'

'And the treasure?'

'The King's.' Wayte raised his glass. 'Here's to September.'

September was the month Wayte was due to retire. Listening to him now, watching him amongst his civvy mates at Fort Nelson, Winter felt the faintest stirrings of envy. Speaking for himself, Winter was happy to admit that he dreaded the prospect of leaving the job. He wouldn't have a clue what to do with the empty days that yawned before him. Harry, on the other hand, couldn't wait for it to happen.

Winter watched him drain his glass, then went to the bar for refills. By the time he got back, Wayte was deep in an abandoned copy of the *Sunday Telegraph*.

'So what are you going to do?'

'When?' Wayte looked up, folding the paper.

'After September.'

'Ah . . .' He grinned. 'You want the list?'

First off, there was long-overdue maintenance on his little fleet of model warships. A major battle was scheduled on Canoe Lake for Trafalgar Day, and he needed his frigates in full fighting order. Afterwards, once he'd taken his missus on the promised jaunt to Venice, he was joining the Hilsea Lines project.

'What's that, then?'

'Down there.' Wayte nodded into the darkness. 'Bunch of blokes have got together on a restoration project. The place has been a wilderness, bits still are. They've put paths in, sorted out some of the casemates, done a bit of research. A couple of blokes on the job have been involved. Me? Can't wait. Cheers. Happy days, eh?'

His huge hand closed around the glass. Hilsea Lines was the inner circle of defence works that protected the north shore of Portsea Island, yet another confirmation that Pompey's hackles were permanently raised. Anyone with a serious interest in this martial little city would have to fight for it.

'What's with Valentine, then?' Wayte had plainly tired of social chit-chat.

'I'm thinking of buying a motor off him.'

'And that's why –' Wayte looked astonished '– you wanted a meet? To talk about Valentine's *cars*?'

'Yeah.' Winter smiled at him. 'Any other reason I should be interested?'

The question was a direct challenge and Wayte knew it. He sat back in his chair, eyeing Winter, trying to gauge his real interest.

'Valentine's leaving,' he said at last. 'Selling up. Getting out. Did you know that?'

'Yeah. And I was wondering why.'

'Because he's had enough.'

'Enough of what?'

'This shit-hole city. Bloke's made himself a packet, done well out of the motors. He's what . . . forty . . . forty-five? That kind of age, you've still got plenty of time to make the most of it. Wouldn't blame him, would you?'

'Where's he going?'

'Spain, as far as I know.'

'Marbella?'

'Could be. Half of Pompey seem to live down there. Good luck to the bloke is what I say.'

'So why aren't you shipping out, then? If it's such a crap place to live?'

'Because it doesn't bother me, not the way it bothers blokes like Valentine. I've lived here all my life, just like my dad did, just like *his* dad did. Those days, you got yourself a decent education, learned to handle yourself, went to sea, got a proper job afterwards. Me? I've loved it all until recently, but that's the job's fault, not mine. Pompey's home, Paul. And my missus can't stand all that Spanish sun.'

Winter nodded. He understood exactly what Harry meant.

'Cathy Lamb mentioned some intelligence you raised a couple of days ago,' he said carefully. 'Big cocaine shipment. Wouldn't have any details, would you?'

' 'Fraid not.'

'You don't have the details or you're not up for sharing them?'

'Don't have the details. Couple of my blokes have their ears to the ground. Street prices are down, too. That tells me it's more than a rumour.'

'But no names attached?'

'No.' He reached for his glass again. 'Why?'

'I was just wondering about Bazza.'

'No.' He shook his huge head. 'Definitely not. Bazza's out of the front line now, too much else going on for him, too busy playing the businessman.'

'You don't think he's retained an interest?'

'That's different. Fuck knows how you prove it but I'd be amazed if he wasn't staking other guys, keeping it in the family. Where else would he get a return like that? It's simple arithmetic, mate. Give me the back of an envelope and I'll show you the way it works. Big profits. Zero risk.' He took another long pull from his glass. 'How come you don't know all this already? I thought you were on Cathy's squad?'

'I am.'

'Then what's this about?'

Winter had anticipated the question. For once, he'd barely touched his second pint.

'Does the word *Tumbril* mean anything to you?'

'Of course it does. Some half-arsed covert, isn't it? Run out of Major Crimes?'

'You tell me. All I hear is gossip.'

'That's all I hear but it sounds pretty fucking kosher to me. Problem is, the thing'll never work.'

'We're talking Bazza again?'

'Yeah. Right target maybe but these guys are five years too late. The time to nick Mackenzie was when he was down in the trenches, taking a risk or two. Nowadays you'll never get anywhere near the bloke. You should go down the command chain, look for the up-and-coming Bazzas. They're the blokes to target.'

'And you think that would make a difference?'

'Not the slightest. You're the guys who've been chasing round after the Scouse kids, aren't you? It's supply and demand, mate, not rocket science. Take the local blokes off the plot and all you do is open the door to those nutters. It's like Iraq. Say we win this war. Say we kill Saddam. And say the country falls apart afterwards. What'll happen in twelve months time? Everyone will be running around looking for a strongman, someone to sort the Iraqis out, someone to impose a bit of order.'

'A Bazza?'

'Yeah, a Bazza. He had this city taped until the Scousers turned up. Now it's a mess.'

'Is that *Tumbril*'s fault? If they've been trying to take him down?'

'Haven't a clue, mate. Who knows, they might even get a result despite everything I say. But that's not going to solve the problem, is it? Not when kids want to get off their heads all the time. I'm telling you, Paul, it's a dog's breakfast. Supply and demand. The magic of capitalism. Thank Christ I'm out soon.'

'So there's fuck-all point even trying?'

'There's fuck-all point thinking you're gonna solve anything. Trying's different. Trying's what we do. Problem with blokes like me is we've tried so bloody hard all our lives that conversations like this really begin to hurt.' He nodded, combative now, moist-eyed. 'Your age, Paul, it might be different. You're still just young enough to kid yourself you can make a difference.'

'I never thought that in my life.'

'You didn't? Then why do you bother?'

'Because I enjoy it.'

'Well that makes you very rare. Blokes like me, we're stuffed in the end because we really did believe we could make a difference, but then you wake up in the morning and you realise there's absolutely no fucking chance. Number one, the problem's too massive. Number two, we haven't got a clue what to do about it. We're like the military, always fighting the war before last.'

'So what's the answer?'

'You're asking me?'

'Yeah.'

'You jack it in.'

'And the rest of us?'

'No idea, mate.' He reached for his glass. 'And you know something else? I don't fucking care.'

Faraday took a taxi back to the Bargemaster's House. There was a message from Eadie waiting for him on the answerphone. She sounded excited, wanted to share something with him, and for a moment he was tempted to ring back. Then he changed his mind and helped himself to a couple of bananas from the fruit bowl.

Outside, on the square of lawn between the house and the towpath, he demolished the second of the bananas before stepping through the squeaking gate and heading north along the path. The tide was high, lapping at the sea wall, and as the slap-slap of the halyards in the dinghy park began to recede, he could hear the honk of brent geese, way out on the harbour. Come May, he thought, these birds would have gone, returning to their breeding grounds in Siberia. By October, they'd be on the harbour again with their young, part of the slow pulse of the passing months that Faraday recognised more and more as a kind of solace. No matter how bad the job got, the geese would always be back.

A mile from the Bargemaster's House, the towpath ducked inland around the jetty where the dredgers discharged their sand and gravel, and Faraday paused in the windy darkness. He was now certain about the phrase of Mackenzie's that had lodged in his memory. He could even picture the moment when he'd first heard it – not yesterday in Willard's Jaguar outside the hotel, but days earlier, at *Tumbril* HQ on Whale Island.

For Faraday's benefit, Prebble had devoted the best part of the morning to profiling Mackenzie. The young accountant had led the new DI step by step through the target's life, exploring the short cuts he'd taken, explaining the way he'd turned casual drug use into a multi-million-pound fortune, introducing the professional friends he'd picked up on the way. Then, towards the end of this impressive presentation, had come a sudden intervention from Imber. Something had angered him. Maybe the nerve of the man. Maybe the sheer scale of Mackenzie's success. Whatever the reason, he'd left no doubt that it was the business of *Tumbril* to strip Mackenzie of his assets. That way, Imber had said, he'd be back where he'd begun: a punchy little mush from the backstreets of Copnor.

Seconds later, thanks to Joyce, Faraday had been looking at a sheaf of wedding photos, Mackenzie's daughter surrounded by dozens of Pompey's finest. He could still remember the plump, moneyed faces beaming at the camera outside the cathedral but it was the earlier phrase that stuck in his mind. *A punchy little mush from the backstreets of Copnor.*

Faraday turned and began to make his way back towards the distant twinkle of the Bargemaster's House, wondering who in that room had passed it on. He could visualise the three faces around the table: Prebble, Imber, Joyce. Why on earth would any of them betray *Tumbril* to Mackenzie?

Chapter twenty-three

MONDAY, 24 MARCH 2003, 09.35

Faraday was late getting to Kingston Crescent, delayed by an accident in Milton. Knocking at Willard's door, he stepped into the Det-Supt's office to find Brian Imber and Martin Prebble already sitting at the conference table. With Willard still at his desk, locked into a particularly difficult phone call, Joyce was busy in the adjacent kitchen.

'Sheriff?' She'd stolen up behind him.

Faraday made way for the tray of coffees and sat down at the table. Imber wanted to know what was going on. All three of them had been denied entry at the Whale Island guardhouse. More alarming still, they'd had to surrender their security passes.

'All in good time, Brian.' Willard had joined them at last. He took the seat at the head of the table and winced when he tasted the coffee. Joyce rarely used less than two spoonfuls of instant.

Imber was still looking at Faraday. Already Faraday could sense the suspicions shaping behind the tight smile. The collapse of *Tumbril*, he thought, had wreaked havoc. And one of the casualties might well be his friendship with this man.

Willard opened the meeting with a surprisingly chaotic account of the way they'd tried to sting Mackenzie. Faraday couldn't work out whether it was embarrassment or simple exhaustion, but it was only slowly that the real shape of the entrapment swam into focus. With Willard's preamble complete, it was Imber – inevitably – who sought clarification.

'Mackenzie was after the fort?'

'Indeed.'

'Which was or wasn't for sale?'

'Was, as far as he was concerned.'

'But for real, later? Because of the woman's circumstances?'

'That's correct.'

'So what happened?'

This time, Willard was brisk. The meet had been set up for yesterday lunchtime. Minimum back-up kept the operation details tight. Wallace and Mackenzie met in the bar, then went through to the restaurant. The subsequent conversation was monitored and recorded. Half an hour into the meal, it became obvious that Wallace was blown. Not just Wallace, but *Tumbril* itself. Game, set and match to Mr Mackenzie.

'I've just been talking to the CPS.' Willard nodded towards the phone on his desk. 'They want the operation discontinued. From here on in, they regard *Tumbril* as tainted.'

'*Tainted?*' Faraday had never seen Imber so angry. 'Is that why we were turned away this morning? Because you guys fucked up the covert?'

'Steady on, Brian.' It was Willard. 'This isn't easy for any of us.'

'I'm sure it isn't, sir. I'm just curious, that's all. We arrive at work. We're denied access. The guy on the gate says the office has been sealed, guards posted, locks changed, the whole nine yards. That makes it a crime scene, doesn't it?'

'Yes.' Willard nodded. 'It does.'

'Brilliant. I go home Friday night thinking we're getting somewhere at last. I've seen the stuff that Martin's prepared for you, the asset statement, and to me it's starting to look good – so good I took my boys to London yesterday and never gave *Tumbril* a moment's thought. That's rare, believe me. Then this morning comes along, and I find the whole thing's collapsed. Bang, nothing left, year zero. Not only that but we're all under suspicion for blowing a sting about which we know absolutely nothing.'

'What makes you think that?'

'Forgive me, sir, but I don't think you've thought this through. Our records will be seized, our e-mails, our phone logs, everything. Are you telling me this is some kind of exercise?'

'Not at all. Damage limitation might be closer.'

'Damage to what? To whom?'

'To *Tumbril*. To us all. To the force in general. I repeat: Mackenzie knows everything. That means someone must have told him. And that means we have to find out who.'

Imber fell silent for a moment. He was far too experienced a policeman to doubt for a moment the course of the next few weeks. With this much egg on *Tumbril*'s face, someone had to start the clean-up.

'Are we suspended?' he asked at last. 'Only it might be nice to know.'

'No.' Willard shook his head. 'Mr Alcott and I considered it but for the moment we don't believe there's a need.'

'So who heads the inquiry?' Imber was looking at Faraday.

'Don't ask me, Brian.' Faraday felt helpless. 'I'm as much in the frame as you are.'

'More, sir, with respect. You were there yesterday. Presumably you were in on the setting-up.'

Willard stirred. 'And so was I, Brian, if that's any consolation. This is getting us nowhere.'

'Mr Willard?' Prebble had raised a hand. 'I know I'm not really in the loop here but it's not clear to me where this leaves the operation.'

'Nowhere. I just told you. The CPS have knocked it on the head.'

'So . . .' He was frowning, trying to follow the logic. 'We never move against Mackenzie?'

'That's right.'

'Or his solicitors? Accountants? All those nominees?'

'Right again. Unless the CPS have second thoughts.'

'That's mad. More than a year's graft? That's insane.'

'I agree.'

Prebble looked sideways at Imber, a mute appeal for support, but Imber appeared to be in shock. His face, always lean, seemed to have caved in on itself. Here was a man, Faraday thought, who's just seen his life's work demolished in less time than it took him to shave in the morning. Nailing Mackenzie, in Imber's own words, was the closest he'd ever got to ripping up this evil by the roots. Now, *Tumbril*'s prime target was beyond reach.

Willard was mapping the road ahead. Given the potential fallout from *Tumbril*, the Chief had instructed the Professional Standards Department to conduct a thorough investigation. Every member of the *Tumbril* team, including Willard himself, would – in due course – be required to make themselves available for interview. In the meantime, everyone with the exception of Prebble would be reassigned to other duties.

This time it was Joyce who raised a hand.

'I vote for a wake.' She was looking at Faraday. 'That's the least *Tumbril* owes us.'

With the meeting over, Faraday was last to leave the table. At the door, Willard called him back. He was standing at his desk, firing up his laptop. At length, he keyed a file.

'Prebble e-mailed me this late last night. There's something you ought to look at.'

Faraday recognised the asset analysis Prebble had been compiling on Friday afternoon. But for the accountant's abrupt departure for the train, he'd have read it earlier.

'Here.' Willard had scrolled through to the final page. Under 'Miscellaneous Assets' Prebble had listed a £7000 payment from Bellux Ltd to a local company called Ambrym. Faraday felt the blood begin to ice in his veins. Bellux Ltd was the most active of Mackenzie's many companies, the engine he used to power his commercial empire. An explanatory note explained that the money was a one-off contribution to a health education video.

'Ambrym?' Willard looked up at Faraday.

'Eadie's company.'

'And the video?'

'That's the one J-J's been working on.'

'About what, exactly?'

'Heroin.'

'Co-funded by the guy who's been running drugs most of his life? If this wasn't Monday, I'd say we were looking at a piss-take here. What the fuck's going on?'

'I've no idea, sir.' Faraday couldn't take his eyes off the screen. Ambrym Productions. November 5, 2002. £7000. Grip, he thought.

Willard stepped away from the desk. Yesterday had left its mark on him: eyes shadowed by fatigue, a fold of skin bloodied under his chin where he'd been careless with the razor.

'We shouldn't be having this conversation, Joe, but let me remind you of the obvious. Investigating officers look for motive. You live with this woman. You want the best for her. You want her to succeed. £7000 isn't a lot of motive but it's a start. You get my drift?'

Faraday nodded. There was nothing to say. Dimly, he heard Willard telling him to sort out a list of Whale Island staff who might have had access to the *Tumbril* offices: cleaners, caterers, photocopier engineers. He wanted full details on his desk by tomorrow morning.

'OK?'

'Yes, sir.' Faraday was back beside the door. 'Cathy Lamb's little job . . .' he began.

'Tonight, you mean? Mike Valentine? The P&O ferry?' Willard looked at Faraday for a long moment, then shook his head. 'The last thing she needs is help from us, Joe. I've told her to sort it from her end.'

It was mid morning before Cathy Lamb was summoned to Secretan's office. The Chief Supt had received a full brief on the forthcoming operation aboard *The Pride of Portsmouth*, and had indicated his approval. While he understood that the operation was purely speculative, based on thinnish evidence, he badly needed a headline or two of his own in the rapidly developing media war. Twice last week, the

316

News had led its main evening edition with drug-related stories involving generous helpings of extreme violence. The city might have survived the Blitz, he told Cathy, but at this rate half the population would be thinking hard about evacuation.

At lunchtime he was hosting a state visit from the Chief Constable and two carloads of assorted worthies. Portsmouth had been chosen as a prime example of a well-run BCU making serious inroads into the Home Office crime target figures. Before the Chief's party arrived, it might be nice to get the latest body count.

Cathy liked Secretan. He radiated exactly the kind of quiet exasperation she herself had turned into a way of life. There was no point, she decided, giving him anything but the truth.

'Good news first, sir. You remember the Scouse lad we picked up at the station? The one we tied to Nick Hayder with the DNA hit? The accident analysis guys think Hayder must have been dragged along for a bit before being thrown off. Then the lad at the wheel went back and ran him over.'

'Nice.' Secretan was staring out of the window. 'You've charged him?'

'Last night, sir. He's still in hospital under guard. He's got no alibi for the Tuesday night. Says he was out of the city but can't remember where.'

'Motive?'

'Hard to say. My guess is that Nick came across him by chance when he was out running, put two and two together, and challenged him. The rest we know.'

'I thought there were two of them?'

'There probably were. We've been trying to nail down the other one for days now, spot of modest entrapment, but it came to nothing. If you're asking me, I'd say the Scousers have buggered off.'

'Why?'

'Pastures new, sir. Plus the Yardies have arrived. As you know.'

Secretan was looking glum. After months of harassment by a specialist Met unit, Jamaican dealers were spilling out of London and looking for profits elsewhere. Operation Trident might have been a high-profile success, tackling black-on-black gun crime, but in Secretan's view the problem had been displaced rather than cured. Every Chief Supt's waking nightmare featured Yardie gangs, and in Pompey's case the nightmare was in danger of coming true.

Secretan pushed his chair back from the desk and got to his feet. On a clear day, his office window offered a distant glimpse of the line of forts on top of Portsdown Hill. He stood there for a moment, deep in thought, then turned back to Cathy Lamb.

'Crack houses?' he suggested bleakly. 'Machetes? Glocks? Where does all this bloody end?'

Faraday got to Hampshire Terrace in mid afternoon. He found J-J at the PC, sorting through video rushes from Al Jazeera. On screen, some wary-looking US troops, taken prisoner by the Iraqis, were being paraded for the benefit of the world's press. Watching their faces, Faraday realised just how helpless both armies had become in the face of political decisions taken half a world away. These men were barely out of their teens. For all their hi-tech body armour and helmet-mounted gizmos, they understood nothing of the people they'd been dispatched to liberate. Now, as prisoners of war, they were clearly expecting the worst.

Faraday laid his hand on his son's shoulder, making J-J jump.

'We need a world without politicians,' he signed. 'Can you get that in your video?'

J-J thought about the challenge for a moment or two. Then, to Faraday's immense relief, he grinned.

'Eadie's been looking for you,' he signed back. 'I think she's gone home.'

'Home?'

'The flat.'

Faraday spotted Eadie's battered Suzuki parked on the seafront opposite the converted hotel that housed her apartment. He slipped the Mondeo into an adjoining space and sat behind the wheel for a moment or two, wondering quite how to handle what would inevitably follow.

Willard had made it absolutely plain that Faraday himself was implicated by Ambrym's acceptance of Mackenzie's money. Any investigating senior officer – any court – would view the tie-up with profound suspicion. On the other hand, the last few days had shaken Faraday to the core, and in ways that surprised him he realised how much he missed this woman's company. Eadie being Eadie, she was probably unaware of any sense of crisis between them but that, in a way, was the point. Eadie was one of the world's great optimists. She had boundless faith in her own abilities and the guts to see a challenge through. The rest, as she so often pointed out, was conversation.

He found her upstairs, perched on a stool by the phone. The moment Faraday appeared, she blew him a kiss and pointed at the kettle. She wanted – needed – tea. Faraday busied himself with the Earl Grey and managed to find a packet of ginger snaps in the tin she used for biscuits.

The conversation on the phone was becoming heated. No, she had absolutely no intention of making money on this deal. The movie was going into schools at cost price. Given any kind of demand, she could dupe VHS cassettes at fifty pence. Even with postage and packing there couldn't be a school in the country that couldn't afford a couple of quid for a glimpse of the truth. When the voice at the other end started to argue again, she cut him off.

'I don't care a fuck what you think,' she said. 'If it's that important, I'll send you a cheque.' She put the phone down, shaking her head. 'Arsehole.'

'Who was that?'

'Guy called Mackenzie. Turns out he backed my movie. Now he's asking fifty per cent of the profits. *Profits?* How gross is that?'

'What else did he say?'

'He said he wanted to see it. I told him my pleasure. Then he started up with all this nonsense about marketing and copyright and selling the arse off the thing.'

'Was that his phrase or yours?'

'Please, Joe? Does that sound like me?'

'In some moods, yes.'

'Really? Am I that horrible?'

'Tell me more.' Faraday nodded at the phone.

'That's about it.' Eadie helped herself to a biscuit. 'Doug had obviously sold him the video on the phone and he couldn't wait to turn it into a big fat royalty cheque. So I told him to bugger off. You probably heard.'

Faraday nodded. He'd only met Doug Hughes once. Eadie had spotted him in a pub they sometimes used and had insisted on doing the introductions. Hughes had been with a striking-looking blonde, and on the evidence of five minutes conversation Faraday had rather liked him.

'How does Doug know Mackenzie?'

'Haven't a clue. The man must be seriously wealthy. Doug's silly around that kind of money, always has been. He can't help himself. Moth to the flame.'

'Have you any idea what Mackenzie does for a living?'

'None. Apart from ripping off Aussie producers.'

'He's a drug dealer.' Faraday saw no point in keeping secrets any more.

'*Mackenzie?* You're serious?'

'Very. You're really telling me you didn't know?'

'Hadn't a clue. All I saw was the cheque. Without the seven grand, none of this would ever have happened.' She stared at him a moment. 'You want to see the final cut?'

She had a VHS of the video in her day sack. While Faraday poured the tea, she knelt in front of the player and turned on the television. Moments later, Faraday turned to find himself looking at a close-up of a needle probing for a vein. Eadie sat back on the carpet, totally absorbed. When Faraday joined her with the tea, she leant back into him for support.

'The next bit's incredible,' she murmured. 'Just you watch.'

Winter had spent most of the day calculating exactly when he'd phone Mackenzie. Too early, and he might have time to make inquiries of his own. Too late, and he'd miss the boat.

The ferry left at 11.00 p.m. According to Jimmy Suttle, Trudy, her mum, and Mike Valentine were having an early farewell supper at a restaurant they both liked over in Chichester. After that, they'd be running Trude back to Buriton. One last visit to pick up some things from the house in Waterlooville, then they'd be heading down the A3 to the Continental Ferry port.

Around six, Winter had decided, would be perfect. Now, with news of another British squaddie killed in action on the car radio, Winter made the call. Mackenzie answered at once. He must have keyed the number into his directory.

'Mr Winter.' He was laughing. 'That's twice in less than a week.'

'We need to meet.'

'Why?'

'There's something I need to get off my chest. Informal would be better, if you know what I mean. Where are you?'

'In the office.'

'Kent Road?'

'That's right.'

'Stay there. I'll be ten minutes.'

Winter didn't hang on for confirmation. Across the road, he could see the big gated mansion that Mackenzie had turned into his corporate headquarters. Since his last visit, the walls of adjacent properties had attracted yet more graffiti. On Bazza's smoothly plastered battlements, still nothing.

Half expecting Bazza to leave, Winter listened to the news before making his way across the road. Mackenzie answered the door in person. He was wearing nicely cut jeans and a plain white T-shirt. The laughter had gone.

'This better be important,' he said. 'I've cancelled a meeting because of you.'

'Upstairs, then?'

Winter walked past him and began to mount the staircase. At the top, Mackenzie pushed past him. The lights were on in the office at the end of the corridor. Winter didn't wait for an invitation before he sat down.

'You've pissed me off,' he said softly. 'Big time.'

'Yeah? Why's that, then?'

'What happened to Suttle.'

'He was out of order.'

'Wrong. Baz. *You* were out of order. The guy could have got badly hurt.'

'Shame he wasn't. Chris told me he went down like a squinny. What's the problem these days? Can't recruit the right kind of blokes? Listen, if this is all you've come to say then you'd better fuck off now. What happened on Saturday was down to that mate of yours. Or maybe even you.'

'Me? How does that work?'

'Didn't I warn you? Didn't I tell you about my Trude?'

'*Your* Trude?' It was Winter's turn to laugh.

'Yeah, my Trude. Got a problem with that?'

'Not at all.' Winter sat back, then glanced at his watch. 'I see Mike Valentine's off.'

'That's right. Tonight's ferry. Fuengirola, lucky bastard.'

'What's lucky about that? The place is full of low life, the way I hear it. Dealers. Expats. Men with too much money and no taste.'

'Yeah? Money get up your nose, does it? No fucking surprise, the pittance you guys pull. No, Mike'll be nicely set up. Even speaks Spanish. Can you believe that? Pompey boy?'

'Still be in touch, will you?'

'Definitely.'

'Business? Or old times' sake?'

'Both. Mike's a natural. Bloke's got class. You can see it. He treats people right. He charms them. He can make money just by the way he smiles.'

'You're right. And not just money.' Winter produced a carefully folded A4 sheet and tossed it onto Mackenzie's desk. 'Read that.'

'What is it?'

'Have a look and you'll find out.'

Wary now, Mackenzie reached for the document. Winter watched him flatten it on the desk. The top line gave him the clue. Halfway down the page, he looked up.

'Where did you get this?'

'Mist's place.'

'She *gave* it to you?'

'I lifted it.' Winter smiled at him.

'You're talking bollocks. She's been there all week.'

'Not on Saturday she wasn't.'

'You're winding me up.'

'Not at all. The Lanesborough up in town. Lift the phone. Here's the number. Suite fourteen. Booked in the name of Mr and Mrs Valentine.'

'Mike?' He still didn't believe it.

'The very same.'

'Cunt.' His voice was barely audible. He'd gone back to the paternity certificate. Finally he looked up, a strange gleam in his eyes. 'This better be some kind of joke, mush, else . . .' He nodded towards the door, dismissing Winter, then reached for the phone.

Eadie and Faraday had spent the best part of two hours discussing the video. Faraday had watched it twice; he wanted to make sure his first impressions were correct. The original material had been powerful enough – images he'd found genuinely shocking – but Eadie's editing had shaped these pictures in such a way that their cumulative impact was irresistible.

The sheer momentum of the thing was, to Faraday, beyond rational explanation. It had a passion, and a pulse, that seized you by the throat and never once let go. By the end he was, in turns, saddened, angered, and determined to do something positive. Sharing Daniel Kelly's story with the widest possible audience would be a very good start. Bang on doors. Spread the message. Force kids to the video machine. Whatever.

'I don't know how you did that,' he told her. 'It's totally beyond me.'

'You think it's OK? Hits the mark?'

'I think it's horrible. And I think it definitely hits the mark.'

'So all those rules I broke . . . ?'

'Pain in the arse. Definitely.'

'And Mackenzie?'

'You blagged seven grand of his money. Congratulations.'

'Friends again, then?' She got up from the sofa and kissed him on the mouth. Then she paused. 'What's the name of that boss of yours?'

'Willard.'

'No.' She shook her head. 'The uniformed guy.'

'Secretan. He's a Chief Superintendent.'

'First name?'

'Andy.' He gazed at her. 'Why?'

Chapter twenty-four

Faraday was late getting to the Sally Port Hotel. He stepped into the lobby, shedding his coat, already aware of the warm buzz of conversation from the nearby bar. Clerics were everywhere, robed in black. At the end of the corridor, Faraday found a small function room. A youth in a scarlet waistcoat was circulating with a tray of canapés and a waitress Faraday seemed to recognise was edging through the press of bodies, topping up wine glasses. The entire cathedral had emptied, Faraday thought, and decamped across the road.

'How are you?'

Faraday turned to find himself face to face with Nigel Phillimore.

'I'm fine.'

'Better?'

'Yes.' Faraday felt slightly embarrassed. 'Thank you.'

'Good.' Phillimore took his hand and gave it a gentle squeeze. 'Come and meet our guests.'

For the next half-hour, Faraday did his best to disguise his ignorance about plainchant. Politeness urged him to compliment these men on their performance last night, but as soon as he could he shifted the conversation onto safer ground. He wanted to know about Tallinn, about Estonia, about the kind of life you might lead up there beside the Baltic, about the local birdlife. He was keen, as well, to sound them out about Portsmouth – what they made of the city, what they'd tell their friends when they returned home – and as the second glass of Cotes du Rhône settled peaceably on the excellent beef sandwiches, he realised he was enjoying himself.

Their music had been austere, almost chilling, but the Estonians had a warmth and curiosity that created an instant rapport. They liked Portsmouth. One of them even called it Pompey, the way you might refer to a favourite child. The place had spirit, he said, and lots of mischief. Plenty had happened here. You could feel it in the narrow streets and alleys around Old Portsmouth, in the sepia photos on the walls of the cafe down the road. He'd bought a couple of books and one day he'd definitely come back for a proper look. He had some Russian friends in St Petersburg and he knew they'd like it too. All Russians, he said, were pirates at heart and they'd definitely feel at home in Pompey.

The thought amused Faraday, and when another of the Estonians enquired about his job, he saw no point in keeping it a secret.

'Cop?' said one, rolling his eyes.

'Detective?' said another.

Faraday nodded, fending them off when they pressed him for war stories, but their enthusiasm loosened his tongue further still and he was happy to leave his card when the time came for him to leave.

'Give me a ring if you ever come back.' He shook the circle of outstretched hands. 'Be a pleasure to show you around.'

Back in the lobby, he searched for his coat. There was no one behind reception but he caught sight of the waitress with the canapés coming towards him with an empty tray. Her face again. He knew he'd seen it before.

She led him down to the cloakroom, pushing the door open and stepping back to let him retrieve his coat. Room 6, he thought. The afternoon he'd first met Wallace and rung down for room service.

Struggling into his coat, Faraday watched the woman disappearing towards the kitchen. Then, struck by another thought, he called her back.

'Is the manager around by any chance?' he asked.

'Yes. I think he's in his office.'

'Might I have a word?' He smiled at her and dug in his pocket for a card. 'Detective Inspector Faraday. Major Crimes Team.'

Winter found the techie from Special Ops waiting for him on the quayside. He'd phoned him half an hour earlier from Kingston Crescent, straight out of a meeting with Cathy Lamb, and the man had assured him that everything was in place. His name was Gulliver. Thanks to P&O, he'd taken the day crossing to Le Havre and back, plenty of time to install mikes and a tiny video camera wired through to the adjoining cabin. All Winter and his mates had to do was make themselves at home next door and wait for the curtain to go up.

Now, Gulliver hurried Winter towards the gantry that offered foot passengers access to the ferry. The ship towered above them, tall as a block of flats, forbidding in the spill of light from the quayside floods. The last of the inbound lorries were still grinding off the ramp at the bow, but the turnround times were tight and the waiting queue of vehicles in the embarkation park would soon be loading.

Inside the ferry, cleaners were hoovering around the reception desk. Gulliver had already made his number with the ship's purser, a middle-aged woman with nice legs and a busy manner. She shook Winter's outstretched hand, then glanced at her watch. Time was evidently moving on.

'I'm still not clear how many of you we're expecting.'

'Six. Myself and five others.'

'They'll be here soon?'

'Two have already arrived, both plain clothes.' It was Gulliver. 'I put them in the cabin.'

'Really? What about the rest?'

Winter took over. Danny French, the other DC from the squad, would be here any minute. Winter had left him at Kingston Crescent, looking for his passport.

'He doesn't need a passport. Unless you plan to get off.'

'It's a contingency, that's all.' Winter was at his smoothest. 'The other two guys are from Scenes of Crime.'

'And they're the ones who need access to the vehicle decks?'

'Please.' Winter glanced at Gulliver. 'You arranged for a fix on Valentine's motor?'

'I did it this afternoon on the way over. The loading officer's got the details. He'll let us know the lane number and access door as soon as they're through down below.'

The purser looked at her watch again.

'Are these Scenes of Crime people in uniform? Only our passengers might get a little bit—'

'No.' Winter shook his head. 'They're both plain clothes. They belled me half an hour ago. They're in a white van. It's all booked through. In fact they're probably in the car park now.'

'And they'll liaise with you?'

'Yeah.' Winter nodded. 'Once we've sorted Mr Valentine I'll give them a ring and they can come down to the cabin. They'll need Valentine's car keys before they start on his motor.'

The purser nodded. She was looking thoughtful now.

'What does "sorted" mean?' she said at last.

The traffic was light on the motorway out of the city. The rain had gone through hours ago and Faraday could see a fat yellow moon rising in the east. The wind was cold through the open window and there were torn shreds of cloud over the distant shadows of Portchester Castle.

At the top of the harbour, Faraday took the Southampton arm of the motorway, easing into the slow lane for the long ascent through

Portsdown Hill. He couldn't be sure, not absolutely sure, but his instinct told him that it was too good a clue to ignore. His whole career had been built on moments like this, a scrap of a memory tucked away and suddenly retrieved. He knew it needed, at the very least, explanation. He sensed, beyond that, the possibility that it might bring this whole sorry episode to some kind of closure. Closure, he thought, was all too exact a term – the kind of word a psychiatrist might use – and he shuddered to think what the next couple of hours might bring.

Twenty minutes later he took the motorway exit for Southampton's eastern suburbs, finding himself in a tangle of roundabouts and trading estates. He drove around for a while looking for a landmark he recognised, eventually finding a pub called the Battle of Britain. From here, a slight hill led down to the housing estate. The road into the estate was on the right. A couple more turns and he'd be looking for the house with Joyce's Datsun in the drive. From that point on, providing he'd got this thing right, there'd be no turning back.

Joyce came to the door on his second knock. She was wearing a loose pair of tracksuit bottoms and a pink crew-neck top. The kitchen door was open at the end of the little hall and Faraday caught the tang of frying garlic.

'Sheriff . . .' She beamed up at him. 'Hey, nice surprise. Come in. You eaten at all. Only—' She frowned, looking down. 'What the heck's that?'

'It's a warrant card, Joyce.'

'You think I don't know who you are?' She looked up at him. 'What is this?'

'Business, Joyce. We can do this two ways. We can have a chat and you can tell me what you know. Or –' he nodded beyond her '– I can just get on with it.'

'Get on with what?'

'Searching your house.'

'I vote for talking.' She stepped back. 'You want a drink or anything, because sure as hell I do.'

Faraday settled for a cup of tea. Joyce opened a new bottle of Bailey's. By the time the tea was brewed, she was on her second glass.

'I still don't get it.' She reached for the milk jug. 'You're telling me you've got a list there. Little *moi* is top of the list? Is that it?'

'I'm afraid so.'

'But why? How come? What makes you think I'm interested in talking to a scumbag like Mackenzie when we've just spent a year trying to nail him to the fucking wall?'

'No one says you've been talking to Mackenzie. It doesn't have to work like that.'

'It doesn't, huh?' Her hand was shaking. Some of the milk slopped into the saucer. 'So do us a favour, sheriff, just tell me how it *does* work.'

Faraday had never associated Joyce with anger before. Even when the pressures at Highland Road had made everyone else lose it, she had always stayed calm, the still centre at the very heart of the storm. Now, she could barely contain herself.

'Can I tell you something? I thought we were friends.'

'We are friends, Joyce.'

'Yeah, but real friends, friends who look out for each other, friends who care. All this shit . . . Where does it all come from?'

'It's a job, Joyce. It's what I'm paid for. The quicker we resolve it, the sooner –' he shrugged '– everything gets back to normal.'

'And you think that's possible? Take a look at yourself, Joe Faraday. There are better ways of handling this. Ever think about the phone? Little call to clear things up? Old times' sake?'

'It doesn't work that way.'

'Sure. So I see. Go right ahead. Interrogation time. You want me to draw the curtains? You want to spill a little blood here? Have a real party?'

She sat back, nursing her empty glass. Apart from a nest of Beanie Babies, she seemed to occupy most of the sofa.

'Let's start with your husband.'

'What about him?'

'He left you, didn't he? Went off with the probationer?'

'Sure. The lovely Bethany. One sweet babe.'

'And now?'

'He wants to come home again. Just goes to show, doesn't it? Guys like him think only the young know about sex. Shame it's taken him this long to find out what he's missing. Poor child.'

'So no chance of him coming back?'

'Absolutely none.' She smiled at him, held her arms wide open. 'Help yourself, sheriff. Meet a girl who knows a thing or two about hospitality.'

Faraday ducked his head. The next bit, he knew, was going to be tricky.

'Is there anyone else?' he asked at last.

'Like who?'

'I've no idea. That's why I'm asking.'

'You think I can't live without a man? You're right. I can't. Is it easy to find one? The kind of man that suits a girl like me? The kind of man who knows a thing or two? Right again. It isn't.'

'So what do you do?'

'I look, Joe. I get out there and keep my fingers crossed and just sometimes I say a little prayer. Oh God, send me a man. You religious at all, Joe? Only it's true, it sometimes helps.'

'You found a man?'

'I have. And he's lovely. In fact he's the loveliest thing I can imagine.'

'Who is he?'

'No way.' She was shaking her head.

'You're not going to tell me?'

'No.'

For a moment, it occurred to Faraday that she might be fantasising. Conversations like this could go on all night.

'What if I have a look round?'

'That's your decision. It happens that I think you won't, but you might.'

'Why wouldn't I?'

'Because you're a decent man. And because you haven't got a search warrant.'

'I can get one. And you know I wouldn't have to leave. A phone call would do it.'

'Sure. And it would be the middle of tomorrow before the thing turned up. Are you planning that long a stay, Joe? Should we think again about something to eat?'

Faraday knew she was trying to get the better of him, to marshal those memories, all those long-ago debts of gratitude he undoubtedly owed her. She'd been tireless and big-hearted as his stand-in management assistant. After Vanessa had been killed in the car accident, Joyce had filled more holes than one.

Faraday reached in his pocket for his mobile.

'What are you doing, sheriff?'

'Phoning for a warrant.'

'You're a callous bastard. You're stringing me along . . . Oh shit, why not? Go ahead. Help yourself.'

She swung her legs up onto the sofa, then changed her mind and reached for the bottle. When she'd recharged the glass she raised it to her lips, eyeing him over the rim. Faraday hadn't moved.

'No clues, Joe.' She sipped at the Bailey's. 'You're on your own now.'

The Le Havre ferry sailed ten minutes late. By midnight, with the lights of the mainland fast disappearing through the porthole, Winter was beginning to think that he'd got it wrong.

Valentine and Misty Gallagher had come straight down to the cabin with an overnight bag between them. Valentine had then disappeared, returning minutes later with two bottles of champagne and a litre of Bacardi. It was hard to be certain on the tiny black and white monitor screen, but the champagne looked like Krug.

With the other three DCs crouched on the bottom bunks, Winter had watched Misty undress and slide between the sheets while Valentine readied two crystal glasses from the overnight bag and opened a bottle of champagne. He was a tall man, well preserved, with a greying mop of curly hair, and when he slipped his shirt off, it was evident that he worked out. He'd handed the brimming glasses to Misty and climbed in beside her. They'd finished the first bottle by the time the ferry was easing away from the quayside and were making love when *The Pride of Portsmouth* slipped out through the harbour narrows.

The watching DCs monitored this performance with interest. Valentine was clearly in love with oral sex and it was obvious that Misty's inventiveness had survived the years of heavy-duty shagging with Bazza Mackenzie. It was, muttered one of the DCs, a bit like watching early porn: black and white and slightly fuzzy.

Now, forty minutes later, Misty and Valentine appeared to be asleep. The lights in the cabin were still on but their eyes were closed, Misty's head nestled on Valentine's chest.

'What do you think, then?' Danny French was inspecting their own bottle of Scotch. Gulliver had left it on the tiny table under the porthole, a parting gift from Special Ops. It was a nice gesture, they all agreed, and it would be a shame to waste it.

As senior DC, the decision rested with Winter.

'Give it another half-hour.' He was looking at his watch.

'Yeah, but who says Mackenzie's even on board? Weren't they supposed to bell you if he turned up and bought a ticket?'

Winter didn't answer. He'd got the promise of a phone call from one of the P&O clerks in the booking hall at the ferry port but told himself there were a million reasons why she might not have got through. Maybe she'd been snowed under with other punters. Maybe Mackenzie had given her some kind of runaround. Maybe he'd paid cash for a ticket and not given a name. Maybe she'd mislaid Winter's mobile number. Fuck knows.

The minutes dragged past. Misty stirred in her sleep, wrapping herself more tightly around Valentine. Their conversation earlier had told Winter absolutely nothing about either Mackenzie or the contents of the BMW X5 below. They were, on this evidence, a middle-aged couple with a lively sex life en route to some kind of holiday abroad. Only Misty's muttered 'Good fucking riddance' as Gunwharf drifted past the porthole offered a glimpse of something more permanent.

By now, the steady roll of the ferry told Winter they were out in open water. One of the DCs had climbed onto the top bunk and had his eyes closed. The other two, French's idea, were playing cards. Suddenly, unnanounced, came a thunderous knocking at Valentine's cabin door. Winter got to his feet, his eyes glued to the TV screen, and gave the dozing DC a shake.

'Get up,' he hissed. 'It's kicking off.'

French was trying to suppress a laugh. Valentine had swung his legs out of the bunk and was standing in the middle of the cabin looking blearily at the door. Whatever dream he'd just abandoned must have been good because he was sporting a sizeable erection.

'Who is it?' he called.

Misty was up on one elbow now, the sheet clutched to her chin. There came another thump at the door, then a voice. Mackenzie. No attempt at disguise.

'Open this fucking door.'

Valentine exchanged looks with Misty.

'Who is it?'

'Baz.'

'What do you want?'

'You, mate. Open up, else I'll kick the fucker in.'

Valentine was reaching for a towel. The erection was beginning to flag. When he shot a helpless look at Misty, she simply shrugged. Valentine unlocked the door and stepped gracefully back as Mackenzie tumbled in. The manoeuvre reminded Winter of a bullfight he'd once seen in Segovia, the wounded animal charging blindly around, unpredictable, immensely dangerous. Caged in this tiny cabin, thought Winter, Mackenzie could only get worse.

'You're pissed, Baz.' Valentine had shut the door again.

'Think so?'

Mackenzie snatched at the towel, then stood motionless, his eyes moving slowly from Valentine to the bunk. Misty was starting to laugh.

'You should have told us you were coming,' she said lightly. 'We could at least have been decent.'

Faraday had nearly finished downstairs. There'd been nothing in the kitchen, nothing in the way of letters or calendar notes or scribbled reminders. Dialling 1471 had produced a London number, which Faraday wrote down, while the redial button took him through to a recorded message announcing that British Gas would be open again for enquiries at 8.00 a.m. When Faraday accessed the message tape, a woman's voice reminded Joyce that bowling had changed to Wednesdays, half seven, same place.

'I'm better than you might think,' Joyce announced from the sofa. 'Must be that goddam prairie adolescence. Queen of the Grand Islands bowl. Winter of '78.' She was drunk now, toasting him with the empty glass as he turned his attention to the drawers in her sideboard. After a while, she struggled off the sofa and made her way carefully towards the CD player. Not Peggy Lee this time but Sarah Vaughan.

Faraday eyed the stairs. He knew he had no choice, not if he was going to box this thing off, but he was aware of the first stirrings of doubt. There were going to be casualties here, whatever the result, and one of them was a relationship he cherished.

'Up you go, sweetie. I know you can't wait.'

Joyce didn't care any more. She was back on the sofa, her legs folded beneath her, staring into nowhere as the music took her away. Faraday gave her a last backward glance.

'Bedside cabinet,' she said tonelessly. 'Window side. What the fuck.' She wouldn't look at him.

The bedroom was at the front of the house. Mirrored fitted units, floor to ceiling, lined the wall behind the door. The rest of the room was dominated by an enormous bed. The little cabinet beside it was a flat-pack unit, recently repainted, and on top was the stub of a candle, planted in a puddle of wax in a saucer.

In the top drawer, beneath a Boots bag, Faraday found a pile of letters. He sank onto the bed and sorted quickly through the envelopes. Same handwriting. Same postmark. Dates going back to December last year. He returned to the most recent of letters, knowing that he'd found what he'd come for. Here, he thought, was the relationship that had brought *Tumbril* to its knees.

He hesitated a moment, curiously loath to read the letter. He was fond of Joyce. She'd been a true friend, there for him, not simply as a stand-in for Vanessa but more recently, only days ago, when he'd felt himself going under. Friday night, at the restaurant, she'd kept his little boat afloat.

'Do it, sheriff.'

Faraday looked round, feeling the stir of air. Joyce was standing in the open doorway, gazing across at him.

'You mind if . . . ?' He showed her the envelope. He felt cheap, dirtied by the task he'd set himself.

'Not at all.' Joyce shook her head. 'You go right ahead.'

Faraday slipped the letter out. There were three sheets, writing on both sides, black ink.

'Read me the first paragraph.' It was Joyce again. 'It's beautiful.'

'Listen, Joyce, I'm not sure this—'

'You owe me, sheriff. Just do it.'

'OK.' Faraday shrugged, bending to the letter, trying to decipher the hurried scrawl. 'My angel,' it began, 'you've made an old man very, very happy. Not just the sex. Not just last night and the night before that and me too knackered to drive the bloody car afterwards. Not just the perfume and the ten cloves of garlic I had to explain. Not just waking up this morning and wondering where the hell you were. But everything since Christmas, and before that, and now, and God willing, forever. Blokes like me gave up on miracles years ago. Now this.'

'There.' Joyce was smiling. 'I told you.'

Faraday nodded, impressed.

'Beautiful,' he agreed.

'Yep. And not just on paper, either. You want to tell me what law we've broken? Or do you do this kind of stuff for kicks?'

Faraday didn't answer. There was only one question left and they both knew it. At length, Joyce stepped carefully across. The mattress sighed under her weight and they sat motionless, side by side. Faraday could feel the heat of her body, hear the steady rasp of her breathing. Finally, he returned the letter to its envelope, giving her the small, revelatory pleasure of naming this new man in her life.

'It's Harry, sheriff.' She beamed at him, proud now, her face inches from his. 'But you probably guessed that, eh? Being a detective?'

'He's going mad.' It was Danny French, crouched in front of the monitor screen. He had a point.

Mackenzie, his broad back perfectly framed by the hidden video camera, was standing between the bunks in the cabin next door, eyeball to eyeball with Valentine. So far, there'd been no violence. Mackenzie had said his piece, produced his evidence, and simply wanted to know the truth. Had Valentine – one of his best mates, one of his closest business partners, the man he'd trusted for most of his life – really been shagging Misty Gallagher all this time? Or were they all the victim of some fucking evil wind-up? And if the latter was true, what exactly was he supposed to make of some poxy certificate suggesting that Trudy belonged not to him but to Valentine?

To none of these questions did Valentine appear to have any real answer. You're pissed, he kept telling Mackenzie. You're pissed, and you're upset, but there's nothing that a couple of hours decent kip couldn't sort out. Yes, he and Misty were seeing each other. That much was obvious. But what else did he expect a good-looking woman to do if the man in her life went off with some Italian bimbette? To this, Misty added a round of applause. Bazza had just thrown her onto the street. What kind of gratitude was that after everything she'd done for him?

Now, Mackenzie seemed to be losing his bearings. His voice, light as ever, had begun to falter and he kept shaking his head as if something inside had come loose. He needed to find out for sure, he kept saying. Yet the last thing he seemed able to cope with was the truth.

'Did you?' he kept saying to Valentine. 'Were you?'

'What?'

'Shagging? Back then? Before Trudy?' He looked wildly from one to the other, wanting a cast-iron denial, wanting his life preserved in the order he liked it best. This sudden possibility that he'd got it wrong all those years, that he'd been tossed leftovers from the feast that was Misty Gallagher, was visibly hurting him. He needed support, hard evidence, anything that put him back where he belonged. In charge.

Without warning, he reached up to the top bunk and seized Valentine's overnight bag. It was biggish, blue leather, badged with the BMW logo. He turned it upside down and emptied the contents at Valentine's feet. Then he was down on his hands and knees, hunting through the tangle of clothing. Winter recognised the book he'd found earlier at Misty's apartment. *The Rough Guide to Croatia.*

'What's this?' Mackenzie was staring up at Valentine, the book in his hand. 'I thought you were going to fucking Spain?'

Valentine said nothing. Misty was flat on her back, the sheet still anchored to her chin, staring at the underside of the bunk above.

Mackenzie had returned to the contents of the bag, feeling around, looking for more clues, more paperwork, anything to put him out of his misery. Finally, he extracted a long white envelope.

'I'd have stuck one on him while he's still got the chance.' Winter was nodding at the screen. 'Bazza's lost it.'

'Fuck-all evidence, though.' It was French. 'If we're still talking drugs.'

'That'll be the least of it. Believe me.'

Mackenzie had opened the envelope. He was back on his feet now, swaying with the roll of the ship. He unfolded a couple of sheets and took a tiny step backwards until he was directly under the light. His mouth began to move, shaping the contents of the letter. There was a second sheet of paper. He barely spared it a glance.

'Senj?' He was looking at Valentine.

'It's on the coast, Baz. Little holiday home. Brand new. Path down to the beach. Bit of land at the back. Friendly locals. You'll love it.'

'Love it, fuck. You're moving there, aren't you? The pair of you? Look.' He thrust the letter into Valentine's face. 'Five bedrooms, double garage. Trude moving out too, is she? Trude and that fucking

333

twat boyfriend detective of hers? Shit, I'm stupid. Stupid. Stupid.' He bent to the floor again, plucked at a piece of clothing, came up with one of Misty's basques.

'Lucky dip, Baz.' Valentine was still trying to see the funny side.

'Lucky dip, bollocks. Is that all you can say? After everything we've been through? Everything we've done together? Lucky fucking dip?'

The bellow of rage came through the wall into the adjoining cabin. It was Mackenzie. He'd grabbed the bottle of Bacardi. He swung wildly at the stanchion supporting the bunk. The glass smashed, leaving the neck of the bottle in Mackenzie's hand. Valentine had stepped backwards, pressing himself against the porthole.

'No, Baz,' he kept saying. 'Listen.'

Mackenzie was staring at Misty. He looked like a man who'd suddenly found himself in a place he didn't recognise. Nothing made sense. Nothing fitted. Some of the Bacardi had splashed on his jeans. The rest had ended up on the pile of clothes at his feet. He knelt again and abandoned the bottle, his hands moving blindly over the garments. He lifted a T-shirt of Misty's and buried his face in it, breathing in, then balled the garment in his fist and let it drop. He looked up at her one last time, then dug in the pocket of his jeans. Winter caught the flare of the lighter, realised what would happen next.

'He's going to torch the place.' He tore open the door of the cabin. 'Fucking no way.'

Valentine's cabin door was unlocked. Winter was first in. Mackenzie had set fire to the letter he'd found in the overnight bag and was holding it at arm's length. Any second now he was going to drop it onto the spirit-soaked pile of clothing on the floor.

Valentine, by the porthole, seemed mesmerised. Misty was scream-ing. Winter hauled Mackenzie backwards, trying to grab his hand, but Mackenzie dropped the burning letter. There was a soft whoosh and a lick of blue flame as Winter ripped a blanket from the top bunk and began to smother the fire. The other DCs filled the tiny cabin. A smoke alarm began to wail.

'Arrest him,' Winter yelled over his shoulder. 'Get the cuffs on.'

'What charge?'

Winter was still jumping on the blanket, the broken glass crunching beneath his shoes.

'Arson.' He was running out of breath. 'What do you fucking think?'

Faraday was back in the lounge, waiting for Joyce to reappear from the bathroom. At length, she stepped carefully downstairs. Cold water seemed to have brightened her mood.

'You mind if I ask you a question or two?' Faraday said.

'Sure, go ahead. Let's make a night of it.'

'How long has it been going on? You and Harry Wayte?'

Joyce studied him a moment. 'Are we on the record here? Do you want to caution me?'

'No. It's just a question.'

'OK.' She nodded. 'Best part of a year.'

'That's most of *Tumbril*.'

'You're right. Though Harry came first.' She smiled. 'Always.'

She said that she'd met him in the bar at Kingston Crescent. He'd been celebrating a Crown Court result on a contraband conspiracy. They'd had a few drinks and Harry had volunteered to drive her home.

'Here? To Southampton?'

'Sure. He's a gentleman. Thought I deserved a little attention.'

They'd met a couple of times over the succeeding weeks, pubs and cafe-bars off the beaten track, often in Southampton. Pretty soon, Harry was turning up with a bottle or two in the evening. No need to waste money on other people's booze.

'And . . . ?' Faraday was nodding at the stairs.

'Sure. He wanted it. I wanted it. The surprise was we fitted so well. Ever find that, Sheriff? That Eadie of yours?'

The affair had deepened in the autumn. Harry was married but his wife was out most nights, busy with a thousand little pursuits. His kids had gone. The house was empty. And Joyce was happy to make room in her life for two. No formal commitment. No talk of divorce and remarriage and all that shit. Just each other, three or four times a week. Great sex, great conversation, chance to cook for two.

'What did you talk about?'

'Everything. Me, him, my creep of a husband, his pudding of a wife, places we'd been, places we'd like to go.'

'Together?'

'Sure.'

'Like where?'

'Me? I had a thing about Marrakesh. Still do, matter of fact. Harry? He wants to take me to Russia.'

'Moscow?'

'Volgograd. Apparently there was a battle there.'

'And you think you'll make it?'

'Sure. You want something bad enough, it'll happen.'

Faraday nodded. Marta, he thought. And a year of stolen weekends.

'You mentioned conversation. What else do you talk about?'

'Everything. Is that a big deal?'

'It could be.' He paused. 'Does "everything" include the job?'

'Of course. Harry's pissed off, big time, and from what he tells me I don't blame him.'

'*Tumbril?*'

For a moment, Joyce said nothing. This, they both knew, was where friendship parted company with something infinitely less elastic.

'I've mentioned it from time to time,' she said carefully. 'Heck, it's impossible not to.'

'So he knows about the operation?'

'Sure. But I just confirmed a rumour. Nothing comes to Harry as a surprise.'

'He told you he knew already?'

'Sure.'

'And you believed him?'

'Of course. Why not?'

'Because he's a detective, Joyce. And a bloody good one. Detectives lie all the time. You know that. It's part of the MO.'

'So you're telling me I should have kept my mouth shut?'

'I'm telling you it might have been better to stick to Marrakesh. You're in the shit now, Joyce. And so is Harry.'

'You going to talk to him?'

'Somebody will.'

'Officially?'

'Afraid so.'

'You want me to phone him? Stand him by?'

'You'll do that anyway.'

'Too damn right I will.' She smiled at him. 'You mind me asking you a question?'

'Not at all.'

'What brought you here tonight? Why me?'

Faraday studied her for a long moment. Then he explained about the phrase Mackenzie had used in the conversation with Wallace, a phrase that could only have come from the earlier briefing on Whale Island. *Punchy little mush from the backstreets of Copnor.*

'Coincidence, sheriff?'

'Doesn't work. Not in real life. If it looks like a duck, odds are it *is* a duck.'

'But there were four people at that briefing. I can see them now. I'm counting. So why me?'

Faraday paused again. No detective in his right mind would answer a question like this.

'I gave you a lift last week,' he said at last. 'I dropped you off in town. Remember?'

'Sure . . . and I saw that receipt on your dashboard. The Sally Port.

Room six. You know what I said to Harry that night? I said Harry, Joe Faraday's screwing some woman in a hotel in Old Portsmouth. And you know what Harry said? He said good luck to him.'

'Did you give him the room number? The date?'

'Probably. This girl's a stickler for detail. Part of my charm.' She paused. The smile had returned, warmer this time. She put her hand on Faraday's arm. 'Tell me something, sheriff.'

'What's that?'

'Was it true about the woman? Room six?'

Chapter twenty-five

Faraday awoke a minute or two before eight to find Eadie already gone. A note on the pillow said she'd departed on a mission. An invitation to lunch at a Southsea restaurant followed, sealed with a flamboyant kiss.

For once, Faraday resisted the temptation to turn on the bedside radio. The war, as far as he could gather, had turned into a showcase for American technology, inch-perfect uppercuts delivered from hundreds of miles away thanks to the miracles of laser targeting and GPS. Sooner rather than later, American armoured columns would thunder into Baghdad, Bush would declare peace, and then – in all probability – the real war would begin.

The big, bare living room was already bathed in sunshine. In the kitchenette Faraday was hunting for a fresh box of tea bags when he caught the trill of his mobile.

'Faraday?' It was Harry Wayte. 'What the fuck's going on?'

Harry wasted no time on small talk. He'd had a call from Joyce. Last night's little visit had been totally out of order. What kind of copper took advantage of a friendship to go banging around in someone else's private life?

Twice, Faraday tried to interrupt, to explain himself, to put everything into some kind of context, but he knew there was no point.

'You want a meet?' he managed at last.

'Too fucking right, I do. And nowhere near the nick, either.'

'Car park on Farlington Marshes? Half ten?'

'I'll be there.'

Wayte rang off, leaving Faraday gazing at the mobile. He knew with total certainty that Harry Wayte had blown *Tumbril* – not just part of it, but all of it. He walked across to the window and stared out. High tide, he thought numbly, watching the water lapping at the landing stage on Spit Bank Fort. He stood motionless for a moment or two, wondering whether Gisela Mendel was in residence, whether she, too, was up and half-dressed, gazing out at the makings of a tricky day.

Faraday returned to the kitchenette and retrieved his mobile. Willard answered his call on the second ring. He was still at home in Portsmouth but was due to leave for Winchester any minute. Faraday kept it short. He had compelling evidence that the *Tumbril* disaster was down to Harry Wayte. And now Harry wanted a meet.

'Who with?'

'Me.'

'Alone?'

'Yes.'

'When?'

'Half ten.'

'How sure are you? About Harry?'

'Very sure.'

'Stay there. I need to talk to someone.'

Willard was back on the phone within minutes. Faraday was perched on a stool at the breakfast bar, nursing a cup of tea.

'Where are you at the moment?'

'Eadie's place. South Parade.' He gave Willard the address.

There was a brief pause. Then Willard was back on the line.

'Someone'll be round within the hour. Face you might recognise.'

'Like who?'

'Graham Wallace.'

'*Wallace?* Why?'

'I want you to wear a wire to the meet.' Willard wasn't interested in arguments. 'I'm going to sort that bastard Wayte if it's the last thing I do. Wind him up, Joe, Press his buttons. I want evidence. I want the thing wrapped up by lunchtime. You hear what I'm saying?'

It took Eadie Sykes the best part of half an hour to dupe the VHS cassette she needed at Ambrym. With the dub under way, she checked her watch, wondering whether it was too early to risk a call to Kingston Crescent. One way or another, she was determined to prise J-J free from the threat of further police action. Given the prospects for the video, it was the least she owed him.

Secretan's name took Eadie through to a woman who appeared to be in charge of the Chief Supt's diary. She had a light Ulster accent and wanted to know how pressing a need she had to talk to her boss.

'Very pressing,' Eadie told her. 'If he's there, just mention a name.'

'Yours?'

'Daniel Kelly. I've made a video about him and I think Mr Secretan should take a look.'

The assistant put Eadie on hold. Then it was suddenly Secretan himself on the line.

'Eadie Sykes?'

'That's me. I was just wondering—'

'Where are you?'

'Down the road.'

'I can spare you a couple of minutes. Now would be good.'

It was less than a mile to the police station at Kingston Crescent. Eadie left the Suzuki in a supermarket car park across the road and found a uniformed WPC waiting for her at the front desk. Secretan's office was on the first floor. The woman with the Ulster accent offered her a cup of tea or coffee.

'Coffee, please. Black.'

Secretan appeared from his office and stood aside as Eadie stepped in. He gestured at the chair in front of his desk and opened the window.

'Beautiful day. Far too nice to be banged up in here.' He turned back into the room. 'What can I do for you?'

Eadie told him about the video. At the mention of J-J and his contribution to the camerawork and the research, he nodded.

'You're talking about Joe Faraday's boy?'

'Yes.' She hesitated. 'Joe and I are good friends.'

'Is that something I should be aware of? Is it –' he smiled at her '– germane?'

'I've no idea. I just thought I'd get it out of the way.' She plunged a hand into her day sack and produced the video cassette. 'This is the final cut, minus the funeral.'

'What do you do? Leave a space?'

'Yes.'

'Bit like real life, then.'

'Exactly.' Eadie was beginning to warm to this man. He was down to earth, real, and he had an easy sense of humour. 'Do you want to see it?'

'Now?'

'Why not?'

Secretan glanced at his watch, then left the office. Eadie strained to catch the brief conversation next door, then Secretan was back again.

'We've got forty minutes, tops,' he said. 'The machine's down in the corner. Best if you do the honours.'

Eadie loaded the cassette and resumed her seat. She must have seen the video dozens of times by now but in new company it always felt a subtly different experience. Secretan sat in silence through the viewing.

Twice he reached for a pen and scribbled himself a note. At the end, he nodded.

'Powerful,' he murmured. 'You've got permissions for all this stuff?'

'Every last frame.'

'And what happens now?'

Eadie explained about distribution. It would be going into schools, youth groups, colleges, anywhere an audience could spare twenty-five minutes of their busy, busy lives.

'They'd be crazy not to.'

'That's my feeling.' Eadie knelt to the player and retrieved the cassette. 'You haven't asked me about the funding yet.'

'Should I?'

'Well, yes. The way it works, I had to raise half the budget under my own steam. That meant hundreds of letters, phone calls, tantrums, you name it. In the end, I got £5000 from the Police Authority, £7000 from a businessman donated through a cut-out, and about £2000 from other sources.'

'Cut-out?'

'My ex-husband. He's an accountant. Mr Bountiful wanted to stay out of it.' She smiled and slipped the video cassette into its plastic box. 'With my £14,000, I fronted up to the local partnership. They match-fund. It's government money, as I'm sure you know.'

Secretan nodded. Eadie could see he hadn't a clue where any of this might lead.

'So?'

'So I end up with £28,000, which is fine, and I put together what you've just seen. You think it works?'

'I think it's extremely effective. In fact I'd go further. I think it's bloody excellent.'

'Good. Unfortunately, there's a problem.'

'How come?'

'The guy with the seven grand turns out to be called Bazza Mackenzie.'

Secretan allowed himself a small, private smile. There was indeed a problem.

'This film is co-sponsored by Mackenzie?'

'That's right. And in the poshest company.' She smiled. 'As you can see.'

'Why Mackenzie? What was in it for him?'

'Lots, the way he figured it. That's why I told him no deal.'

'When was this?'

'Yesterday. He was after a share of the profits. I pointed out there won't be any profits.'

'Do you know what Mackenzie does –' Secretan frowned '– for a living?'

'Now I do, yes.'

'And do you know he's just been arrested for arson? On a cross-Channel ferry?'

Eadie thought about this development for a moment or two. In essence, it changed nothing.

'The fact remains he paid for the thing. Or helped to.'

'Indeed.' Secretan nodded. He pushed back his chair and went across to the window again. 'We're talking about J-J, aren't we?'

'Yes. He's on police bail. Pending further inquiries.'

Secretan said nothing. Eadie watched him at the window, deep in thought. At length, he turned back to her.

'Great film,' he extended a hand, 'and outstanding camerawork.'

Eadie got to her feet and shook his hand. Secretan started to laugh.

'I meant the video.' His hand was still out. 'There are one or two other people who ought to take a look.'

The entrance to the RSPB bird sanctuary on Farlington Marshes lies at the end of a gravel track that runs beside the main east–west motorway at the top of the city. Most birds are driven south by the incessant thunder of traffic, feasting on the rich mudflats that ring the tongue of salt marsh extending deep into Langstone Harbour. A scrap of land off the slip road from the motorway offers parking for visitors to the sanctuary. Faraday was there with five minutes to spare.

At length, eager for something to take his mind off the imminent encounter, he got out of the Mondeo and looked around. The gravel was littered with broken glass from yet another vehicle break-in and he kicked the worst of it away before slipping his Leica binoculars from their case and propping his elbows on the car roof.

On the second sweep, he caught sight of a pair of lapwings, windmilling above the salt marsh. He'd glimpsed them earlier from the road, driving down beside the harbour, and there they were, in perfect close-up. Absorbed by the small drama of their flight, he failed to hear Harry Wayte's arrival. Only when the DI got out of his car and crunched towards him across the gravel did Faraday turn round.

'Walk?' Wayte set off down the track towards the picket gate at the end without a backward glance.

All too conscious of the tiny Nagra snugly taped to the small of his back, Faraday followed. For the second time in twelve hours, he felt wretched. Even now, in ruins, *Tumbril* had the power to overwhelm him.

It was a beautiful morning, a cloudless blue sky with a feather of breeze but scarcely a ripple on the water. Away to the south, barely visible on the horizon, the white smudge of the Bargemaster's House.

Wayte pushed through the gate at the end of the track. From here, a path on top of the sea wall circled the edge of the reserve. The two men had yet to break the silence.

'Why go bothering her, Joe?' Wayte said at last. If anything, he sounded reproachful.

'Because we just lost a year's worth of work and God knows how much money. But then you'd know that, Harry.'

'I would?'

'Of course you would.'

'Why's that?'

Faraday brought Harry Wayte to a halt. Awkwardness had given way to anger. This man had just destroyed a year's work. No point, he thought, in ducking the obvious.

'You're not denying that you and Joyce . . . ?'

'Have been shagging? Christ no, Joe. Far from it.'

'And I gather you discussed *Tumbril*.'

'Is that what she told you?'

'Yes.' Faraday gazed at him, waiting for some kind of comment. Wayte didn't say a word. 'You're telling me you knew nothing about *Tumbril*?'

'Nothing that every other bugger in the force didn't know. You blokes have been chasing your tails. If you're trying to set me up for the fall – or Joyce – then you'd better think again.'

'So you never discussed the operation?'

'Pillow talk? *Tumbril*? Forget it.'

'OK.' Faraday had never expected this to be easy. 'Then let's pretend you've had a lapse of memory. Let's imagine you've got what Nick Hayder's got – a bloody great hole instead of perfect recall. Let's even pretend that I was right, that you *did* discuss *Tumbril*, that in fact you knew everything. Are you with me?' The question drew a wary nod from Wayte. 'OK, so you've had dealings with Mackenzie before. I checked the records this morning. You've been passed over for DCI. You're pissed off with the job and you can't wait to leave. You also, as we all know, think *Tumbril*'s a complete waste of space. Why? Because the way you see it, Mackenzie helps keep the peace. You may have a point, Harry. You may even be right. But that's not it, is it? Because the last thing you do in this job is go telling tales to the enemy.'

'Enemy?' Wayte threw his head back and began to laugh. 'Are we talking the same bloke here? The hooligan I nicked for affray twenty years back?'

'Yes.' Faraday nodded. 'Nine million quid's worth of hooligan if you want the exact figure.'

'And you really think I've been mouthing off to him? Marking his card?'

'Yes.'

'Can you prove it?'

The question had been a long time coming. Faraday took Wayte by the arm but Wayte shook him off. The two men began to walk again.

'Professional Standards are mounting a major investigation,' Faraday said. 'That'll take months, Harry. They'll turn everyone over – me, you, Joyce, all of us.'

'And Willard, too. He was SIO, wasn't he?'

'Yes.'

'So how come you think they can tie any of this to me?'

'Because you'll have been careless, Harry, as well as greedy. There'll be a trace. There always is. And somewhere down the line, sooner or later, they'll find it.'

'So what are you saying?'

'I'm asking you to have a think, Harry. For the record, I've got you down as a bloody good cop. I don't agree with everything you've said lately but you wouldn't expect me to.'

Wayte nodded, then gazed out over the harbour. Tempers had cooled. To Faraday's surprise, this was turning into a negotiation.

'You know I'm retiring in September?' Wayte asked at last. 'Joyce tell you that?'

'She didn't but you did, Harry. Couple of days ago? Up in the bar at Kingston Crescent?'

'Did I? Shit . . .' He pulled a face, not the least embarrassed. 'And did I tell you I can't bloody wait?'

'That, too.'

'Bugger me . . . I must be getting old.'

'Happens, Harry.'

Faraday brought them both to a halt again. Metres from the sea wall, a pair of dunlin were loitering with intent amongst the seaweed on the foreshore. Faraday watched them for a moment, then he reached under his anorak and turned off the recorder.

Wayte had followed his every movement. The rueful smile had disappeared.

'Bastard,' he said softly.

'I've turned it off, Harry, not on. You want to check?'

'Bastard,' he repeated.

Faraday studied him a moment, then shrugged. He was doing this man a big favour. Whether he chose to see it that way was his problem.

'I went down to the Sally Port the other night and had a little chat to the manager. He remembers you coming in on Saturday, Harry. You wanted to know about the occupant of room six on Wednesday last. You made it official and so he told you. Guy called Graham Wallace, he said. Gave you his home address, car registration, credit card details, the lot. That was a bit over the top, Harry. All Mackenzie really needed was the name plus the fact that I'd called in to see him.' Faraday took a last look at the dunlin, then patted Wayte on the arm. 'You've got my mobile number, Harry. Give me a ring.'

Faraday was back in his office at Kingston Crescent, waiting for a chance to see Willard, when his mobile began to ring. He checked the number. Harry Wayte.

'Harry?'

'Me. Listen, you alone?'

'Yes.'

'I've had a bit of a think about this morning. Fact is, mate, I'm up to here with it.'

'With what?'

'The poxy job. I'm binning it. Early retirement. I'll be doing the paperwork this afternoon.'

'Harry –' Faraday had pushed his chair back from the desk '– are you sure you've thought this through?'

'Yeah . . . But listen, Joe, the way I see it is this.' He began to talk about his current caseload, how few of the jobs were going anywhere, and as he did so Faraday was doing the sums. He and Wayte, both DIs, were on the same pay grade. By handing in his ticket six months early, Faraday estimated Wayte would be kissing goodbye to £20,000 worth of commutation. When Wayte paused for breath, Faraday went through the sums with him. In fairness, it was the least he could do.

Wayte listened, then cut Faraday short.

'Joe, I'm not deaf. I heard what you said this morning. Twenty grand? What makes you think I can't make that up elsewhere?'

Faraday stared at his mobile.

'What did you just say?'

'You heard me. We never had this conversation but twenty grand's fuck all in some circles, as you well know.' He began to laugh. Then the phone went dead.

Willard's office was across the corridor.

'Joe.' The Det-Supt barely looked up from his PC. 'You talked to Wayte?'

'Yes, sir.'

'Good. I'll be with you in a minute.'

Faraday settled himself at the conference table. Willard finally joined him. For a big man, Faraday thought, he looked strangely diminished, even forlorn.

'So how did it go?'

'Nothing actionable. He'll fight the inquiry all the way.'

'*Nothing?*' Willard was frowning. 'I thought you told me he'd blown *Tumbril?*'

'He has. That's exactly what he's done.'

'To Mackenzie?'

'I assume so.'

'*Assume* so? What kind of dog wank is that?'

Willard rarely stooped to canteen language. He was plainly under immense pressure.

Faraday leaned forward, taking the chance to explain exactly what had happened over the last twenty-four hours. How he'd isolated that single phrase about Mackenzie on the tape from the Solent Palace. How the phrase had to have come from a *Tumbril* meeting. How he'd shrunk the suspect list to just four names. And what had emerged from last night's visit to Joyce's place.

'So she's been shagging Harry Wayte?'

'Yes.'

'Fucking hell. And giving him all our secrets?'

'They talk. Shagging isn't a crime. Neither is conversation.'

'It bloody well is when it goes straight to Mackenzie.'

'That's not Joyce's fault.'

'Of course it is, Joe. She signed an undertaking about *Tumbril*. By talking to Harry, she broke it. She's either stupid or guilty. You're telling me she trusts this man?'

'She's in love with him. It's often the same thing . . . As we all know.'

'What the fuck does that mean?'

'Nothing, sir. But you know it and I know it. Get really serious about someone and the rest of it goes out of the window.'

'The rest of it being *Tumbril?*'

'Yes.'

'What about Wayte? What's his line?'

'He wants early retirement. Insists, in fact.'

'He's copping out?'

'Yes. It's the white flag. He's jacking it in.'

Willard brooded about this news for a moment. Then he looked up at Faraday again.

'So what does he have to say about Mackenzie?'

'Nothing. He denies everything. He's insisting he's never said a word to Mackenzie and it's up to PSD to prove otherwise. He'll take them to the wire.'

'And there's absolutely no hard evidence that ties him to Mackenzie?'

'None. Joyce admits she discussed *Tumbril* with him.'

'About what? Specifically?'

'About a booking at the Sally Port. Room six. Graham Wallace.'

'Last week, you mean?'

'Yes.'

'How the fuck did she know about that?'

'I . . .' Faraday felt about twelve '. . . left a room service receipt in the car from the afternoon I was with Wallace. Joyce happened to see it. Thought I was over the side. Passed it on as gossip. Like you do.'

'Great. Wonderful. The receipt had Wallace's name on it?'

'No, sir, just the room number.'

'So how did Joyce tie the receipt to Wallace?'

'Wayte fronted up at the hotel. Sat the manager down and did the business.'

'As a copper?'

'As a DI. Warrant card, the lot.'

'You *know* that?'

'I talked to the manager last night.'

'Got a statement off him?'

'No . . . but it's there for the taking.'

'Thank Christ for that. Anything else?'

'No, sir.'

'The tape from this morning?'

'Useless. Packed up halfway through. Technical fault.'

Willard nodded. Back at his desk, he put a call through to the Chief Supt. heading the Professional Standards Department. Briefly, he passed on the news about the manager at the Sally Port. PSD should get someone down there sharpish. Harry Wayte, in his view, was on a nicking. And so was Joyce. The conversation over, he turned to Faraday again.

'That Harry Wayte,' he said softly, 'is a dead man.'

The restaurant Eadie had chosen for lunch was in the heart of Southsea. Sur-la-Mer offered decent French cuisine at sensible prices with a respectable wine list to go with it. Eadie chose a '95 Rioja, a tacit signal to Faraday that all was well with their world. To Faraday, depressed by the last couple of hours, it was the sweetest possible news.

Since she'd got back from Kingston Crescent, she'd received word from the people at the Portsmouth Pathways Partnership. They'd

347

watched their copy of the VHS, and although they'd never expected anything quite as hard-hitting, a first viewing indicated that it might make a bit of an impact.

'Impact?' Faraday laughed, light-headed now. 'Christ.'

'I talked to one of the girls there. Off the record, she told me they might be up for paying for proper distribution.'

'I thought that was all taken care of?'

'No.' Eadie snapped a bread stick in two. 'I've only budgeted for Hampshire. This would take it nationwide.'

'Brilliant.' Faraday raised a glass. 'Congratulations. You've bloody earned it.'

'You really think so?'

'Yes. I've had my doubts but . . .' They touched glasses. 'Turns out I was wrong.'

'How does that work?' Eadie couldn't believe her ears.

'Well . . .' Faraday was frowning now. 'If you think there's a problem, a real problem, then you have to confront it. In our job we try and do just that but it's getting harder all the time.'

'Yeah?'

'Yes.' He nodded. 'I can give a list as long as your arm. Changes in the law, everyone moving the goalposts, crap morale, whatever. As a cop you start off wanting to make a difference but in the end it grinds you down. In your game, it isn't like that at all. You answer to no one. You sense a problem out there, you go and tape it. Going gets rough, you ride it out. And in the end, because you won't take no for an answer, you get a result. Nice.' He raised his glass. 'I applaud you.'

'Shit.'

'What's the matter?'

'Nothing.' Eadie turned her head away. For once in her life, she was close to tears.

The waiter arrived. Faraday chose lamb shank. Eadie, trying to focus on the menu, finally ordered a cheese omelette. Faraday helped himself to more wine. Time to change the subject.

'Why were you after Secretan's name last night?'

'I've been down the nick.' Eadie was blowing her nose. 'I wanted to talk to him, show him what we've done.'

'You need to book weeks ahead. April, if you're lucky.'

'Not at all. He saw me then and there. I even got to show him the movie.'

'And?' Faraday was astonished.

'He loved it, or said he did.' She'd regained her composure by now. 'He knows about J-J, by the way.'

'Of course he does.'

'I didn't mean that, not just the problems. I told him about J-J's contribution to the film. He was impressed.'

Faraday began to get her drift. Remarkable, he thought. Not an angle left uncovered.

'And what did he say about the boy?'

'Nothing. Except I got the impression he ... you know ... understood.'

'Understood what?'

'That J-J made a bit of a difference.' She gestured him closer, then leaned over the table and kissed him on the lips. 'Mitigation? Isn't that the word?'

The food arrived with a huge plate of vegetables and they began to talk about the possibility of some kind of break. Next month, with the pressures of *Tumbril* over, Faraday might be able to take a bit of time off. Maybe they could ship over to Bilbao and drive down to Extremadura. This time of year, said Faraday, the spring flowers on the *dehesas* could be sensational. He could show her eagle owls and griffon vultures, and in Trujillo there was a little bodega that served the best smoked ham in the world.

'Sounds brilliant. Only one problem.'

'What's that?'

'Daniel's inquest. It's likely to be the end of April. I'm supposed to be there as a witness.'

'Of course. And so you must.'

'But later? Say May?'

'Whatever. Just the thought's enough for now.'

'You mean that?' Her eyes were swimming again.

'Yep –' he reached for the bottle '– sad man that I am.'

By late afternoon, Winter was beginning to suspect the worst. An area car had met Mackenzie off the inbound P&O ferry and driven him the mile and a half to Central police station. Another had taken Valentine and Misty Gallagher to Waterlooville nick while Scenes of Crime and a team of vehicle engineers did the business on the BMW X5.

At Central, to Winter's alarm, Mackenzie had demanded Hartley Crewdson as his solicitor. Crewdson, arriving within the half-hour, had listened to his client's account of events on the ferry and then asked Winter for a look at the key sections of last night's videotape. Under PACE regulations this was his right, but Winter – anticipating the request – had done his best to bury the cassette.

Crewdson, who could read Winter like a book, pointed out that arson was an extremely serious offence. Already, he knew that neither Valentine nor Misty Gallagher was prepared to make a statement against Mackenzie. Asked to explain the incident, they'd agreed it was a joke, a private thing between the three of them that had got out of hand. So just how much weight should Crewdson attach to Winter's version of events?

The Custody Sergeant agreed that the video ought to supply the answer. A couple of minutes in an empty office was enough to get the tape from Winter. A quarter of an hour later, Crewdson emerged from a private viewing with a smile on his face. The key sequence, he told Winter, proved absolutely nothing. Back view, Mackenzie's and Winter's bodies blocked the action. His client was insisting that Winter himself had forced him to drop the burning letter and there wasn't a shred of evidence to suggest otherwise. A clumsy, unwarranted CID intervention had nearly set the ship on fire.

Now, an hour and a half into the interview that was supposed to put Pompey's top criminal behind bars, Winter was on the back foot. Ninety minutes ago, Mackenzie had confirmed his name, date of birth, and address. After that, with a studied lack of interest, he'd met every question with a muttered 'No comment'.

DC Danny French, for the second time in three days, was sharing the interview with Winter. He, too, had plainly abandoned all hope of getting any kind of result. Just how do you penetrate an absolute refusal to start a conversation?

Desperate, Winter decided to go for broke. Shooting a look at Danny French, he eased himself forward across the table, his face inches from Mackenzie's. Winter seldom raised his voice in interview, knowing that matiness unlocked many more doors than aggression, but now his voice had sunk to a whisper.

'Bazza, I have to be honest with you, it's the video that bothers me. We've talked about the business with the bottle and that letter you set fire to. Fair play, the tape doesn't prove it either way. You've told your brief I made you drop it. I happen to know I didn't. But that's between you and me. No, Baz, it's the earlier stuff on the tape. Maybe we ought to talk about that.'

Crewdson glanced across at Mackenzie. Even Danny French seemed puzzled.

'Yeah?' It was the first time Mackenzie had volunteered an answer. 'What of it?'

'Well . . .' Winter was taking his time now. 'Let me see. It must have been pretty early on. We'd only just got going. In fact we were still in the bloody harbour.'

'And?'

'They were at it, mate, like rabbits, the pair of them. Not easy in a squitty little bunk, but lots of action. That Misty . . .' He shook his head. 'We can show you if you like, Baz. Be a pleasure.'

Crewdson raised a weary hand.

'DC Winter.' He sounded, if anything, disappointed. 'This is an outrage and you know it.'

'Outrage?'

'My client has been arrested for arson. I fail to see the significance of this line of questioning. And, aside from the law, I find it deeply distasteful.'

'You do?'

'Indeed. As, I suspect, does my client.'

Winter was looking puzzled. 'We're not interested in motive here?'

'Motive for what?'

'Arson.'

'My client denies the charge. Whatever happened earlier on your videotape has absolutely no bearing on the matter in hand.'

'How about we watch the whole tape, then? Take Mr Mackenzie through it? See what happened before? Put this whole incident in context?' He looked round. 'No?'

There was a long silence. Even Danny French was studying his hands. Finally Mackenzie sat back in his chair. For the first time since the interview began, he was smiling.

'You know something?' He was looking at Winter. 'You've fucking lost it.'

The interview came to an end twenty minutes later. After a brief conference with Winter and French, the Custody Sergeant summoned Crewdson and told him that for the time being Mr Mackenzie would not be facing charges. He was granting him police bail while further inquiries were made, but for now he was free to leave.

As Crewdson and Mackenzie headed for the door, the Custody Sergeant beckoned Winter to the desk.

'Message from Scenes of Crime.' He put on his glasses and peered at the scribbled note. 'They've stripped the BMW but found nothing.' He glanced up. 'I understand the parties involved have been released.'

Winter and French emerged from Central minutes later. It was getting dark by now and it took a moment or two for Winter to recognise the figure standing by the roundabout. Mackenzie.

'Waiting for a lift,' French grunted. 'Must be.'

Winter said nothing. He walked French to his Subaru, glancing over his shoulder to check on Mackenzie again. By the time they were both in the car, he was still at the kerbside, still waiting.

For a full minute Winter sat motionless behind the wheel. French wanted to get back to Kingston Crescent.

'Well? Are we here all fucking night or what?'

'Wait.'

'Why?'

'Because I say so, OK?' Winter shot him a look, then returned his attention to Mackenzie. French began to argue again but then gave up and reached for the door handle. Better a cab than this farce.

'Look.' Winter stopped him.

A sleek Mercedes convertible had pulled up beside Mackenzie. The bulky figure behind the wheel leaned over and opened the passenger door.

'It's Talbot.' Winter started the engine and began to pull out of the car park.

'What now?' French was looking alarmed.

'We follow them.'

'You're joking. You and another fucking pursuit? Nearly killed Dawn Ellis last year, didn't you?'

'Who said anything about a pursuit?' Winter was enjoying himself at last, back in a plot he understood. 'Twenty quid says they're going up to Waterlooville.'

'*Waterlooville?* Why would they do that?'

'Valentine. Unfinished business. Bazza has some sorting out to do.'

'And we're going to be there? To watch it all? Terrific.'

French sat back, eyes closed, resigned now to whatever might happen next.

The Mercedes headed out of the city. On the dual carriageway that fed rush-hour traffic onto the motorway, Talbot suddenly signalled left, ducking onto the slip road that led down to the ferry port and the northern suburbs.

'He's clocked you,' French said drily as they slowed for the roundabout. 'I'll get out here. Bloody walk to the office.'

Spotting a gap in the oncoming swirl of cars, Winter accelerated hard. Moments later, they were back behind the Mercedes.

'Subtle,' French muttered. 'You must have done this before.'

Half a mile later the Mercedes indicated left again, turning into a cul-de-sac that led to a scruffy industrial estate. Soon they were bumping over a potholed track, the back of the city's greyhound stadium on one side, a builder's yard on the other. Ahead, the last of the daylight silhouetted a line of ancient military vehicles, awaiting the wrecker's blowtorch.

'The scrapyard.' Winter was talking to himself. 'Maybe they've lifted

Valentine already. Got him trussed up and waiting. Baz has done this before.' He glanced across at French. 'You with me?'

French was fumbling for a cigarette. He wanted no part of this.

The Mercedes had disappeared into the scrapyard. Winter pulled into the shadow of the stadium and killed the engine. In the sudden silence came the sigh of the wind off the nearby harbour.

'What now?' It was French. He couldn't find his lighter.

'We get out. Take a look.'

'Back-up?'

'Don't need it. You up for this or not?' Winter didn't bother to wait for an answer.

With some reluctance, French joined him in the chilly twilight. They made their way into the scrapyard, keeping to the fence on the left. Beyond a line of army surplus tanks, Winter could make out the whale-like shape of an abandoned submarine beside the scrapyard jetty – rusty, half submerged, a relic from some long-forgotten war.

'Is there another exit?' French was looking for the Mercedes.

Without warning, a pair of headlights pinned them against the fence. The Mercedes was parked twenty metres away, behind the nearest of the tanks. Clever. An engine purred into life. The car began to roll towards them.

'Now what?' French had stopped.

'Fuck knows.' Winter kept walking.

The Mercedes pulled into a tight turn, rolling to a stop beside Winter. The passenger window slid down, Mackenzie's face shadowed against the glow of the dashboard. Winter looked down at him, then stepped backwards as Mackenzie opened the door. For a moment, neither man said a word. Then Mackenzie beckoned him closer.

'You kill me, you guys,' he said. 'You think I'm really stupid, don't you? Really thick?'

Winter could smell the gum on his breath. Spearmint.

'He's probably at home, Baz. Tucked up again. Celebrating.'

'You took his motor apart?'

'Of course.'

'And?'

'Clean as a whistle.'

'What a fucking surprise. Don't you cunts ever learn?'

There was a long silence, then a brief flare in the darkness beside the fence. Danny French had evidently found his lighter.

Mackenzie hadn't finished. He had something to get off his chest, something important, and now was the time.

'You know what it boils down to in the end?' he said. 'Business. That's all it is. Just business. You're telling me Valentine's spent the last twenty years knobbing Mist, I believe you. You think any of that makes any difference, you're out of your fucking mind. And you know why? Because I didn't get this far to blow it all over a dog like Mist. Valentine's history, mush. I'll pension him off. He gets Mist for free. Big fucking deal.' He paused. 'You got all that? Only it might be time for your twat friends in *Tumbril* to wise up. This game's bigger than you think. In fact it's bigger than anyone thinks.' He offered Winter a sudden grin. 'Give me a bell sometime if you're desperate. See if we can't work something out . . . eh?'

Epilogue

The inquest on the death of Daniel Kelly took place at the end of April. With three weeks advance warning and *Tumbril* quietly laid to rest, Eadie and Faraday took a brief holiday in northern Spain, returning a couple of days before the inquest convened.

Martin Eckersley, the coroner, met Eadie in the magistrates court. 'You look amazing,' he said. 'Years younger.'

'Thanks, Martin.'

'I mean it.' He produced a video cassette from his briefcase. 'I looked at this a couple of nights ago. I understand it now.'

'What?'

'All the fuss in the press. Didn't spare the details, did you?'

'Never. You're still going to use some of the rushes in there?' Eadie nodded down the hall towards the Coroner's Court.

'Definitely. I'm using the sequence you sent with the finished video. The lad injecting then stumbling off to bed.'

'You're sure that's enough?'

'That's all that's germane. We're here to establish the facts, Eadie.' He patted her on the arm. 'The clever stuff is down to you.'

Eadie went off in search of coffee to kill the time before the inquest was due to begin. She'd given the *News* a copy of the video, and to her delight they'd turned the resulting controversy into a two-page feature. The health educationalists were outraged, as were many of the specialist agencies in the drugs field. Pictures as unsparing as these, they warned, might easily do watching kids real harm. Many teachers and parents, on the other hand, couldn't wait to sit their charges down in front of a TV. Here, for once, was the unvarnished truth.

Of Bazza Mackenzie, mercifully, there was no mention in the *News* feature. Eadie had kept Mackenzie's financial contribution towards the project to herself, and she and Faraday had celebrated when J-J's CID file was closed after the CPS ruled the interview at Central inadmissible. Free from police bail, J-J had decided to accept Eadie's invitation to join Ambrym full time and develop a small library of, as she put it, in-your-face social documentaries. J-J's editing work on the anti-war video had shown every sign of opening a number of doors in London post-production houses, but in the end he'd decided to stay in Portsmouth.

And Bazza himself? Eadie filled a plastic cup with coffee from the machine and made her way back towards the Coroner's Court. According to Faraday, Mackenzie was expanding his interests abroad, chiefly in Dubai and the Costa del Sol. A planning application had been lodged for a new extension to the family home in Craneswater and there was talk in certain quarters of the city that Bazza had designs on one of the sea forts off Southsea Beach. The latter rumour, said Faraday, had proved to be baseless, but Mackenzie's new management team at the Solent Palace were giving the hotel an ambitious makeover. To mark the official reopening, they'd put in an extremely competitive bid to host the CID midsummer ball.

The inquest started at eleven o'clock with a series of witnesses summoned to plot the course of Daniel Kelly's final hours. Eadie herself described the taped interview and Daniel's growing distress as the minutes ticked away without any sign of the expected delivery. When it came to the moment when he retreated to the kitchen to at last prepare his fix, she kept the details to a minimum, knowing that Eckersley planned to show the video sequence later.

Next into the witness box was Daniel's sometime girlfriend and ex-flatmate, Sarah, who'd discovered his body. Then came the attending paramedic, followed by a uniformed PC and the duty CID officer, Dawn Ellis. The pathologist read from her report on the outcome of the post-mortem, noting the presence of quantities of unusually pure heroin in the contents of Daniel's stomach. Death, she said, had been caused by asphyxia following the ingestation of vomit.

Eckersley, as Coroner, brought the proceedings to an end with a carefully delivered summing-up. The bulk of his comments, offered in sympathy rather than judgement, were directed to Daniel Kelly's father, who'd sat motionless throughout the proceedings, hunched in a nicely cut cashmere overcoat. Daniel's death, said Eckersley, was a tragedy in itself and a warning to us all. Drugs and desperation had killed him. It was, in an exact sense, the total waste of a life. Daniel had misjudged the strength of that final wrap and Eckersley had no hesitation in returning a verdict of Accidental Death.

In conclusion, with a brief word of gratitude to Eadie, Eckersley announced his intention of showing the final few minutes of Daniel Kelly's conscious life, part of a new video destined for the nation's classrooms. Here, he said, was a tiny flicker of hope at the end of a sad, sad story.

The lights in the court were dimmed. The pictures began to roll. A quivering needle searched for a vein. In the gloom Eadie could see Daniel's father, stony-faced, staring at the screen. The plunger eased the muddy brown liquid into Daniel's arm. Moments later, he was loosening the tourniquet, slack-jawed, moist-lipped, happy, feeling his way out of the kitchen, across the lounge, wanting nothing but oblivion.

As the camera lingered at his son's bedroom door, Eadie was still watching Daniel's father. Daniel had collapsed on the bed, plucking feebly at the duvet. The shot slowly tightened on the face on the pillow. There was a flicker of movement, a tiny nerve beneath an eye. Then the big face rolled to the left, directly towards the watching camera. Daniel was smiling. Eadie saw his father's head tip back in despair. His eyes closed. He took a deep breath.

Then the screen cut to black.

Later that same day, early evening, Faraday found himself in the Southsea branch of Waitrose. He joined the shortest of the queues at the checkout, wondering if he had time to fit in a visit to Nick Hayder up at the QA. On the point of unloading his basket at the till, he felt a tug on his arm. It was Harry Wayte.

'Joe,' he said amiably. 'Long time.'

'Harry.' Faraday offered a nod. 'How's tricks?'

'Fine. Finally jacked it in last week.'

'Jacked what in?'

'The job. Bunch of us had a few bevvies at a pub over in Fareham. Would have dropped you an invite but . . . No offence.'

Faraday studied Wayte for a moment. To the best of his knowledge, Professional Standards were still pursuing an enquiry, though he was woolly about the details.

'My brief says they're wasting their time.' Wayte could read his mind. 'Can't find anything to tie me to Bazza. Not a shred, Joe. Not a phone call. Not an e-mail. Not a penny I can't account for. Not a single, fucking dicky bird. Look.' He nodded at the waiting checkout assistant. 'You're pissing her off, too.'

Minutes later, in the car park, Faraday was finishing a call on his mobile when he caught sight of Wayte emerging from the supermarket. With his flapping raincoat and bulging carrier bags, he looked an old man already. He crossed the tarmac and paused behind a new-looking BMW convertible while he fumbled for his key.

Faraday pocketed his mobile and stirred the Mondeo into life.

Slipping the clutch, he eased the car forward. Wayte was loading the boot of the BMW with litre bottles of German lager. Faraday paused beside him. The car was blue with a *Play Up Pompey* sticker on the back.

Wayte glanced up. Faraday was still gazing at the Pompey sticker. 'Nice motor, Harry. Must have cost a bit.'

Wayte looked down at him, savouring this small moment of truth. 'You're right,' he said at last. 'It did.'